RESTRAIN: BOOK FOUR IN THE BOUND SERIES

SHANDI BOYES

Illustrated by
SSB DESIGNS

Copyright

By: Shandi Boyes
Editing: Mountains Wanted Publishing
Photographs: Shutterstock Account
Cover Designer: SSB Designs

Also by Shandi Boyes

Perception Series - New Adult Romance

Perception of Life - (Noah & Emily)

Reality of Life - (Conclusion of Noah & Emily)

Fight of Life - (Jacob - standalone)

Player of Life - (Nick - standalone)

Beats of Life - (Slater - standalone)

Enigma Series - Steamy Contemporary Romance

Enigma of Life - (Isaac)

Unraveling an Enigma - (Isaac)

Enigma: The Mystery Unmasked - (Isaac)

Enigma: The Final Chapter - (Isaac)

Beneath the Secrets - (Hugo - Part 1)

Beneath the Sheets - (Hugo Conclusion)

Spy Thy Neighbor (Hunter - standalone)

The Opposite Effect - (Brax)

I Married a Mob Boss - (Enrique)

Second Shot (Hawke's Story)

Bound Series - Steamy Romance & slight BDSM

Chains (Marcus and Cleo)

Links (Marcus and Cleo)

Bound (Marcus and Cleo)

Restrain (Marcus and Cleo)

Dedication

To the fabulous members of Shandi's Book Babes.
Thanks for continuing to inspire me to write.
Every word I type is written for you lovely ladies!
I hope you enjoy Restrained.

Shandi xx

Chapter One

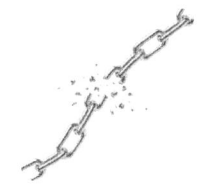

THE CLICK OF MY HEELS RACING DOWN THE NARROW CORRIDOR nearly drowns out the deep, thick voice begging for me to stop. I don't look back. I don't need to. Although I recognize the voice, it isn't the one I want to hear. It isn't Marcus.

My speed remains unchecked as I push through the heavy door leading to the ballroom where the Serena Scott Foundation is being held. Denying Brodie's plea for me to stop, I weave through a horde of elegantly dressed people mingling in the opulent ballroom. Although I gain just as many curious gawks as I did the first time I stumbled into the foyer hours ago, not all their eyes are slit with disdain—some are doused with worry.

Pretending the moisture in my eyes is from expensive perfume burning my corneas, I continue with my trek. I keep my head held high, my shattered heart not enough of a deterrent to warrant embarrassing myself in public. My soul may be shattered, but my Garcia pride remains intact.

I'm halfway across the room when Brodie's distinct rumble sounds over the string quartet entertaining the wealthy benefactors of the Foundation. "Cleo, wait up."

I crank my neck to peer at him. Although I only met him last week, I hate that he is caught in the middle of a battle he doesn't belong in.

"I'm fine, Brodie," I assure him before continuing my effort to leave the gala before my tears fall.

The air in my lungs is brutally evicted when I spin back around and crash into a rock solid wall. Pain tingles across my face when my nose violently slams into an extremely hard pec. The pain is so intense, moisture floods my eyes. *At least now I have an excuse to cry in public.*

"Shit, Cleo, are you okay?"

Holding the bridge of my nose to ensure no blood trickles onto my priceless silk dress, I lift my tear-welling eyes. Dexter is peering down at me, his face lined with regret. When he spots the small trickle of blood pooling in the crevice of my nose, the worry tainting his face grows tenfold.

"Here." He clutches my elbow and guides me to the bar Andy is working behind.

Noticing our collision, Andy hands Dexter a ziplock bag full of ice. I grimace when Dexter removes my hand to replace it with the bag. It isn't pain causing my scrunched-up expression; it is the freezing coldness of the ice pressed against my flaming-with-anger face.

"I'm fine," I assure Dexter, removing the ice from my nose.

I roll my eyes at my pathetic reply. *Are those the only two words I know today? I guess if I can convince those around me that I'm fine, I might believe it as well.*

I use one of the stark white cloth napkins fanned across the bar to pat under my nose. "See?" I express when my quick dab fails to produce any blood. Although our collision was painful, it was more the shock of it happening than actual pain. Physically, I am fine; it is just my insides that look wretched.

Not getting the message, Dexter places the bag of ice on the bar then cradles my cheeks. His thumb gently pushes on my nose to make sure it is still in one piece before his fingers skim my blemished cheeks. His gentle touch as he inspects my face for damage soothes some of the nicks my argument with Marcus created. Don't get me wrong, another man's touch will never erase Marcus from my soul, no matter how long our stint of absence is, but it is nice to be rewarded with tenderness after my heart was just ripped to shreds.

The exact moment Dexter's hands drop from my face, a broad arm wraps around my waist. My idiotic heart hopes it is Marcus clutching my hips for dear life, but my body knows it isn't. It didn't react like it does when its awareness of Marcus activates. It more jumped in fear than excitement.

"Honey, how many times have I told you to watch where you're going?" asks the thick, deep voice from above—a voice I immediately recognize.

My spine snaps straight when Brodie's beard tickles my lips as he places an impromptu kiss on the edge of my mouth. Although his lips are barely touching mine, the angle of his head doesn't expose that. It looks as if we are kissing—*intimately.*

Shunted in silence, I return Dexter's baffled stare with as much confusion as Dexter is bestowing on me.

"I thought. . . aren't you with. . . hold on... What the hell is going on?" Dexter's words are as baffled as his facial expression. His jaw is hanging loose, and his eyes are wide with shock.

After running his slit gaze over Brodie for the third time, Dexter says, "You're the douchebag who just cut in while I was dancing with Cleo. One minute she was there; the next, she was gone."

"It isn't called 'whipping them away for a quickie' for no reason," Brodie fires back, not the slightest bit deterred by Dexter's name-calling.

My and Dexter's eyes rocket to Brodie in sync. He arrogantly waggles his brows before cuddling me into his side. Because of his tall height, I snuggle right into the nook of his arm like I belong there. My mouth opens and closes in preparation to deny his claims, but I'm honestly stunned into silence; my mouth won't cooperate with my brain.

When the cockiness radiating out of Brodie becomes too much for Dexter to bear, he devotes his attention back to me. This time when he drinks in my wide eyes, flustered cheeks, and disheveled appearance, the worry in his eyes doesn't grow. It dampens—*majorly.*

"You went for a quickie?" Although he is staring straight at me, I honestly don't believe Dexter's question is directed at me. He appears as if he is talking to himself.

Dexter misses the brief shake of my head when Brodie says, "We better get going, Cleo. I'm eager to finish what we started." He looks Dexter dead set in the eyes. "If you know what I mean?" If he didn't, the arrogant wink Brodie adds to his short sentence ensures there is no misconception.

I'm taken aback when Brodie locks his lustful eyes to mine. He is playing the part so well that if I didn't know any better, I'd swear we had just returned from having a quickie. Marcus may never secure a role in a major motion picture, but if Brodie doesn't dull down his acting skills, Hollywood will come knocking.

Not giving me the chance to protest, Brodie pushes off his feet and heads for the door I fled through mere minutes ago. His hurried pace only slows when a raspy voice calls my name. Cranking my neck to the side, I see Andy holding out my purse for me. My head is so fuzzy, I entirely forgot I'd placed it on the countertop after my collision with Dexter. I'd like to say my daft behavior is based on the alcohol lacing my veins, but that isn't the case. I stopped drinking well over an hour ago, and even if I didn't, every drop would have burned off during my exchange with Marcus. That is how heated our interaction was: potent enough to singe Satan's bottom.

When I reach out to accept my purse from Andy, my brows scrunch. Even with blood roaring in my ears, I couldn't miss the crinkling of paper when I accepted my satin clutch from his grasp. Noticing a small piece of paper Andy inconspicuously handed me during our exchange, I raise my eyes to his. He smiles softly, acknowledging the paper is for me without a word tumbling from his lips.

"Be careful, Cleo." I've never been good at lip reading, but I'm certain that is what Andy silently mouths before his attention reverts to a benefactor requesting his assistance.

Still jolted with shocked silence, I briefly nod my head before allowing Brodie to escort me out of the gala. Since Dexter is paralyzed with astonishment, he doesn't hinder Brodie's endeavor. I don't know if I should be peeved or pleased by that notion. Considering it is the second time in under ten minutes I've failed to warrant a chase down, it bruises my ego more than I'd care to admit.

I swallow the horridly bitter taste in the back of my throat as I store the scrap of paper in my clutch. Andy seems like a great guy, but with my heart sitting in tatters, the last thing I want is more complications.

My eyes lift to scan my location. Brodie and I are moments away from reaching the emergency door I exited moments ago.

I dig my heels into the thickly piled carpet in an attempt to slow Brodie's urgent pace. My efforts are utterly fruitless; his speed is so unchecked, we finalize the last half-dozen strides in two heart-thrashing seconds. "I swear to god, Brodie, if you've lured me into another trap, Lucy will be an only child," I grumble under my breath, my words wheezy.

"I swear to god, Cleo, if you force me into this getup one more time tonight, I'll reconsider my stance on whipping women."

Even hearing a whip of edginess in his voice—*no pun intended*—I freeze in place. His tone is playful, but it was void of any confirmation that Marcus isn't lurking behind the door for me like he was last time Brodie stole my attention from Dexter.

"Are you luring me into a trap?" I ask, staring straight into Brodie's twinkling-with-amusement eyes. "Is Marcus standing behind that door?" I continue, pointing to the door we are mere feet from.

"Not even a snide remark on my whipping comment?" Brodie asks, his voice cracking with laughter.

I'm glad he can find humor in my situation, but I am not amused. The more my shock at his admission we got freaky in the middle of a fundraising gala subsides, the more my anger is returning.

Incapable of ignoring my rueful glare for a second longer, Brodie breathes out, "No. Marcus isn't behind the door."

I don't want it to, but disappointment slams into me.

"My instructions were to collect you, bundle you into a car, then take you home." All the humor in his voice has vanished, leaving nothing but a thick timbre hindered by a snip of regret.

"Marcus wants me to leave?" *God—expressing it out loud hurt more than thinking it.*

The knife twisting in my heart pushes deeper when Brodie briefly nods his head.

"What does he think I was doing? I was leaving before you stopped me," I retaliate, my anger so wrathful, I can't stop it, even knowing it's being forced on the wrong person.

Peering at me with a set of remorseful eyes, Brodie pulls the listening contraption out of his ear and stores it in his pocket. The demands of the person squawking in his ear are loud; I hear their grumbly voice mumbling through his trousers the entire time he scrubs his hand over the cropped beard on his chin while he configures a reply to my question. His anxious response sets my nerves on edge. It isn't one I anticipated from a bodyguard left to clean up the mess of his boss. It seems more personal than that.

"What is going on, Brodie? This isn't like you. It also isn't like Marcus. I know him. That wasn't him." I mumble my last two sentences, my voice wary it's allowing my heart to speak on behalf of my head before it's had time to evaluate everything rationally.

They say love can make you blind, but that isn't the case right now. I know what I saw. *I hate what I saw.* But my gut is cautioning me not to jump to conclusions. Marcus said just last week I was fulfilling his requirements, so what has changed so drastically between now and then?

"What did I do wrong?" I ask Brodie, my words tumbling from my mouth before I can stop them.

"I'm not the man you should be asking, Cleo." When he spots a glint of moisture teeming in the corners of my eyes, he adds on, "I'm just doing the job I'm paid to do. Please don't make it any harder on me." I can tell by his tone he is remorseful for my situation, but he is also being honest. He is just doing his job.

Brodie steps in front of me, engulfing me in his bottled-cologne scent. "What do you want to do, Cleo? Stay here or go home?" The brutal pain in my heart softens, encouraged by him seeking my opinion instead of forcing one onto me.

Incapable of speaking for fear of crying, I curtly nod my head.

"Home?" Brodie confirms, unsure what my gesture refers to.

When I nod again, Brodie releases a deep exhalation of air. Gratefulness spreads across his face as he splays his hand on the curve of my lower back. Remaining quiet, he pushes open the emergency exit door, then nudges his head for me to enter before him. My eyes fleetingly scan the dingy hallway when I cautiously step into the mildew-scented area. Just as Brodie guaranteed, Marcus is nowhere to be seen. Half of me is grateful his pledge was spot on; however, the other half is devastated.

I have so many emotions pumping into me right now, I'm honestly at a loss as to what the hell is going on. Marcus didn't confirm that Keira is his sub, but he didn't deny it either. Add that to the culpability his eyes were carrying during our exchange, and all the arrows point to the same conclusion: Keira is his sub. Furthermore, if he didn't have anything to hide, why wouldn't he have just been honest? What good can possibly be achieved with deceit?

The playful vibrancy bouncing between Brodie and me when we walked into the hotel hours ago has been snuffed, traded for a stuffiness that makes my stomach churn. Brodie doesn't speak until we merge onto the cracked sidewalk at the back entrance of the hotel.

"We are looking for a dark gray Jaguar," he murmurs as his eyes scan the crammed street hidden behind the hotel.

After wrapping my arms around my torso to ward off the chilly winds prickling my skin with goosebumps, I help Brodie locate our transport. With the gala attended by the wealthiest of the wealthiest, the alley is lined with expensive vehicles. It is like an auto show of the most pristine cars—some vintage, some not even scheduled for production yet. If my heart weren't a twisted mess, I'd be tempted to yank my cell out of my clutch to snap some pictures for Jackson. He has a fondness for restored classics. But since it feels like my heart has shrunk to a quarter of its size, I keep my cell stored away.

When Brodie notices me shivering, he shrugs off his jacket and drapes it over my shoulders. Before I can express my thanks, a dark gray Jaguar pulls to the curb in front of us. After ducking his chin to peruse the driver's credentials, Brodie opens the back passenger door and gestures for me to enter. My body slicks with sweat, shocked by the contrasting temperatures between the cab of the Jaguar and outside. It's like I've trekked out of the Antarctic straight into a Syrian desert. It is roasting in here.

My neck cranks to the side so fast my muscles squeal in protest when the passenger door slams shut with Brodie still standing on the sidewalk. The request for an explanation is rammed back into my throat when he cracks open the front door. *Phew! I thought he was leaving me here—alone.* I've always embraced New York's eclectic life-style without a second thought. But with my mind hazy from my exchange with Marcus and unexplained dizziness, I'm not as welcoming of a solo voyage as usual. I love New York—it is my sister city—but navigating my way through the craziness unaccompanied seems daunting tonight.

Panic wells inside me when Brodie fails to slide into the passenger seat. Remaining on the sidewalk, he hands the driver a yellow post-it note with an address hand-scribbled across the front. "Take Cleo to this address. Don't stop for anything. Do you understand?" he instructs, the authoritativeness of his tone shocking me.

Brodie is a bodyguard, but I've never heard his voice have this much sharpness. When the driver nods his head, Brodie slaps his hand on the hood of the Jaguar, soundlessly advising the driver to exit.

Anxiety grips my throat as I scoot across the sticky leather seat. Failing to notice my gaped jaw and bugged eyes, Brodie's stance stiffens. His entire composure screams of a man on watch. His shoulders broaden as his chest puffs out, his feet plant at the width of his shoulders, and one of his hands rests on the concealed gun strapped to his hip. His stature conveys a "do not mess with me" attitude.

Once Brodie's protective stance becomes nothing but a blur in the distance, I shift my confused gaze to a pair of eyes scrutinizing me via the rearview mirror. I frown in confusion as my brain racks why his eyes seem so familiar, although I'm confident we've never met.

A tiny shiver moves through me when recollection dawns on why his blue eyes are recognizable. He is the man who drove me to Marcus's residence weeks ago. The one who refused to pull over no matter how much I begged.

Incapable of ignoring the sick feeling brewing in my gut, I lock my stern eyes with the driver before asking, "What address are you taking me to?"

He peers at me, blinking and confused. Recalling that his English is poor, I ask another way: "Montclair? Are we going to Montclair?"

"No." A curt shake of his head amplifies his short reply. "This address," he adds on, tapping the post-it note stuck to his steering wheel. "No Montclair."

"Please. . ." My petition to alter our route is barely hatched when he rolls up the Jaguar's privacy partition, arrogantly denying my God-given right to make my own decisions.

Clearly, he remembers me as well as I remember him.

Chapter Two

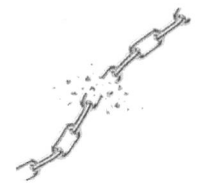

TEN MINUTES CONTEMPLATING A WAY OUT OF MY PREDICAMENT equals ten minutes of wasted time. Previous experience told me pleading with the driver to alter the direction of our travels would be pointless, yet I still squandered the last ten minutes begging for him to do precisely that.

Confused and a little worried, I slouch into my seat and shift my eyes to the sea of vehicles clogging the streets of New York. With traffic the densest I've seen, mere seconds pass before an idea I've been toying with fully forms in my mind. I'll walk to the closest train station and take public transport home. Although my heels are the tallest I've ever worn, I'd prefer to endure blisters than have my heart undergo another brutal beating it may not withstand. I can't take the risk—one more crack could permanently disfigure it.

When the driver stops at a red light, I curl my hand around the door handle and yank it back roughly. My teeth grit when my ploy to escape is thwarted. The Jaguar's lock mechanisms are firmly in place, leaving me trapped in the car with a man who is watching me like a hawk from the rearview mirror. His gaze is mocking, goading me without a syllable oozing from his hard-lined lips.

Unable to leash my Garcia stubbornness, my overworked brain

seeks a viable alternative. It smacks into me like a ton of bricks not even ten seconds later: *Lexi*. I drop my eyes to my watch to calculate the time left on our journey. If I message her now, she should arrive at Marcus's residence within minutes of my arrival. The short delay will give me enough time to pack my belongings and meet her out front. As much as it would be nice to be heedless right now, my budget isn't flexible. Every penny I have must go towards mine and Lexi's living expenses, so replacing the clothes I have stored in Marcus's expansive walk-in-closet is out of the question.

Pretending I can't feel my heart sinking into my stomach, I lean over to snag my purse from the seat next to me. My brows furl when the faintest buzz gains my attention. Assuming it is the rattle of my hands shuddering up my arms, I snatch my purse off the seat and rummage inside for my cell. My hunt for my phone halts when I feel a second vibrating sensation moments later. Although its buzz is faint, I'm certain it isn't from my shaky composure.

I run my hands down my body, only stopping when I reach the pocket of Brodie's coat curled around my shuddering frame. With my brain in a tizzy, I completely forgot he lent me his jacket. I jump in fright when an unexpected shudder courses through me again. Since my hand is resting in the pocket of Brodie's jacket, it amplifies the strength of its vibration.

My hand slips into the right-side pocket of Brodie's jacket. My pace is so slow, you'd swear there was a nuclear weapon crammed into the small opening. Blood roars to my ears when a brisk coolness graces my fingertips. Quicker than I can snap my fingers, horrid unease thickens my blood. *Please, for the love of god, don't let it be the vibrating butt plug Marcus slipped into his pocket before we left his residence.*

I slump in my chair, eternally grateful when my hand wraps around a sleek metal material that can only represent one thing: Brodie's cell phone. With my heart thrashing against my ribs, I yank Brodie's phone out of the pocket. I'm not planning on snooping; I just want to advise his caller that he is away from his phone. I know how much I panic when Lexi doesn't answer my calls, so I'd hate to put his family through the same thing.

My heart stops beating when my eyes drop to the screen of

Brodie's phone and the name of his caller displayed. *Marcus.* I stare at the phone, unmoving and confused, until his call is forwarded to Brodie's voicemail. Just as quickly as the cell stops vibrating, it commences ringing all over again. With chaotic heartache thrusting me into idiocy, I slide my finger across the screen and press the cell to my ear.

"Jesus, Brodie, what took you so long? Do you have her? Is she safe? Where are you?" Marcus's voice is so panicked, his words fire off his tongue before they are properly developed. "Did you give the driver clear instructions on where to take her?"

I don't speak. I can't. I can barely breathe, let alone advise Marcus I'm not Brodie. It isn't his molten lava voice that has me tranced into stupidity, it is the absolute panic tainting his usually calm tone.

"Brodie?!" Marcus snaps, his voice roaring through the cell so brutally, I startle. "Do you have her. . .?" Before the entire sentence leaves Marcus's mouth, he inhales a sharp breath. "Cleo?"

My eyes frantically search the area, certain he can see me, as there is no way he'd know it is me on the other end of the line. I'm not even breathing for the fear he would recognize my wheezy pants.

"Cleo." This time his tone doesn't come out sounding like a question. It is a confirmation.

Tears prick my eyes when he mumbles, "Are you okay, baby?" I hear a commotion sound down the line like he has muffled the phone to talk to someone before. "Where's Brodie? Is he with you?"

"No," I reply softly, timidly shaking my head.

Marcus exhales harshly as if he was sucker-punched. "Do you know where he is?"

"Umm. . . yes. He's at the hotel," I stammer out, my voice as shocked and weak as I feel.

I don't understand what the hell is going on. The man talking to me on the phone is not the same man I was arguing with twenty minutes ago. I know I said previously I can tell the difference between Marcus and Master Chains, but this is ridiculous. Surely his contrasting personalities don't extend past the bedroom. *Do they?*

"What?" I ask when Marcus's deep voice calling my name draws me back to the present.

"Where are you, baby?" he asks, his voice a soft, nurturing purr. "Who are you with?"

My brows stitch. He has only called me a term of endearment a handful of times. The first few times was before we met in person. It was when he was wooing me to be his sub. It was more a playful tease than a term of endearment. The second time was following my attack in the alleyway. So, for him to say it to me twice in under a minute has my confusion intensifying to a point I'm not comfortable with.

"What's going on, Marcus?" I ask, dread echoing in my tone.

"I can't update you right now, Cleo. I just need you to tell me where you are."

Even with my spikes hackled from his crass tone, I breathe out, "I'm in your Jaguar."

Marcus releases a massive exhalation of air. It is so robust, my face grimaces when it shreds my eardrums. "She's in my Jag," I hear him tell someone in the background.

I sit up straight in my seat when a mix of male and female voices react to his revelation. "Who are you with? Are you with *Keira?*" Keira's name is barely whispered since it took every morsel of my soul to articulate it.

I press Brodie's phone close to my ear when muffled voices reverberate down the line. The multiple accents are so jumbled, I wouldn't be surprised to discover Marcus is cupping the speaker of his phone.

Although it is only faint, I overhear Marcus say, "I want this wrapped up. I need to go."

My jaw tightens when a female voice replies to his request. Although I can't one hundred percent testify it was Keira, the green sludge lacing my veins doesn't hear logic. As far as my jealousy is concerned, that female voice belongs to Keira.

My heart rate races as my stomach churns. "That was Keira, wasn't it?"

There is a scrape of a chair across the ground before the thud of shoe-covered feet padding on a tiled floor booms through the cell's speaker.

"Answer me, Marcus. Was that Keira?"

"Cleo. Stop," Marcus demands, his voice on edge.

Angered by his continued deflection, I hit the end call button on Brodie's phone, switch it off, then send it sailing across the interior of Marcus's Jaguar. A tinge of hesitation courses through me when Brodie's phone smacks into the polished wooden trim on the back driver's side door before dropping to the floor. Neither Brodie or his cell phone deserves the wrath of my anger. That right solely belongs to the man who confuses me as much as he irritates me.

Feeling guilty that I've damaged property that doesn't belong to me, I lean over to collect Brodie's phone from the floor. I stop halfway, hindered by the buzz of my cell phone in my purse. Even knowing who is calling doesn't prevent me from yanking my phone out of my bag and peering down at the screen. Although the display screen states my caller's identity is unknown, I know who it is. Other than my sister, nobody calls my phone.

Feeling spiteful, I send Marcus's call to voicemail. Pretending I can't hear my cell phone ringing again, I fish the twenty dollar bill out of my wallet I attempted to give Andy for my bottle of water and slam it against the privacy partition. The driver slides down the window, apparently noticing the crumpled-up note.

"We go to this address," he maintains, jamming his index finger into his steering wheel.

Although his words are firm, they also expose his wavering constraint. If I had more than small change in my purse, I'm confident I could use it to my advantage, but considering this twenty is all I have, I stick with my initial plan.

"Yes, we go to that address, but faster." I inwardly sigh, grateful when my voice comes out smooth and confident, meaning he will have more chance of understanding me.

"Fast?" the driver confirms, peering at me in the rearview mirror after lowering the partition all the way down. His face is flushed with anger, but his bright eyes expose his interest.

When I nod my head, he adds on, "This address?" The horn of the Jaguar beeps when he taps the post-it note firmly.

"Yes," I verify, leaning over the partition to hand him my note.

He smiles, exposing his slightly crooked teeth. "Okay. Thank you."

He puts my twenty in the top pocket of his short-sleeve dress shirt before increasing the pressure on the gas pedal. Happy the first stage of my plan has successfully launched, I slip back into my seat, refasten my seatbelt, then drop my eyes to my phone. If I weren't already aware of my mystery caller's identity, the four calls I've missed the past two minutes guarantees I can't be mistaken. No one I've ever met is as impatient as Master Chains.

After sending Marcus's fifth call to voicemail, I begin dialing a number I know by heart. I've only dialed two digits when the screen announces another call. Hitting the end button, I continue with my mission.

My attempts to call Lexi are impaired over and over again by Marcus's constant calling. Annoyed beyond belief, I swipe my finger across the screen and press my cell to my ear. "What!?" I scream down the phone. My voice is so loud the driver of the Jaguar raises the partition once more.

"Cleo?" queries a hesitant voice—a voice that doesn't match Marcus's.

Swamped by guilt, I sink into my seat. "Hey, Dexter. Sorry. I've just had a . . ." My voice trails off when I can't find an appropriate word to describe my night. It went from an awe-inspiring high to a devastating low so quickly, my head is still spinning.

"Shitty night?" Dexter fills in.

I feebly laugh. "Yeah, something like that." I lick my parched lips before saying, "I'm sorry about what happened earlier. I didn't ditch you for Brodie—"

"I know," Dexter interrupts. "Look, I'm not going to lie, Cleo; he is a damn good actor. I was truly worried at the start, but then I realized you're not *that* type of girl."

"*That* type of girl?" I mimic. Although I'm sure he was being playful, the feminist side of me I buried two months ago is rearing her head, ready to defend the rights for any woman to do as she sees fit with her body.

Dexter's husky laugh douses my agitation—slightly. "I didn't mean it in a bad way, Cleo. I just meant you deserve more than a five-minute romp in a storage closet. But, hey, if that's what turns you on, so be it. Any man would be crazy to miss an opportunity to be with you."

It could just be my woozy head, but his last sentence sounded like it was laced with sexual innuendo.

"Thanks?" I blubber. My tone makes my praise sound like a question more than a declaration. I'm not used to getting unexpected compliments, so they always thrust me into a state of idiocy when I do.

Dexter's breathless laughter switches to a belly-clutching chuckle. "I've made you embarrassed," he snickers between laugher.

"No, you haven't," I reply, waving my hand through the air like it's no big deal, eternally grateful he can't see me, otherwise he would have noticed my inflamed cheeks and wide eyes.

Dexter's laugh tells me he doesn't believe a word I said. Rolling my eyes at the cockiness beaming down the line, I ask, "Was there a purpose to your call? Or did you just set out to make me uncomfortable?"

"So you are embarrassed?" Dexter replies, his smooth voice sending a flurry of goosebumps to the nape of my neck.

"Fine! I'm embarrassed. Happy?" That isn't entirely true. I'm more confused than anything. I've got too many thoughts passing through my mind to add a flirty comment into the mix.

"Very much so," Dexter mutters. His throaty purr causes the hairs on my arms to bristle. Which, in turn, adds to my confusion. "Anyway. . ." he breathes out heavily, like he is snapping himself out of a trance. "I have a very valid reason for my call."

Noticing the snip of unease in his voice, I straighten my slumped form. My intuition is proven dead on point when Dexter mutters, "How well do you know Keira Herrington?"

"Not very well. Why?" The swishing of my stomach resonates in my low tone.

I hear Dexter rub his hand over the scruff on his chin before he answers, "Being Delilah's date gave me more than just cooties."

I try to shut it down, but a small smile tugs at my lips before I can stop it. My grin is brief, but obviously long enough for Dexter to hear. Clearly, when he says, "Ah, that's better," as if he heard my cheeks incline over the phone.

My smile enlarges more. "I suggest a disinfectant bath with a steel sponge," I chide, hoping a bit of playfulness will settle the nerves wreaking havoc with my stomach.

My efforts have the effect I was aiming for when Dexter's boyish laughter barrels down the line. "Don't worry, I have an entire recon planned to rid me of her germs."

His reply increases the bow of my brow. *How close did he and Delilah get if he is required to don a hazmat suit after their date?*

After settling his vigorous chuckles, Dexter asks, "Do you have any plans tomorrow, Cleo? I'd rather share the information I have in person than over the phone."

I frown, panicked. "It's that important?"

"As important as breathing," Dexter fires back in an instant.

My stomach flips, loathing the disturbing images his reply bombarded me with. All were similar to the ones I saw earlier tonight, but this time around, Marcus and Keira weren't elegantly dressed. *They weren't dressed at all.*

"Yeah, I can meet you somewhere. Did you want me to come to you?" I ask through the solid lump in my throat.

"Nah," Dexter replies, dragging out the one word as if it is an entire sentence. "Isn't that pizzeria you mentioned a few months ago in Montclair?"

My brows furrow. "Villa Victoria? Yeah, it's on Park Street," I reply, shocked he remembered a restaurant I mentioned months earlier.

"I'll meet you there tomorrow. Say around 2?" Dexter suggests, his voice high with uneasy excitement.

I nod, even though he can't see me. "Okay. I'll see you tomorrow at two," I confirm.

"Alright." I hear his smile through the phone. "I'll see you tomorrow. Bye, Cleo."

"Bye, Dexter," I bid him farewell, confusion evident in my tone.

Just before I disconnect our call, a question pops into my head. "Dexter?"

"Yeah," he answers immediately.

My lips are dry, so I lick them before asking, "Am I going to need anything tomorrow? Like . . . *tissues?*" My voice is so weak, I won't be surprised if Dexter asks me to repeat my question.

He doesn't.

"Depends," he replies, honesty in his response.

Sickness spreads through my gut. "On what?"

My breathing stills; my heart stills. I swear, time stands still as I await his reply.

"On if you are in love with Marcus Everett," Dexter eventually replies, his tone so low I'm certain the devil heard it.

The wooziness inflicting my head swells when the air is sucked from my lungs. Hearing my unenthusiastic response, Dexter asks, "Are you, Cleo? Do you love Marcus?" His voice sounds confused. *He isn't the only one.*

"No," I mumble, my voice cracking with emotions. I try to shake my head to strengthen my statement, but my body won't allow it.

My hand darts up to rub away a tear descending down my cheek when Dexter mutters, "Bring tissues."

Chapter Three

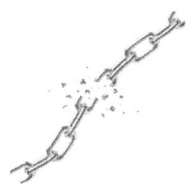

I'VE BARELY CALMED THE ERRATIC BEAT OF MY HEART WHEN THE
Jaguar pulls in front of the platform steps of Marcus's New York residence. My plan to have Lexi pick me up in the minutes following my
arrival has been left for dust after my conversation with Dexter. I've
done nothing the past forty minutes but stare at the pitch black sky,
striving to untangle some of the confusion bombarding me. Forty
minutes of silence awarded me with forty minutes of additional
confusion.

Pushing aside my bewilderment, I accept the hand the Jaguar
driver is holding out for me. With my tight dress holding my thighs
hostage, it is a little harder to slip out of the car than it was to enter it.

"Thank you," I say graciously when the driver passes me Brodie's
cell I sent hurling across the car earlier.

The driver dips his chin before jogging around to the driver's side
door of the Jaguar and slipping inside. I wait until his taillights disappear in the distance before climbing the platform stairs. The same set
of butterflies that take flight in my stomach every time I climb these
stairs are still present; they just aren't based on giddy silliness. I
genuinely feel ill.

My shaky steps up the stairs halt halfway when the large glass entranceway door suddenly swings open. With my poor eyesight hampered by tears, it takes me several blinks to recognize the person standing in the doorway. It is the beautiful middle-aged Hispanic lady who disappeared within minutes of my first arrival at this residence: Aubrey, Marcus's personal assistant/housekeeper.

"Come on, dear, it is cold out there." She signals with her hand for me to hurry.

I push off my feet before my brain can cite an objection to her bossy tone. When I stop in front of Aubrey, shivering from the sprinkling of rain mottling my hair, she snatches my purse, Brodie's jacket, and his cell phone out of my hands.

"I need that," I instruct, pointing to my purse when she dumps my belongings on the glass entranceway table.

Just because I've spent the last forty minutes in a daze doesn't mean my plans have altered. I'm still calling Lexi to pick me up.

"You are to be fed, showered, and sent to bed. Mr. Everett didn't explicitly state which order, so you can choose whether to eat or shower first. What do you want to do?" Aubrey asks, her tone indicating she's not to be messed with.

I take a step back, bamboozled by her bitchiness. *Is every female in Marcus's life without a heart, or just those who work for him?*

When I ask Aubrey that, her brows stitch. She looks as bewildered by my response as I am to her affirmation she was given instructions on how to handle me. The longer she stares at me, the weaker her evil glare becomes. Apparently, the anger activating every nerve in my body is potent enough she can feel it shuddering the ground as well.

The twinkle in Aubrey's eyes grows as she mumbles, "You're different than the others," under her breath.

"That's because I am *not* one of them," I reply, hating that I'm once again defending my title in Marcus's life. "I am *not* Marcus's sub."

Aubrey runs her hands down the crease of her skirt, seemingly unsure of a reply. I wouldn't necessarily say she doesn't believe me. She just seems unaware of how to act in this predicament. Obviously, she is more well-equipped to handle Marcus's subs than she is his girlfriends. *Ex-girlfriend,* I mentally correct.

Wanting to switch off the washing machine in my stomach, I mutter, "Do you have any reservations about me eating in my room?"

Aubrey peers up at me with her dark eyes blinking. "No. I will arrange for your meal to be brought there."

Smiling to issue her my thanks, I gather my purse off the entranceway table and make a beeline for the stairs. Aubrey's eyes burn with concern, tracking me the entire time. Once I hit the landing of the spiral staircase, I dig my cell out of my clutch. My hand is slicked with so much sweat, I nearly drop it while nervously fumbling for Lexi's number. She answers not even two seconds later.

"Cleo. . .Hi." The scrumptious laughter accompanying her greeting dulls the ache in my chest. Her girly giggle is full of vibrancy and love —a stark contradiction to the emotions pummeling me into a blubbering mess.

"Have I interrupted something?" I ask when the sound of sheets shuffling jingles down the line.

"No. . . Jackson, stop it," Lexi chastises him, her words muffled as she cups her phone. "You know I'm here whenever you need me, Cleo; what's up?" Her last sentence comes out in a hurry since a girly laugh quickly followed it. "Jackson. . .don't; it's Cleo."

"Oh, hey, Cleo," Jackson mutters down the line, his words as high as my arched brow.

I pace into the main suite of Marcus's residence. "Hi, Jackson. Is everything okay?" I ask, my tone laced with suspicion.

"Perfectly A-OK," Jackson replies, drawing out his words.

I stop frozen at the side of Marcus's bed when Lexi's faint moan is barely covered by Jackson's throaty laugh. My confusion grows when a loud yelp barrels through my phone's speaker moments later, closely followed by a manly growl. *What the hell are they up to?*

I hold my phone to my ear with my shoulder so I can gather my overnight bag from the footlocker at the end of Marcus's bed. As I enter the expansive walk-in closet, Lexi and Jackson's playful banter continues as if I'm not eavesdropping on every murmured statement. I am. I listen like a real creep, adoring the utter bliss radiating out of my baby sister's voice. She sounds so incredibly happy, tears spring in my eyes. And for the first time tonight, they are tears of happiness.

I stop stuffing clothes into my bag sprawled open on the pristinely clean floor when I catch the quickest snippet of a request Jackson makes between a peppering of smooching kisses. He was quiet, but not soft enough for my snooping ears to miss. "Say it again?"

"No," Lexi replies breathlessly, her one word drenched with heavy sentiment. "I'm talking to my sister," she continues, revealing she is aware I'm listening in like a weirdo.

I push the phone in close to my ear, displaying the title "Cleo the Creep" Lexi gave me four years ago is still going strong when Jackson demands, "Say it again, then I'll leave you alone." His voice is so soft, it is barely a whisper.

Standing frozen in the middle of the dead quiet closet, I can hear Lexi's heart thrashing against her ribcage before the faintest whisper of, "I love you," spills from her lips.

I gasp in a shocked breath as a rush of moisture floods my eyes. The satin material of my dress does a terrible job mopping up my tears when Jackson replies, "Not as much as I love you."

Not trusting my legs to keep me upright, I move to sit on the chaise Marcus spanked me on the morning following our first session in his playroom. Although devastated by the circumstances of events that has happened thus far tonight, hearing my baby sister express her love to the man of her dreams has fulfilled one of my greatest wishes.

Just like me, Lexi closed herself off after our parents and Tate died. In the beginning, I thought her reasons were the same as mine—she was afraid of people leaving her. It was only after watching her wade through breakup after breakup the past three years did I realize our logic for keeping people at arm's length was entirely different. I kept people away because I was afraid they would leave me. Lexi kept them away because she was afraid of leaving them.

Every time Lexi started a new relationship, she began immediately plotting its demise. She has often quoted she didn't want love, marriage, and a family. Where in reality, she didn't want them to suffer the heartache of losing her. I don't know if her change in mindset is based on how well the Kayldeco program is working for her, or if she just needed a man like Jackson to prove loving her will be worth the heartache of losing her. *Maybe it is a bit of both?*

Telling Jackson she loves him is a massive step for Lexi—one so significant, I'm not going to ruin it by being melodramatic.

"Lexi," I breathe heavily down the line, drawing her attention away from Jackson, who I can hear schmoozing her neck.

"Yes," Lexi replies, her voice sounding elsewhere. A faint slap bellows down the line before Jackson's hearty chuckle. "Sorry, Cleo. You *now* have my undivided attention."

A smile stretches across my face when Jackson warns, "You have five minutes, Cleo. Use it wisely." The last half of his sentence is barely audible, overtaken by the thud of feet padding against a hard floor. If my assumptions are right, it sounds like Lexi is chasing him down our hallway.

I jump, startled when a door suddenly slams moments before Lexi's breathless pants wheeze down the line. "Sorry, he's truly gone this time. I used our new reinforced door to lock him outside."

"Lexi. . ." I drawl out with laughter in my voice.

"What?" I can imagine her shrugging. "He needs a moment to cool down. Hell, I need to cool down." She dramatically huffs. "Our week of solidarity is nearly up, so we're getting in as much alone time as possible, but, my god, my body is feeling it."

My theatrical gag ends when I hear Jackson pounding on our front door. "Lex, let me in. Mrs. Rachet is taking my picture."

"Smile, Jax," Lexi squeals, her voice so high she sounds more like a teen than a grown woman. "She will post that on the Montclair Neighborhood Watch website, so you better look good. Once an image is released to the world, there is no chance of removing it."

My childish giggles nearly have me missing Jackson's shouted demand, "Goddamn it, Lex. Let me in! I don't have any pants on."

When Lexi ignores Jackson's continued requests for entry, I say, "Lexi." I drag out her name in a long, warning purr. "You can't tell a man you love him, then throw him outside without any pants."

I hear Lexi's throat work hard to swallow. "You heard that?" she asks, her voice not as chirpy as it was.

"Yep. Every word," I confess, not the slightest bit hesitant to admit I am a creep.

Lexi huffs. I can just imagine her rolling her eyes. "Stop acting like I won valedictorian. It was only three little words, Cleo."

"Three *very important* little words," I reply, my voice as high as my dangerous heartrate.

"Whatever," Lexi grumbles under her breath.

She doesn't fool me. I heard her heart skip a beat. After a short stint of silence, the clunk of our front door lock booms into my ears, closely followed by the creek of the warped floorboards in our entranceway.

"He's in. Are you happy?" Lexi asks, her voice half-angry, half-amused.

"Very much so," I reply, smiling.

My eyes lift from my heel-covered feet when I detect another presence in the room. I don't want it to, but a dash of disappointment thickens my blood when I spot Aubrey entering the master suite. She has a white napkin curled over her forearm, and she is balancing a silver tray on her hands. With a contrite smile, she places the serving tray onto a stack of drawers on her right. My stomach grumbles when the smell of curry filters into the air. Its desolate response reminds me I haven't eaten since lunch.

Spotting that I'm on a call, Aubrey dips her chin, then exits the room, leaving the door open in her wake. My attention reverts to my cell when Lexi's soft giggle jingles down the line. It appears a few moments in the blistering cold winds Montclair is famous for didn't dampen Jackson's interest in the slightest. I don't know why, but that awards me an immense amount of pleasure. At least one of the Garcia women is feeling the love tonight.

"I love you, Lexi. I'll talk to you tomorrow," I say down the line.

Lexi shushes Jackson before saying, "Hold on one minute, young lady. You didn't just call to tell me you love me."

Warmth blooms across my chest, cherishing the fact she knows me so well she can intuit what my call is about.

"Your voice is doing that weird skittish thing it only does when you are excited or nervous. So, spill the beans, Cleo, or I'll torture it out of you."

"All the way from Montclair?" I jest.

"I'll find a way," she assures me, her tone confident.

I wait a beat, giving my body a chance to rid itself of nerves before saying, "No, you're right. I didn't just call to tell you I love you. I called to ask you something."

I hear Lexi's pulse raging through her veins as she waits for me to continue. Her thudding heart is drowned out by a fit of laughter when I ask, "Did you know pineapple makes guys' cum taste sweeter?"

Chapter Four

SHAME WALLOPS ME AS I STAND ON THE LANDING IN THE SECOND story of Marcus's residence, swinging my eyes up and down his opulent home. I have my bags packed and sitting at my side, but I'm at a loss as to where I'm going. I can't go home as I don't want to interrupt what should be an uninterruptable moment between Lexi and Jackson, but I can't stay here either. Just the thought of facing Marcus head on has my stomach twisted up in knots. God—I wish I had a bundle of cash sitting in my bank account, begging to be squandered. Then I'd simply call a taxi and spend the remainder of my weekend holed up in a two-star motel on the outskirts of town. But, unfortunately, there are no hotel rooms in New York city available for three hundred dollars a night—yes, I checked. Furthermore, I can't afford the cab fare to drive me there.

This is one of those sporadic moments where I wish I didn't love my sister as much as I did, then I wouldn't have hesitated to ask her to come pick me up. Considering it's been over three hours since I left the gala, even with my forty-minute delay in calling her, we would have been long gone before Marcus arrived home.

I honestly don't know if I'll survive seeing him again. I wasn't being dishonest when I said if this turned out to be nothing but a crazy, lust-fueled fling it would kill me. It isn't just killing me. It is gutting me alive. I haven't even left his residence yet and I already feel hollow. Imagine how much worse it will be when I build up the courage to walk out his front door?

I repeat a mantra my dad always quoted as I stoop down to gather my overnight bag from the floor. "It's time to pull up your big girl panties and show how strong you truly are."

Although he was originally talking about dealing with schoolyard bullies or clients disgruntled by the scathing article printed about them by Global Ten, it's still suitable for this occasion. Not facing Marcus would be a cowardly way of ending things. Even with my heart being held together by a thin thread, it knows confronting him in person is the right thing to do. My parents raised me to be a strong, independent woman, so I can't just push that aside when the circumstances don't fall in my favor.

My steps down the glamorous hallway are shaky and long. With Aubrey advising she was heading to bed hours ago, the entire house is plunged into eerie darkness. My heart slithers into my stomach when I open the door of a room I'd give anything not to see again: Marcus's old sub room. *If it's old.*

Careful not to impact the heavenly thick wool carpet, I place my dowdy overnight bag on the ground next to the closed bedroom door, then trudge to the bathroom. Although I've already showered once tonight, I still feel dirty. It's probably more to do with this room than anything.

I take my time in the shower, ignoring how starkly contradicting it is to the grandness of Marcus's bathroom. Don't misconstrue my statement, this bathroom is a thousand times better than the one in my home, but compared to Marcus's four vanity sinks, egg-shaped tub, and large double shower, this one just looks shabby.

I huff incredulously. I've clearly allowed the opulence of Marcus's properties to spoil me. Maybe that is why I'm finding it so hard to leave? It isn't because of my confusion; it is because I don't want to give this up. God—no wonder everyone assumes I am Marcus's sub. I'm acting just like one.

Annoyed at myself, I dress in a pair of stretchy yoga pants and a long-sleeve shirt. I'm so peeved, I don't bother putting on panties or a bra. I don't even dry my hair. I'll deal with the aftermath of my decision tomorrow. For now, I just want to crawl into bed and forget the world exists.

That would be a whole heap easier to do if I weren't doing it in the bed Marcus's previous subs used. I've been tossing and turning non-stop the past forty minutes. I've never seen photos of Marcus's former subs, or been given any indication of how they look, but I'm imagining a flurry of beautiful blondes with ocean blue eyes and perfect facial features. They are gorgeous women, but their faces are horrid enough to instigate nightmares.

Realizing I'm never going to achieve sleep in this room, I crawl out of bed, collect my bag, then leave the room. Because the house is so unnervingly quiet, the padding of my feet is readily distinguishable. The first door I open is the room Marcus and I prepared in earlier tonight. It has too many memories for me to sleep in there. The second door is the home gym. Other than the bench Marcus lifts weights at, there isn't another flat surface. I close the door and continue my trek, knowing there are only three more doors to explore. Two I'm well acquainted with: Marcus's bedroom and his playroom. Considering I don't plan on stepping foot in either of them, it leaves me only one option: the media room.

Gratitude clears away some of the nerves fluttering in my stomach when I notice the configuration of the room. It has two rows of reclining chairs lined in front of a monstrous projection screen. Thankfully, each chair is void of the armrests found in cinemas. If it weren't for the small walkway down one side, they would extend wall to wall.

After snagging a cashmere blanket draped over a railing on my right, I dump my bag on the floor and trudge down the small staircase. The bulky chair in front of the large screen is calling my name, beckoning me to it. My steps are sluggish, weighed down by the heaviness of my exhausted muscles. I am truly the most fatigued I've ever been. Even my blinks are long as my eyes fight to stay open.

My muscles sigh in gratitude when I slump in the super comfy recliner. The leather is so voluptuous, it curves around my body, cradling it with comfort. It is so blissful, before I know it, I fall into a much-needed, yet restless sleep.

I don't know how much time passes before I am awoken by the noise of someone yelling. "Where is she?! You said she was here!"

I blink several times in a row as my body struggles to produce enough saliva to quench my bone-dry mouth. I've clearly been asleep long enough my mouth had time to gape open, but not long enough for my thumping headache to relinquish its stranglehold on my temples.

"She was, Sir. She was in your room last time I saw her."

My pulse quickens when a furious growl rumbles through my chest. "Sir? Stop calling me goddamn sir! How many times have I told you not to call me *that*?"

A rush of giddiness clusters in my head when I lurch to a half-seated position. It isn't my temples drilling my skull causing my staggering response, it is recognizing the voice shouting so loud he is going to wake three continents. *Marcus.*

"I'm sorry, si—ah, Mr. Everett. It is an old habit from my previous employer," Aubrey explains, her tone as low as my heartrate.

Panic clutches my throat when Marcus arrogantly mutters, "I'll be your previous employer if I hear you say it again. Do you understand me?"

"Yes, I understand," Aubrey replies dismally.

"Good. Now, where is she?" Marcus's words are smeared with so much anger, they went to hell and back before they were delivered.

"She was in your room. I swear," Aubrey answers, her voice cracking with emotions.

"I checked in my room; she isn't there!" Marcus yells, his stern timbre shuddering through the thick paneled door between us.

"What about the subs' room, have you checked there?" Aubrey

questions, confirming what I suspected last night. She is aware of Marcus's involvement in the BDSM lifestyle.

"I checked. She isn't there either!"

My brows stitch when my ears misinterpret the anger in Marcus's voice as panic.

"She didn't leave, Mr. Everett. How could she? She doesn't have access to the security codes." I can hear the sheer bewilderment in Aubrey's tone. Clearly, she has never seen this side of Marcus either. Usually, he is calm and collected. Tonight, he is anything but.

"Yes, she does. I gave them to her last week!" Marcus replies, his tone wrathful enough to rattle my ribcage. "I asked you to watch her until I returned. You shouldn't have slept."

Hating that Marcus is directing his anger at the wrong person—much like I did hours ago—I throw off the thin blanket draped over my shoulders and trudge up the stairs. For how heavy my muscles are, my movements are remarkably quick.

I throw open the door with so much force, it slams into the drywall. "Don't speak to her like that. Just because she is your staff does not give you the right to disrespect her. Did your father not teach you any manners?"

Marcus and Aubrey's eyes rocket to me in sync. Aubrey's are brimming with relief. I don't know if her response stems from discovering I'm still present in Marcus's residence, or because I am standing up for her. Marcus's eyes are as black as the sky, tainted and murky, much like the sludge his deceit created in my heart.

I take a step backward, startled by the blatant fury beaming out of him in invisible waves. I take another step back when I realize it isn't anger being projected from his narrowed gaze. He's panicked.

"Cleo," he sighs deeply.

I flinch when he charges for me. His movements so fast, the air ripples in his wake. My mouth gapes when he smashes his lips against mine. His tongue slides into my mouth before a smidge of hostility can be announced by my overworked brain. I didn't think any kiss would top the one he gave me in the driveway of my home two weeks ago. I was wrong. This kiss. . . *my god*. He kisses me with so much vigor, my brain can't formulate an objection before it is turned to mush. He kisses me until my mind is blank and my panties are wet. He kisses me until I forget my name. Then he kisses me some more.

When he pulls away, the squeal of my lungs battling to be replenished with oxygen rings over the manic thump of my heart. Marcus places me on my feet before cradling my slackened jaw with his shaking hands. His eyes go crazy, scanning every inch of my face. I return his stare, muted with shock.

"When I couldn't find you, I thought you were gone. I thought you'd left me," he mumbles under his breath, his voice drenched with uncontrollable fear, like the thought of me leaving him truly gutted him.

The pure devastation in his tone cuts me raw, but it doesn't stop me from saying, "I *am* leaving you, Marcus. Just not until tomorrow morning." It is the fight of my life not to roll my eyes over the dimness displayed in my voice. How pathetic have I become that I can't break up with a man until after I've slept on his couch because I have nowhere else to go? I am better than this; my parents raised me better than this.

"I am leaving you," I say with more determination. "Now."

It will be a struggle, but I'll find a way to make it happen tonight, because standing across from him is more than I can bear. Seeing everything I am losing up close hurts way more than I could ever explain.

"No," Marcus says, shaking his head as his stern eyes dance between mine. "You're not leaving me, Cleo."

The anger his kiss dampened steamrolls back into me from the vicious snarl of his words. He replied as if my decision to leave him isn't my choice. Like he is the only one who has a say on the length of our relationship. Well, I have news for him.

"I'm not your submissive, Marcus, so any stipulated timeframe you force your subs. . ." I overemphasize the "S" on the end of "subs" to enhance my statement. ". . .to adhere to don't apply to me."

The rapturous standing ovation of the little voice inside me dims to a faint clap when Marcus replies, "I have plenty of resources at my disposal to restrain you here, Cleo. Don't test me."

The veins in my neck thrum, my body choosing its own response to his frisky tease. Annoyed at both Marcus and my lust-driven body, I roll my eyes, pivot on my heels, then head for the door.

"I might have stupidly thought that was sweet when you joked about it weeks ago. Now it is just disturbing," I snarl, my words wildly reckless.

My knees clang together when Marcus warns, "I'm not joking, Cleo. If you leave me, I'll hunt you down and tie you to my bed." His low tone vibrates from the roots of my hairs to the tips of my toes.

Silently huffing, I continue for the door. I may be head over heels in love with this man, but I am not so down on my luck I'm willing to pretend I didn't see what I see. So many women stay in relationships they should have left years earlier. I'm not going to be one of those women.

Gritting my teeth in the hope it will stop my tears from falling, I pry open the media room door. Unsurprisingly, Aubrey has made herself scarce. I don't blame her. The tension bristling the air is so dense, it has slicked my skin with a fine layer of sweat. And don't even get me started on the mess it has caused to my insides.

My angry strides into the hallway freeze when Marcus murmurs, "Cleo, please." I never knew two small words could express such agony.

After exhaling a deep breath, I pivot around to face him. He tries to tuck it away, but I see the quickest flare of emotion pass through his eyes before he entirely shuts it down. For someone who has poor acting skills, he is genuinely portraying that the idea of me leaving him is cutting him raw.

"We could have had something magical." When he endeavors to interrupt me, I continue speaking, foiling his attempt. "But you ruined what could have been the best thing of your life all because your desire to follow the rules of a BDSM lifestyle was stronger than your desire for me."

"No, Cleo," Marcus denies, shaking his head. "Nothing is stronger than the desire I have for you. Not BDSM. Not the rules. Not a person. Nothing. I would kneel before I'd let any of those things take you away from me."

"She was wearing your collar! Your trademark!" I retaliate, loathing that my voice displays I am on the verge of tears. "You looked at her like you look at me." The anger in my voice makes way for sheer devastation. My heart smashes into my ribs so fast, it feels like it's moments away from breaking out of my chest cavity.

Confusion smears on Marcus's face before he shakes his head, soundlessly denying my accusation.

"I saw you, Marcus. I saw you with *her!*"

"You saw me comforting a friend. Nothing more," he interrupts, his voice quickening in anger.

I brush a tear from my cheek, hating that it makes me look weak. "A friend wearing a collar everyone in *your* lifestyle knows belongs to *you*. I looked like an idiot proudly prancing around in your trademark. The same one *she* was wearing." My voice is barely a whisper, doused more with shame than anger. I'm not ashamed of myself; I'm disappointed in Marcus's pathetic attempt at admitting his mistakes. I thought he was more of a man than this. Clearly, I was wrong.

"Say something. Tell me I'm wrong. Tell me everyone didn't think *she* was your sub when they saw her collar."

He remains quiet, breaking my heart even more.

"You're pathetic," I mutter under my breath, beyond devastated.

Ignoring the flare of anger detonating in Marcus's eyes from my taunt, I spin on my heels and exit the media room. I'm so rattled with sick outrage I forget to gather my bag from the floor. It can wait. I'd rather wander around Montclair naked than spend another moment standing across from a man so cowardly he'd rather lie to my face than tell the truth.

I've barely made it halfway down the hall when Marcus catches me. He seizes my left wrist in a vice-like grip and yanks me backward. Just like earlier tonight, I act before thinking. My right hand flies toward Marcus's face so wildly that I don't stop to consider the consequences of my action.

Everything slows to snail's pace when my hand connects brutally with Marcus's left cheek. My slap is so firm, his head snaps to the side as a fiery burn incinerates my palm. Although my slap was a spur-of-the-moment decision, I know Marcus had time to stop me. The blaze in his eyes moments before my hand connected with his cheek was all the indication I needed to know he could have stopped me if he wanted. I just can't fathom why he didn't?

Seizing both of my wrists Marcus slaps my hands across his face over and over again. "Hit me, Cleo. Scratch me. Yell at me. But you are *not* leaving me!" he growls between slaps.

He doesn't hold back. He uses my hands to hit him continually until the redness on his face matches mine. They aren't soft taps either. They are so potent, the sound of skin slapping skin echoes off the pristine walls before booming back into my ears. Every hit he inflicts on his face with my hands breaks my heart more.

"Stop it," I blubber through a sob. "Stop it. Stop it. Stop it."

I yank away from him when he fails to adhere to my screamed demands. The air leaves my lungs in a grunt when my sudden movement causes us to crash into the same painting we stumbled into the last time we interacted in this hall. With how much my heart is tearing in two, I'd give anything to transport back to that day.

"Stop it, Marcus! Stop it!" I scream, my voice relaying I'm no longer capable of holding in my tears. "You're hurting me," I barely murmur, my heart broken beyond repair. "Pineapple."

Marcus releases my hands in an instant, the expression on his face mortified. I don't know if his brisk response is from me using my safe word or from my declaration that he was hurting me.

I scoop my stinging hands in close to my chest as my eyes roam his red-welted face. I can hardly breathe through the pain curled around my throat when I spot the absolute agony in his eyes. He is truly devastated. His desolate eyes show his heart is breaking as much as mine.

"Why? If you didn't want me to leave, why be with *her*? Why deceive me? Do you think so little of me you thought I'd stay when I discovered you are cheating on me?"

"I didn't cheat, Cleo. I don't cheat. But even if I did, I'd *never* cheat on you." The fury of his low tone doesn't match the sentiment in his eyes.

"I saw you, Marcus!" I roar, my heartache unmissable.

He leans into me, pinning me to the painting with his impressive, suit-covered body. "You saw nothing. Your mind was playing tricks on you. I shouldn't have sustained your climax. I shouldn't have teased you. You're clearly not trained enough for that yet. I played with fire, wanting to ignite your desires, but instead, I ended up getting burned."

Even confused by his riddle, I thrust against him, striving to break free, hating that he is using my attraction to him to insult me. My efforts are utterly pointless. He is too strong for a woman of my size to contend with.

Using the only weapon I have left in my arsenal, I angrily sneer, "I'm *soooo* sorry my submissive qualities aren't up to your standards, *Master Chains*." My voice is doused with bitter sarcasm. "I'll be sure to be more courteous to my next Master."

Marcus leans into me, crushing not just my body, but my heart as well. He glares into my eyes, his arrogance too haughty for my liking. His body temperature is so hot, a bead of sweat forms on the nape of my neck before rolling down my back.

My lashes blink back tears when he raises his hand to grip my throat. His hold isn't tight enough to impede my breathing, but it is firm enough for my traitorous body to respond to his touch. He curls his hand around the identical spot he did the last time we were in this hallway. I didn't know it at the time, but that was my first taste of sub space. Our exchange that night showed how much I trusted Marcus. I didn't even flinch when my life was placed in his hands. Now he has ruined that. His deceit broke my trust, and everyone knows broken trust can't be fixed. *Can it?*

Seemingly reading my inner monologue, Marcus asks, "How can you trust me with your life, Cleo, but not your heart?" His voice sounds tormented, as if he is stuck in an alternative universe, incapable of distinguishing the enemies from the allies.

He tracks his thumb over the vein throbbing in my neck before tightening his grip on my throat. My pupils widen as a feverous current rages through my veins before clustering in my heated core. Although I should be pulling away from his hold, demanding for him to stop this instant, my body doesn't cite a single protest. Not even my eyes demand for his withdrawal.

"Trust extends much further than a playroom, Cleo. When you trust me, it is the greatest compliment. Just like your distrust is the biggest disparagement," Marcus mutters, his nurturing voice in direct opposition to the hold he has on my neck.

He bounces his eyes between mine, the anger in them simmering to a slight boil as he loosens his grip. I keep my eyes locked on him as much-needed air hisses between my parted lips.

"You either trust me or you don't, Cleo. There is no middle ground," he murmurs as he drops his hand from my neck to brush it over my budded nipple, woefully displaying my enticement by his hold. It stiffens even more from his meekest touch.

A bout of shock hits me when his eyes lift to mine. I was expecting them to be filled with smugness, reveling in my body's inability to deny his touch. They aren't smug—not in the slightest. They are as tormented as ever.

"Do you trust me, Cleo?" Marcus asks as his beautifully haunted eyes frolic between mine.

My first instinct is to shake my head, but no matter how hard I plead for my body to respond to the prompts my brain is firing, it refuses. It trusts Marcus. So does my heart. It is just my brain begging for me not to get caught in a trap.

"Keira is a submissive," I mutter, using her name for the first time tonight, wanting to ensure Marcus knows to whom I am referring. My voice is barely a whisper, but it is confident enough to express that my statement was not a question. It was a confirmation.

"I know," Marcus replies, moving his hand to cradle my quaking jaw.

It is the fight of my life not to lean into his embrace, but I give it my best shot, still scorned by betrayal.

"She was wearing your collar," I murmur, grateful my voice is void of the anguish in my heart.

"I know," Marcus repeats, his voice a seductive purr that successfully conceals his bewilderment.

"Because she's your sub?" I ask. This time there is no doubt my question is a question. Just the heartbreak resonating in my low tone makes it unmissable. My heart cracked more just voicing that admission out loud.

"No," Marcus denies, briefly shaking his head. He locks his eyes with mine, ensuring I can see the honesty relayed by them as he discloses, "Keira has *never* been my sub. She will *never* be my sub." My lips quiver when he presses the softest kiss on the edge of my mouth as he mutters, "I don't need anyone but you, Cleo. I will *never* need anyone but you."

"Then why was she wearing your collar? And why didn't you say she wasn't your sub when I asked you?"

My lungs suck in their first full breath in over ten minutes when Marcus draws back enough he relieves the pressure placed on them. His tongue delves out to replenish his lips as he contemplates a reply. The longer he takes deliberating, the more my anger resurfaces.

"You made me angry," he eventually replies, his voice as weak as his excuse. "First I had to send Cartier over to deflect the bartender's advances, then you danced with Dexter."

Pushing aside my bewilderment that he knows Dexter's name, I snarl, "So you collared a submissive with your trademark just to make me jealous? Real mature, Marcus."

He balks, shunned by my reply. "What? No. I didn't collar Keira. I don't even know why she was wearing a collar, because as far as I am aware, she is currently without a Dom."

If he is hoping his answer will subdue my anger, he needs to devise a new tactic. I'm more ropeable now than I ever was.

"She doesn't have a Dom as the one she wants is already occupied. And since we don't have an official contract, I guess she figures she'll just stand in the wings, waiting for you to have your fill." I shrug my shoulders, the expression on my face leaving no doubt I'm enraged with jealousy. "Or maybe she will turn up to a gala wearing your signature and force a permanent intermission in our relationship."

Marcus's dark brows slant together. "So I get punished for the actions of another? How is that fair?" he questions, his tone half-wrathful, half-confused.

"I'm not punishing you for Keira wearing your trademark. If she did that of her own accord, you are not to blame. I'm punishing you because you didn't ask her to remove it, and you didn't deny she was your sub."

Marcus's baffled eyes bounce between mine. "How do you know what I said to her? Did you hear a word I spoke?"

I freeze as the quickest flashback from earlier tonight runs through my tired brain. My stomach winds up to my throat when I recall I didn't hear anything either of them said. I could barely hear a thing over my pulse shrilling in my ears, much less the low tone Marcus was using.

"No. You didn't hear anything I said, did you?" You could construe his statement as snarky, but the relief in his eyes doesn't allude to that.

I shake my head. "Still doesn't explain why you didn't deny she was your sub."

"I was being stubborn. Just like you were when you refused to answer my questions about Dexter," Marcus immediately fires back, his tone laced with as much jealousy as mine. We are both being immature.

"Then why did you let me leave?" Although my words are shaky, I'm pleased they come out with the confidence I am hoping for. "You had every opportunity to stop me, but you didn't. You just let me go. That hurt me, Marcus. So much. . ." My sentence trails off when my words crack with emotions.

Marcus runs his hand over his clipped afro, a tell-tale sign he is worried. He peers past my shoulder for several heart-thrashing seconds before he connects his eyes back with mine. "For the past few weeks, my security team has been receiving death threats. Tonight's was more concerning than the previous ones they have investigated."

My sharp inhalation of air nearly misses the rest of his admission. "This is nothing out of the ordinary in my industry, so usually I'd just brush it off as a consequence of fame, but this time was different." He twists a piece of my humidity-frizzed hair around his index finger. "I never had anyone to protect before. *Now I have you.*" He whispers his last sentence so softly, I barely heard him.

"You let me leave to protect me?" I ask, sheer bewilderment in my tone.

"Yes," Marcus answers, nodding.

His confession pushes us into resolute silence, plagued with confusion. Although I'm still angry, and my brain continually argues with my too-easy-to-forgive heart, I'm honestly too tired to keep bickering. What I saw between Marcus and Keira was wrong—there is no doubt in my mind, but when I push aside my jealousy, and look at the entire picture, I realize their exchange could have been as guiltless as mine was with Andy. They were fully clothed, and they weren't kissing. As much as it kills me to admit, other than Keira's poor choice in accessories, their exchange was innocent. Furthermore, what Marcus said is true: when you trust someone, it should extend past the bedroom.

The same can be said for acting recklessly. Marcus doesn't just make me irrationally reckless inside the playroom; he makes me unreasonably reckless in all aspects of my life. So much so, I'm lashing out without first sitting down and evaluating the entire picture. I'm allowing my fear of losing him as a way to push him away, instead of cherishing every moment we have. Clearly, he is doing the same thing.

Instead of telling me he was worried about my safety, he let me believe the horrid notions running through my head, as he knew I wouldn't stand by and watch it happen. My desire to flee the gala was one of the most potent I've had. I guess to Marcus, it was the perfect solution to ensure my safety. It was stupid, but it was also effective.

After swallowing down my unease, I lift my eyes to Marcus's. My breath traps halfway to my lungs when I notice he is observing me cautiously. The uncontrollable rage in his eyes has entirely subsided, but the slap marks on his face are as angry as ever.

"Tell me how to fix this, Cleo. Show me what to do. I'll do anything you want; just don't ask me to give you up. I'd rather die than give you up."

God—Marcus. The pain in his voice makes it feel like an elephant is sitting on my chest.

"I can fix this," he assures me, his tone confident. "I just need the chance to do that. Give me a chance, Cleo. Trust me enough to know I'd never intentionally hurt you. Give me that much, and I'll award you with so much more."

I return his fervent gaze with equal vigor. I'm honestly at a loss for a reply. Not just because his captivating green irises are luring me into a tangible trap from which I'll never be strong enough to break free, but because I genuinely can't think of anything he can give me than he hasn't already given. My only request at the start of our relationship was to have our D/s contract removed from our negotiation. Marcus did that—then so much more. So what more could he possibly give me?

I freeze when an idea pops into my head. It causes a rush of giddiness to hit my stomach and head at the same time. Don't ask me if it is a good or bad giddiness as I wouldn't be able to say.

Like he can sense my internal battle, Marcus places his hand under my chin and raises my head. "Tell me," he requests, his tone not wrathful or annoyed.

I swallow the brick lodged in my throat before checking, "Anything?"

"Anything," Marcus confirms while tucking a strand of my wild hair behind my ear. "I'd give up everything I have before I'll give you up."

Once the unruly curl is secured behind my ear, the back of his fingers trace my earlobe, slide down my neck, then skim over my barely exposed collarbone. His touch is brief, but robust enough to spark a fire deep in my womb I never expected to ignite tonight. It also strengthens my determination to push our relationship onto a whole new playing field. One I'm sure Marcus has never fielded before.

Marcus's hand freezes on the collar of my shirt when I ask, "Have you ever made love?"

His Adam's apple bobs up and down before he briefly shakes his head. "No."

"Will you make love to me? Will you give me that? Will you give me a part of you no one else has had?" I ask.

Marcus peers into my eyes, the sentiment in them growing every second that ticks by before he faintly whispers, "Yes."

Chapter Five

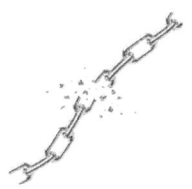

THE TENSION IN THE AIR RAPIDLY CHANGES TO LUST WHEN MARCUS curls his hand around mine and paces toward his master suite. Incredulously, my hands are clammier now than they are when I kneel in his playroom. That probably has something to do with this being as foreign to Marcus as it was for me entering Chains months ago. Although I hate that I'm forcing him out of his comfort zone, I'm not going to stop our exchange. I need this—*we need this.*

After swinging open his bedroom door, Marcus switches on the lights, then merges deeper into the room. My brows furrow when his brisk pace has us passing right by his monstrous bed sitting in the middle of the vast space.

"You don't need a bed to make love," Marcus advises my stunned expression. "You just need a place where you can worship, devour, treasure, and. . ." He fleetingly glances my way before muttering, "love."

My heart rate kicks into a mad beat, an awakening combination of lust and excitement when he walks us into the bathroom. The attraction crackling between us is as vibrant as ever, but it is even more powerful, encouraged by a connection more compelling than just jealousy. There are so many emotions passing between us. Mutual respect. Understanding. Silent pleas for forgiveness—not only from Marcus, but me as well. But more than anything—the most intoxicating of them all is the sentiment of desire. It is so strong, I'll confidently declare that Marcus wants this as much as I do. He wants to share this experience with me—and only me.

Marcus releases my hand to switch on the shower faucet. After ensuring the temperature is adequate, he devotes his attention back to me. He stares at me, unmoving, nonjudgmental. He just stares.

"What are you waiting for?" I ask, my voice barely a whisper. I'm so used to him taking charge, I'm a little stumped on how to move our exchange forward without jumping him like an out-of-control nymph.

"For you to tell me what you want," Marcus answers as a ghost of a smile cracks on his lips.

My eyes dance between his. "I want you."

"Good. That's a start," he replies, his smile enlarging. "Where do you want me? What do you want me to do?"

My brows stitch as confusion makes itself known. *Why is he handing all the power to me? This isn't what I wanted.* I gasp when reality dawns.

I connect my eyes with Marcus's. "I don't want to top you, Marcus. I just want *you* to make love to *me*. Not *me* top *you*."

"So you still want me to take charge?" he clarifies, his brows furrowing.

I smile at the unease in his voice. "Yes and no. I want you to lead, I just don't want any rules. I'm pretty sure that is the only difference between BDSM sex and vanilla sex: both participants control the exchange."

My smile enlarges when Marcus grimaces at me mentioning the word "vanilla."

The worry tainting his gorgeous face vanishes when I grip the hem of my shirt and whip it over my head. Air hisses through his teeth when my naked breasts fall heavily to my chest. Obviously, he was unaware I am naked beneath my clothing.

Keeping my eyes locked with his, I shimmy my yoga pants down my thighs. His avid gaze raking over my body boosts my confidence. I've never felt more desired than I do right now. "So beautiful, Cleo," Marcus murmurs more to himself than me.

I brazenly step toward him, my desire to undress him as potent as my need to taste him in my mouth. Usually, I'd have to wait for him to permit me to touch him, but since our exchange is happening on neutral territory, my body can express its desires without fear of repercussion.

As I fiddle with the buttons on his fancy dress shirt, Marcus gathers my hair to the left so he can ravish my neck. I lean into his embrace, adoring the smattering of kisses he places along my jaw and down my throat. Each soft nib and suck adds to the twinge inflicting my throbbing sex. My body heats up when one of his hands lowers to the curve of my back to draw me in, where the other cups my breast to toy with my erect nipple.

Because I'm so caught up in calming the furious storm brewing in my core, it takes me nearly five minutes to undo the last button of his shirt. I feel Marcus smile against my neck when his shirt drops to the floor in a heap. As my hands work on the belt wrapped around his waist, Marcus toes off his shoes. Warm water glides down my face when he steers us into the shower, his impatience meaning he isn't even undressed yet.

I pull back from his embrace. "So impatient," I tease, inwardly sighing when my voice comes out with the hint of sexiness I was aiming for.

Any reply Marcus is planning to give is rammed back into his throat when I lower myself to my knees and glance up at him. I lick my lips when the glorious image of his thick cock bracing against the zipper of his trousers is thrust into my vision.

When I brush my hand over his massive bulge, Marcus mutters, "I thought I was supposed to worship you?"

"Oh, believe me, this will be just as fulfilling for me as it is for you," I guarantee while sliding down his zipper.

I squeeze my thighs together when his glorious cock springs free. He is thick, long, and jutted. My mouth waters when I spot a bead of pre-cum pooling at the top of his engorged knob. Loving that I don't need to wait for permission, I wrap my hand around his thickened shaft before my tongue makes quick work of the salty goodness. Marcus's groan rolls all the way down his chest until it vibrates on my tongue.

Once I lap up every drop of his excitement, I lower my mouth down his densely veined shaft. I sink my lips as far down as possible, only stopping when it is physically impossible for me to take any more.

"God, Cleo," Marcus sighs, his tone announcing it is more a sigh of pleasure than disappointment. "I love the way you suck my cock, all greedy and eager."

His praise encourages my pursuit. I run my lips up and down his magnificent manhood on repeat as my hand works the section missing out on experiencing the warmth of my mouth. I may have no gag reflex, but that doesn't mean I can deepthroat Marcus. The girth of his cock is already a challenge, let alone the length of him.

"Slow down, Cleo, I don't want to cum in your mouth," Marcus advises me a short time later, his tone laced with lust. "I want to be wrapped in the warmth of your pussy before I cum."

I continue my pursuit, acting like I didn't hear what he said.

"Cleo. . ." Marcus growls out, his tone as unforgiving as my pumps on his cock. "Slow down."

Although his growl is clearly a warning, my speed remains unchecked. My tongue gathers every bead of pre-cum seeping out of his knob as my mouth sucks urgently on his shaft. I'm so dying to taste him, my cheeks hollow painfully with every suck.

When I peer up at him, silently advising him I have no intention of stopping, his grip on my hair loosens, and the strain marring his beautiful face fades.

"Good boy," I mutter through a mouth full of cock.

If I hadn't seen the quickest smirk etch onto his mouth, I'd be worried about my brazenness, but since the spark of admiration in his eyes is making me the most confident I've ever felt, I continue my mission to unravel him without pause.

Approximately five minutes later, my dedication is awarded in the most glorious way. The strong, brackish taste of Marcus pumps onto my tongue in raring spurts as he grunts my name in a guttural moan. My throat struggles to swallow every delicious drop of his spawn, but I give it my best shot, not willing to waste a single morsel of his cum.

Once every scrumptious drop has been consumed, I lift my eyes to Marcus. He peers down at me. Shock and admiration are smeared all over his face. My kneecaps pop back into place when he aids me into a standing position. I sway slightly, intoxicated by lust. In the past few weeks, I've only been allowed to suck his cock twice. Once was in the playroom when I wasn't allowed to touch him, and another was when I woke him three days ago at 3 AM in the most glorious way. Although stunned by my brazenness, excitement soon pushed aside his anger.

Marcus's big hands swallow my cheeks as he cups them before sealing his lips over mine. His tongue slides into my mouth, not the slightest bit concerned that his cum was just inside my mouth. Just the thought of him tasting a smidge of himself has my thighs touching. He kisses me until the dizziness causing me to sway like a leaf in the breeze becomes uncontrollable.

Keeping his hands on my shoulders to ensure I don't succumb to the giddiness clustered in my head, Marcus kicks his drenched pants to the side, then moves to stand behind me. Although he just came, the heat of his erect cock scorches my back when he bands his arms around my waist and draws me into his body, stilling my swaying movements simultaneously. The cushy softness of my backside can't take away from the sheer girth of his cock. He is even thicker than he was when I had him in my mouth.

My head lolls to the side when the softness of cashmere scrapes over my aching breasts, down my quivering stomach before scrubbing ever-so-slightly over my throbbing clit. Marcus delivers an additional three gentle rubs over my pussy before he moves the shower puff back to my torso. I try to hold in my whine. I miserably fail.

"Who's impatient?" Marcus mutters, his voice so tempting, a gathering of goosebumps race to the surface of my skin.

Once every inch of my torso has been thoroughly lathered with fragrant body wash, Marcus takes a step backward. Although disappointed by his lack of contact, the gentle sweeps of the heavenly soft shower puff on the weary muscles in my back keeps my disappointment at bay. His touch is gentle enough to know he is nurturing me, but firm enough to knead out the tension of my night.

After washing the suds off my torso and back, Marcus moves to stand in front of me. The excited butterflies in my stomach drop to my sex when he glances into my eyes and lowers himself to his knees. The reasoning behind his submissive stance becomes apparent when he lathers my legs with the same amount of attention he gave to my torso and back. Although my pussy was well-cleaned previously, it is awarded a second lot of attention when he slides the shower puff from my left leg to my right.

My breathing turns labored when the tips of his fingers extend past the shower puff to graze ever-so-slightly over my throbbing clit. The chances of securing an entire breath are lost when Marcus snags the extendable showerhead from the middle of the pole to remove the suds from the lower half of my body. The heated water pumping onto my pulsating sex adds to the tingling sensation sweeping across my stomach. He pulls it in close, ensuring every inch of my pussy is rid of bubbles.

I groan a low, raspy moan when Marcus peers up at me while replenishing his top lip with moisture. His eyes tell me he knows how desperate I am for him to touch me, but he remains entirely still, wearing nothing but an amorous smirk on his gorgeous face. The longer he stares at me, the stronger my desires grow. I'm so damn desperate for him to touch me, I'm not above being disobedient. Any punishment he wishes to instill will be worth it if he'll just touch me. I'm so close to the brink, I'm confident one sweep of his thumb over my clit will have me freefalling over the edge.

Suddenly, my spine snaps straight. *I don't have to fear discipline. Not tonight.*

Marcus's throaty laugh is muffled by the dampness pooling between my legs when I grip the back of his head and mash it with my pussy. I moan a throaty purr when the tip of his tongue grazes my throbbing clit. My hands shoot out to brace against the foggy shower door when his tongue slides up the folds of my aching sex before rolling around the bud of my clit.

"Yes," I hiss through gritted teeth when he suckles my clit into his mouth.

Although the lashes of his tongue and the nips of his teeth are more reserved than I am used to, they aren't weak enough to stave off my desire to climax. I try to hold it back. I fight with all my might to ignore the tidal wave crashing into me, attempting to drag me away.

But the sensation is too intense. Within seconds, I'm swept into the current, unable to breathe, move, or have a single lucid thought.

"Give it to me," Marcus demands, his voice a soft purr that pushes my climax over the line in a sexually seductive way.

I inhale a sharp breath, overcome by the sensation carrying me away. My orgasm is so strong, my vision blurs, and my entire body quivers and shakes as it rides the awe-inspiring intensity. The orgasmic shudders violently coursing through me turn me into a quivering, blubbering mess. I'm shaking so uncontrollably I lose my grip on the shower wall, and my knees buckle.

"I've got you," Marcus guarantees as he firms his grip on my ass to keep me upright.

Once every blissful shudder has been exhausted from my body, Marcus stands from his knelt position, gathers me in his arms, then strides out of the bathroom. My damp hair fans across the silky soft bedspread covering his monstrous bed when he lays me down in the middle of it. The thermostat is set to a pleasant temperature, but it doesn't stop goosebumps racing to the surface of my skin since neither Marcus or I dried off upon exiting the shower.

Beads of water roll off his afro and drip onto my stomach as he places a trail of kisses from my neck to my still throbbing core. I girlishly giggle when he presses the quickest peck to my tingling sex. His touch is only brief, but strong enough to ignite a new fire deep in my womb.

With his lustful eyes fixated on me, he kneels between my legs before carefully raising my backside off the bed. My breathing levels when the crest of his cock braces the seam of my soaked pussy.

I graze my teeth over my bottom lip when he attentively asks, "Are you ready?"

I nod my head, too overcome with emotions to express words.

My back arches off the bed and my eyes snap shut when he slowly inches inside me. The sensation is overwhelmingly sweet and toe-curlingly delicious at the same time. My sex ripples around him, coercing him deeper until every inch of his glorious cock is hilted. I purr softly, adoring the heaviness of him inside of me.

The past two weeks we've had sex a minimum of two to three

times a day, and every single time awards me with an entirely new sensation. Today is no different. With my pussy well-prepared for his intrusion and happily accepting it, the pain usually associated with taking a man of his size isn't present.

When my eyelids slowly flutter open, they are met with the most alluring pair of dazzling green eyes. Marcus watches me carefully, ensuring not a skerrick of pain crosses my face as he slowly drags his cock back out. My vagina hugs him, massaging every perfect vein feeding his magnificent manhood. After pulling out all the way to the tip, Marcus rocks back into me, his pace not as slow as his first pump, but a nice speed that guarantees he is not fucking me; he is making love to me.

Goosebumps follow the track his lips make when he moves them between my neck and breasts. His mouth adores the top half of my body while his cock worships the rest. I honestly feel cherished; I'd even go as far as saying loved.

I'm going to be honest: when I asked Marcus to make love to me, I truly thought it would be an hour or two filled with awkwardness. Although he has never explicitly said it, making love is not Marcus's forte. He is a man who likes to fuck, and he fucks well. But not seeing a snick of hesitation on his face as he worships my body is a treasured memory I'll never forget. This experience expresses way more than words ever could. I feel admired, cherished, respected, and loved.

Striving not to cornily express my undying love during our activity, I grip the round globes of Marcus's perfect ass and enjoy the sensation. He rocks in and out of me, over and over until the unmistakable signs of an orgasm awaken within me. Although his speed is a lot slower than we usually go, the rim of his cock hits the sweet spot inside me with every grind.

As he continues driving me to the brink with nothing but a mouth-watering smirk, a leisured speed, and a contented face, I work through my bewilderment at how quickly my climax is cultivating. Usually, I need. . . *more*, but I can't deny the tingling sensation sweeping across my core. It is so strong, I feel like I'm mere moments from climaxing.

No, make that I *am* climaxing.

My nails dig into Marcus's ass as a furious wildfire roars through my body. I'm not the only one caught off guard by my climax; Marcus is just as shocked as me. He stills for a mere second before he continues grinding into me, forcing me to ride the intensity of my soul-stealing climax. His muscles contract and release with each perfect pump his cock does as he uses every inch of his body to make love to me. I shiver and shake as I whisper his name on repeat, adoring that I achieved the unachievable. *I came during sex.*

My orgasm is long and exhaustive, one of the strongest I've ever had. It feels like hours pass before I can garner the strength to open my eyes. When I do, I spot Marcus staring down at me, smiling and uncontained. His eyes are the rawest I've ever seen them, so open and honest. Tears well in my eyes when I read the sentiment in his heavy-hooded gaze. He isn't just happy he accomplished greatness, he is as smug as hell.

"Shut up," I murmur while throwing a fist into his rock-hard abs.

I growl a hungry grunt when he flexes his cock. That one little flex thrusts me to within an inch of the finish line. My god—the power this man has over my body is truly astounding. Even when he is making love, he is still a Master.

"I'm not laughing at you, Cleo. I'm smiling. Missionary has never been my position of choice, but after seeing the way your face flushes with ecstasy as your pussy milks my cock, I might have to alter my opinion on that humble position. That was by far the sexiest thing I've ever seen."

The tears looming in my eyes nearly roll down my face when Marcus unexpectedly flips over. Since he is still hilted inside me, I follow his movement. I purr like a kitten when the hard muscle of his Apollo belt grinds against my clit in the process.

Loving my reaction, Marcus jerks his hips upwards. A husky moan tears from my throat when his cock inches even deeper inside me at the same time his pelvis stimulates my clit. Wanting to return his tease, I defy my Jell-O thighs by raising myself onto my knees. A blistering of stars twinkle in front of my eyes when I slam down hard, taking Marcus's cock to the very base.

A grunted moan roars through Marcus's lips as his grip on my hips turns deadly. "Jesus Christ, Cleo. We're supposed to be making love."

My hands shoot out to lean on his sweat-slicked torso as a surge of excitement spasms in my pussy, loving the curtness of his tone. I also need a minute to catch my breath. Because we've never done this position, the change in angle is truly breath-stealing.

"We've already made love. Now I'm going to prove you can make love without needing to go slow," I whisper breathlessly. "It's the emotions displayed during the exchange that differentiates sex from making love."

Marcus's teeth grit when I swivel my hips in a circular motion. "It's the reactions you force from the one you're worshipping." When I tighten the walls of my vagina around his twitching shaft, he thickens even more. "It's expressing your every want, need, and desire without using words."

Marcus's eyes bounce between mine for several seconds. I can tell the instant he reads the honesty from my eyes, as he releases my hips from his firm grasp and places his hands behind his head. Although his eyes are still raging with naturally engrained dominance, they are also sparked with agreement. They permit me to do as I please without a word needing to be passed through his quirked-with-amusement lips.

"Show me, Cleo. Tell me what you want to say but are too afraid to speak," he commands.

I do exactly that. I express everything he means to me without a syllable escaping my mouth. I tell him how much I love his dominance, his caring nature, his bossiness. But more than anything, I express those three little words I'll never be game to say out loud.

I tell him that I love him—over and over again until we collapse from exhaustion.

Chapter Six

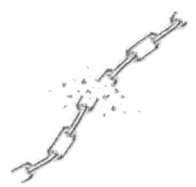

"Remember, Brodie goes where you go, Cleo," Marcus instructs from the driver's seat of his car, the deep hum of his voice persuasive enough for a flock of birds nesting in the tree at the side of his residence to take flight.

I roll my eyes, faking annoyance to his unyielding demand. I'm not annoyed. Although at times, his protectiveness hackles my spine, after years of going it alone, it's nice having someone care enough about me they are worried about my safety. I'm also too exhausted to take on the stress denying his command would instigate. Last night smoothed some of the kinks in our relationship, but there are still many other bumps that need ironing out.

"I know, Marcus. I've already brought Brodie a studded collar and lead. Since he is shadowing me like a puppy, he may as well dress the part," I jest, my tone high-spirited.

Marcus's deep growl rumbles through my chest before clustering in my throbbing womb, which is still reveling in the aftermath of our lovemaking that proceeded until the wee hours of this morning. Resisting the desire to squeeze my thighs together from his scrumptious growl, my eyes stray to Marcus. He peers up at me, exuding anger and silent expectations. The absoluteness of his gaze sends a chill down my spine.

"What?" I murmur, questioning myself more than Marcus.

Although stumped by his response, I have no doubt he is angry. Blatant jealousy pumps out of him in enraged spurts, and his gaze is so hot, the brisk winter winds aerating my damp hair become a distant memory.

The cause of his sudden shift in composure comes to light when Marcus mutters, "I thought your knowledge of animal play was minimal?"

My eyes bulge when the quickest flash of a memory sparks in my spent mind. I'm held captive as I recall the lady standing in front of me, lowering herself onto her hands and knees to crawl into Chains at the heel of her Dom.

When I snap out of my trance, I try to hold in my laughter that Marcus is fretful of Brodie kneeling at my heel. The more I struggle to contain my childish giggles, the harder my fight becomes. I don't know what is more amusing: the fact Marcus thinks Brodie would heel, or that Marcus is so blinded by jealousy, he can't see that I care for Brodie as if he is family. Brodie is a great guy, but there isn't an ounce of attraction between us.

Marcus's eyes thin when my dainty laughter trickles into the dew-filled air. "It isn't funny, Cleo," he grinds out through clenched teeth.

Snubbing the way his narrowed glare hits every one of my hot buttons, I bend down, slap my hands on each side of his cheeks, then plant a big sloppy kiss on his hard-lined lips. My excitement mounts when Marcus growls as I fail to open my mouth at the request of his lashing tongue.

"Our shared shower already has you behind schedule," I mumble against his lips before pulling back. "You don't want to leave Cameron waiting on the tarmac even longer, do you?"

The quickest flare blazes through Marcus's eyes. Although I'm confident I've seen it before, the nanosecond between its arrival and departure is too fast for me to decipher what it means.

Marcus's hand tightens around his steering wheel as his eyes roam my face, categorizing every fine feature with detailed accuracy. When his eyes land on my faintly blue-tinged lips caused by the nippy mid-December temperatures, he asks, "Where is your coat? Why didn't Aubrey get your jacket as I requested?"

When his hand curls around the door latch, preparing to exit his vehicle, I bump my hip against the driver's side door, keeping him trapped in his car. "Aubrey gave me my coat as per your request; I left it on the entranceway table. I'm feeling a little warm."

The concern Marcus's eyes have been carrying all morning doubles. "Are you unwell? Are you sick?" His eyes thoroughly inspect me with the same attentiveness Abel had weeks ago. "Should I stay? Do you want me to stay?"

"No, I'm fine. I'm just a little warm after our *strenuous* activities this morning. Who wouldn't be after that exchange?" I fan myself, acting all flustered. My inflamed cheeks aren't a ploy to lessen his worry. Our exchange went above and beyond my wildest dreams. "Last night was wow, Marcus. Like. . . *whoa!*"

The worry clouding Marcus's usually vibrant eyes dulls from my confession when he reads the honesty on my face. Last night was out of this world. Not only is my heart still beating at triple the speed, but my muscles are screaming from exhaustion. *Who knew making love was such an arduous experience?*

I lean into the open driver's side window so I can place my hands on each side of Marcus's recently shaved jaw. The contrasting temperatures between my hands and his face are staggering. Come to think of it, his cheeks are just as heated as mine.

"Call me when you land, okay?" I request. I try to keep the worry out of my voice. I fail. Marcus is a very skilled pilot, but that doesn't mean I'll not freak every time he's in the air.

"Alright," Marcus agrees before he gently nibbles on my lips. "Stay safe, baby," he murmurs ever so quietly.

His kiss is brief but wondrous enough to cause a rush of dizziness to cluster in my head. After taking one last whiff of his delicious scent, I regretfully withdraw from his scrumptious mouth and take a step back from his car. The loud rumble of his engine breaks through the uncomfortable silence bouncing between us when he cranks the ignition of his sports car and revs the engine. The pout on my lip switches to a smile when he playfully revs his engine a few more times for good measure, ensuring our exchange is ending with fond memories instead of sad ones.

"That's better," Marcus murmurs when he spots my smile. "I'll see you soon, Cleo."

Not trusting my mouth to hold back the heavy sentiment I feel, I broaden my smile and idiotically wave. Marcus winks before increasing the pressure on his gas pedal. From the way I stand on the stoop of his stairs, watching his car roll down the asphalt, you'd swear he was leaving for war, not spending the week laying down tracks on another no doubt record-breaking album.

I wait for the taillights of Marcus's car to disappear on the horizon before pivoting around and climbing the platform stairs. "Come," Aubrey says from the entranceway. She gestures her hand in the same manner she did last night, but this time, her tone is void of any annoyance.

Earlier this morning, when Marcus was submitting his flight manifest for his trip to Ravenshoe, I had a quiet word with Aubrey. It was awkward, but one hundred percent necessary. I wouldn't say it was unnecessarily awkward for Aubrey—I was the only blubbering idiot in our conversation—she handled it with the maturity awarded by her age. Although I pathetically used my argument with Marcus as an excuse for my appalling behavior, Aubrey graciously accepted my apology before issuing one of her own. Our bond started on unstable ground, but with us both being mature enough to admit our wrongdoings, I think all previous awkwardness will now be avoidable. Once I'm satisfied that's been achieved, I'll begin working on her relationship with Marcus. It is clear before last night they had an amicable working relationship, but their exchange in the hallway has added some obvious cracks I'll strive hard to repair, since part of the blame for their spat lands on my shoulders.

Aubrey drapes a large blanket around my shuddering frame before running her hands up and down my prickled arms. Once she is satisfied my body temperature has returned to an acceptable level, she curls her arm around my shoulders and guides me into the living room. A grin curves on my mouth when I spot a large mug of hot chocolate sitting on the coffee table. It is positioned right next to my recently loaded Kindle.

"I'll get fat if I keep consuming sugar-laced drinks while sitting on my backside reading," I grumble under my breath.

"It's Sunday. Besides, from what Mr. Brown told me this morning, I don't think you need to worry. Mr. Everett isn't planning on being gone long," Aubrey replies, her usually smooth voice hindered by the crack of hilarity.

When my eyes sling to hers, the hue of pink on her cheeks shifts to a vibrant red coloring. "You've been talking to Abel?" I question, happy to deflect the conversation away from my vigorous sex life.

Like her face could get any redder, Aubrey's cheeks blaze even more. "Yes," she replies with a faint smile.

I step into the living room and slide onto the comfy couch, inconspicuously snagging my Kindle and hot chocolate off the coffee table on my way by. "Did you and Abel talk to plan Marcus's visit, or. . ." I leave my question open, letting my waggling brows speak on my behalf.

The heat on Aubrey's cheeks ascends halfway down her neck. "Our call was not in regards to Mr. Everett."

She stands still, frozen by my shocked stare. Before I can configure a response to her admission, Aubrey mumbles something under her breath before she pivots on her heels and exits the living room without a backward glance. Since our relationship is still wading in murky waters, I store her flustered response away as ammunition for when I'm next wrangling Abel.

After switching on my Kindle, I snuggle into the couch Marcus defiled me on weeks ago and get caught up in the fictional world of my all-time favorite author.

I've been reading for nearly two hours when the buzz of a cell phone interrupts me. Unable to tear my eyes away from the super-hot sex scene of a detective and his long-lost love, I continue reading as my hand aimlessly searches the coffee table for my cell. When I find it, I dash my eyes between my Kindle and the screen of my phone. Noticing it is a message from an unknown caller, I rest it against my thigh. With my utmost attention devoted to the story melting my Kindle more prominent than my need to be persuaded by a telemarketer, I ignore my caller.

"Damn," I murmur to myself when the storyline merges into wicked territory. The tension between the two characters is so hot, it would fog up my glasses if I were wearing any.

When my cell phone buzzes again and again, I place my Kindle on the coffee table with disappointment and read the messages. The second helping of hot chocolate I guzzled down with a set of homemade scones gurgles in my stomach when I read the first message.

Unknown Caller: *Are we still meeting today? Dexter xxx*

The contents of my stomach wind all the way up to my throat when I read his second and third message.

Unknown Caller: *Don't forget the tissues.*

Unknown Caller: *Actually, bring two boxes just in case.*

Riddled with worry, my eyes shoot to the clock hanging in the middle of the blank wall of the living room. It displays it is nearly noon. With traffic, it will take me almost an hour and a half to get to Montclair. That leaves me half an hour to get ready, so I have no excuse not to meet with Dexter. *Dammit.*

Although Marcus and I worked through a lot of my concerns last night, I still have a lot of unanswered questions. And although I'd donate a kidney to ease the confusion muddling my mind, shouldn't I seek answers from the man who is the source of them?

After a few moments of deliberation, I fire back a quick message to Dexter, notifying him that our meeting is still on. Worry slows my strides as I weave through Marcus's residence, seeking Brodie. I know he is here, as he was the first person Marcus called when he discovered his trip to Ravenshoe had been moved up a day.

I find Brodie twenty minutes later in the room I couldn't sleep in last night: Marcus's old sub room. His brows are furrowed together tightly, and he has a confused expression etched on his face. When he spots me standing in the doorway, he drifts his eyes to me. "Do I want to know what this room is?"

From the scratchiness of his tone, you'd swear he was standing in the middle of Marcus's playroom, not his guest bedroom. Although his question is highly warranted, I quirk my lips and shake my head. Brodie's brows stitch together even more from my blasé response.

While running my sweaty palms down my jeans, I pace deeper into the room. "Will you be ready for a trip to Montclair in twenty minutes? If not, I can take myself, then you can continue unpacking." It is the fight of my life not to roll my eyes over the dimness in my voice. I sound like a child asking a parent for a cookie while dinner is being served.

Brodie stands from the bed before shifting to face me. "Marcus said he wanted us to stay here for the week."

"We are; I just have plans with a. . . *friend* for lunch." I grimace at my poor choice in tone. If Brodie wasn't already suspicious of my motives, I'm certain his interests are now piqued.

"Who's your friend?" Brodie asks, his tone similar to one you'd expect a detective to use when grilling you for murder charges, not a bodyguard protecting you because your boyfriend is worried about overzealous fans.

"Is your friend a male or female?" Brodie continues to probe when I fail to answer his first question.

I cock my hip and spread my hands across my waist. "Does it matter? A friend is a friend, no matter what their gender is."

Brodie's lips curve high enough I can see the pegs of his white teeth. "So it's a male friend."

I cross my arms in front of my chest, but don't negate his claim. *Lying has never been my forte.*

"Does Marcus know you're meeting a *male* friend?" Brodie queries, his voice higher than his arched brow.

I squint my eyes at his smug expression. He laughs off my attempt to snarl at him, finding it more humorous than dangerous. His brutish response unleashes my Garcia fighting spirit.

"Does Marcus know you helped remove the nipple clamps from my breasts last night?" I ask.

Brodie's eyes widen to the size of saucers as he takes a step back, shocked by my brazenness. "I didn't touch you. I might have noticed the clamps on your necklace when you shoved it into my chest, but I sure as hell didn't remove them for you."

"Marcus doesn't know that," I fire back, my tone relaying I'm not joking.

I stare at Brodie, silently praying he won't see the truth in my eyes. My desire to talk to Dexter is strong, but not strong enough to throw Brodie into the deep end without a life jacket.

When his malevolent glare intensifies, the take-no-shit expression on my face grows. It feels like the moon circles the earth three times before Brodie shakes his head. As a sneaky smirk cracks onto his lips, he snags his jacket from the bed he is standing next to.

"He has no fucking clue what he's dealing with," he murmurs under his breath as he curls his arm around my shoulders.

When he drags me into the corridor, I mumble, "I was planning on taking a shower and getting changed before we leave."

"I was planning on masturbating on a floral bedspread while watching porn, but I guess plans change."

My eyes rocket to Brodie. Disbelief—and if I am being honest—a little bit of impishness is lining my face. As I said to Marcus earlier, there is no spark of attraction between Brodie and me, but even a blind woman couldn't deny Brodie is a handsome man. Not as attractive as Marcus, but that would be a hard feat for any man to conquer, so just the thought of him getting a little handsy with himself has my pulse rising.

Spotting my slack-jawed expression, Brodie assures me, "I was joking, Cleo."

I stare at him, my suspicion uncontainable. His eyes aren't expressing mischievousness. Actually, they aren't revealing anything.

My disbelief is proven on point when Brodie mumbles, "I wasn't planning on watching porn."

Chapter Seven

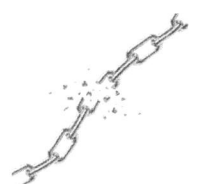

"I'VE BEEN TO THIS PIZZERIA MANY TIMES BEFORE. THERE IS NO BACK exit. All clientele must walk in and out that door," I say, pointing to the glass door of Villa Victoria. Brodie and I are parked just a few spaces up from here.

When Brodie continues to silently protest about my request for privacy, I add on, "You are a bodyguard, Brodie, not a watchdog. This will be a very long week if you don't occasionally learn to heel." My spine straightens over my poor choice of words, but the sternness on my face remains firm.

Brodie quietly studies me, drinking in my determined resolution. "Jesus, and here I was thinking Lexi was the bossy one in your dynamic." Although his tone is a little snarky, the laughter in his voice dampens the snappiness of his reply.

"Who do you think she learned her bitchiness from?" I query with a bowed brow.

Brodie doesn't answer my question. It is a smart decision on his behalf. Clearly, he isn't just a handsome man, he is a shrewd one as well.

"Give me your phone." A stranger may construe his statement as a request, but I didn't. It was a demand.

After handing him my cracked cell, he unlocks the screen without requesting my access code, then scrolls to my contacts to add a number to my frequently called list. If he had slapped my face he couldn't have shocked me more.

Snubbing my disapproving glare, Brodie advises, "This is my cell number. If you so much as sniff an ounce of trouble, call me. I'll be in that pizzeria faster than a crack dealer running from the police."

He tilts my cell toward me, not relinquishing it from his tight grip until I give him my wholehearted agreement that I'll call him at the first sign of trouble. Storing my cell in my purse, I slide out of Brodie's car and head into the pizzeria. Although my insides are bristling with annoyance, I realize Brodie is just doing the job Marcus pays him to do. So, if anyone is going to cop the wrath of my anger for my privacy being invaded, it should be the man leading the helm: Mr. Marcus Everett.

Inane butterflies take flight in my stomach when I swing open the thick glass door of the pizzeria and enter. The smell of garlic and melted cheese smacks into me, forcing a rampant grumble to gurgle in my hungry tummy. With it being late in the afternoon, the crowd isn't as heavy as the ones I've come to expect during evening rush hour, but there are still a good number of people mingling in the space.

My head slings to the side when a distinctive voice calling my name rings through my ears. Dexter is sitting at a table on my right, just in front of a large painted mural. He is dressed down today compared to last night, wearing a pair of well-fitted jeans and a light blue long-sleeved shirt rolled up to his elbows.

After placing my jacket on the coatrack on my left, I pace over to greet Dexter, taking in a set of tattoos on his arms I didn't know he had.

"Hey, Cleo," he greets, rising from his chair to place a kiss on my cheek. "No tissues?"

I force a smile on my face, vainly portraying his playful comment didn't cause a stabbing sensation to my heart.

After returning his greeting in a similar manner, I take a seat across from him. A flustered waitress arrives at our side not even two seconds later. She informs us of the specials, then takes our drinks order. Wanting to get our festivities over sooner rather than later, I order my

RESTRAIN: BOOK FOUR IN THE BOUND SERIES

main meal at the same time as my drink. Thankfully, Dexter follows suit. It isn't that I don't want to spend time with Dexter; I just don't want Brodie left sitting in his car longer than needed. It may not be snowing, but with the temperature beyond freezing, I'd say there is only a matter of days before Montclair is covered by a blanket of white.

Dexter waits for the waitress to gather our menus and leave before locking his eyes with mine. The light blue color of his shirt makes his icy blue eyes more prominent than usual, and the scruff on his chin adds a manly edge to his usually boyish looks. He is already the rightfully-titled resident hottie at Global Ten, but if the women from Accounting could see him now, I doubt they'd continue running their yearly poll. He'd be the hands-down winner time and time again.

"Did everything work out okay last night? You sounded pretty rattled when I talked to you on the phone," Dexter queries, genuine concern echoed in his tone.

I smile when inappropriate images of my rendezvous with Marcus this morning flash before my eyes. "Yeah, everything is fine. I was just overreacting," I assure him, waving my hand through the air like it is no big deal. "You know us girls, dramatic and all."

I cringe, loathing that I used the weakest excuse known to mankind for my pitiful behavior. I also shouldn't be lying; Dexter saved my hide more times than I can count last night. And how does he get awarded for his gallantry? By me lying to his face.

"What about you? How did your date with Delilah end?" Although I'm chomping at the bit for Dexter to disclose the real reason behind our sudden lunch date, it is more polite to ease us towards that conversation than hammer him with the big questions straight up.

Dexter waits for our waitress to finish serving us our drinks before answering, "Not quite how she was hoping."

The churning of my stomach ramps up a gear. Delilah is attractive —if you can look past her narrowed eyes and near-constant abhorrent facial expressions. Even if Dexter wasn't accustomed to her taxing personality, it doesn't take more than a few minutes for a stranger to discern that Delilah is as satanic as her nearly pitch-black eyes.

Dexter dips a corn chip the waitress left on the table into a spicy salsa mix while saying, "If I were interested in financial gain, the circumstances of my night would have altered significantly. But since I've never had an interest in money, her proposal didn't tickle my fancy in the slightest."

If I push aside his odd choice of words, his reply doesn't shock me. If he were money-hungry, he could have pocketed millions by exposing Marcus's secret. Considering that idea never crossed his mind assures me he isn't meeting with me for financial incentive.

With my interest piqued on Delilah's motives last night, I lock my eyes with Dexter and ask, "Delilah propositioned you?"

A faint grin stretches across his face before he nods. I honestly can't tell if it is an expression of mortification or satisfaction.

"For sex or something else?" My low tone reveals my embarrassment at asking such an insensitive question. After everything he has done for me, I'm definitely starting to consider Dexter more of a friend than a work colleague, but I'd have a hard time questioning Lexi in this manner, much less an attractive male.

Thankfully, Dexter doesn't seem the least bit worried about my imposing question. He just pops a corn chip into his mouth before muttering, "Honestly, sex was never mentioned, but I had a feeling she believed it was part of our negotiations."

"Negotiations?" I ask, my interest unmissable.

My eyes lift when a plate of steamy, aromatic food is set down in front of me. Even though I gorged on scones mere hours ago, the delicious scent lingering into my nostrils has my stomach grumbling like it's never been fed.

"Thank you," I murmur to the pretty waitress serving me.

After placing Dexter's meal in front of him, she skedaddles away from our table. Her eagerness to leave has me wondering if she caught wind of our conversation, or if she is hoping Dexter won't see how flustered her cheeks got when he thanked her for her hospitality with a flirty wink. When she continually glances over at us while serving the patrons sitting behind us, I realize it is the latter.

"You have a fan," I say to Dexter, nudging my head to the waitress.

When Dexter cranks his neck to peer at her, the heat on her cheeks grows. "She's cute. But I don't do blondes."

"You don't *do* blondes?" My voice is snarled with a hint of bitchiness. "Does that refer to dating or. . ." I leave my question open for Dexter to answer how he sees fit.

Dexter smiles a shit-eating grin before shaking his head. "I don't date. So. . ." He leaves me hanging, much to my dismay.

Disgusted by his nonchalant avoidance of women of a particular hair color, I grab a handful of the corn chips he's been munching on and peg them at his head. His smile enlarges to a full-toothed grin as he snags a rogue chip clinging to his shirt to consume it. Its loud crunch is barely audible over his concealed laughter. I shake my head in disbelief before tackling the scrumptious meal in front of me.

After settling down his boyish chuckle, Dexter locks his eyes with me. He only stares at me for a minute, but the heat of his gaze is as blistering as standing on the sun. When his stare becomes too great to ignore, I arch a brow, silently requesting a reason for his prolonged gaze.

"You do realize Delilah won't quit hounding you until you give her the identity of the man at the helm of Chains, don't you?" he responds to my silent interrogation.

"Yeah, I'm aware of that, but it doesn't change anything. The people she is hounding don't deserve to be harassed, so until that stops, I'll continue deflecting her ruses," I reply, my tone indicating to my shock at our quick change in subject.

"You speak like you're one of them, Cleo." Dexter peers into my eyes, his concern unmissable. "Are you?"

I forcefully swallow a chunk of chicken in my mouth. Its greasy goodness now feels as dry as a rock. "Would it bother you if I were?"

Dexter leans back in his chair as his dark brows incline. He takes his time configuring a response. I can't help but stare at him, wondering if he is weirded out by my question. His face is void of the disgust I expect people to hold when I voice an interest in BDSM, but it isn't pleasant either. He looks genuinely confused.

By the time he replies, the hot meal he was served has turned stone cold. "It's not my place to judge. I just didn't realize you were in so deep, Cleo."

"I'm not." Well, not in the way he is suspecting. I'm in deep as I am in love with Marcus, but I'm not a submissive as Dexter is assuming.

I place my fork on my plate, my earlier hunger vanished. "When you asked me to meet you here, you mentioned Keira. What does she have to do with any of this?"

My stomach gurgles when Dexter replies, "I'm beginning to suspect a lot more than you realize."

He scrubs a napkin over the stubble on his chin before snagging his dowdy satchel off the floor. With a nudge of his head, he summons me to his side of the table. Swallowing down the concern his worried eyes have instigated, I move to sit in the chair next to him instead of across from him.

"Do you remember when Keira joined Global Ten? The ruckus about her getting a senior position when she wasn't qualified for it?" Dexter queries as he fires up his laptop.

I nod, recalling the snarky comments circulating the water coolers the days following her arrival.

"Do you remember when that was?" Dexter adds on when he spots my agreeing gesture.

My lips quirk. "Around four months ago?" I answer, my interest highly notable.

Dexter nods in agreement. "Before that, her time was shared between a vast number of volunteer organizations. She'd never actually worked for payment before Global Ten."

With two clicks of his mouse, he brings up photos of Keira in front of numerous reputable charity organizations. Some I recognize from articles in prominent newspapers, others are more personal. The most notable photo shows Marcus to her far left.

"So you spotted suspect number one and two," Dexter remarks as he watches my throat work hard to swallow. "What about number three?"

My confused eyes dance between Dexter's for several moments before I return them to the photos on the screen. It takes me scanning the images an additional four times before I locate the face of the person Dexter is mentioning.

"Mr. Carson?" I question, my tone unsure even though I'm certain it is him. Although his face is barely distinguishable since it is the size of a tack head, there is no doubt that is his handsome profile. I recall faces; his is one I recall with ease.

When Dexter nods, my stomach flips. I've hardly had the chance to settle my twisting stomach when Dexter brings up another set of photos. These are more stomach-churning than his first two. They appear to be a part of a police file, and the polaroids are dated June thirteenth—exactly two days before Keira joined Global Ten. The set of eight polaroid photos display injuries to a female victim's back, thighs, and chest. The extent of her injuries range from small scratches to bruises the size of an orange.

"Who is that?" I ask Dexter, my voice quivering with nerves. Even with my vision hazy from a rush of moisture flooding my corneas, my intuition is warning me I'll not like unearthing the mysterious blonde's identity.

My eyes rocket from the medical report hidden behind the scattered polaroid photos to Dexter when he says, "By the medical report, she is Jane Doe."

My hand shoots up to cover my mouth. "She's dead?"

"No," Dexter quickly responds, appeasing my dread in an instant. Although I feel horrible about her injuries, I'm sure she would much rather be injured than dead.

"That's just what the treatment clinic marked her down as when she refused to give them her real name," Dexter informs me.

My brows join together. "Why would she do that?"

Dexter shrugs his shoulders. "I'm assuming to protect the identity of the man who assaulted her?"

Ignoring the barrage of silent questions my eyes are issuing him, Dexter's fingers fly wildly over the keyboard of his state-of-the-art laptop. My eyes sneakily scan our surroundings to ensure no one is eyeballing us when Dexter hacks into a government website. He moves through the site with ease, exposing this isn't the first time he's hacked their servers.

When Dexter brings up the screen he is searching for, he nudges me with his elbow, stealing my attention from a man gawking at me from the far corner of the restaurant. Although most of his face is covered by the newspaper he is reading, the top half of his sunglass-covered profile seems familiar.

My suspicion on his familiarity is pushed to the back of my mind when a video begins playing on Dexter's laptop. It's from one of those fancy private medical centers in the middle of Manhattan, one someone like me could never afford. If I were to believe the rumors, just getting a simple flu shot in an establishment like that costs thousands of dollars.

The air sucks from my lungs when the quickest flurry of blonde captures my attention. The curve of Dexter's lips tells me he noticed my breathless response to a blonde scurrying out of the main entrance of the medical center to slide in the back seat of the heavily tinted Escalade.

"That was Keira." Even though my tone is low, there is no way Dexter could construe my response as a question; it was a declaration.

Dexter swivels in his seat to face me front on. "Did you notice the timeline on the video?" he asks.

Unable to speak, I merely nod my head.

"That was within an hour of these pictures being taken." He points to the polaroids of the lady with the badly bruised back. "These photos were taken at the same medical center Keira exited," he discloses, his tone forthright.

My eyes snap to his. "Are you sure?" I ask with panic smeared in my tone.

Dexter nods his head as he zooms into one of the images on top of a stack of papers. My heart lurches into my throat when in the far right-hand corner of the picture the name of the medical center becomes visible. It matches the business name marked above the entrance Keira dashed out of.

I slouch into my chair, unsure where my loyalties lie. Although I know the injuries Keira sustained can be perfectly normal for some subs, there is a sick, twisted feeling in my stomach warning me that isn't the case. The way she responded to Marcus last night leads me to believe she's a demure sub, one who would rather please her Dom than suffer the consequences for discipline. Furthermore, the pain etched on her face increased with every step she took in the surveillance video. Opposed to me, Keira seems to balk from pain. I'm the only idiot who relishes it.

My eyes lift from my intertwined fingers when Dexter says, "I ran the license plate of the car that picked her up. It registered to a car service in lower Manhattan."

Dexter's ruffling through a stack of papers in his bag stops when I ask, "Always On Time Limousine Service?"

"Yeah, how did you know that?" he asks, his shock uncontained.

"That is the limousine service Chains uses for its clients," I explain.

Although I should feel guilty exposing that, I don't. The limo service Chains uses is a well-known fact to every member of the Daily Express Team investigating Chains, so it would have only been a matter of time before Dexter knew himself. Besides, I kept the most important part of my knowledge concealed, the knowledge that the fleet of Escalades used on a day-to-day basis by Always On Time Limousine Service is reserved solely for the use of Chains' VIP clientele. The fleet of Escalades is what transports Chains' submissives to hair appointments, shopping expeditions, and spa treatments. It is also their chosen mode of transport when sharing subs with other Doms. But since my extensive knowledge of Chains' protocol was awarded personally, it doesn't feel right to share that information with Dexter.

My hand rattles when I secure a glass of water off the table to take a sip. My mouth is so parched, I down half the glass before my scorching throat feels any relief. Once I set my water back down, Dexter advises, "It took me a few hours, but I tracked the Escalade through the city."

My lips quiver when I begin to speak, "Where did it go?"

Even though Marcus guaranteed me last night that Keira has never been his sub, I silently pray he doesn't mention Marcus's New York residence.

When Dexter's silence becomes too unbearable for me to ignore, I plead, "Please, Dexter."

"I'm just making sure you're ready for this, Cleo," he murmurs, amplifying the giddiness twisting my stomach.

"I'm ready," I reply, even though I am anything but.

My silent prayers are answered when Dexter says, "It went to an abandoned warehouse on the corner of Coulson and 42nd street."

He brings up Google maps and zooms in to the address he mentioned. It shows a similar landscape you'd come to expect from the commercial industry in New York. Although most old warehouses have been converted into trendy apartments, some have been abandoned as investors wait for the prime opportunity to either convert their project or sell it on to another investor.

"I ran the address through the database, and it led me to a foreign investor company from Nepal," Dexter informs me, his voice confident but with a smidge of hesitation. "I followed the company's legal paper trail the past three days. I've got nothing. I'm guessing whoever is operating their security is the same person who doctored the surveillance image from the hotel."

My eyes snap to Dexter. "You think the warehouse is owned by the same entity as Chains?"

"I'd put money on it," Dexter replies, nodding. "That's why Keira went there. The bruises on her body weren't from being assaulted; they were placed there during a party at Chains."

He shuffles through the small stack of papers in his satchel. His eyes grow wider when he finds the article he is looking for. My heart leaps in my chest when my eyes drop to the elegant calligraphy on the paper. It is a replica of the invitation Mr. Carson handed me months ago when he put me undercover at a Chains party.

"A Chains party was held the night before Keira sought assistance for her injuries." Dexter hands the invitation to me, proving what he is saying is true. "That party is reported to have been held only two blocks from the medical center Keira was taken to. Although medical reports state she arrived alone, surveillance images do not corroborate that. She was dropped off by this gentleman."

The miniscule portion of my lunch threatens to resurface when Dexter hands me a photo. Although the image appears to be nothing more than a man sitting in a flashy dark gray sports car, it is the make, model, and license plate causing the fierce response from my body. It is Marcus's car. The exact car he drove me to Global Ten Media in earlier this week, and the exact car he drove away from me in mere hours ago.

Spotting my ghastly expression, Dexter says, "Now you can see why I'm worried about you, Cleo. I don't want anything like that to happen to you." I hear nothing but genuine concern in his voice.

"Just because Marcus helped Keira doesn't mean he hurt her," I mumble through my sob, my voice half-confused, half-devastated.

I don't know what warrants more devastation: the fact someone hurt Keira when she clearly displays she isn't into that type of play, or the fact Marcus failed to inform me of the real connection he has with Keira. If he helped her through this, that is clearly more than just a simple friend-helping-friend situation. When people go through a crisis together, it either gives them an unbreakable bond or tears them apart. There is no middle ground.

Dexter gives me a moment to settle some of the confusion pumping into me before he hits me with even more bewilderment. "Mr. Carson approved the investigation into Chains the Monday morning following the incident. Keira started working at Global Ten that same day."

"Woah. . . what?" I know I sound like an imbecile, but his admission just blindsided me. "Are you saying there is a connection between Keira being assaulted and Mr. Carson approving the investigation into Chains?"

"Look at the evidence, Cleo. Would you see it any other way? *Someone* at Chains hurt Keira."

He doesn't need to say Marcus's name for me to know who he is accusing when he sneers "someone."

"Mr. Carson took offense, and now he's determined to ruin whoever did it."

I remain quiet as my brain processes all the information Dexter has handed me thus far. When I add it to seeing Mr. Carson comfort Keira in his office, the evidence is damning. Mr. Carson's fierce reaction Monday morning reiterates that the Chains investigation is personal to him, much like Keira did when she bombarded me in the elevator weeks ago. The only thing that baffles me is why are two opponents associating with each other? If Mr. Carson cares enough about Keira he wants the blood of the person who hurt her, why would he hunt a community she is clearly a part of and respects? It truly doesn't make any sense. Unless. . .

My eyes rocket to Dexter. "I'm really sorry, but I have to go."

Not waiting for him to reply, I stand from my chair and gather my purse from the tabletop. Dexter mumbles out an excuse for me to wait. His words trap in his throat when I lean over to place an impromptu kiss on the edge of his cheek. When he suddenly moves, my lips brush the edge of his mouth. The smell of garlic and tomatoes lingers into my nostrils when I abruptly pull back, panicked strangers will construe my friendly peck as more than friendly.

"Thank you," I graciously praise, peering straight into Dexter's wide blue eyes. "I owe you big time."

"You still owe me lunch!" is the last thing I hear Dexter shout as I race across the restaurant, secure my jacket, then stumble onto the sidewalk outside.

With my focus devoted to deciphering the information bombarding me, I accidentally bump into a gentleman exiting at the same time as me.

"Sorry," I mumble as I sidestep the man wearing a dark drench coat, black cap, and a pair of sunglasses, so I can hotfoot it to Brodie's car. My eagerness is so apparent, I'm practically sprinting.

"That's okay, Cleo," replies the stranger.

My steps halt midstride when the deepness of his voice registers as familiar. After taking a moment to clear the confusion from my face, I spin on my heels to face the person I bumped into. My eyes dart in all directions, seeking his dark coat. He is nowhere to be found.

Chapter Eight

LEXI'S HEAD LIFTS FROM THE NEWSPAPER SPRAWLED ACROSS HER AND Jackson's intertwined legs when our front door's creak announces my arrival. The confusion etched on her face grows when she spots me entering the main entrance of our home. Her shock switches to happiness when she spots Brodie trailing closely behind me. Her response startles me. Although Lexi's temperament is friendly most days, it is unusual for a person to compel such a response from her, much less a man who usually hackles her spikes more than he soothes them.

After hanging mine and Brodie's coats, I pace into the living room. The apprehension twisting my stomach eases when I spot a brand new entranceway table sitting in the position our old table used to be. Although its super shiny lacquer doesn't match the rest of the outdated furniture, it is a beautiful piece that adds a touch of class our house has been missing the past four years.

"You like?" Lexi asks, standing from the couch and pacing toward me.

"It's very nice," I reply, greeting her with a hug and a peck on the cheek.

My brows stitch when Lexi holds on to me a little longer than normal.

"Did you miss me?" I ask, my melting heart echoing in my tone.

Lexi scoffs before drawing back. "Not exactly." She rolls her eyes at my waggling brows. "Alright. Fine. I missed you. Okay?"

"Okay," I reply with an equal amount of sassiness. "I've missed you too."

After checking that Jackson is occupied talking with Brodie, Lexi returns her eyes to me. The worry in them has my nerves sitting on edge. Anxiety has never been a problem for Lexi; she has confidence by the bucket loads, so I'm somewhat surprised by the concern her eyes are holding.

"Can I talk to you for a minute?" she asks, nudging her head to our kitchen.

I nod before pacing into the funky-smelling space. Lexi shadows closely behind me, acting like she can't smell her disastrous culinary skills. Some of the nerves making me a jittering mess dull Lexi secures a saucepan from the drawer under the oven and fills it with milk before placing it onto the stovetop. She adds all the ingredients for her famous hot chocolate before spinning around to face me.

"What did you do?" I accuse. She doesn't usually make me hot chocolate unless she is sucking up. Actually, come to think of it, the last time she made me hot chocolate was when she drew a gun on Marcus.

"This isn't about me," Lexi replies, her tone apprehensive. "This is about you and Chains."

Not trusting my legs to keep me upright, I take a seat in one of the chairs at our small eating nook. I truly don't know if my brain can handle any more information than it is currently tackling. The ten-minute trip from the pizzeria to my house was a complete blur, not just wasted trying to work out the connection between Marcus, Mr. Carson, and Keira, but also struggling to identify the stranger I bumped into. Although years ago, I was regularly confronted by Mont-clair locals wishing to express their condolences for my loss, the stranger's voice didn't seem to be the right age for that. His voice was smooth and alluring—like a man in his mid to late twenties.

My attention drifts back to the present when Lexi places a large mug of hot chocolate in front of me. Horrid unease twists up my throat when I notice two marshmallows floating in the rich, sweet goodness. Lexi doesn't believe hot chocolate needs any more sweetness, so her Garcia stubbornness means she usually serves mine without the puffs of sugar.

"Spit it out, Lexi. I'm dying here," I advise, my voice relaying the honesty of my confession.

She sits on the chair across from me. After tucking her feet under her bottom, her big brown eyes stray to mine. For the quickest second, all I see is our mom reflecting back at me. *God, I miss her.*

"Hit you straight up?" Lexi queries, wanting to ensure I know she isn't going to hold back.

"Straight up," I confirm, nodding.

She takes a sip of her hot chocolate before placing it on the table-top. I'm tempted to follow suit, but chose to wait, unsure if I can trust my churning stomach with liquid.

"I thought the whole idea of your week with Marcus was for him to have time to convince you to go with him to Ravenshoe?" she asks, her tone low and without judgment.

"It was," I verify, recalling Marcus saying exactly that during our negotiations in our room last week.

I pick up my mug, feeling that I've overreacted to the worry on her face. Maybe it is more exhaustion than apprehension?

"Then why are you here?" Lexi asks. Her tone is so forthright; if I didn't know her better, I'd swear she was annoyed by my visit.

My mug freezes halfway to my lips as my brows stitch in confusion. I was too busy battling through disappointment that Marcus had to leave earlier than expected, I haven't stopped to consider what altered his prior arrangement.

My eyes lift to Lexi when she gently squeezes my hand. "Did something happen that changed his plans? Or. . ." She leaves her question open for me to fill in.

"Nothing really happened. . . Well, we did get in an argument last night. But that was resolved before he left this morning," I answer, my words as unconvincing as my facial expression.

Lexi's eyes dance between mine. "Are you sure? As he was adamant last week he wanted you to return to Ravenshoe with him. That's why he kept begging for you to hand in your notice at Global Ten. He wanted to make things official between you."

I nod. It isn't a confident nod. "He said he'd see me soon. He did seem a little edgy before he left, but that's just the way he is." My voice softens at the end of my statement as worry makes itself known. "What do you think it means?"

Lexi shrugs as the concern in her eyes doubles. "I don't know what to think. When I first saw you walk in the door, I was worried. Then I saw Brodie, so I figured I had nothing to worry about. Why would he keep protection on you if he didn't care about you?" She grazes her teeth over her bottom lip before she quickly mumbles, "Then I got close enough to see the worry in your eyes, and it had me doubting everything." She locks her eyes with mine, the mayhem in them unmissable. "I'm so fucking confused."

I laugh. It isn't my usual full-hearted laughter, but you work with what you have. "Welcome to the club. I've been like this for months."

Lexi smiles. It isn't as bright as her usual smile either. "Alright, I hit you with straight up honesty. Now you need to do the same."

Lexi giggles, gags, and grimaces during my recount of the events that occurred from the time Marcus and I negotiated a week of solitude until I walked through the front door. She also threatened Marcus's life on more than two occasions when I reached the parts that included Keira. The only thing that kept her backside planted on her seat and not rummaging through the safe bolted in my parents' closet, was when I disclosed Mr. Carson's involvement in the bizarre circumstances I find myself in.

Once I've finished relaying the entire story, nearly an hour has passed on the clock and we've consumed two mugs of hot chocolate.

Lexi slumps into her chair before raising her eyes to me. "Okay. First of all, I understand your confusion. Woah!" She waves her hands in front of her head like her brain is exploding. "Second, you are evil. It was only a few weeks ago you argued that being spanked wasn't natural, then you go and do *that*. . ." She doesn't need to express what her "that" is referring to. Her face shows the entire picture.

"I didn't tell you everything so you could judge me—"

"I'm not judging you, Cleo. I'm in friggin' awe. Kudos to you —seriously."

If I couldn't see the honesty in her reply, I'd be tempted to recant her statement.

"So what's the look on your face about?" I query.

I stand from my chair to place our dirty mugs in the sink. Lexi waits for me to turn around to face her before she says, "There are parts of your story that don't make sense."

"I know. That's why I'm here, seeking answers," I agree, crossing my arms in front of my chest.

Lexi rises from her chair and paces to stand next to me. "But the person you should be seeking answers from isn't here, Cleo. He is over a thousand miles away somewhere in Florida."

Even though I know exactly whom she is referring to, I bounce my eyes between hers, pretending I don't.

"If you want your questions answered, you need to ask Chains," she suggests, her tone revealing she wasn't buying my attempts of acting clueless.

"And exactly how am I supposed to do that?" I hate that I'm acting so cowardly that I want my baby sister to pull me out of the quicksand trying to swallow me whole.

"What did Daddy always say?" Lexi queries with her brow arched high.

"Most conversations start with a hello," we quote in sync.

"I'd probably start there," Lexi adds on, her tone more mature than her twenty-one years.

I briefly nod my head. "Good point. I'll give it a go."

Lexi runs her hand down my arm before she exits the kitchen. Her girly giggle shrills through my ears not even ten seconds later.

"Jackson Josiah Collard, we have guests," Lexi chastises.

Even from the kitchen, I'm not buying her scold. She needs to remove the absolute bliss from her voice if she wants anyone to believe her reprimand. Ignoring the mortified expression crossing Brodie's face as he watches Jackson and Lexi play tonsil hockey, I gather my cell from my purse on the entranceway table and saunter into my room.

The worries I held yesterday about being spoiled by the opulence of Marcus's properties are proven unfounded when I pace into my childhood bedroom. Although it isn't as grand as Marcus's bedroom, it has much more sentimental value than money could buy. I've lived in this room my entire life. No price can be placed on that.

After carefully closing my bedroom door so it doesn't give out a squeak, I move to my bed to sit down. My brows furrow when I notice the stuffed rabbit I came home from the hospital with is sitting between the ruffled pillows on my bed. It is usually housed on the shelf above my desk.

Placing my cell down, I lift Mr. Bunny from my bed, give him a quick squeeze, then put him back in his rightful spot. Just the smell of his mottled fur flashes images of my parents to the forefront of my mind, inciting tears to prick my eyes.

I take a moment to settle my nerves before striding back to my phone and dialing Marcus's number. He answers not even two seconds later.

"Hey," I greet him. My voice is confident, but it also gives a hint to the torrent of emotions pumping through me.

"Hey, Cleo. Everything okay?" Marcus replies, his tone laced with worry.

I smile, loving that he detected my apprehension when I only spoke one little word.

"Yeah, I'm fine. Just a little worried. I thought you were going to call me once you landed?" Since most of my statement is true, it comes out sounding honest.

"Ah. Yeah. Umm. Our departure got pushed back." My heartrate kicks up from the uneasiness in his reply. He usually exudes confidence by the bucket loads, so his skittish response is odd.

"You're still in New York?" I query, excitement echoed in my tone. This conversation will be ten times easier if I can do it in person, as more times than not, Marcus's eyes relay more than his words ever could.

"Ah. Yeah, but we're flying out soon," Marcus answers, his words flying out of his mouth in a flurry.

Disappointment slashes through me. "Oh. . . that's a bummer." I roll my eyes. I sound like a fifth-grader.

"Cleo, is this important? I could listen to your voice all day, but I'm a little busy right now," Marcus discloses, his tone sharper than usual.

"Oh, okay. Sorry," I reply flimsily, muted into stupidity by his admission he likes listening to me talk. I've always thought my voice was a little nasally and high.

I press my cell in close to my ear when I hear a female in the background greeting Marcus. Her voice is high and bouncy, the type you'd expect from someone in the twenty-one to thirty-year age bracket. I hear Marcus shush her before he muzzles the phone with his hand. Although they continue talking, I can't understand any of their words. It probably doesn't help that my hearing is affected by the rush of jealousy roaring through my body. Jealousy was never a horrid neurosis of mine. . .until Marcus came along.

After what feels like an eternity, Marcus's attention returns to me. "I have to go, Cleo. I'm sorry, baby. I'll talk to you soon. Okay?"

"Okay." I'd like to articulate a better response but I'm left a little dumbfounded, but the chance to respond is lost when Marcus abruptly disconnects our call.

I stare at my phone, blinking and confused. Our conversation went nothing like I had predicted. Before we officially met, Marcus and I communicated on the phone for hours every night, so to have our call ended in under a minute is truly shocking. His abrupt reply can only mean two things: he truly is busy, or he doesn't want to talk to me. With how badly my stomach is twisting up I have a horrible feeling it is the latter.

I jump, startled, when Lexi asks, "What did he say?"

She has her shoulder propped up on my door. I stare at her with as much confusion as my call with Marcus created. . *How did she get my door open without it creaking?*

Misreading the expression on my face as contempt, Lexi pushes off her feet and saunters into my room. "Did he give you any answers?"

I shake my head. "I never got the chance to ask any. He hung up on me."

"He hung up on you?" She sounds as shocked as I feel. My mattress squeaks in protest when Lexi flops onto the overused springs. "So what are you going to do now?"

I take a minute to consider a mature response. It is clearly a waste of a precious minute when I reply, "I'm going to yank my head out of the sandbox and start using the brain our parents hard-earned money went toward developing."

Lexi peers up at me as confused as ever.

"Do you know where my box is?" When Lexi's confusion grows, I add on, "The box I left Global Ten with? The one with all my work on Chains?"

"Should be by the entranceway where you left it. I don't touch your stuff." I'm halfway down the hall before the entire sentence leaves Lexi's mouth.

My box is exactly where she said it would be, tucked between our coatrack and our new entranceway table. Jackson and Brodie's heads lift from the sports highlight program broadcasting on the TV so their eyes can track me dragging the heavy box into the formal dining room. Although the box isn't overly heavy, with my muscles still weak with exhaustion, it feels like I'm dragging a Mack truck.

Like a perfectly timed skit, Lexi enters the dining room at precisely the same time I'm struggling to lift the box onto our large oval table. "Jesus. What have you got in here?" she grunts while assisting me, realizing the strain crossing my face wasn't fake.

I flip off the lid of the box, allowing the documents inside to answer on my behalf. Lexi's eyes bug as they wander over the hundreds of pictures I printed out after my night at Chains.

"Holy shit. You were right. Seeing it in the flesh doesn't match what you imagine when you're reading it," she murmurs softly.

She picks up the photos of a lady hanging from a steel-like contraption wearing nothing but rope for clothing. "That takes a lot of trust," Lexi mumbles under her breath.

"It does," I agree wholeheartedly. "That is one of the biggest things in the BDSM world. Trust."

Lexi places the photo onto a bunch of ones displaying Marcus's mask-covered face. "Then why are you re-opening your investigation into Chains? I know Marcus owes you some explanations, but *investigating* him? This doesn't feel right, Cleo. It's something I'd do, but this isn't you. You bring the smarts; I bring the looks. You bring the understanding; I bring the suspicion. You bring the creep; I bring the—"

"Leech," we say in sync.

The rigidness in the air evaporates when our conjoined laughter fills the room.

I wait for her laughter to dim before saying, "I'm not investigating Marcus; I'm investigating Chains."

Lexi rolls her eyes. "They are one and the same, Cleo," she fires back as a cloud of chaos overtakes the glint of happiness in her eyes.

"Not Chains the person. Chains the company," I inform her. I move my hand to the pocket of my jeans to dig out the photo I sneakily borrowed from Dexter on my brisk exit of the restaurant.

Lexi inhales a sharp breath when I hand her the printout of Keira's bruised back. "Are those whip marks?" Lexi asks, running her index finger along the welts in Keira's back.

I commence answering her question with a shrug. "I think so. The pattern is unusual, though. I've never come across that type of pattern during my research."

Lexi raises her panicked eyes to me. "Are her injuries typical for people in the BDSM lifestyle?"

I quirk my lips while taking a moment to contemplate a response. I want to be honest with Lexi, but I don't want her to panic either. "Depends. Some people need. . . *more*, where others need a lot more," I eventually answer.

When panic flares in Lexi's eyes, I add on, "I researched the lifestyle for weeks, and from what I've seen, this seems extreme. But it never would have happened without the submissive's permission. There are very strict rules to ensure nothing like this happens without prior consent. It may seem cruel, but some people need that type of stimulation to feel whole."

Lexi remains as quiet as a mouse. It is an uncomfortable three minutes filled with awkward tension.

"Say what you want to say, Lexi. I'm a big girl; I can handle it," I express, loathing the concerned look she is issuing me.

Lexi's tongue delves out to replenish her lips before she asks, "Do you need that much. . .*more*, Cleo?"

Relief floods her eyes when I shake my head. "No. After last night, I'm beginning to wonder if my desires for more are based around the lifestyle or the man associated with it."

Lexi continues with her silent stance, forcing me to say, "Last night was the first time I climaxed without additional stimulation. That should mean something, shouldn't it?"

"Yeah, it should," Lexi replies as the color in her cheeks returns. "It means I want what you're having." She excessively waggles her brows.

I inwardly sigh, grateful her playful response killed the tension hanging thickly in the air.

After placing the photo of Keira into the box next to numerous surveillance images of Marcus, Lexi spreads her hands across her tiny hips. "Okay, let me check we're on the same page?"

She waits for me to nod before saying, "Her injuries happened at Chains?" She points her index finger at Keira's photo. Although her eyes are showing her relief, I can tell she is still rattled, as her slim finger is incapable of hiding the tremor of her hands.

I nod my head. "There is a match in timelines between a Chains party and her seeking medical assistance," I disclose, happy my voice doesn't expose my jittering insides.

"And she is the reason Global Ten Media is investigating Chains?" Lexi asks.

"Yes. Well, I'm assuming that is the case. My intuition is warning me she is somehow involved, I just need to work out how," I say before pulling out a chair from the dining table and sitting down.

"Easy," Lexi replies as if it is the simplest solution in the world. "She wants revenge on the Chains community for what happened to her, so she sold them out to Global Ten."

Lexi's eyes drop to mine when I reply, "No. Although her assault seems to be the premise of the investigation, she didn't initiate it."

"How do you know that?" Lexi questions, shock smeared in her tone.

I swivel in my chair to face her. "She isn't against the members of Chains; she is working in cahoots with them."

Lexi looks the most confused I've ever seen her.

"Remember me telling you about Keira bombarding me in the

elevator the morning I was called into Global Ten for an emergency meeting? How she pleaded for me to write my story on Chains based on facts, not a sugarcoated pop culture piece? She defended the BDSM lifestyle and the rights for its members to choose their own sexual proclivities."

Lexi crosses her arms over her chest as she nods, her interest unmissable.

"That was her," I say, pointing to the photo of Keira.

Lexi gasps in a shocked breath as her pupils dilate to the size of saucers. "That doesn't make any sense. The evidence clearly shows she was the reason the Chains investigation commenced, so why would she then defend them?"

"That's what I am endeavoring to find out. Keira is the link between Chains and Global Ten. If I can work out why, I might be able to work out how to end the investigation before Marcus or any of his clientele get caught in the crossfire."

My eyes track Lexi when she spins on her heels and makes a beeline for the door. "Where are you going?"

She cranks her neck to peer at me over her shoulder, but her pace remains unchecked. "We need wine before we tackle this head on."

"We?" I retort, pretending I can't read the excitement on her face.

Lexi freezes halfway out the room, cocks her hip, then glares at me. "Yeah, *we*. Do you really think I'll let you do this without backup? I'm your little sis. We Garcia women stick together through a crisis."

She strengthens her stance as the gleam of cheekiness in her eyes turns calamitous. "Besides, if you're going to take down a billion-dollar company with those grainy images, you'll need someone without shitty vision to help."

I glare at her with my mouth gaped open. "Then you better get your glasses," I tease when she fails to acknowledge the threat in my glare.

Lexi stares at me; her confidence at an all-time high. "I was planning to—right after the wine."

Chapter Nine

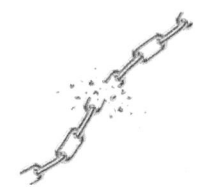

"I NEVER SAID THAT, PROFESSOR. I MAY THINK YOUR BREATH SMELLS like dog doo, but I'd never say it out loud."

Lexi springboards into a half-seated position when I throw a kernel of caramel-coated popcorn at her head. Is it wrong of me to admit I know who she is talking about even though I've never attended her college? Her physics professor is a lovely man, but my god, the times I served him at our local gas station during summer holidays my senior years of high school, were unpleasant enough for the memory to stick. I've always believed a scent is the quickest way to trigger a memory. That is one of the reasons I was so baffled about the mysterious stranger I bumped into yesterday. I swear I've smelled his scent before.

My attention drifts back to the present when Lexi's bewildered eyes roam around the dining room. She has a massive gob of dried drool in the corner of her mouth, and the papers she was sleeping on have creased her cheek. Guilt makes itself comfy in the middle of my chest when I spot the dark rims circling her eyes. She looks exhausted, which is understandable considering it is 5 AM.

"Did I fall asleep again?" Lexi queries, her words muffled by a tiger-like yawn.

"Only for a few minutes," I lie. She's been out nearly two hours.

"We should probably call it a night anyway. You've got your volunteer session at Links tomorrow before school."

"Today," Lexi corrects, grimacing.

"Sorry," I apologize, hating that I've put her natural body clock out of whack.

She waves off my worry. "It's okay. I have exams the next two weeks."

Guilt slams into me.

It doesn't last long when Lexi quickly adds on, "But I don't have any today. Thank god."

"Thank god, indeed."

Lexi gingerly stands from her chair to aid me in gathering the documents and photos we have sprawled across the table. Although we can confirm without a doubt that Keira is a member of Chains, we are not any closer to discovering the connection between her and Global Ten. This is going to make me sound like the most horrible person in the world, but I'm just being honest. I don't know what I find more concerning: the photos of Keira's bruised back, or the dozens upon dozens of images of her gawking at Marcus from the surveillance pictures gathered from my night at Chains. Although Keira was wearing a simple silver mask, her platinum blonde hair, small facial features, and prominent blue eyes guarantee her identity can't be hidden. She was in multiple shots, and as I had suspected, her eyes were always firmly rapt on Marcus, proving her fascination with him is more than just friendly.

"Oh, hold on," Lexi says when her stack of papers tumble onto the mouse of the laptop, awakening its monitor. "Do you remember how we searched for Mr. Carson and Keira?"

Nervous butterflies take flight in my stomach as I nod my head.

I breathe out slowly when Lexi says, "We finally got a match."

"What month is it? Around June/July?" My nerves show up in my voice.

Lexi shakes her head. "No. It was in September."

"Around the time the Chains investigation started?" I ask, stunned. I'm shocked as the first searches done were based on the prior six months, so why didn't it come up then?

"Not September this year," Lexi clarifies, drawing my attention back to her. "September fifteen years ago."

"What?" I ask, certain my lack of sleep is playing tricks on my spent brain.

Lexi spins her laptop around to face me. There is a picture of a teenage boy and a girl I'd guess to be around the age of ten. It is a newspaper article about a local baseball charity game played in Jersey. All benefits from the game were donated to a domestic violence shelter the community was endeavoring to get off the ground.

"That looks like Keira," Lexi summarizes.

I nod my head in full agreement. Although she is much younger, she has the same eyes and hair color. "It is either Keira or her twin sister."

"Is that Mr. Carson?" Lexi asks, pointing to the handsome teen in the photo who has his arm wrapped around Keira.

I lean in to inspect the photo more thoroughly, not wanting speculation to run wild in my mind. The teen's cheeks are shiny since they are covered in sweat; his eyes are as wild as the messy mane of inky black hair on his head, and his jaw is stiff and rigid, even though he'd be barely over the age of fifteen. He is Mr. Carson. I am certain of it. I was so fascinated by the local boy from Jersey who turned into a self-made billionaire, I gobbled up every article I could find on Mr. Carson when I was younger. This picture matches ones I've seen of him in his teen years.

"That is Mr. Carson," I confirm to Lexi.

"So they've known each other for fifteen years, as this photo is way too chummy for a random stranger pic," Lexi says as shock replaces the tiredness in her eyes.

When I nod, Lexi asks, "Where do we go from here?"

I scroll through the additional images attached to the article Lexi discovered, striving to devise what this new information could mean for my investigation. This changes everything, because not only are Keira and Mr. Carson well-known to one another, but unlike this photo, they are playing on opposing teams. Is that what their confrontation was about in his office last week? Maybe Keira thought using tears was a way to break through Mr. Carson's stern resistance?

Much like she used a chain-link choker as a way of capturing Marcus's attention.

Suppressing my jealousy before it gets the better of me, I click through articles matching the story on the charity baseball game. Just thinking about Marcus being intimately connected with another woman triggers feverish jealousy, but I've got too much on my plate to add anything else.

My manic clicking stops when I stumble upon a picture of a lady with a broad smile and vibrant eyes. It takes several minutes staring at the familiar-looking brunette's face before I realize how I know her. Just as quickly as recognition surfaces, so does the familiarity of her surname.

With my heart sitting in my throat, I do a quick internet search on the brunette's name, but instead of using her whole name, I focus on her surname. My eyes go crazy when they are bombarded with hundreds and hundreds of responses for my search. Newspaper clippings, arrest warrants, photos, everything and anything you could imagine is displayed directly in front of me. It is exciting and stomach-churningly worrying at the same time.

I remain quiet, struggling to join each piece of the puzzle to the right section. It is a complex puzzle that comes together surprisingly quickly when all the main players are exposed.

When the final piece locks into place, shock hits me so hard and fast, I'm nearly knocked onto my ass. I connect my eyes with Lexi. "Do you need a ride to Links today?"

My words are hurried as I jump up from my seat to gather all the documents sprawled across the desk at a more frantic speed than the one I was using earlier.

"I was going to catch the train. Why, are you going that way?" Lexi answers, watching me with bewilderment etched on her face.

The fettering of her brows increases when I nod my head. "I have a brunch date I completely forgot about. Get dressed; I'll update you in the car."

Several hours later, I'm mingling in the lobby of an extremely elegant apartment building located directly across from Central Park. That smell of wealth I whiffed at the fundraising gala two days ago is as blatant in the building as the scent of taxi fumes in Times Square.

After running his eyes down mine and Brodie's body for the tenth time the past twenty minutes, the pompous-looking receptionist says, "Yes, Ma'am. I'll send them straight up." He is talking into the small black device lodged in his ear canal.

With a snarl, he gestures his hand to the mirrored glass elevator banks behind his station. "Penthouse floor. George will show you the way."

A gentleman in a dark burgundy suit and top hat dips his chin in greeting before waving his hand to the elevator banks. When he pushes off his feet, Brodie and I shadow him. I've always felt out of place around the wealthy, but my neurosis has been pushed aside today because Brodie's discomfort is strong enough for the both of us.

Our ride in the elevator with George happens in silence. I'd like to say resolute silence, but with ghastly elevator music filling the void, it isn't entirely silent. My eyes rocket to Brodie when he whistles along to the tune. If it isn't bad enough my ears are being subjected to torture from the elevator music, having him whistling along makes it ten times worse. I don't hate many things, but whistling is on my concise list of dislikes.

"You should sleep more. You get grumpy when you're tired," Brodie snickers as we follow George out of the elevator, straight into the lavish foyer of an opulent home.

A large crystal vase full of fresh lilies and pussy willow branches sits on an antique round table in the middle of the vast space. The extravagant floral arrangement fires the air with a refreshing scent of pollen, ridding it of the wealth its maplewood wainscoted walls and tiled marble floors convey. After scrubbing his polished shoes on the bristled mat, Brodie places the box we arrived with at the side of the glistening space before joining me in soaking up the lifestyle many dream of but will never achieve.

I stop appraising an original Monet when the distinct rumble of

Cartier rolls through my ears. "Darling, if I had known you were coming, I would have seen my guest out earlier."

She floats across the room like an angel gliding over a cloud. She is dressed more casually than she was when I saw her Saturday. Her fit body is covered with a floral kimono cinched so dangerously loosely at the waist, Brodie is mere moments away from inspecting *precisely* what she is wearing under her satin gown.

A grin curves on my lips when Cartier greets me with two air kisses to each of my cheeks. The unique scent of flowers and spices lingers in her wake when she welcomes Brodie in the same fashion. My grin enlarges to a full smile when the beard covering Brodie's chin can't hide his smirk from Cartier's friendliness.

My brows bow when a handsome man in his mid-thirties struts into the room. From his disheveled hair and rumpled clothing, it isn't hard to decipher what he was doing, but his peacock attitude is a good give away. After smirking a greeting to us, he leans in to whisper something into Cartier's ear. I slap Brodie's arm at the same time Cartier hits the unknown man's chest.

"Do you recognize him?" I ask Brodie, my voice barely a whisper.

"*HBO?*" Brodie silently mouths, acknowledging my suspicion he is one of the lead actors who stars in a popular sitcom on HBO.

When the dark-haired man finalizes his conversation with Cartier, he shifts his gaze to Brodie and me. We both stand a little straighter, trying to act like we weren't just spying on their exchange. It is a woeful effort. The instant his highly recognizable eyes lock with mine, I know he is precisely whom I suspected, which makes me grin like an idiot. I'm going to be honest, I'm a little starstruck right now.

Cartier waits for her guest to leave with George before drifting her eyes back to me. "Look at you, just as ravishing in casual clothing as you are in designer dresses. I understand Marcus's beguilement." Every R she pronounces rolls off her tongue with a throaty purr.

"Come, let's get something to drink." She pivots on her heels and saunters into a room on our left.

"It's not even 10 AM," I grouse, shadowing her into the massive living room.

My jaw slackens in an unladylike manner when the wonderment of silk, gold, and maplewood bombards me. At least my response was more subdued than Brodie's. He didn't manage to hold in his curse word.

This room is massive, stretching the entire length of the apartment. The views of Central Park from the floor-to ceiling-windows are breathtaking. This would have to be one of the most valuable properties in New York City. Nothing could replicate this view—*not a single darn thing.*

Cartier giggles softly, adoring our slack-jawed expressions. I guess she has become accustomed to the awe she wakes up to every morning. Arriving at a bar on our right, Cartier offers us a drink. I kindly refuse. I've never been fond of drinking so early in the morning, and my lack of sleep last night has already given me a severe case of dizziness, so I don't need anything to add to it. Brodie also refuses her request, citing, "I don't drink while on the job."

After pouring herself a three-finger serving of fancy whiskey in a crystal glass, Cartier takes a seat in one of the four voluptuous sofas in her living room. Brodie and I also sit, but on the couch across from her.

"I thought Marcus said you were a journalist?" Cartier queries, peering at me with a set of suspicious eyes.

"I am," I confirm, nodding my head.

"Then why do I get the feeling I'm sitting across from two detec-·tives?" She holds her hands out in front of her body like she is pleading innocence. "I swear, Officers, I don't know anything. I'm a good girl."

Brodie's throaty laugh rumbles my nerves out of my stomach. While kicking his shoe with my heel to halt his immature response, I mumble, "I'm not here to interrogate you, but I did come here to ask you something in confidence."

Cartier reads the honesty from my eyes before her dazzling gaze shifts to Brodie.

"This is the first I'm hearing of it," Brodie advises her questioning glare.

"He didn't know we were coming here until he pulled into the valet," I inform Cartier when her suspicion remains high.

Cartier shifts her eyes back to me. "How did you even know where *here* is, darling?"

"This," I reply, scooting to the edge of my chair to show her the article I saved on my phone during our hour commute.

She gasps in shock when she recognizes the image reflecting back at her. It is a photo snapped of her when she was cutting the ribbon at a domestic violence shelter in New Jersey nearly twenty years ago—the same shelter Keira and Mr. Carson were raising funds for fifteen years ago. Although Cartier is decades younger, and her hair is as dark as the storm looming in her eyes, I have no doubt it is her. The modern fashionista smiling at the camera is wearing a replica of the small thin necklace she hides under her big bulky ones. I only caught the quickest glimpse of the collar she was fiddling with Saturday night, but its infinity eight design was captivating enough for me to remember. It is simple but classically elegant.

Since the photo was snapped years before Cartier began using nicknames to hide her true self, her full name was displayed: Phoebe Annabella Gottle, wife of the suspected mob boss of New York City. Although I was unaware of Mr. Gottle's influence in New York when he arrived at my home with Marcus after he was arrested last month, my impromptu internet search of him this morning unearthed more information on him than months of investigative journalism could ever locate on Cartier. Unlike his wife, Mr. Gottle's personal life isn't personal.

"The Gottle surname is not unique. . . except in New York." My eyes wander around the affluent surroundings. "I knew the exact building to find you as Henry looks after his family members very well."

Brodie's eyes snap to mine at the same moment Cartier's do. His eyes are wide, and his mouth is gaped. Cartier's expression isn't as shocked as his. Her plump lips have scoured into a thin line, and her eyes have narrowed.

"I am not his family, darling. I was nothing more than his whore," Cartier replies. Her words are hurled off her tongue like daggers, but it does nothing to hide the massive sentiment dangling on her vocal cords.

"A whore who happens to still carry his last name?" I query softly, my confidence lacking from the dubious glare she is directing at me. "Please correct me if I am wrong, but how can the title of 'wife' be misconstrued as 'whore?'"

Cartier straightens her spine before her eyes drop to the diamond chain-link pendant nestled in the groove of my neck. "Some things are more valuable than titles. If you lose that, you lose them. Simple. A last name means nothing, and neither does the piece of paper stating it does. The law doesn't tell you whom you belong to, darling; your heart does."

My heart breaks from the pure agony in her words. This was not my intention. I didn't come here to drag down her eminent personality I adore. I just want answers to questions I know she can provide.

When I explain that to Cartier, she stops peering at my pendant to look at me. "Does Marcus know you are here?" she questions, her voice not as agitated as earlier.

Missing a backbone, I timidly shake my head.

I thought my admission would pain her more. It doesn't. The faintest smile creeps across her face as she says, "Oh, darling, you remind me so much of myself at your age. You revel in defiance. I'm just grateful you learned in weeks what took me years to work out."

"Learned what?" I query, my interest unmissable.

Brodie tries to deflect his curiosity with a sizeable yawn, but I'm not buying his attempts. He is not only listening to every word Cartier and I speak, but he is also digitally categorizing it for future use. Although interested in learning what he is planning to do with the information, my primary focus must remain on the task at hand. If I juggle too many balls, some will eventually fall. Considering every ball I'm juggling has immense sentimental value to me, I'm not willing to let one topple from my grasp. So, for now, I'll push aside Brodie's interest as purely inquisitiveness until each ball is safely placed back into my pocket.

Cartier licks her lips before replying, "Rebelliousness keeps the flame flickering longer. Don't ever lose that, darling, because when you do, the remains of an overinflated balloon are never as pretty as they once were."

I'm shunted into silence, confused by her statement. Brodie appears just as baffled as me, but instead of keeping his bewilderment to himself, he asks, "What does that mean?"

Cartier shifts her eyes to Brodie. "Have you ever had someone who makes you feel so wonderful, you believe nothing could ever bring you down?"

Brodie nods.

"Imagine every compliment or precious thing they did for you was the equivalent of pumping air into your balloon. Once the balloon is at its greatest, there are only two things that can happen: it either pops or they let it float away. To some, popping the balloon you've worked so hard to inflate seems cruel. The balloon may have an opposing opinion. Why spend years growing something to its best only to let it float away the instant it reaches greatness?"

When Cartier toys with the thin necklace I referred to earlier, I blurt out, "Did Henry give you your necklace?" before I can stop my words.

Cartier's hand drops from her neck at a faster rate than my plummeting heart slithers into my stomach. The devastation brewing in her eyes with a rueful smirk cuts me raw. It is the same turmoil Marcus's eyes held when he noticed my cut lip after I was assaulted in the alley weeks ago.

"I'm sorry, I didn't mean to pry," I apologize with sincerity in my tone.

Cartier accepts my apology with an air of grace. "Intellectual curiosity is the forefront of knowledge, Cleo, but idle gossip is the first step to hell. Perhaps you should remember that when you are prying into people's lives."

"I am *not* prying," I assure her, stunned by her statement.

"You are a reporter arriving at my home with a vault of old news that was buried faster than it was built," Cartier fires back. "Is that not prying?"

I nod, agreeing with her. She seems shocked by my obliging response. She shouldn't be. Everything she said was true, so why would I deny it?

"Yes, I am a reporter, and I did disrespectfully present myself to you this morning as if I am here as your guest. But you can be assured, I am not here to break a story, Cartier; I'm here to stop one unjustly being broken. One I believe is very dear to your heart."

A tense stretch of silence passes between us. I wouldn't necessarily say her silence is off-putting; it is more like she is generating her own reason for me arriving unannounced by reading the truth from my soul-baring eyes instead of listening to the words I spoke.

Realizing there is only one way to gain her trust, I expose my most lethal hand. A spark of curiosity blazes in Cartier's narrowed gaze when I take the printout of Keira's injuries from my purse. The heat of Brodie's body blooms across my chest when he leans in intimately close to my side as I carefully open the folded-up piece of paper.

"Where the hell did you get that?" Brodie asks at the same time an exasperated gasp escapes Cartier's O-formed lips.

Ignoring Brodie's question, I keep my focus fixated on Cartier. "That's Keira Herrington, a founding member of Chains."

Cartier remains quiet, neither denying or agreeing with my accusation. She doesn't need to speak for me to hear the words she is saying, though. Her forthright eyes reveal the truth.

"This is also Keira," I say, handing her the fresh printout I printed minutes before leaving my home—the one that shows Keira volunteering at one of the many charities Cartier founded.

"And so is this one," I add on, handing her the final photo of Keira and Mr. Carson when they were younger. Cartier gasps with even more shock over this image.

"I don't know how, but I know these two are linked in some way," I say, gesturing my hand between the photo of Mr. Carson and Keira and the single ones of Keira. "If my hunch is right, Keira's injuries were the catalyst behind Global Tens' investigation into Chains. I just haven't worked out that link yet. I was hoping you'd help me."

I sheepishly lift my eyes to Cartier. She is glancing straight at me with shock and dread tainting her beautiful face. "Chains is being investigated?" she asks, her tone high with disbelief.

Shit. I assumed her extensive knowledge on Marcus Saturday night meant she was aware of the investigation. I had no clue I would be the one breaking the news.

After swallowing down the unease lodged in my throat, I mumble, "Yes."

I'm expecting Cartier to sigh in disappointment, or at the very least voice anger about people's right to privacy, and how they shouldn't be judged or ridiculed because of their sexual proclivities. She does nothing of the sort. She merely looks me straight in the eyes and says,

"Give me everything you have. All of it, Cleo. By the end of today, there will be no story."

Chapter Ten

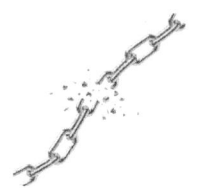

"I'VE GOT IT," SAYS CARTIER, HER VOICE SOUNDING MORE LIKE A ticket hackler in Yankee stadium, than showing the refinement it usually holds. "I don't know how I bloody missed it, but now it is as clear as day."

The past several hours of research must be taking its toll on Cartier. From her dark-ringed eyes and gaunt expression, I'd say I wasn't the only one burning the candle at both ends last night. She looks as wretched as I feel. Even Brodie appears exhausted. He is slumped on a body-hugging chair, basking in the rapidly setting sun. If I didn't hear his faint snoring, I'd be none the wiser that he was napping.

My aching muscles squeal in protest when I stand from my seat to take up the vacant spot next to Cartier. She has numerous print outs of the Chains' event I attended last week, but the one she is holding in her hand is the group photo of Marcus, Keira and Mr. Carson taken at a charity event over twelve months ago. Following the direction of her gaze, I realize her eyes aren't rapt on Marcus nor Mr. Carson; her gaze is firmly fixated on Keira.

Stumped as to why she believes this is the key to unlocking our confusion, I lift my eyes to her and say, "You're going to need to fill me in. I'm a little lost."

Cartier's beautiful chuckle jingles into my ears, warming my heart and awakening Brodie. After scrubbing the back of his hand over his tired eyes, Brodie moves to join my intimate gathering with Cartier. I'm glad she and I managed to costar over the massive barrier I lodged between us this morning without too much drama. Cartier's warranted unease only lasted the length of time it took for her to hear my quiet grumblings about Global Tens' investigation into Chains while I was unpacking my box of goodies I took from my office when I was placed on suspension for striking Delilah.

"Look, darling. It's Lauren Schwartz," Cartier says, handing the photo to me.

I drop my eyes to scan the image once more, searching for the woman Cartier is referring to. "Who is Lauren Schwartz, and what does she have to do with this investigation?"

Cartier laughs harder. "Not Lauren Schwartz the person, Lauren Schwartz the thing. A wonderful thing only a small number of people can afford."

She extends her overly manicured index finger to a shimmering of glitter on a hand resting on the edge of Keira's small-framed hip. Although the image is bright enough to see the enormous diamond engagement ring nestled on a tiny finger, it does not indicate to whom the hand belongs as the owner has been cut from the photo.

"That is a one of a kind platinum ring encrusted with an Asscher-cut 18-carat diamond, specially designed by Lauren Schwartz," Cartier explains.

"How can you be so sure?" I ask, dragging my face to within an inch of the image to inspect it properly. "There is no doubt that is a spectacular rock, but how do you know it belongs to Lauren Schwartz?"

Cartier cranks her head to the side. Her glare is so roasting, even if we were in the Antarctic, a coat would not be necessary. "I know my jewelry, darling. I was only researching new names last week. Lauren has a nice ring to it—no pun intended."

I giggle softly before handing the photo to Brodie as per his silent request. "Okay, so we know someone schmoozing Keira is extremely wealthy, but that doesn't bring us any closer to discovering the link between Mr. Carson and Keira. Everyone at the charity campaign is wealthy."

"But you wouldn't cut just anyone out of a photo," Brodie mutters more to himself than Cartier and me. "This was done on purpose."

Brodie spins the photo around to face me before he glides his finger down a blurry section of the picture. "Someone used Photoshop to remove the person standing next to her. This photo would look more legitimate if they removed the hand curled around her waist."

"Exactly!" Cartier overemphasizes. "They assumed removing her face from the photo was stripping her of her identity, but they couldn't be any more wrong. That piece of jewelry is as identifying as a set of greasy fingerprints. We just need the right person to crack the code."

My pulse hastens when she secures her diamond-encrusted cell phone out of the pocket of her kimono and dials a number I know will haunt her for months to come.

"Phoebe," Henry Gottle answers not even two rings later. His deep, raspy voice bounces around the room on speakerphone. His voice is a flawless display of what you'd expect from a mob boss—sexy and dangerous. "It has been too long, my love. How are you?"

"Cut the crap, Henry. You know as well as anyone, Phoebe died a long time ago," Cartier snaps down the phone, her tone forthright but jam-packed with emotions.

"Is that why you won't sign the divorce papers, because you are dead?" Henry retorts, his tone so low it spurs a smattering of goose-bumps to race to the surface of my skin.

"No." Cartier shakes her head, sending a rustle of blonde curls into her eyes. "It is to stop any other fool making the same mistake I did."

"Mistakes have consequences—"

"And consequences have actions. I've heard it all before, Henry. I don't need to hear it again," Cartier interrupts.

Henry sighs softly. If I hadn't read the many horrendous things he has done the past forty years of his life on the commute to Cartier's, I'd swear he was a man harboring a broken heart. "What do you want, Cartier?"

Cartier tries to snuff the flare of disappointment raring through her eyes from him addressing her by her infamous nickname, but she wasn't quick enough to entirely shut it down before I saw it. "I need the name, address, and contact details for a woman wearing a Lauren Schwartz ring."

"Seeking prospective gifts?" Although Henry only utters three words, the disdain in them made his sentence appear much longer.

"If I said yes, would you give me the information?" Cartier asks.

Henry takes his time configuring a response before he replies, "Have I stopped you yet?"

This time, Cartier sighs. "Can you get me the information I need, Henry? Or shall I contact someone from the Pop—"

"I'll get you the information you need," Henry snarls down the line, cutting Cartier off midsentence. "Give me everything you have, and one of my guys will call you in five minutes."

Henry kept his word. Within five minutes of Cartier relaying the dimension, cut, and size of the stone in the Lauren Schwartz ring, one of Henry's crew, Cooper, emailed Cartier the name, age, and address of the vanishing lady: Marissa Schulte, a forty-five-year-old native from the Upper West Side.

"That's only half a block from here," Cartier explains when I pull out my iPhone to look up her address.

Remaining quiet, Cartier continues scrolling through the email as Brodie and I peer over her shoulder. Cooper's dossier is so detailed, page after page of text on Marissa's day-to-day life flies by in an instant. If any of it is relevant, I wouldn't know, as Cartier's eagerness to get to the numerous image attachments in the bottom of the cryptic email is stronger than my ability to speed read.

"Words are deciphered solely on how the reader chooses to translate them. Photos capture unsaid words. A look, a feeling, a moment in time no words could ever express. If you ever want to see someone's true feelings, don't ask them to articulate them, ask them to express them," Cartier responds to my private grumbling.

I stop trying to unjumble her statement when an image of Marissa pops up on the screen. The first few photos were from years ago when Marissa was married. They are seemingly uninteresting. . . until Cartier continues clicking. Not only does Marissa and Mr. Carson's relationship become exposed in the timeline of photos, so does my knowledge of why Marissa's face registered as familiar.

"I could be wrong, but I swear Marissa is the lady I met when Mr. Carson propositioned me to investigate the Chains story. She was the unnamed blonde who convinced them to have a set of eyes in the room." I lock my eyes with Cartier. "Did Cooper's dossier list an occupation?"

Brodie shakes his head, answering on behalf of Cartier. "From what I read while Cartier was scrolling, Marissa has been a stay-at-home mother since the birth of her daughter twenty-five years ago. She is on the board of numerous charities, but husband number three's significant earnings ensure she doesn't have to lift a finger if she doesn't want to."

"Have you met her, Cartier?" I ask, knowing she is a benefactor for hundreds of charities founded around the New York region.

"No. She must be new to the area. With her bank account that large, highfalutin' snobs around here would have paraded her around for society to see if she's been here longer than six months," Cartier answers, nudging her head to a printout exposing Marissa's net worth.

I choke on my spit, stunned by the number of zeros attached to the first three digits. "There is a decimal point there somewhere, right? My vision is just too poor to see it?"

Cartier remains quiet, but Brodie's response is less reserved. His chuckle rumbles out of his cracked lips before it bounces off the luxurious wallpapered walls to shrill into my ears.

My attempts at nipping his laughter in the bud with a quick kick are thwarted when my toe jabs into the thick wooden chair Cartier's silky derriere is sitting on.

"Ah... crapola," I scream, wishing I could articulate the string of curse words running through my mind without fear of prosecution. "That. . . *friggin* hurt."

"You really want to swear right now, don't you?" Brodie asks, his deep voice barely recognizable with laughter.

Gritting my teeth, I nod.

"Then, why don't you?" Brodie asks, shocked.

Because Marcus has rules in place to discourage my love of profanity. Rules I don't want to break since they all include some form of sexual deprivation.

Instead of expressing what I really want to say, I shrug my shoulders. Brodie peers at me as if I said my private thoughts out loud. Before a single accusation can be fired off his tongue, our attention reverts to Cartier when she says, "Here is the link you've been searching for, darling."

"No way. That can't be true," I murmur as I peer at a photo of Marissa, Mr. Carson and Keira taken at the end of last year. "Mr. Carson only turned thirty last year. This can't be right. There must be a mistake. There is no way Keira is Mr. Carson's niece."

I aim for my tone to come out firm and to the point, but the nerves jittering my stomach are uncontainable, coating every word I spoke with the quiver of panic. I'm fiercely protective of Lexi because she is my blood, so I have no doubt Mr. Carson's protectiveness of Keira is just as intense. Now his response last week makes sense. He saw the medical report on Keira's injuries. That is why he agreed to the Chains investigation. He's protecting his niece from what he assumes are monsters.

My eyes swing to Brodie when he says, "According to Cooper's report, Marissa and Jack Carson have the same mother but different fathers. Marissa's father passed away in a workplace incident when she was eight. Her mother remarried five years later; two years after that, she gave birth to a baby boy: Jack Carson."

"So there is a fifteen-year gap between siblings?" I query, my brain too spent absorbing all the information I'm being handed to do simple math.

Brodie nods. "Marissa gave birth to Keira a few months shy of her twenty-first birthday. Jack was only five at the time. Keira is his niece."

"Then why is that not common knowledge? None of the articles we have read the past five years mention that Mr. Carson has a niece," I ask, my voice high with confusion.

Cartier stands from her chair, her movements effortless and harmonious. After running her hand down my frazzled hair, she locks her glistening eyes with mine. "There is no rhyme or reason for the way people live their lives, which also means there is no motive for judgment either. They could have a very good reason why they kept their relationship out of the public eye."

When I attempt to interrupt, Cartier continues speaking, foiling my chance. "Look at you, darling; you're exhausted because you are working so hard to protect Marcus." She runs her index finger over the heavy bags under my eyes the best she can without gouging my eyes out with her chunky rings. "When you love someone, your sanity fluctuates between manic and frenzied, and sometimes the only way to calm the agitation is by concealing it. That logic doesn't just extend to partnerships; it is for everyone you love. Mothers, fathers, siblings. . ."

"Nieces," we say at the same time.

"Yes," Cartier agrees with a faint smile. "Now you just have to decide what you're going to do with the information you've unearthed."

I wait a beat, hoping a solution to my predicament will smack into me. It never comes.

"I don't know what to do, Cartier. What would you do?" I ask, loathing that I'm leaving an important decision to a woman who was a stranger mere days ago, but adoring that we've created such a strong bond in a short period, I feel comfortable asking her this.

"Only you can make that decision, darling," Cartier replies as her eyes dance between mine. "But let me say one thing: love is when another person's happiness is more important than your own. When you truly love somebody, sometimes it takes big mistakes to figure that out. Then it often takes an even bigger mistake to fix the first mistake."

My brow furrows as confusion stirs in my gut. "Why do I get the feeling our conversation just shifted away from Keira and Mr. Carson and reverted to Marcus and me?"

Cartier smiles sweetly, but it is the anxiety in her eyes causing my biggest worry. "Because no matter which path you choose to walk, controversy will follow you."

"Why?" I query, genuine confusion echoed in my tone.

Warmth blooms across my chest when Cartier briefly skims the back of her nearly translucent fingers over my cheek in the exact area

Marcus always does. If I didn't know any better, I'd swear she knew about my attack weeks ago.

"The most crucial mistake I made was when I was your age. I fell in love with a man whose heart belonged to another." She intertwines her fingers in front of her body before locking her glistening eyes with me. "My second was believing I could force him to love me even if his heart didn't belong to me. He married me to prove his devotion. He left me to verify mine."

"I'm so sorry, Cartier," I express softly, hating the absolute agony in her eyes. Although I don't know exactly what I am sympathizing with, the pain radiating from her beautiful eyes warrants acknowledgment. "You are a beautiful person who deserves the world." I wave my hand around her opulent home. "You deserve even more than this."

"Thank you, darling," she replies graciously, accepting my praise in a manner I'd hoped.

I do not mean to suck up; I just hate that my visit has caused a ripple in her previously calm waters. She was airy and carefree in the minutes leading up to my disclosure of her true identity. Now her eyes are so dull, it feels like I've sucked the life straight out of them.

Reading the guilt in my eyes for what it is, Cartier says, "Don't feel bad, Cleo. My conversation with Henry was short but long overdue. Just knowing it helped Marcus immensely outweighs any negativity associated with it. It means more to me than any gift I've been given." She takes my hands in hers and gently squeezes them. "Now I'll award you with the same respect you bestowed upon me by trusting me to help you."

Horrid unease twists from my stomach to my throat when she says, "Tread carefully, darling. Your heart is in the right place wanting to protect your Master, but that also means you are placing it directly in the line of fire. Have you ever heard of the saying, 'To keep a secret is wisdom, but expecting others to keep it is madness?'"

I peer at her, blinking and confused when she hands me the printout of Keira's injuries from months ago. She stares at me, unmoving and unspeaking. Her eyes are soul-baring, but the worry in them doesn't weaken their usual forthrightness. It honestly feels like her silent warning is more based on Marcus and me than my fight against a man equally as powerful as the one I'm striving to vindicate.

"Look closely, darling. All the evidence you need is in your hands."

After tapping the printout in my hand, she spins on her heels and exits the living room as quickly as she entered, leaving Brodie and me to devise our own way out.

Chapter Eleven

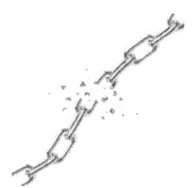

"YOU ALRIGHT, CLEO?"

After dragging my seatbelt over my erratically panting chest and clicking it in place, I raise my eyes to Brodie. He is watching me with the same set of worried eyes he's been directing at me the past hour. Although I could see a broad range of questions filtering through his eyes as we packed my belongings sprawled throughout Cartier's living room, these are the first words he has spoken to me since we unearthed the connection between Keira and Mr. Carson. He didn't even utter a syllable when our mad dash through a sprinkling of rain to his car drenched us head to toe. I expected a curse word—or the very least a grumble—he said nothing. His silence worries me more than the glint of anxiety in his eyes.

"Yeah, I was just thinking," I answer when the worry in Brodie's narrowed gaze grows from my delay in responding.

A gathering of wrinkles pleat the corners of his eyes when he screws up his nose. "That's your thinking face?"

His playfulness has the effect he was aiming for when I lean across the middle console to pop my fist into his thick bicep. I regret my decision when the thick ridges of his arm cause more damage to my hand than to him.

Grimacing, I cradle my injured hand with my uninjured one. "My god, did you pack rocks under your shirt this morning?" Unexpected laughter hinders my question.

Brodie's brow cocks high into his hairline as a ghost of a smile cracks onto his lips. "I aim to please."

I smile more broadly, equally loving and hating his cocky attitude.

I wait for him to finish latching his belt before mumbling, "Can I ask you something, Brodie?"

He runs his hand along the scruff on his chin, gathering the stubborn drops of rain still clinging to the bristles of his beard before replying, "As long as it is a question I can answer, sure, shoot." His tone is as hesitant as his facial expression.

Surprised by his anxious reply, the question sitting on the tip of my tongue rams into the back of my throat. Taking my silence as the end of my interrogation, Brodie shrugs, cranks the ignition on his car, then begins to back up. His foot glides from the gas pedal to the brake when the shrill of a cellphone rings through my ears. My heart beats triple time when I register the ringtone as familiar. A grin curls on my lips when Brodie's cell phone starts hollering not even two seconds later. My smile doesn't last long, only long enough for a terrifying notion to bombard me. Usually, bad news is delivered in quick succession.

My panic subsides when Brodie mumbles, "It's Lucy." His voice sounds relieved as if he too was worried by our combined calls.

He nudges his head to the cell I'm clutching for dear life, silently enquiring my caller's identity, his eagerness unmissable. I lower my eyes, just as eager to discover who my caller is. My smile returns when I spot Lexi's scowling face stretched across the screen. She wasn't impressed when I snapped a sneaky picture of her last week.

My smile must answer Brodie's questions as he drifts his eyes back to the road before activating the bluetooth device in his ear. I follow his suit, minus the bluetooth part.

"Miss me?" I query into my cell, not bothering to issue a greeting.

Lexi gags. "Only a lunatic would miss your snoring ass."

"Whatever," I force out with a laugh. "I'm not the one who talks in her sleep. 'I swear, professor. I might think your breath smells like dog doo, but I'd never say that out loud,'" I recite, my voice cracking with laughter.

I giggle even more loudly when my confession has Lexi stumped for a reply. My insides do a little jig, pleased as punch I've finally shocked her into silence. This is the first time I've succeeded what I previously thought was an unwinnable achievement.

When Lexi's silence lingers longer than anticipated, I ask, "Is everything okay, Lex?" I use Jackson's nickname for her, conscious it may catch her off guard enough to disclose whatever the problem is.

"Yeah. . . umm . . . Never mind. I've just realized why the microwave isn't working. It wasn't switched on." She huffs loudly, feigning stupidity. Her tone is so convincing, if I didn't know her as well as I do, I might have believed her.

"What's going on, Lexi?" I ask. My worried pitch is strong enough to gain the attention of Brodie. He disconnects his call, houses his cell in his jacket pocket, then devotes his eyes to me. When I catch sight of the time on the dashboard of Brodie's car, my worry intensifies. "Why aren't you with Jackson? I thought you guys were going out tonight?"

"I'm fine." She's lying—don't ask me how I know, I just know she is.

"And I'm not with Jackson as he got called into work. His schedule is all over the place." Now she is telling the truth.

I stare at Brodie, speechless. I know Lexi is lying, but I can't just call her out, can I? Brodie must spot the apprehension in my eyes, as the instant he gets a clearing in traffic, he completes a U-turn, altering our course from Marcus's residence to Montclair.

"Brodie and I are coming; we're around forty minutes away," I instruct Lexi, my voice shuddering with nerves.

Lexi breathes slowly down the line, attempting to drown out the expletive curse word that quickly follows it. "I'm not at home," she discloses after a stretch of uncomfortable silence. "I'm in New York."

I grit my teeth. I knew she was lying. If I had just called her out on it, we could have saved two minutes driving in the wrong direction. When I advise Brodie of her location, he dangerously veers into oncoming traffic. Thankfully, the motorists driving on the other side of the road are vigilant, meaning we avoid getting into a collision.

I brace my hand on the ceiling to lessen the crazy bounces hammering my body from Brodie's manic maneuvers. "Where *exactly* are you, Lexi?" I ask, my tone unforgiving.

If she lies to me again, I'm not above disciplining her. I don't care that she is twenty-one, she is still my baby sister. My worry could be unwarranted, but being deceitful isn't Lexi's forte, so for her to lie to me, I know it is for something significant.

All noise ceases to exist when Lexi replies, "I'm at Toloache."

"Why are you at Toloache?" I ask as panic roars through my body.

Hearing my question, Brodie increases the pressure on his gas pedal.

"This is where the note told me to come," Lexi answers, her tone relaying that she feels stupid.

I push aside my desire to agree with her assessment for a more appropriate time. "What note, Lexi?"

"A card. It was on my bed when I woke up from a nap this after-noon. I thought it was from Jackson, but he just messaged me. It wasn't from him. He's only just got out of surgery, he's been in their since midday. Cleo, something doesn't feel right. I've only just arrived, but my intuition is warning me something is off," Lexi discloses, her voice doused in panic.

Jesus Christ. I lock my panicked eyes with Brodie as dread chills my spine. "Please, hurry."

Nodding, Brodie flattens his foot on the gas pedal. We weave in and out of traffic with more stealth than bees swarming a honeypot.

"Lexi, are you there?" I query, panicked by the eerie silence coming down the line.

"Yeah." My heart leaps in my chest from the sheer panic relayed in her tone.

"Can you leave?" I ask, my voice cracking with nerves.

"Uh huh," Lexi answers softly.

"Okay. Leave. Now. Please." Wheezy breaths separate my words.

I hear a chair scrape across the ground before a male voice filters down the phone. The panic curled around my throat lessens when I realize it is the waiter checking in on Lexi. After assuring the server she is okay, Lexi accepts her coat then leaves. I've never been more appreciative to hear the buzz of traffic as I am right now. Hearing noise tells me Lexi is okay. It is silence I don't want to hear.

"Take a right as you exit; Links is a few blocks over. I'll meet you there."

"Okay," Lexi croaks out, her voice shattered by anxiety. "Cleo?"

"Yeah," I reply.

"Will you stay on the phone with me as I walk?"

I brush away a tear rolling down my cheek from her panicked tone. "Yes, of course I will.

I do precisely that for the entire ten-minute journey that usually takes twenty-five. We don't speak; we just listen to each other breathe, both grateful for the lack of commotion.

Brodie has barely pulled to the curb at Links when I throw off my seatbelt and race into the foyer. Even with my top lip dotted with sweat, I keep my jacket on, too motivated to find Lexi amongst the hundreds of patrons who use Links every day. I close my eyes and sigh loudly when I spot her standing at the side of the rec room with a wide-eyed Serenity. Not even caring that I'm in public, I let my tears flow freely, beyond grateful she is uninjured.

"Do you recognize this man?" Shian asks, sliding a photo across the desk I've been sitting behind the past two hours.

Although Lexi was uninjured, Brodie suggested we report the incident to the authorities. The fact someone was in my house when Lexi was alone warranted my agreement, but instead of calling Montclair PD as I had expected, Brodie called Shian.

Not looking at the picture, I crank my neck to Lexi. She shakes her head, silently acknowledging she is unaware of the man's identity. "Shian showed me his picture earlier; I've never seen him before," Lexi discloses, her voice not as haunted as it was earlier. Lexi acts tough, but her insides are a little squishier than she'd care to admit.

After running my hand down her arm, soundlessly assuring her she is fine, I lower my eyes to the picture. The longer I glance at the mug shot, the closer my brows join.

"That's Andy," I advise, my voice high in shock. "He was working behind the bar at the fundraiser I attended Saturday." My gaze dances between Shian's worried eyes. "Why do you have his photo? What does he have to do with this?"

Shian plucks the photo out of my hand. "We believe he is the man who left the note for Lexi."

"Why? Lexi said she's never seen him before, so why would he do that?" I cringe when my voice comes out snarky. I do not mean to be short with Shian; I'm just lost on what this all means.

Bile gurgles in my throat when Shian slides a second picture across the table. I curse the day I was born when I recognize the faces projecting back at me. It is Richard and Andy standing side by side. From the way they are clutching each other's shoulders and smiling broadly, it is as obvious as the sun hanging in the sky they know each other well.

"Andy thought Lexi was me," I murmur under my breath, answering my own question.

Shian nods, even though I didn't need her confirmation. "We couldn't comprehend why we were still intercepting messages in regards to your stalker case after Richard's death. Now we have a better understanding. These two are like brothers," she says, pointing her index finger between Andy and Richard. "They did everything together."

Clearly.

"Can you stop this from continuing? Is Andy going to be held accountable for this? He broke into our house. Into my sister's room. . ." My words stop as I fight to hold in my sob.

Shian licks her lips, her eyes hesitant. "The fact Andrew was detained sitting in the booth he reserved to meet with you aids in our case, but with how fickle the justice system is, I never make guarantees anymore. With no fingerprints at the scene or on the note, our evidence is minimal at best."

"He broke into our house!" I stand from my chair, my anger too great to inhibit. "You need to make him confess, Shian. He knows what he did wrong; force him to admit that."

"It isn't that easy, Cleo—"

"Bullshit!" I interrupt, shaking my head. "Look him in the eyes and force him to kneel. You're a Domme for crying out loud! How can you not make a pathetic man like him kneel?"

Ignoring Shian's flaming-with-anger face, I make a beeline for the door. Legally, Shian can't force a confession from someone, but I sure as hell can.

I'm shocked as hell when the first door I fling open in the long corridor is the one Andy is sitting in. *Andrew*, I correct myself. *He is not my friend.*

"Cleo," he says, shocked, adjusting his slumped position. "What are you doing here? Did you read my note?"

"It's a bit hard to read when you gave it to the wrong person," I reply, my words a vicious snarl.

Andrew's brows crimp as his lips purse. "What?" he asks, confused as ever.

"That was my sister's room. The note you left for me was placed on my baby sister's bed!" I roar, sending my loud voice bouncing off the stark white walls before booming back into my ears.

Andrew's eyes bounce between mine, his confusion unmissable. "Woah. . .hold on a minute. I didn't give your sister a note. I gave you a note. Remember?"

"You gave it to the wrong person, you dipshit!"

My brisk charge across the room is thwarted by the FBI agents sitting across from Andrew. They dive out of their seats, halting my endeavor to smack the confusion right off his face. I kick and wail against them, acting like a woman possessed. Going after me is one thing, but endangering the life of my sister intensifies my anger to a whole new level. Nothing gets in the way of me protecting my sister— not even two burly FBI agents.

Using their distraction of Shian's reprimand to put me down, I shrug out of their hold and charge for Andrew. Although the handsome blond agent curls his arm around my waist before I can reach Andrew, his firm hold leaves my arms unrestrained, meaning I can strike Andrew across the face. Since the agent yanks me back at the same time my hand sails wildly through the air, nothing but my sharp nails connect with Andrew's face.

Air hisses through his teeth when my nails drag across his face, leaving three significant scratches embedded in his nearly perfect skin. "What the fuck, Cleo? What the hell are you doing?"

He appears genuinely shocked, like he is appalled at the level I will stoop to protect my sister. He has no idea. If I weren't being subdued by a man the size of a bear, the scratches on his cheek would be the least of his worries.

"Tell them the truth," I implore as the FBI officer drags me out of the room.

"What the fuck do you think I'm trying to do?" Andrew yells through the rapidly closing interrogation room door.

"Read the note, Cleo!" I hear him scream as I'm hauled down the corridor, suddenly panicked I'm about to face my own prosecution. "It will explain everything. Just read the note!"

Chapter Twelve

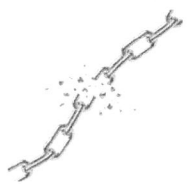

I CAREFULLY DRAPE A CASHMERE BLANKET OVER LEXI'S SLEEPING frame before tiptoeing out of the spare room of Marcus's residence. Warmth flourishes in my heart when my quiet exit from her room has me passing by a man I know she's been dying to see: *Jackson.*

"How is she?" he asks, his voice low with worry.

I crank my neck to peer back at Lexi sleeping before returning my drooping eyes to Jackson. "She is good. She wanted to wait for you to arrive, but Aubrey's hot chocolate is more lethal than she realized."

Some of the heaviness on my chest clears away when Jackson's bright white smile lights up the faintly lit room.

"Go on," I say when his eyes relay he is chomping at the bit to check on her himself.

My cheeks incline when he places a quick peck on the edge of my mouth before ambling to her bedside. Lexi stirs, her body recognizing Jackson's presence even in her sleep. Her groggily saying his name is the last thing I hear when I enter the hallway, gently closing their door behind me.

I jump, startled to within an inch of my life when I spot a shadowy figure propped up halfway down the hall. Although I'm grateful for the smiling assassin's eagle watch, he still isn't the person I was hoping to see. The whole "Andy" incident happened over six hours ago, and I still haven't heard from Marcus—not even a text asking if I am okay. I'm not going to lie—even with his house filled with people I care about, I'm devastated by his lack of contact.

"Did Andy confess?" I ask Brodie, hoping he will have an update from Shian.

My hopes are dashed when he shakes his head. "Not yet, but the DA is holding him on remand a few days; we'll see if a few nights in solitary can rattle a confession out of him."

I briefly nod. "Hopefully that works. If not, I wouldn't mind another attempt."

Brodie smirks before shaking his head. "You're lucky Shian likes you, Cleo. If anyone else pulled that stunt, you would have been eating Christmas turkey behind bars."

A stretch of silence passes between us. It is plagued with awkwardness.

I'm the first to break the silence when I ask, "Have you heard from Marcus?" My words come out quietly.

Brodie scrubs his hand across his chin while muttering, "Yeah."

"Yeah?" I question, certain I heard him wrong. I didn't. The guilt in Brodie's eyes grows tenfold when hundreds of silent questions from mine bombard them.

"What did he say?" I eventually ask when Brodie doesn't crumble under the pressure of my eyes.

Brodie half shrugs. "Not much." He breathes heavily, exposing he hates being stuck in the middle of Marcus and me. "It was the same stuff he always says. Make sure you're eating, sleeping, etc." He lifts his eyes from the ground to me. "To make sure you're safe."

Even annoyed Marcus didn't call me himself, heat blooms across my chest from Brodie's admission. "Did he say when he was coming back?"

Brodie nervously shifts on his feet before briefly shaking his head. "He didn't mention anything to me."

"Alright," I breathe out slowly, my disappointment revealed by my short response. "Well, I'm going to go to bed." I don't know why I felt the need to update Brodie on my happenings, it just occurred before I could shut it down.

Brodie briefly nods. "Okay. I'll see you in the morning?"

Since his statement comes out sounding like a question, I nod my head.

Just before I enter the master suite, Brodie calls out of my name. "Marcus did say one thing that baffled me."

He waits a beat, unaware he is torturing me, before adding on, "'Tell Cleo if she is cold, she can borrow my jackets. Navy blue is my favorite color.'"

"What does that mean?" I ask, shock evident in my tone.

Brodie's shoulder touches his ear when he shrugs. "I don't know."

After a final shrug showing his confusion, Brodie gallops down the stairs, disappearing into the blackness of Marcus's residence in three heart-thrashing seconds.

While showering and preparing for bed, I contemplate what Marcus's riddled statement could mean. Minutes of deliberation award me even more confusion. Shrugging off my perplexity as the effects of an exhausting week, I crawl into bed, wanting to forget the world exists.

I don't know how much time passes before I'm startled by someone slipping in between my sheets. The panic surging through my veins simmers when the unique scent of Marcus lingers into my nostrils. He scoots across the mattress until the heat of his naked torso warms my cami-covered back. A grin tugs on my weary face when he curls his arms around my waist and draws me back until he is cocooning me. It is incredible how well he eases my agitation. Every worry I've had the past forty-eight hours disappeared the instant he wrapped me up with his warmth.

"Hey," I greet him, my words barely a whisper since I'm half asleep.

"Hi, baby," Marcus replies, pressing his lips to my temple. "Go to sleep. I just want to hold you for a minute."

Blood floods my heart. "You flew all the way here just to spoon me?" I try to conceal the sheer delight doubling my heart's size. I miserably fail. I'm as smitten as hell he is here.

"Yes," Marcus replies, his tone shocked. "I'm sorry it took me so long to get here. I was tied up convincing a friend not to arrest my girlfriend for battery."

I bite on the inside of my cheek to ward off my smile. When I attempt to roll over to face Marcus, he holds on tightly, refusing my request. I pout, even though the room is so dark he can't see me.

"How did Cameron handle the news of you wanting to fly out again so soon?"

Marcus stiffens for the quickest second before he murmurs, "He is paid well enough he knows his opinion doesn't count." His reply is nearly drowned out by the sizeable yawn breaking free from my mouth.

"Go to sleep, Cleo," Marcus demands, his bossy tone sending the thump of my temples to my aching sex.

"I'm not tired," I lie. I'm so exhausted, I'm finding it hard to keep my eyelids open.

When I grind along Marcus's thickened rod, which is braced against my panty-covered backside, his deep growl rolls through my ears. I yelp when his teeth unexpectedly sink into my earlobe. His bite is soft enough for excitement to cluster in my core, but firm enough to divulge its execution was more for punishment than pleasure.

After lavishing the sting of his teeth with the lash of his tongue, Marcus repeats. "Go to sleep, Cleo, or your disobedience will require punishment. And it won't be in the way you are hoping."

Hearing the snip of danger in his warning, I stop grinding against him and nuzzle deeper into his embrace. With his closeness warming both my heart and my body, mere seconds pass before I fall blissfully asleep.

Several hours later, I wake up startled, disoriented, and confused. As one of my hands rubs the sleep from my eyes, my other creeps along the warm bedding in search of Marcus. I sigh softly when my exploration comes up empty. The bed is void of another soul. I scoot up the mattress to rest my back on the headboard, muted with confusion. Marcus was here last night, wasn't he?

Leaning over, I switch on the lamp on the bedside table. Once the room illuminates with unnatural lighting, I scan my eyes over the expansive space, ensuring I am alone. It is a replica of how it was left hours ago. The only difference is I'm tucked under the comforter instead of sleeping on top of it. That isn't unusual for me. As a child, I often fell asleep on the floor only to awake hours later in my bed. I assumed it was my dad moving me, but I guess now that isn't the case.

Baffled by the empty room, I snag the pillow next to me and lift it to my face. I inhale deeply, relishing the scent of Marcus's skin on the pillow. There is no doubt he was here. His scrumptious smell is too fresh and invigorating to have been left days ago.

Squealing with excitement, I fling off my comforter and race into the bathroom to get ready. I'm so eager to see Marcus again, I throw my hair into a messy bun on top of my head as I frantically scrub my teeth and gums with a toothbrush. Happy my breath is minty-fresh, I exit the bathroom. Although my pace is brisk, it isn't fast enough to miss a small card tucked into the edge of the last vanity mirror. As my brows stitch with suspicion, I pace toward the card and pluck it from its inconspicuous hiding place.

My eyes lift to scan the room, certain that card wasn't there when I showered last night. Everything in the bathroom is meticulously in place—as expected for any residence in Marcus's realm. Ignoring the rattle of my hands, I drop my eyes to the rectangular card. My breath snags halfway to my lungs when I read the handwritten note.

The most beautiful smiles hide the deepest secrets;
the most dazzling eyes hide the number of tears they have shed,
and the kindest heart is usually the most broken.
Actions always prove why words mean nothing.

I flip the card over, seeking any indication as to whom the message is from. Although my heart swears the note is from Marcus, receiving this card the morning following Lexi receiving one has my worry intensifying. There are no identifiable markings on the postcard. It seems as if it magically appeared, thwarting my panic at the same time it triggers it.

Seeking answers, I push off my feet and exit the bathroom. I gallop down the stairs two at a time, not stopping until I crash into a wall of hardness—literally.

"Whoa, Cleo, slow down. Did you take too many vitamins this morning?"

Lifting my eyes from the ground, I'm met with the twinkling gaze of Brodie. He has a mug of steamy hot coffee in his hands and is sporting a set of tired bags under his eyes, which is surprising since he went to bed hours before me. The suspicion tainting my blood grows when I notice how rumpled his clothing is. I swear that is the same outfit he was wearing last night. Has he not showered since yesterday?

I splay my hands across my cocked hip. "Why are you wearing the same clothes you had on last night?"

My rigid stance eases when Brodie replies, "Lucy had a fever last night. Although I couldn't be there in the physical sense, I could morally. I stayed up with her, retelling her favorite fairytales." His last handful of words are muffled by a massive yawn.

"Oh. . ." I'd like to say more, but guilt has stolen my words.

"Is she okay now?" I ask once I've regained the ability to talk.

Brodie's hand scrubs his tired eyes as he nods his head. "Yeah, probably just a virus of some sorts. Kids are full of germs."

Smiling at his screwed-up expression, I say, "I can only imagine."

My hand splayed on my hip slithers to my back when Brodie nudges his head to the card I'm clutching. "What's that?" he asks with interest.

"Umm . . ." I graze my teeth over my bottom lip as I contemplate a reply. It's a very long minute.

Realizing Brodie could aid in un-riddling my confusion, I pull the card out from my back and hand it to him. I watch him in silence, categorizing every expression that crosses his face as he reads the small message scripted on the card. His eyes blaze with a similar range of emotions I felt while reading the card for the first time.

Brodie connects his eyes with mine. "Who gave you this?"

I answer his question with a shrug.

"Do you recognize the handwriting? Is it Marcus's?" he continues to interrogate, his words hurried.

Concerned by the worry in his tone, I once again shrug.

"You need to give me more than shrugs as answers, Cleo," Brodie chastises, his tone void of any amusement. "I'm not a fucking mind reader."

"I don't know who it's from. I woke up to it lodged in the bathroom mirror." Ignoring the apprehension in Brodie's eyes which has exploded to full-blown worry, I add on, "I believe it is from Marcus, though."

"Why?" Brodie snaps, shocking me with his curt tone.

"Who else would it be from?"

Brodie glares at me, his stare anything but pleasant.

"Marcus came home last night. He snuck into my bed around 2 AM. Putting two and two together, it's pretty obvious who the message is from. *Let alone your disheveled appearance.*" I mumble my last sentence under my breath, but the look crossing Brodie's face tells me he heard it.

Acknowledging I can't dig my hole any deeper than it is, I ask, "Was Lucy really sick last night? Or was a pedantic rock star the real cause of your tiredness?"

Not taking the time to absorb my snippy comment, Brodie says, "Meet me in the foyer in five minutes." His curt tone ensures I can't mistake his demand as a question.

"But I want to see Marcus."

"I just finished sweeping the house. Marcus isn't here. Five minutes, Cleo."

Snubbing my slack-jawed expression, he takes the stairs two at a time, disappearing before I have the chance to articulate one of the many gripes running through my brain.

Nearly two hours later, Brodie pulls into a cute little double story house in a community east of New York. He hasn't even clambered halfway out of his car when the cutest little squeak of, "Daddy!" roars through my ears. I recognize the flurry of blonde galloping down the stairs from the photos Brodie showed me Saturday night. It is his daughter, Lucy.

Excited squeals bellow out of Lucy's mouth when their meeting halfway down the painted sidewalk results in her being twirled into the air. Her gleeful giggles make fond memories of my dad greeting Lexi and me the same way rush to the forefront of my mind. *God, I miss my family.*

Lexi must be feeling the same sentiment, as the angry mask she's been wearing since I begrudgingly dragged her out of bed clears away the longer she watches Brodie and Lucy interact. Nothing can compare to the love a parent has for their child. You can love someone with every ounce of yourself, and it still wouldn't represent the love parents have for their children. The love from a parent isn't the same as the love you crave from a spouse. They are unique and special in their own right.

At Brodie's request, Lexi and I unlatch our seatbelts and climb out of his car. The frigid breeze rattling my bones does nothing to lessen my excitement when Lucy greets me by wrapping her tiny arms around my thighs and squeezing me tightly. When she releases her death-like grip, I bob down to face her eye to eye.

"Hi, Lucy," I greet while running my hand down her hair to smooth the pieces floating in the wind from Brodie's robust twirls. "It is a pleasure to meet you. Are you feeling better?"

Lucy nods her adorable head. "Yes, thank you." Her words are so undeveloped, I swear she said, "Spank you" not thank you.

Shocked by my disturbing thoughts, I stand from my crouched position so I can watch Lucy greet Lexi in the same manner. Smiling, I accept the hand Lucy is holding out, then follow her into the quaint home where I stay for the next three hours, learning all aspects of Brodie's life.

I'd like to say the stories shared were full of rainbows and lollipops, but unfortunately, that isn't the case. Brodie's wife, Caroline, passed away when Lucy was six months old. Although Caroline has a large family, as far as Brodie is concerned, Lucy is the only family he has. With Brodie's hours being sporadic, he has a live-in nanny who aids in raising Lucy. Ms. Mitchell has a heart of gold, and her fondness for Lucy is unmissable. Her children are grown, but she is not yet a grandmother, so she has plenty of time to devote her motherly attentiveness to Lucy. It is the perfect predicament. One I hope will last for many years to come.

After bidding farewell to Ms. Mitchell with a kiss on the cheek and promising Lucy we'll come back to visit soon, Lexi and I shadow Brodie to his car. Heat blooms across my chest when I see the indecisiveness in Brodie's eyes. I can see how much he hates leaving Lucy without a word needing to spill from his hard-lined lips.

"Why do you do it?" I ask while latching my belt.

Brodie starts his ignition and reverses from the driveway of his family home before locking his eyes with mine. "Do what?"

"This." I gesture my hand around his car, hovering more on Lexi and me. "There are plenty of positions that wouldn't require overnight stays, so why do it?"

Brodie takes his time configuring a response. I don't know whether he is stumped or doesn't appreciate me analyzing his choices. I'm not at all judging his parenting. I saw him interact with Lucy; she is a well-adapted four-year-old who is well-taken care of and loved. I'm just trying to understand why he'd work in a field where they are forced to be apart.

My eyes lift from my intertwined hands when Brodie says, "I did consider a change in career when Caroline passed away. I even took an extended leave of absence from my position, but this type of industry is hard to give up. Once it's in your veins, you can never fully remove it."

His response seems more heartfelt than one you'd expect from a bodyguard. Don't get me wrong, I've always believed in having pride in your position, but his response seems more than just pride. His job is important to him.

Before any more interrogating questions can filter from my mouth, the shrill of a cellphone rings through my ears. Brodie taps on the device in his ear before saying, "Shian, did you find anything?"

My suspicion piques when Brodie continues with his conversation. If I'm not mistaken by the snippets of his reply, he didn't introduce Lexi and me to Lucy to prove she was unwell; he needed us out of Marcus's residence. The only thing I can't fathom is why.

My silent questions are answered when Brodie disconnects his call and locks his eyes with mine. "The card you found in the bathroom wasn't from Marcus." The swirling of my stomach doubles when he says, "The handwriting matches the card Lexi received yesterday. Whoever broke into your house yesterday was in Marcus's house last night."

"But you said Andy is in custody," Lexi interjects, leaning forward to join our conversation.

"He is," Brodie replies, nodding.

"Then who sent the card?" I ask, shock in my tone.

Brodie shrugs. "I don't know, but until we find out, you're going to become well accustomed to this space." He gestures his hand between the small portion of air sitting between us. "I've just become your new best friend, Cleo."

He wasn't joking. He did precisely that for the next four days.

Chapter Thirteen

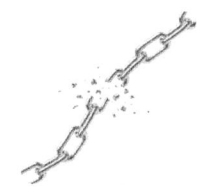

My eyes lift from an article on the rapid advancement of technology's effects on diversity when a commotion at the door gains my attention. Lexi has her shoulder propped up on the entrance of Marcus's office. Her lips are facing down, and her eyes are dull.

"If I spend another moment cooped up inside, I'm going to go bonkers," she mutters, her words enunciated with an exaggerated huff.

I peer at her over the screen of Marcus's laptop when she moseys into the room, her steps sloth-like. "I thought you were studying?"

"I am; I did; I conquered. Can we please do something more invigorating today? I'm bored out of my fucking mind."

Lexi and my eyes missile to the door in sync when the distinct rumble of Aubrey sounds over the quiet. Although there are a good dozen or so feet between us and the cookie-smelling room Aubrey is baking in, I'm confident she heard Lexi's curse word. Just like Marcus, Aubrey is not a fan of derogatory comments, sneered words, or any mention of God's name attached that isn't a prayer.

Over the past four days, Lexi has been learning the hard way that swearing isn't acceptable in this residence. Although her punishment hasn't been as spine-tinglingly delicious as the course I endured last week, she is quickly learning disobedience limits rewards, whereas obedience doubles them.

"Great, there goes my afternoon snack," Lexi grumbles under her breath.

She props her backside onto Marcus's flimsy desk before dropping her eyes to the document on my screen. "What are you working on?" Although she is asking a question, she keeps talking, foiling my reply. "Snoozefest. Why are you writing about that? Magazine articles are no different than novels. If you want to sell stories, write what you read."

"I like reading about this stuff; it's interesting," I argue with an immature roll of my eyes.

Lexi makes snoring noises, cutting off any further replies I was planning to give.

"Oh, is that Chains?" she asks when an email notification pops up on the screen.

My pulse quickens as I drop my eyes to the monitor. Although Marcus's messages have been more sporadic than usual the past three days, I still cherish every one I get. His messages and phone calls are brief but sweet enough to cause a toothache.

Not wanting Lexi to snoop on my private conversation, I minimize the screen on my laptop and click on the email. Realizing it is a message from the security company Marcus hired to install a state-of-the-art security system in my home in Montclair, I return the screen to its original position.

Lexi tries to hide it, but I see the quickest flare of excitement blaze in her eyes when it dawns on her she is mere hours away from returning home. Although I've pleaded and begged for her to stay with me at Marcus's house until the culprit of the notes is apprehended, she is refusing my requests. She is siding with Jackson, believing both notes were delivered before Andy was arrested, and my poor eyesight is the cause for me not noticing it earlier. Considering we haven't had any dilemmas the past four days, my apprehensions are beginning to swing in the opposite direction as they did days ago.

"So can we go out?" Lexi asks, dragging my focus back to the present.

Confused by her question, my brows furrow. "Go where, exactly?"

"To lunch," Lexi questions as her legs swing wildly in the air.

I eye her suspiciously, shocked by her blasé response. She usually only acts skittish when she is hiding something.

"I don't think it's a good idea, Lexi," I say, unable to read the prompts her eyes are relaying.

Lexi drops her bottom lip and gives me the biggest puppy dog eyes she's ever issued. "Please, Cleo. Why can't we go out?" Her whiny voice makes her sound more like a teenager than a twenty-one-year-old woman. "Shian said Andy's bail hearing isn't until Monday, so there is no reason for us to hide out. *Please....* I really really *really* want to get out of this house."

Her whining stops when my cell phone buzzes and vibrates on Marcus's desk. Like every time it dings announcing a message, my hopes kick into overdrive that it's from Marcus. Unfortunately, my dreams are left for dust when the screen displays the message:

Unknown number: *What's a girl got to do to get a lunch date around here?*

If I hadn't recognized the tone of the message, the shit-eating grin on Lexi's face would have disclosed my caller's identity either way.

"Are you and Serenity conspiring against me?" I ask Lexi, swiveling the screen of my phone to face her.

"No," Lexi lies, nodding her head.

I try to hide my smile from her double-meaning reply. It is a hard-fought battle. "Yes or no, Lexi; which one is it?"

"We aren't conspiring against you. We're just colluding so you'll join us for lunch," she states matter-of-factly.

"Conspiring and colluding are the same thing," I mumble, laughter in my tone.

Lexi crosses her arms in front of her chest as she shakes her head. "No, it isn't. Conspiring is when you are doing something evil. Colluding is when you work together for the greater good."

My eyes roll skywards. Her excuse is as weak as the one Marcus used when arguing that negotiating and comprising are separate entities. They are the same damn thing.

"Come on, Cleo. Serenity is hungry; I suggested lunch as a solution for her hunger. She thought it was a great idea," Lexi continues to plead.

I glare into her eyes, knowing there is more to the story than she is sharing. Her eyes frolic between mine, the plea in them growing in intensity for every second that ticks by. "If you're worried about Marcus being angry, don't be. I'll talk to him. We'll even take Brodie with us. *If we must."* She mumbles her last sentence.

She continues pleading until she breaks through the protective wall I built around us the past four days. Then she proceeds chipping away at the panic curled around my neck until its tight grip is loosened enough I can reluctantly nod my head. I never could deny her, so I don't know why I bothered resisting her request.

My nod was brief, but not curt enough for Lexi to miss it. "Yes!" she screams, throwing her arms into the air. Anyone would swear she just won the lotto.

Her eyes track mine when I push the office chair away from Marcus's desk and stand. "Let's do this."

Not giving me the chance to change my mind, Lexi wraps her arm around the nook of my elbow and drags me out of Marcus's office. Her pace is so unchecked, she barrels into Aubrey, sending cookies and milk flying into the air.

"Sorry," she apologizes with a grimace before continuing our trek, her excitement too high to stop her.

Fifty minutes later, our coats are hung by the beautiful hostess at an elegant restaurant where I've only dreamed of dining. Not wanting to be the odd man out, Brodie is holed up in his car with a bag of greasy takeout and a few sports magazines. I finalize my risqué text to Marcus, ensuring his understanding of our desire to eat out will be significantly rewarded upon his return tonight, before storing my cell into my clutch.

My leisured steps into the elegant-smelling space quicken when my sweep of the room has me stumbling upon a familiar face sitting across from Serenity: *Cartier.*

"Hello, darling," she greets, rising from her seat to place air kisses on each of my cheeks. After greeting Lexi in the same manner, she says, "I don't need to ask whom you belong to."

I smile. "Lexi, this is a friend of mine, Cartier. Cartier, this is my baby sister, Lexi." I try to keep the muckiness out of my voice during my introduction; my attempts are borderline. I can't rein in my pride when it comes to Lexi.

Lexi cordially greets Cartier with a smile. Her embrace of Serenity is a little friendlier. They act like lifelong friends as they wrap their arms around each other and bounce on the spot, giggling like teen girls on the way to prom.

"Thank you," I gesture to the waiter when he fans a white napkin over my lap after I take a seat across from Cartier. "I wasn't aware you knew each other," I say to Cartier as my eyes drift between her and Serenity.

The twinkle of fondness in Cartier's eyes grows when she locks them with Serenity. "It is a recently formed relationship. We have one man we both care very much about." I assume she is talking about Marcus until her hand lifts to caress the thin necklace hidden behind her bulky ones. "Speaking of men I care about, how are things with you and Marcus? Everything okay?"

Cartier's hand drops from her neck when I gush, "Umm. . . Great. Actually, it's wonderful."

Cartier smiles, but it is more reserved than her usual smile. It was more like she had to force it onto her face than it being there of its own will. "Stop acting so damn happy or people will get the wrong impression," she snickers under her breath.

"Are you sure it's the wrong impression they'd be getting?" I ask with a waggle of my brows. I indeed need to limit my time with Lexi; her maturity is starting to rub off on me—and not in a good way.

Wrinkles crease my nose when Cartier rolls her eyes. "Gosh, if I didn't know any better, I'd swear you're acting like a love crazy imbecile."

I graze my teeth over my bottom lip, incapable of denying her snickered claim.

The happiness making my head a giddy mess drifts into abyss when

Cartier requests, "Please tell me you haven't expressed. . ." Her words trail off as she assesses my face. "Whatever this is. . ." she swirls her hand around my loved-up expression, ". . .to Master Chains."

If it weren't for the dire expression on her face, I might have laughed at her statement. But since her gaunt appearance is relaying nothing but panic, I leash my childish response and briskly shake my head.

Cartier sighs deeply. "Thank god," she murmurs frailly.

"Would it really be that bad if I did?" I ask before I can stop my words.

Cartier's tongue delves out to replenish her lips before she swivels in her seat to face me. She waits, soundlessly building the suspense until it is nearly murderous. Just when I think she isn't going to speak, she says, "I like to believe I know the true Marcus, the one beneath the Master Chains mask he regularly wears, but even I can't guarantee what his reaction would be if you declare your *love* for him." She whispers the word "love" as if it is a curse word. "I thought I knew Henry, and look how that turned out."

Ignoring the swirling in my stomach induced by her peculiar reply, I accept the wine list from the waiter, happy to use it as a distraction while unravelling Cartier's puzzling statement. I've barely scanned the first page of cocktails when the menu is plucked from my grasp.

Keeping her eyes locked on the waiter, Cartier says, "We will have sparkling water, thank you."

My bottom lip drops into a pout. With nearly every drop of alcohol in Marcus's house potent enough to knock me on my ass with one sip, I was very much looking forward to a fruity cocktail. And, if I'm being honest, I was hoping to lace Cartier's veins with alcohol to loosen her lips.

"Alcohol ages you," Cartier snickers, her voice as mortified as my facial expression.

"Says the lady downing margaritas last week like they were apple juice," I scold, my playful tone dulling down my snappy reply.

Cartier's chance to reply is lost when Serenity and Lexi's prolonged greeting comes to an end. My eyes roam Lexi's face when she plops into the chair next to me. Her face is red with exertion, but no signs of air struggle are notable. It is indeed amazing how much the Kalydeco program has been a godsend for Lexi. If I didn't already love Marcus with every morsel of my soul, Lexi's new lease on life would have soon taken care of that.

Don't get me wrong; I'm not saying I love Marcus because of what he can give me. I love him for how generous and kind he is. His kindness extends way beyond monetary value. I honestly believe even if he weren't a wealthy rock star and BDSM club owner, his charity efforts would still be as strong as they are today. His grandmother left him a lasting legacy, one that will live on for years after he is gone.

Feeling giddy, I snap open my clutch to check for a return message from Marcus. Regretfully, my screen is void of any messages or missed calls. After accepting the menu from the grinning waiter, Lexi swaps seats with Cartier as per Cartier's request.

I raise my eyes from the menu to Cartier, taking in her flawless designer-clothed body on the way. When our eyes meet, she asks, "Have you talked to Marcus about what you unearthed Monday?" Her tone is more friendly than the one she used earlier, but it still has a hint of antagonism associated with it.

I shake my head. "No. I want to do it in person."

Cartier stills from my confession but remains quiet. I can understand her reservation. I've had plenty of opportunities to discuss my findings with Marcus the past four days, but every time I prepare to expose the connection between Keira and Mr. Carson, my words clog in my throat. I don't know why. I think part of my worry stems from the protectiveness Marcus displayed to Keira Saturday night, and the other half is concerned about what his reaction will be when he discovers I've been investigating him.

I'd like to say my investigation into Chains ended the instant Cartier unearthed the link between Keira's assault and Mr. Carson's agreement to investigate Chains, but that would be a lie. Although it isn't as rampant as it was days ago, I've still spent a minimum three hours a day seeking further information on their connection. Mr. Carson and Keira's family association is buried by so much legal propaganda, that one photo Lexi discovered Sunday morning is the only photo I've found of them together. It is as if they are total strangers.

I stop twisting my napkin around my fingers so tightly they are void of natural color when Cartier places her hand over mine. She peers at me like she wants to say something, but not a syllable escapes her lips.

Dying for her to articulate the secrets her eyes are struggling to conceal, I ask, "Have you talked to Marcus about what I discovered? About *Keira?*" I whisper her name since my hackles are still bristled from last weekend.

I feel sorry for what happened to Keira months ago, but I'm still angry at her wearing Marcus's trademark. There is only one reason she did that—she wanted Marcus's attention. And, unfortunately, that is precisely what she got. Marcus is a smart man, but he fell straight into Keira's trap last weekend. The fact she unarmed a man as guarded as Marcus has me truly worried about the influence she has on him. I have no doubt Marcus feels guilty for Keira's injuries if they were sustained against her wishes while she was a patron at his club, but unless her injuries were placed there by him, it is unnecessary guilt. If Keira genuinely cares for Marcus, as her eyes relayed last weekend, she should relinquish him from his guilt, not encourage it.

A wisp of blonde hair falls into Cartier's face when she robustly shakes her head. "No, darling. It is not my place to tell him. It is yours. Relationships are enough work without third-party influences butting in."

"Ain't that the truth," I mutter to myself.

I realize my quiet summarizing wasn't as discreet as I was aiming for when Lexi and Serenity's heads lift from their menu to peer at me. Although their gazes drop back to the menu seconds later, I can feel the heat of their eyes on me. It isn't the warmth of friendliness; it the heat of worry.

"When you get the chance, you really need to talk to him, darling," Cartier requests softly, tapping my hand with hers. "I know he is swamped; when I saw him yesterday, he was run off his feet, but the information you found could be critical for many people very dear to him. You must tell him what you discovered, Cleo. It is the right thing to do."

I swallow the bitter taste in the back of my throat before murmuring, "You saw Marcus yesterday?" Although I wholeheartedly agree that I need to inform Marcus of my findings, my primary focus is on Cartier's admission she saw Marcus yesterday.

A twinkle of fondness flares in Cartier's eyes as she nods her head.

"You went to Florida?" I ask, shock smeared in my high tone.

The glimmer in Cartier's eyes dulls before she timidly shakes her head. "No, darling. Why would I go to Florida?" she asks, sounding disgusted at the idea.

"Because Marcus is in Florida," I object, my words laced with unwarranted bitchiness. When Cartier balks from my admission, I add on, "He is in Florida, isn't he?"

For the first time, Cartier looks genuinely fearful. She forcefully swallows before her eyes drift to Serenity and Lexi, who are once again eyeballing our exchange in silence.

"You must have gotten your dates mixed up, Cartier. You saw Marcus last week, remember?" Serenity's attempt at lying is as woeful as mine usually are. I hardly know her, and I still know she is lying; that is how bad her effort was.

"Oh, yes, that is right. It was last week," Cartier agrees with her squinted gaze locked on Serenity.

Because I can't see her eyes, I can't 100% proclaim she is lying. Her vocals were higher than usual, indicating deceit, but since we met mere days ago, it doesn't feel right to call her out as a liar.

Cartier sighs loudly when our waiter magically appears at her side, demonstrating that she too felt the uncomfortable awkwardness plaguing our small gathering.

By the time everyone's orders have been jotted down, any opportunity to grill Cartier and Serenity further are lost. They are buried in discussion with Lexi about a man named Ricci.

Over the next hour, I try to participate in the conversation being held around the table, but with my mind elsewhere, my responses are lackluster, missing the Garcia spark. Lucky Lexi's personality makes up for my deficiency in schmoozing. I know the cause of my absentmindedness: while unjumbling the complexity of my conversation with Cartier, many theories ran wild in my mind—*none of them were pleasant*.

Accumulating my knowledge of Marcus and Keira's connection, the link between Mr. Carson and Keira, Marcus's sudden decision to return to Ravenshoe alone, and Cartier's admission she saw Marcus as recently as yesterday has bombarded me with a severe case of nausea. I feel sick—*incredibly unwell.*

Excusing myself, I snag my clutch off the table and make a beeline for the washroom. Although my first thought was to splash some water on my face, when I'm in the safety of the stall area, I yank my cell phone out of my purse. After kicking down the toilet seat in the vacant stall in the far back corner, I dial Marcus's number. His cell-phone rings on repeat—over and over again.

All six of my calls sent to voicemail amplifies the sick gloom creating havoc with my chest. I sit in silence, assuring myself repeatedly that Cartier was mistaken, that she didn't see Marcus yesterday, and that Marcus isn't accepting my calls as he is in the process of flying home.

Several minutes of reassurance awards me with nothing but additional butterflies in my churning stomach. Why would a woman as intelligent as Cartier get something so simple wrong? She wouldn't have, would she? And although Marcus is flying, wouldn't advances in technology mean he could still answer my call if he wanted to?

I run my hand across my cheek, gathering a stupid tear descending down my face when Lexi calls out, "Cleo? Everything okay?" From the way her voice is projecting, it sounds like she is standing right outside of the stall.

"Uh, yeah, just an aversion to the clams." I cringe, loathing my inability to think on the spot.

"Eww. Alright. Buzz me if you need assistance."

She waits for me to respond before she leaves me in peace. I take a few more minutes to settle the restlessness on my face before dumping my tear-gathering napkin into the bowl and flushing the cistern. My brisk pace to the vanity to wash my hands slows to a snail's pace when my eyes lock in on a shimmering of blonde standing next to the only sink in the room. I calm the unnatural beat of my heart, confident the world wouldn't be so cruel to throw me another curveball right now. I've been dodging so many balls this week, one is eventually going to hit me square in the guts.

A timely reminder of how cruel life can be hits fruition when the blonde pivots on her heels to snag a paper towel from the muted washroom attendant dressed entirely in black on her right. Seemingly unaware of my gawking glance, Keira thoroughly dries her hands before placing a selection of bills onto a gold tray in the corner of the room. I suck in a grateful breath when she heads for the door without so much as a sideways glance in my direction.

The air I've just drawn in is brutally evicted when her swayed steps stop. She turns her head to face me, her movements stiff and robotic. "Cleo?" she greets, her tone apprehensive, like I'm a mirage standing before her.

Realizing I'm not an illusion, she paces two steps toward me. "What a pleasure to see you again." Her tone is so convincing of her gratuity, I may have believed her if the quickest flash of annoyance didn't blaze through her eyes.

"Hello." I'd like to express more, but vehement jealousy has stolen my words.

Even though her exchange with Marcus last week could be construed as innocent, I hate that she interfered in our relationship at all. What she did last week was wrong. If I weren't fearful of airing my dirty laundry in public, I'd tell Keira precisely how disgusted I am about her ruse. But since I was raised better than that, I dip my chin, finalizing my greeting, then hightail it to the sink.

Keira doesn't utter a syllable as I wash my hands at a record-setting pace before heading for the washroom door.

"Cleo, wait," she calls out as I glide into the corridor.

I hear her apologize to the washroom attendant in Spanish before she shadows me down the corridor separating the restrooms from the main seating area of the restaurant. "I really didn't want everything to come to this. What I said to you in the elevator months ago was true. I do genuinely like you. It is just. . . just. . ."

"Just what, Keira?" I ask, spinning on my heels to face her. "I'm nice, but not nice enough for you to respect me? Or am I only convenient to associate with when I'm not occupying the time of the Master you want?"

Keira tucks her fancy clutch under her arm as her eyes fleetingly float around the room. "You need to keep your voice down," she implores, her tone more mature than her twenty-five years.

"Why?" I ask, my voice laced with bitchiness. "Are you afraid people will discover you aren't as innocent as you portray?"

Keira's eyelashes flutter as she struggles to blink back her tears. My throat tightens, hating that I'm allowing my jealousy to turn me into a vindictive, malicious person.

Lessening the severity of my wrath, I take a step closer to Keira. "If you were honest with your uncle, all of this could have been avoided."

"*All* of this?" Keira retaliates, her voice quickening with anger. "What is happening is not my fault. I've done everything in my power to stop Global Tens' investigation into Chains."

"Have you tried being honest?" I fire back, my tone just as stern as hers.

"Yes!" she answers, her word hissing out of her mouth like venom.

"So you told your uncle everything? You explained that the bruises and whip marks you sought medical assistance for were put there by your own choice?"

Keira balks as her pupils turn massive. Clearly, she is unaware how deep my investigation into Chains has gone. As quickly as her tears appeared, they vanish. She realigns her slouched pose before the glint in her eyes turns evil. She glares at me, issuing a stare so chilling, it reminds me of my many run-ins with the devil herself.

Not willing to back down without a fight, I take a step toward Keira. We are standing so close, the gold trim of her clutch digs into my chest. "I saw the devastation on your uncle's face firsthand when he disclosed the reason he agreed to the investigation into Chains. He thinks they are monsters, Keira."

She stares at me, blinking and mute. Her silence confirms my suspicions. She is a part of the BDSM lifestyle but unwilling to admit it. I don't know if her hesitation stems from shame or because her views on the lifestyle are as negative as Delilah's.

"Weeks ago you implored me to look at the BDSM lifestyle from the angle of a person intrigued by it but not guided by society's opinion of it, yet you are doing the exact opposite. You're letting a community you love take the fall for your cowardice. I know it's hard to express yourself, Keira. I fully understand what it is like to crave things society doesn't deem acceptable, but I'd never let those I care about be caught in the crossfire. Be honest with your uncle. Tell him those bruises and marks on your back were put there by your own free will. If you care about Marcus at all, save him from being unjustly vilified."

"Why? So he can ride off into the sunset on a white horse with you?" Keira replies, her hackling tone shocking me. "I'm sorry things didn't work out for you and Marcus, Cleo, but that doesn't mean I'll disgrace my family name just so you can claw your way back into his good graces."

"What?" I ask as my eyes dance between her. If she failed to hear the confusion in my tone, the expression on my face is unmissable. I am more confused than ever.

"We all make mistakes. Mine is keeping my inclusion in the BDSM lifestyle from my family. Yours is believing you can make a man like Master Chains kneel. Dominance is who Marcus is; he doesn't know any different, so the instant you forced vanilla on him, you lost him. Be angry, Cleo. Lash out. But remember the blame for the demise of your relationship lies solely on your shoulders—not mine."

My lips twitch, dying to rebut her false statement, but not a word spills from my mouth. I don't know why; I just can't get a syllable out no matter how hard I fight. It probably has something to do with the fact Keira knows Marcus and I made love. How could she know that. . .unless.

My eyes missile to Keira. "When did you last see Marcus?" I ask, my voice rife with suspicion.

The egotistical gleam in her eyes doubles, enhancing my hesitation as she replies, "We had brunch yesterday." She scans her eyes over our location before she adds on, "In this very restaurant."

She locks her eyes with mine, ensuring I can't miss the honesty in her reply. "As I said, Cleo, I like you. You're kind-hearted, eager to please, and you'd make a wonderful submissive; you're just not the right sub for Master Chains."

"And let me guess, you are?" I snarl, my words vicious.

Keira remains quiet, but the smirk on her face answers all my questions. Her confidence is at an all-time high, and way too smug for my liking.

Her abhorrent smile is wiped straight off her face when I sneer, "You have until Monday to tell Mr. Carson the truth about your injuries, or I'll expose your secret."

"You wouldn't dare," Keira mutters under her breath as her hand lifts to clutch the vein throbbing furiously in her delicate neck. "That would not only jeopardize your freedom, it will also undermine any chance you have of winning back Marcus. I know Marcus's worth, so I know there is no way you'd risk it. I know from experience: one taste of him is never enough."

I take a step closer to her. The veins in her neck thrum even more violently when I snarl, "I've never been one to back away from a dare, Keira, so please feel free to test me. I dare you."

Chapter Fourteen

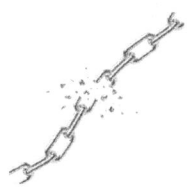

With it being early on a Friday afternoon, the city is thrumming with activity. Taxis clog the streets in a stream of yellow as people cram onto the sidewalk. With winter arriving a week earlier than usual, my love of people watching has been downgraded to designer coat admiring. It is probably for the best. With my mood still edgy from my exchange with Keira, I'm not in the best frame of mind to absorb my sister city in the true glory she deserves.

I trust Marcus, but Keira's remark—"one taste of him is never enough"—is an accurate description I'd expect from any woman who has been bedded by him. He is like a drug—so potent one taste makes you an addict.

My eyes drift from the hotdog vendor serving a lady wearing a five-hundred dollar pair of couture shoes when Lexi asks, "Are we still going?"

The stitch of her brows deepens when I reply, "Hmm?"

Lexi swivels her phone around to face me, allowing the email she just received to speak on her behalf. It is an email from my ex-boyfriend Luke, advising that the location of his birthday party tonight has changed to his parents' sprawling mansion. From the photos attached to his email, it appears as if the party is already in full swing. This is not surprising for Luke.

"It seems Mr. Popular is still as popular out of high school as he was in," Lexi murmurs as she returns her phone to face her.

I nod. Luke was the equivalent of the popular jock. He had the looks, the brains, and was the beloved captain of the basketball team. He was the very epitome of every teen girl's high school crush. He was a great boyfriend. He was just too. . . *sweet* for me.

If I hadn't met Marcus, I would have never understood why my relationship with Luke didn't work. I needed *more* than he could give me. Don't construe my confession the wrong way; I'm not saying I broke up with Luke because he was too perfect. It was because I would have never felt comfortable expressing my true desires to him. And, in all honesty, even if I did suddenly grow a backbone, I don't think Luke would have fulfilled my wishes the way Marcus can. He wouldn't hurt a fly, much less spank my backside until it is red raw.

Ignoring the chill of duplicity running down my spine, I return my focus to Lexi. "What did you reply?"

Her eyes dance between mine. "I didn't reply. It's not a replying type of email."

I glare at her. "You have to reply. It's the polite thing to do."

"Then you do it. You're CC'd in the email."

Fighting hard not to roll my eyes at her snappy mood, I snag my cell phone out of my purse and log in to my email. Although I pretend I didn't notice the absence of any message or missed calls from Marcus, the stabbing pain maiming my heart foils my endeavors.

It takes a few moments for my emails to download, but when they do, I freeze, paralyzed by a horrendous attack of jealousy sluicing my veins. It isn't Luke's mass email to the hundred plus recipients that has me sweating like I've run a marathon; it is an email from a private company, informing me of the location of the latest Chains' party being held tonight.

I didn't realize when I logged in to the server months ago I'd be added to their mailing list for future parties. This is a significant gaffe by Marcus's company. If members aren't paying the extreme annual dues to be a member of Chains, shouldn't emails like this be revoked to ensure privacy is maintained for paying guests?

I startle, scared out of my mind when my cell phone suddenly buzzes in my hand. I level my breathing before dropping my eyes to my phone. The endeavor of my heaving lungs doubles when I realize who is calling me: Marcus.

After reminding myself that I trust him—*over and over again*—I connect his call and push my cell close to my ear.

"Hello," I greet, my tone apprehensive.

"Hey," Marcus greets, his tone more pleasant than mine. "Sorry I missed your call. My phone was on silent."

My heart reprimands my brain for being too quick to judge when he asks, "Are you ready for me to come home tonight? It's been a long week."

"Yes," I reply, smiling. Because my reply is honest, it is echoed in my tone. "What time are you arriving?" Although I'm asking a question, I continue talking, thwarting his chance to reply. "Because I completely forgot I accepted an invitation to attend a friend's birthday party months ago. I was hoping we could attend together? *As a couple.*"

"Who's this friend?" Marcus queries, his interest uncontained, abundantly proving he didn't miss the dip in my pitch when I said the word "friend."

Loathing he didn't have a response to my admission I wanted our relationship to go public, I reply, "Umm. . . he's an ex-boyfriend of mine."

I cringe as I impatiently wait for his reply. Thankfully, he doesn't keep me waiting long. "How old of a relationship are we talking, Cleo?" He tries to keep jealousy out of his question; his efforts are borderline. There was a slight snip of envy left dangling in the air at the end of his question.

"A very long time ago," I answer, happy I'm not the only one who struggles to rein in my jealousy in this bizarre relationship we are endeavoring to get off the ground.

I hear Marcus scrub his hand over his clipped afro as he mutters, "Okay."

"You'll come?" I query, excitement laced in my words.

"Yes," he chuckles, appeasing every nick my confrontation with Keira caused to my heart. "When is it?"

"Tonight." My one word fires off my tongue in a hurry, my glee unbridled.

"Tonight?" Marcus confirms, his tone high with reservation. "I can't do tonight, Cleo." He sounds genuinely remorseful.

"Why? I thought you said you were coming home tonight?" I can't help but sound disappointed.

"I am," he answers after sighing heavily. "I'm just not arriving until late this evening."

I struggle to ignore my brain's repeated pleas for me to grill him for information. It is a waste of time. "Why are you arriving back so late? Can't you bring your flight forward an hour or two? You're the pilot; you can do whatever you want."

Marcus sighs again, this one more grim than his first. "I haven't got time to discuss this right now; I'm swamped, but I'll see you tonight. Okay?"

I remain quiet, unsure how to reply. I also don't want to open my mouth for the fear the sick gloom hammering my stomach will attempt to see daylight.

"I know you're disappointed, but I promise I'll make it up to you. Okay, baby?" Marcus asks, coercing me to bend to his will by calling me a term of endearment, which he rarely does.

"Okay." I despise that I've become so desperate for his attention, I'm letting my heart win every argument against my intelligent mind. "I'll see you tonight."

As I'm dragging my cell away from my ear, Marcus calls my name. "Make sure you take Brodie with you." This time, he doesn't attempt to hide the jealousy smeared in his low tone.

After agreeing to his unbendable demand, Marcus disconnects our call. It is a pity his eagerness to end our call wasn't quick enough for me to miss hearing a female voice call his name. I'm not talking about the name on his birth certificate; I'm referring to a name only a handful of people know him by: Master Chains.

My teeth graze my bottom lip as I lower my cell from my ear. The turmoil making my stomach a horrid mess ramps up when my phone illuminates the email from Chains, notifying the location of tonight's party.

"What's wrong?" Lexi asks, intuiting my forlorn look. "Change of plans?" Her voice sounds as devastated as I'm feeling. She knows I've been counting down the hours until Marcus's return, so seeing me end our call on a sour note has her worry piquing.

"No, he's still coming home tonight; he's just not getting in until late." I keep my voice upbeat, hoping to lessen the worry lines marring her forehead.

"So what's with the pouty lip?" Lexi asks, twanging my bottom lip with her thumb.

Her playfulness makes me smile. "It's. . . umm. . .I don't know. It's nothing. I'm just being stupid."

"Cleo." She only says one word, but her eyes express so much more.

"It's nothing. Truly. I've just got a million things running through my head right now." I huff, portraying my best worrywart impression.

Lexi rolls her eyes. "You'll learn to slow down one day."

I can tell she wants to say more, but thankfully, after a reassuring bump of her shoulder against mine, she drifts her eyes to the scenery whizzing by the window.

The remainder of our trip to Marcus's New York property is made in silence. Quiet is a rare commodity when you are in Lexi's presence. Even Brodie continually peers at us via the rearview mirror, shocked by our tightlipped composure. Usually, he can't get a word in between us.

With our late lunch stretching into the earlier afternoon, it is a little after six PM when Brodie's vehicle rolls to a stop at the platform stairs of Marcus's house. Lexi curls out of the car at a record speed before galloping up the stairs. When she reaches the landing, she cranks her neck back to peer at me. "I'm going to grab a shower before getting ready. Jackson packed all my dresses, so if you need to borrow one, help yourself," she shouts, projecting her voice to ensure I can hear her.

My brows stitch. "Why would I need to borrow a dress?"

Although my poor vision makes Lexi appear as nothing more than a blur, I swear I saw her eyes roll. "Luke's party. Drrr. Be ready to leave at nine. That way we are fashionably late, but not annoyingly late."

Not giving me the opportunity to protest that I don't feel like going out, she charges in the house, stealing my chance to reply.

I drift my eyes to Brodie, who is peering at me in the rearview mirror when he says, "At least she's regained her bounce."

Smiling, I nod, although I'm still suspicious about what caused her sudden change in temperament. I'm beginning to wonder if I am the only Garcia to have a run-in with Keira today? Lexi is as fiercely protective of me as I am of her, so I don't doubt if she discovered Keira was dining in the same restaurant as us, nothing would have stopped her from having a quiet word with her. By quiet word, I mean, severe threat.

Shutting down my inner monologue before it causes the contents of my stomach to see daylight, I mimic Brodie's departure from his now stationary vehicle. We trudge up the steps in silence, both our shoulders weighed down by a difficult day. Even the slight sprinkle of rain dotting our hair with glistening drops doesn't increase our pace.

The slight creak of the front door announces our arrival to Aubrey, who is sitting in the living room watching a Spanish soap opera show. The glee on her face is doused when she spots my downcast head. Switching off the program, she stands from her seat and moseys toward us. I've barely yanked my coat halfway off when she arrives to my side with a towel in one hand and a pair of thick socks in another. My brows stitch. *Where did she get them from?*

After using the towel to pat sporadic sprouts of curls dry, I kick off my shoes and replace them with the heavenly comfort of the socks Aubrey handed me. My confusion grows when I shift on my feet to face Brodie, preparing to offer him my towel to dry himself. He is nowhere to be seen.

Acting like it is perfectly reasonable for people to vanish into thin air, Aubrey curls her arm around my shoulders and guides me into the kitchen. Although I ate mere hours ago, my stomach grumbles when an alluring smell of spices and curry lingers into my nostrils. Abel's specialty is breakfast treats; any scrumptious morsel of food you could imagine consuming before midday was sampled by me during my five-day stint in Bronte's Peak. Aubrey's cooking specialty fills in the remainder of the day. It is lucky Marcus's staff members don't follow him to each location, or I'd end up the size of a house.

Actually, come to think of it, I could really use Abel's advice right now. Although Abel has never said it, I'm reasonably confident he is aware of Marcus's preferred bedroom activities. If he weren't, the sudden arrival of a playroom in the residence he calls home would have been an odd moment for all involved. But Abel took it in his stride, neither expressing condemnation or praise, so it displays he has an open mind—one I need to possess if I want any chance of working through the confusion debilitating me.

After sitting down on the stool I sat in when Marcus attempted to coerce me into being his sub, I lock my eyes with Aubrey. She is standing in front of the stovetop, serving a large helping of coconut curry chicken onto a bed of jasmine rice. The ladle freezes halfway between the pot and the bowl in her hand when I ask, "How many of Marcus's subs have you served this dish to?"

After taking a beat to clear the panic on her face, Aubrey spins on her heels to face me. "None," she says confidently as she paces toward me to set down the bowl of steamy goodness.

I arch a brow as my eyes silently assess the truth in her eyes. I'm taken aback when nothing but genuine honesty reflects back at me.

"How can that be true?" I question, more to myself than Aubrey.

She gathers a fork from the top drawer, wraps it in a napkin like a fancy restaurant, then sets it down next to my bowl. "Can I be honest?" she queries, her pitch hesitant.

Not trusting my voice not to crack with emotions, I nod my head.

"The entire time I've worked with Mr. Everett, he's had stringent rules. How I could interact with his subs, what they could wear, and what food they ate." She drops her eyes to the bowl of scrumptious chicken calling my name, begging to be consumed. "Any products laced with creamy goodness were not on his list of prepared meals."

"Prepared?" I query, my tone confused.

Aubrey nods. "He had a list of meals I was to prepare for each night of the week. I worked Saturday through to Sunday preparing the meals for the following week."

"Then what?"

"Then I worked from home the remainder of the week." She paces to a stack of drawers at the side of the kitchen. After gathering a sheet of paper, she returns to her original position and hands the document to me.

I breathe out my nerves before dropping my eyes to the sheet of paper. The concern blackening my blood is unwarranted. The list is nothing more than a grocery list with a set of meals made up for each day. Although the meals appear lavish with the inclusion of salmon and poached chicken, they are also bland, with every meal complemented by steamed vegetables or a side salad minus any condiments. There is also not a dessert mentioned in the entire document.

My spine straightens when reality dawns. Raising my eyes from the paper, I lock them with Aubrey's glistening gaze. "Today is Friday, isn't it?" I scan the kitchen, expecting the date to appear before my eyes magically.

"Yes," Aubrey agrees with a giggle.

"Then why are you here?" I cringe when my high tone makes my voice come out rude. I'm not trying to sound obnoxious, because all I'm feeling is gratitude. Even more so since my stomach's focus hasn't veered away from the fragrant dish in front of me to cite an objection about Aubrey's disclosure that Marcus preferred his previous liaisons to be uninterrupted.

Aubrey taps the piece of paper I'm clutching for dear life. "Because Mr. Everett said none of this applies to you. In fact, he didn't even give me a list of meals he wanted prepared this week. I was told to make you feel as if you are in your own home."

I grind my back molars together as I fight to ignore the tears welling in my eyes. Not trusting myself not to blubber, I quickly reply, "You've done exactly that. Thank you."

A flare of happiness sparks in Aubrey's eyes before it makes way for a dusting of tears. I'm glad to see I'm not the only one incapable of ignoring the substantial sentiment in the air.

"Now grab a fork and take a seat. If I eat all this chicken, Marcus will force us to eat that rubbish," I mumble, nudging my head to the paper I've dumped on the countertop.

With a smile, Aubrey does as requested. We spend the next several moments sitting side by side, consuming the dish I'm sure took her hours to make. The chicken is so tender it melts in my mouth the instant it hits my tongue. Aubrey discloses that the recipe has been handed down by her family for generations. It is so old, she doesn't even recall where it originated from.

Although Aubrey and I are separated in age by around two decades, we talk as if we are friends. I discover she is the eldest of eleven children, ranging between the ages of 17 and 54. Her parents still live in Mexico, along with half of her siblings, and she is unmarried with no children of her own.

"Did you not want children, or was the timing never right?" I query, praying she won't see my question as being nosy. I'm so genuinely interested in her life that I blurted out my question before I could stop my words.

"A little bit of both. With so many younger siblings, by the time I reached thirty, it felt like I had already raised my children." She slips off the stool and moves to the sink to commence clearing away our dishes. "It may be selfish, but I wanted some *me* time."

"That's not selfish." I join her at the sink. After accepting the dish she is holding out, I continue, "Selfish would have been leaving your parents to raise your siblings alone."

"Hmm. I guess." She shrugs her shoulders. "I've always grown up believing it takes a community to raise a child, not just its parents. It's unfortunate that logic isn't as strong as it used to be."

"If my dad were still around, he'd 100% agree with you. He always said 'it is the free-range parents' fault for raising a generation of entitled people.' Don't get me wrong, he wanted his children to achieve greatness; he just didn't want us to become self-centered and undeserving while doing it. 'Everyone wants the glory, but no one is willing to climb their way to the top anymore' was another one of his favorite sayings."

Aubrey giggles softly. "My papa calls them the 'silver spoon generation.'"

The rest of our dishes are done in silence. It isn't uncomfortable, but the silence does allow my thoughts to run wild. At least this time, not all my thoughts are reckless—like Aubrey's disclosure that Marcus's sub rules don't apply to me. But for every question I answer, another one pops up. Like is Marcus's negligence of the rules a good or a bad thing for our relationship? Before me, Marcus hadn't even frolicked with a sub outside of the playroom, let alone made love to one. I adore that I have that special part of him, but part of me worries I'm drawing him too far out of his comfort zone. Marcus doesn't instill punishment for pleasure, but what Keira said is true: the BDSM lifestyle is all he knows. If my desire for him to give that up became stronger than my need to be dominated, could Marcus walk away from the BDSM lifestyle?

I'd like to say yes confidently, but if I did, that would be a lie. I truly don't believe Marcus's desires for me are stronger than his need for power and control. He has never hidden the fact he craves control, so why would that logic suddenly change? *It wouldn't.*

I thank Aubrey for dinner and our chat when I hear my cell phone vibrating on the glass entranceway table. Because the residence is quiet, every buzz it makes adds to the quickening of my pulse.

My lungs take stock of their oxygen levels when I lift my cell and discover three unread messages from an unknown number. The first message is a simple one-line text.

Unknown number: *I'm here if you need me.*

The next two messages are picture files. Although the image of an elegantly dressed couple wouldn't usually instigate a horrid epidemic of nausea, it is recognizing the two people in the image that has my stomach churning out of control.

The first photo is a snap of Marcus and Keira standing at the front an industrial-looking building. Marcus has his arm wrapped around Keira's waist, and his nose is tucked into her neck, hiding his alluring green eyes from the person snapping their photo unaware. They are both wearing masks—similar to the ones I saw Chains patrons wearing three months ago.

The second photo is a little harder for me to decipher. It is so pixelated even someone with perfect eyesight would have a hard time decrypting it. It is only when I flick between the two images numerous times do I realize what the second photo is. Both photos are identical, but one is zoomed in to display the bare skin on Keira's right shoulder blade. Because her shoulder is mottled with faint bruises and red welts, the image is barely identifiable. It also doesn't help that her welts are a circular pattern. . . My inner monologue trails off as I'm held captive by a terrible notion. Those marks on Keira's shoulder look oddly familiar to ones I've seen before. They are nearly an exact replica to the strands on a flogger I saw in Marcus's playroom at Chains months ago.

No, they couldn't be. . .Marcus wouldn't cheat on me. *He doesn't cheat.*

I nearly drop my phone onto the marble floor when a deep voice asks, "What's that?"

I take a moment to settle the mad beat of my heart before connecting my eyes with Brodie. If he keeps scaring the living daylights out of me, I'm going to put squeakers on his shoes. My god—I can barely breathe with how hard my heart is thudding my chest.

My brain demands I act on these photos immediately. I twist my phone to face Brodie, who removes my cell from my grasp so he can appraise the images more diligently. Initially, his brows stitch, but I know the exact moment it dawns on him what he is looking at. His jaw quivers as his eyes rocket to mine.

"Who sent you those pictures?" he queries, his tone direct.

I shrug. "Does it matter? What's captured in the photo should be more concerning than who took them, shouldn't it?"

Brodie's lips twitch, preparing to speak, but I beat him to it. "What do you think caused the marks on Keira's shoulder?"

Brodie's throat works hard to swallow as he scrubs his hand over his chin. He remains as quiet as a church mouse. He doesn't need to answer my question, though. His eyes tell the entire story.

I angrily shake my head, sick of the constant deflections of my questions. If someone would just answer one goddamn question without skirting it, I wouldn't be so consumed by confused rage right now. It is the constant feeling of being left in the dark that is driving me more crazy than Keira's acknowledgment she wants Marcus to be her Master. Yes, these images are as innocent as the ones I witnessed in person last week, but they'd be a whole heap easier to handle if there weren't a shadow of doubt placed on every question I ask.

Realizing there is only one man who can give me answers, I snatch my cell out of Brodie's hand and head for the stairs, wanting privacy for what should be a private conversation. I'm halfway up the curved stairwell when Brodie shouts, "Just because you received these photos tonight doesn't mean they were taken tonight. They could be from months ago."

"It still doesn't change the facts, Brodie. Although more ghastly than last week, Keira is once again wearing Marcus's trademark in public." My voice cracks with emotion at the end of my sentence.

Brodie replies, but I don't hear a word over the roaring of blood to my ears. After running my sweaty hands down the flare of my skirt, I dial Marcus's number. I command on repeat for my body to calm down; it never listens. It is a lot harder feigning ignorance than I realized.

Marcus's cell rings eight times before it connects to his voicemail. I stand from the bed to pace a track into the plush carpet fibers of Marcus's master suite. My brain is warning me not to act so irrational —he could merely be flying home—but my heart is enlarged with worry, certain Marcus's silence is more dire than my brain realizes.

When my heart's pleas ring louder than my brain, I scroll through my list of contacts, stopping when I find a number I stored in there weeks ago. My hand shakes when I press my cell phone close to my ear. I count the rings—*one, two, three, four*—praying I don't reach eight before my call is answered.

Gratitude pumps into me when the distinctive clip of a landline shrills into my ears on the seventh ring.

"Hello," greets a thick husky voice I immediately recognize.

"Hi, Abel," I address, hating that I've allowed the pleas of my foolish heart to put him in the middle of my confrontation with Marcus. "I'm sorry to bother you; I am just seeking Marcus. He isn't answering his cell, so I thought I'd check and see if you knew when he was scheduled to fly out."

"Fly out? Ah. . . I'm confused as to what you mean, Ms. Cleo," Abel replies.

The panic in his tone also shocks me. "He was scheduled to fly out earlier today, but his departure was delayed. Is he still there? Can I talk to him?"

Abel's heavy sigh obscures the tapping of his feet on the wooden floorboards of Marcus's Florida home. He coughs to clear his throat before he mutters, "Umm. . . Ah . . ."

"He is there, isn't he?" I interrupt, my tone crammed with suspicion.

My suspicions amplify when Abel replies, "No. I haven't seen Mr. Everett today, Ms. Cleo."

The room spins around me as I'm overwhelmed with dizziness. Not trusting my legs, I sit on the edge of Marcus's huge bed.

"When did you last see him?" I ask, my voice half-panicked, half-laced with unbridled jealousy. I'm frankly stumped on which emotion to honor. I feel panicked and enraged with anger at the same time.

Horrid unease twists in my stomach when Abel replies, "I haven't seen him since he left with you weeks ago." His voice has a whip of edginess to it, like he too is annoyed by Marcus's lack of contact.

I remain quiet, unable to speak through the terrible feeling twisting my stomach. Marcus said he was returning to Ravenshoe, so why wouldn't he stay at his residence while he was there? Not unless he stayed elsewhere. . .

I'm freed from my sickening thoughts when Abel asks, "Ms. Cleo, are you there?"

"Ah, yes," I reply, my voice as low as my heart rate. "If you hear from Marcus, can you tell him I need to talk to him?" I roll my eyes, loathing that the confidence I built the past three months was side-swiped in one afternoon.

"Yes, Ms. Cleo, I most certainly will." Some of the dread scorching my throat eases from Abel's guarantee.

After apologizing again for disturbing him, I bid farewell to Abel, then disconnect our call. I don't know if I'm just being spiteful, or merely striving to spark a reaction out of Marcus, but I send him a cryptic text message.

Me: *How's the weather in Florida? Be sure to rug up before you return home because things are getting mighty cold here. By the way, Abel says hello.*

I glare at my phone for the next twenty minutes, yearning for it to ring, buzz, vibrate—to do anything!

It does nothing.

Chapter Fifteen

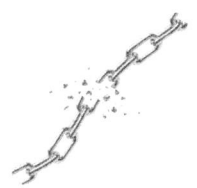

I ANGRILY SWIPE AT A TEAR ON MY CHEEK WHEN A BRIEF TAP SOUNDS on the door of Marcus's bedroom. Not waiting for me to give permission to enter, Lexi cracks open the door and saunters inside. I slowly suck in a lung-filling gulp of air as I drink in her perfectly made-up ensemble. She is wearing a thick wool skirt with a dangerously high slit kept modest by three strategically placed chunky diaper pins. Her long-sleeve white shirt accentuates every perfect curve of her body, and her hair has been curled in a crazy, rock-chick style. With her vibrant brown eyes shadowed with a glittering of midnight black powder, her red-painted lips really pop off her face. She has taken the requisite 80's Rock 'n Roll dress code on Luke's invitation and given it her own edge. I'm not going to lie; she looks so sexy, I'm afraid shoulder pads and teased-up bangs are about to become all the rage again.

Noticing I'm still wearing the same outfit I wore at lunch, Lexi checks the time on her watch. "It's 9 PM, Cleo," she states as if I am unaware of the time.

"I know," I reply, rising from my slumped position. "I'm not going. I called Jackson, he'll be here to collect you soon."

"No," Lexi responds, spreading her hands over her cocked hip. "You RSVP'd for both of us. That means we're *both* going."

She tosses aside my furious glare as if it is as weightless as a piece of lint before padding into the walk-in closet I share with Marcus. I can hear her grunting and moaning as she digs through my minuscule collection of clothes. She arrives at my bedside two minutes later holding a ghastly bright fluorescent pink slip dress I completely forgot I owned with a pair of glossy navy blue heels.

"Tease out your curls and cake some blue eyeshadow on your eyes, and you'll be good to go," Lexi says, throwing the dress at me.

"Come on, Cleo. Chop, chop. There is such a thing as too late," Lexi bickers when I fail to move my sloth-like form.

"I don't want to go out. I'm tired," I grumble when she grasps my arms and drags me from the bed.

Ignoring my childish whine, she whips my shirt over my head before wrangling with the zipper on my skirt. I freeze when her nose digs into my armpit. She inhales two quick whiffs in rapid succession before murmuring, "Good enough." She yanks my dress off the coat hanger and drags it over my head before I can blink.

"You don't understand, Lexi. I have a very legitimate reason why I don't want to go out."

"I know," Lexi sighs, cutting me off. "I ran into Brodie in the hallway."

Great. The last thing I want is people talking about me behind my back.

"It's not like that, Cleo," Lexi replies to my private thoughts. "Brodie wasn't gossiping about you. He's just worried. I assured him you'll be fine. You're a Garcia. We survive anything."

She swirls an eyeshadow brush in her makeup kit I didn't notice she was holding until now. Happy she has an adequate amount of blue eyeshadow on the brush, she sets to work on doing my makeup.

I remain quiet, running her declaration through my mind on repeat. I am a Garcia, and I've survived much worse than this, but I honestly don't know if I'll survive losing Marcus. Just the thought of not having him in my life has my stomach twisting up in knots.

After applying enough makeup to my face to conceal my devastation, Lexi locks her eyes with mine. "When the game is ending sooner than you like, you force the opposition into the penalty box," she recites a quote our dad mentioned numerous times in our teens. I've never understood its logic. Tonight is no different.

I begrudgingly slip on my heels, gather my cell, then shadow Lexi into the hallway. Although I'm not the best company, being surrounded by old friends will remind me I'm stronger than I realize. Just as I'm about to take the first step of the stairwell, Lexi seizes my elbow. My eyes bounce between hers when she continues clutching my arm until she has dragged me to the very end of the hallway.

"Brodie is downstairs," she whispers like it is a treasured secret.

"Yeah. . . so?"

The hallway is dimly lit, but it isn't dark enough for me to miss Lexi's eye roll. "You can't force penalty time by colluding with the umpire," she grumbles.

Chilly winter winds whip my hair into a frenzy when Lexi cranks open the window we are standing next to. After thrusting her purse and cell into my chest, she clambers out the window.

"Are you insane? We're grown women, for crying out loud. We don't need to sneak out." Half of my sentence is muffled by a bout of childish giggling. My reaction can't be helped. With Lexi's super tight skirt, watching her scoot along the tree branch her legs are wrapped around is extremely entertaining.

"If I get a splinter in my snatch, you're digging it out," Lexi warns, her pitch drenched with cheeky innuendo.

"If you're wearing panties, you won't have to worry. . ." The remainder of my sentence gets lodged in my throat when Lexi suggestively waggles her brows.

"Lexi! You're. . ." I can't think of an appropriate word to call her. "You're bad," I settle on.

"Obviously not since you're only just realizing this." She grunts when she lands on the dew-covered ground with a thud, her years of cheerleading awarding her the perfect dismount.

After throwing down her purse and our cells, I hike my skirt up high on my thighs and climb out the window sill. My ovaries shrivel up when the freezing cold temps outside have me wishing I could dart downstairs to retrieve my coat. It is as thin as my patience is right now, but it would be better than nothing.

"Come on, Cleo," Lexi says, encouraging me to hurry. "Jax has the heat on in his truck."

I grimace when the tree bark digs into the smooth skin high on my thighs. My dismount isn't as graceful as Lexi's. It isn't a lack of cheer-leading skills causing me to fall to the ground like a sack of potatoes, it is hearing Brodie calling my name. For how loud he is, I'm confident he is on the second level of Marcus's house.

My assumptions are proven correct when Brodie's torso leans out of the window I just climbed out not even two seconds before. His wide eyes dart between me and Lexi standing frozen on the manicured turf, the confusion in them doubling for every second that ticks by.

"Don't you dare!" he warns in a gravelly tone when he realizes what we are doing.

"Never dare a Garcia, Brodie, because you'll never win." Lexi curls her arms around my elbow and bolts toward Jackson's truck idling at the end of Marcus's driveway, lugging me behind her. For a woman who weighs ten pounds less than me, she hauls me across the grounds without even breaking into a sweat.

"Cleo, you have five seconds to get back here!" Brodie shouts from the top floor.

When his demand is met with a bout of laughter, he roars, "Goddamn it!"

Lexi increases her pace when Brodie disappears from the window. With how eerily quiet the night is, I can hear the thuds of his steps as he gallops down the stairs. He takes the last steps just as we reach Jackson's truck. Lexi throws open the door so forcefully, the truck's hinges squeal in protest.

"Go, go, go," Lexi requests, squealing when we dive into the roasting hot cab. Lexi wasn't joking; Jackson has the heat up high.

Jackson's truck glides down the asphalt at the exact moment Brodie sprints down the platform stairs. "You know he'll just jump in his car and force Jackson to pull over," I inform Lexi, my words wheezy from our mad dash.

"Bit hard without these," Lexi says, her voice high with excitement.

Swinging my eyes from Brodie chasing us on foot, I spot Lexi dangling a set of car keys on her index finger—keys that don't belong to her.

"And it isn't like he can just show up to Luke's, since the venue of his party changed," she adds on, her smile the largest I've seen. "I deleted Luke's email from our servers too, just in case you were wondering."

I honestly don't know whether to hug her or strangle her right now. My exhausted body is welcoming the surge of adrenaline from our risky breakout, but there is still a smidgen of doubt blackening my blood.

Some of my dread dampens when Jackson seizes Lexi's wrist and drags her across the bench until she is nuzzled under the nook of his arm. After pressing a kiss to her temple, he whispers three little words I'd give anything to hear right now: "I love you."

The past week has been hard on them. I wouldn't necessarily say it's been any harder than it has been on Marcus and me, but there is no doubt "absence makes the heart grow fonder" is not a theory they're interested in testing again anytime soon.

Unsurprisingly, we've barely exited Marcus's street when my cell starts hollering. Surprisingly, the call isn't from Brodie. It is from Marcus. Taking matters into her own hands, Lexi snatches my cell phone out of my hand, declines Marcus's call and silences my phone. I eye her curiously when her fingers tap wildly over the screen. The swoosh of a message being sent sounds through my ears, closely followed by Lexi's phone buzzing, indicating she has received a text message.

She drops my cell into her lap before picking up her phone. I peer over her shoulder, watching her configure a two-sentence email.

If you want to talk to my sister, you'll have to go through me first. And there is NO chance of that happening until you explain these, dipshit.

Her lips quirk as she attaches the two photos the anonymous messenger sent me earlier tonight. Her message has barely left her inbox when her cell starts ringing. I don't need to peer at the screen to know it is Marcus. I can feel it deep in my bones.

My brows scrunch when Lexi denies Marcus's call before returning her cell to her purse. "Never negotiate with terrorists," she explains to my baffled expression. "How many hours did you spend sniveling in your room tonight waiting for him to return your call?"

Jackson's gaze strays from the road to me. His worried glance is discreet, but strong enough to make me feel ashamed.

"I wasn't sniveling," I lie, loathing the sorrow-filled glances being directed at me.

Lexi arches her brow and glares at me, acting like she didn't hear a thing I said.

"Around two hours," I mumble, knowing she'd eventually read the truth from my eyes.

Lexi checks her watch. "So at eighteen minutes past midnight, Chains' can have his questions answered. Until then, he can suffer in his jocks."

"He can what?" I ask, confused.

"Suffer in his jocks," Lexi confirms, grinning. "I heard Cartier say it earlier today. It has a nice ring to it."

Snubbing my slack-jawed expression, she devotes her attention to Jackson.

I spent the first half of our commute unscrambling everything that has happened thus far today. You'd think my primary focus would be on learning when the photo of Marcus and Keira was taken, but it isn't. With Lexi's mention of Cartier, my prime focus has centered around her concern about me expressing my love to Marcus. Is it just a coincidence his withdrawal of contact directly follows my request for him to make love to me?

Cartier has said numerous times the desire to be loved was the conundrum that unraveled her relationship. Can the same be said for Marcus and me? I didn't hold anything back last week when we made love. I expressed everything he meant to me using my body instead of the words I really wanted to say. So maybe that is the cause of his lack of contact? Perhaps he doesn't see our relationship heading in the direction he desires, and this is his way of ending things amicably.

I know it is extreme to think this way, but what other reason could he have for pretending he was in Florida? Although I don't have proof, my intuition is telling me he's been in New York the entire time. Unlike Keira, Cartier has no motive to lie about seeing Marcus. She saw him yesterday—in New York, and she spoke as if he has been here the entire time, so I believe her. And Abel seemed just as concerned by Marcus's lack of contact as I was.

Panicked alarm slams into me when reality dawns. I feel sick— so horribly ill. *Is Marcus breaking up with me because he hated vanilla sex?* If he is, he doesn't need to be worried. I enjoyed making love to him—it was beautiful and special—but I *love* being dominated by him. If I knew my request for him to make love to me would have such an adverse reaction, I would have never asked him to do it. I just wanted a piece of him that no one else had. I wanted to claim him as my own—much like he did by placing his collar around my neck. I never wanted it to end us.

Lifting my eyes from my intertwined fingers, I lock them with Jackson. "Pull over," I stammer out, my words choked by the bile surging to the base of my throat.

"Pull over," I demand more assertively when my first request is met with silence.

Seeing the panic on my face, Jackson pulls his truck to the curb. I've barely scampered out of the cab when the coconut chicken I ate at dinner resurfaces in the ghastliest way. It is nowhere near as appetizing the second time around.

Once the heaving racks hammering my body ease, Lexi hands me a wad of tissues from the glove compartment.

"Can I please have my cell?" I plead while wiping a remnant of vomit from my bottom lip.

"Please, Lexi," I beg when she puts up a silent protest to my request. "*Please.*"

She huffs softly before leaning into the cabin of the truck to fish out my cell phone. The shake of my hand is obvious when I accept it and dial Marcus's number. Although I'm a skittish bag of nerves, my determination remains resilient. This phone call is long overdue.

Marcus answers not even two rings later. "Cleo, where the hell are you? I told you to take Brodie with you. Why did you leave without—"

"Did I break us?" I interrupt, my voice displaying I'm on the verge of tears but mighty pissed off. My eyes are brimming with so much moisture, I'm certain they are moments away from bursting, but the anger roaring through my veins is keeping them at bay.

"I didn't mean to break us. I like what we did, but if I knew you were going to hate it so much, I wouldn't have asked you to do it." My words are forced out my mouth so fast, they are nothing more than a blubbering string of nonsense.

A chair scrapes across the ground before the stomps of shoe-covered feet bellow down the line. "Cleo. . . baby, please don't cry." Marcus's words are jutted like he is pacing. "You haven't done anything wrong. I swear to God, we're okay." His voice is a stark contradiction to the fury radiating down the phone. He sounds equally panicked and wrathful.

His term of endearment forces a stray tear to topple from my eye, but my broken heart is not crippled enough to stop me seeking answers. "Why are you lying to me, Marcus?"

"I'm not—"

"Stop, Marcus! I *know* you're in New York. I *know* you never went to Florida. I *know* you've seen *her*. How much more proof do you need?" Anger quickly overtakes my heartache. "If you didn't want to be with me anymore, you could have just said. You didn't have to go to such lengths to get rid of me. We don't have a contract, so you don't owe me a specific amount of time. You owe me nothing but honesty."

I hear his hand run over his clipped afro as he curses softly. "Cleo, I need you to stop talking and listen to me." His demeanor is calm and controlled, an absolute contradiction to the woman he is talking to. I'm shaking so much, my teeth are chattering as if I'm standing in the middle of the arctic, and my shuddering response has nothing to do with the freezing winter temps curling around my body.

"You need to trust me. Remember, being trusted is a compliment greater than being loved," Marcus implores, using the same pleas he made the last time he lied.

"Just like the smallest lie encourages doubt in the biggest truth. A lie, no matter what size, cracks the foundation trust is built on. You lied to me, Marcus. Over and over again," I reply, my tone devastated yet firm.

Suddenly, my spine snaps straight when a male voice says, "I've got a trace on her cell. She is on highway 32, half a mile down from off-ramp 12."

Before I can register my disgust that he tracked my cell, Marcus says, "Stay where you are, Cleo. I'm coming to get you, then I'll explain everything." His words are breathless as if he is running.

I push my cell in close to my ear when a faint tune sounds down the line. Although the music isn't overly familiar, I'm confident I've heard it before, I just can't recall exactly where.

The air is evicted from my body in a brutal grunt when recollection dawns. The soft, ambient music has me recalling a time when the pleasantry of the tune didn't match the explicit scenes unfolding before my very eyes. Scenes only attendees at an exclusive invitation-only gathering would see. It is the same music that was playing the night I was a guest at a BDSM club in lower Manhattan. It is the music played in Chains.

Lexi gasps when I suddenly question, "Are you at Chains?"

A string of garbled words leave Marcus's mouth. Although I'm certain he is speaking English, I'm only listening for two words: yes or no.

When I fail to hear either of those words, I snarl, "Answer the goddamn question, Marcus! Are you at Chains?!" My voice is so loud a pack of dogs start howling in the distance, startled by my brittle tone.

Marcus waits a beat before he breathes out, "Yes, but—"

The rest of his sentence is lost when my phone slips from my grasp, shattering into a million pieces when it collides with the asphalt. I close my eyes and raise my head to the sky, struggling to hold back the tears threatening to spill down my cheeks at any moment. It is a point-less effort when the cool breeze blowing across my face contrasts against the fat, hot tears sliding down my cheeks.

I count backward from thirty, giving my heart the chance to mourn the end of my relationship before returning my chin to its normal position and fluttering open my eyes.

"I need a drink. . . or fifty," I instruct Lexi, who is staring at me with worry.

Remaining quiet with sheer alarm tainting her beautiful face, she nods before aiding me back into Jackson's truck. After cocooning my shuddering frame with her tiny body, she signals for Jackson to continue our journey, leaving my shattered cell on the edge of the road looking as mangled as my heart feels.

Chapter Sixteen

THE FIRST TWO HOURS OF LUKE'S PARTY FLIES BY. I BOUNCE between guests, acting as if the last six years of my life never happened. But like all alcohol-induced happiness, my wine-inspired social butterfly routine is nipped in the bud even more quickly than it began. For the past hour, I've floundered around, willfully moving from group to group, hoping to feel welcomed in one of the cliques parties like this always attract. Unfortunately, just like my night at Chains, I don't belong here either. It isn't that I don't feel welcome; it's just no amount of idle chit-chat and warm alcohol can cure debilitating heartache.

Needing some fresh air, I weave through the partygoers bumping and grinding on the makeshift dance floor in the middle of Luke's parents' house until I merge onto the wooden deck at the back of their sprawling property. I shake my head in disbelief when I spot a handful of birthday guests swimming in the pool—barren of any clothes. Although the pool is heated, no amount of alcohol-fueled bravery would have me stripping down in front of hundreds of guests for an impromptu swim. I've never been overly audacious. That's why I'm so surprised at how much I loved Marcus's dominance. I've always said I am a strong-willed and determined young lady. Clearly, that isn't the case. Just my miserable attempt at enjoying the celebration of a dear friend shows how pathetic I've become.

Not anymore. This miserable Cleo act ends tonight.

The familiar giggle of Lexi sounds through my ears when I reach the pool room at the back of manicured grounds. Considering Lexi's laughter came from the direction of the pool, I keep my gaze front and center, not trusting my sister's wild antics. The last thing I need is to see her in the buff once more.

I inhale deeply when the scent of Luke's aftershave he wore in college lingers into my nose. Back in the day, this used to be Luke's bedroom. He wanted privacy, and supposedly a detached dwelling mere feet from the principal residence was the perfect solution for his predicament. I feel a rush of heat creep across my cheeks when I recall some of the events that took place in this room. This is the very room I lost my virginity in. It was a highly awkward and stumbling time. Thank god Luke was also a virgin, so he was just as ill-informed on the probability of orgasming during sex as I was. He never once voiced a concern that I didn't climax during sex, because he didn't know I was supposed to.

My pupils widen when my trip down memory lane is interrupted by the man I was thinking about. Luke walks out of a steam-filled bathroom with nothing but a thin towel wrapped around his drenched hips.

Allowing the alcohol lacing my veins to get the better of me, my eyes drink in his carved body, veined arms, and glistening pecs unashamed—not once, but twice!

"Cleo," Luke greets, shocked when he spots me standing at the side of his bed, obsessively ogling him.

"Hey." I cringe, loathing my lack of elegance. "Sorry. I was just seeking a place of solitude. It's getting a little rowdy out there."

Luke smiles a grin that makes him look younger than his twenty-six years. "It is. It reminds me a lot of our high school parties. Although I don't recall the pool being quite that cold."

When he peers out to the pool, I follow the direction of his gaze. As I suspected, Lexi is in the pool. Thank god my eyesight is poor enough I can't tell if she is naked or not. Not that I can see either way since her tiny body is swamped by Jackson's large frame.

"She is very much like you," Luke laughs when he spots Lexi sucking face with Jackson.

I fiddle with the hem of my dress to stop myself from rolling my eyes like a fifth grader. "Only ten times wilder."

My eyes snap to Luke when he throws his head back and chuckles. "You keep telling yourself that, Cleo, then maybe one day people might believe it."

"I wasn't that bad, was I?" My eyes widen in shock when my voice comes out all throaty as if I'm a little sex kitten purring at his heel, begging for him to stroke my back.

I'm not the only one who noticed the change in my vocals. Luke's eyes blaze with excitement as his towel fails to conceal his impressively stiff manhood. I bite on the inside of my cheek, vainly trying to hold the skerrick of modesty I have left as I divert my eyes away from his erect cock.

"Oh shit," Luke grumbles as he snags a pair of jeans off a rumpled bed to yank them up his thighs. "I swear to God, Cleo, if you blush, you're not leaving this room with your virtue intact."

I giggle softly as heat blooms across the shallow blackness in my chest. "You can't use the same line years later, Luke. It's just tacky."

Luke's laughter warms my chest even more, soothing some of the nicks Marcus's betrayal caused. "Why not? You're acting like you've never seen my cock. We both know you sure as hell have," he replies, his voice throaty.

"It's different now." I twist my head to the side to ensure he is dressed before shifting on my feet to face him. He is clothed. Well, if you consider wearing a pair of jeans commando as dressed, he is. "You were only a boy back then, so things could have changed."

I'm disgusted with myself when my eyes drop to the zipper of his jeans as I chew on my bottom lip. Marcus's betrayal hurt, but two wrongs never make a right.

Pretending I wasn't just eyeballing him with suggestion, I pick up a throw cushion scattered on the floor and peg it at Luke's head when he grabs his crotch and asks, "Did you want to check?"

"You're disgusting," I mumble, faking annoyance. I'm not annoyed. It is great bantering with him again. I feel like I've flashed back to my teen years. I'm just peeved at myself. I'm acting like a harlot with no morals.

Sensing my thoughts have veered toward the negative, Luke says, "And you're the prettiest girl I've ever seen." He wraps his arms around my waist before drawing me into his bare wet torso. "I'll lasso the moon if you want me to."

"If you do, I'll throw it straight back, because out of all the stars in the sky, none will shine brighter than you," I quote my half of our shared declaration from our two-year courtship.

Luke smiles, appreciating that I remembered the saying he created. "So what's all this about?" His worried gaze dances between mine. "I've never seen your eyes so lifeless, Cleo, not even after. . ."

He doesn't need to finish his sentence. I know what he is referring to. And no, it isn't about the demise of our relationship. Although I incited our break up, our relationship ended on amicable terms. Luke and I were great together; we just weren't perfect.

I don't know if it is the alcohol warming my veins, or the fact I don't have any girlfriends to talk to, but over the next twenty minutes, I share every detail of my relationship with Marcus with Luke. By everything, I mean *everything*. BDSM included. The only part I leave out is Marcus's true identity. Luke listens intensively, only butting in to ask the occasional question.

Once I've spilled my guts, Luke locks his eyes with mine and says, "You need to tell him how you feel, Cleo."

I throw my arms into the air. "Did you not just hear a word I spoke? He's at a BDSM club."

"Did you hear a thing you said?" Luke fires straight back. "He *owns* a BDSM club, Cleo. It's his business. I'm not sure what your ideas on running a business entail, but I sure as hell don't run my pharmacy from home. I have to rock up occasionally." The playfulness in his tone eases some of the sting his brutal honesty caused. "Chains never lied about owning a BDSM club. You knew that about him when you agreed to meet him, so you can't throw it in his face."

"What about all the other stuff? The photos? Collaring other subs? Him pretending he is in Florida when he isn't?"

"Come on, Cleo. I thought you were the mature one in our group. That's all high school shit. Remember when Stacey Coulter found a love letter in her locker, and she told you it was from me? You didn't talk to me for three days. It was only after asking her for proof did you realize the note wasn't from me."

"Because she spelled your last name wrong," I add on, recalling our first real fight.

Luke's wet blond hair flopped on his head barely moves when he nods. "Instead of asking me straight-out, you cut all ties with me for days. It fucking killed me, Cleo. I loved you, yet you wouldn't give me the time of day." He locks his eyes with the diamond chain pendant I haven't worked up the courage to remove. "You're doing the exact same thing to him. I was lucky I knew where you were. I camped under your bedroom window every night during our breakup. Chains isn't so lucky. He has no clue where you are."

Moisture wells in my eyes. "When did you get so smart?" I jest, hoping a little bit of playfulness will stop my tears from falling.

I lose any chances of holding back my childish sobs when Luke replies, "When I lost the girl of my dreams because she didn't feel confident enough to talk to me like she just did."

He plucks two tissues out of a box next to the couch we are sitting on, then hands them to me. After mopping up the handful of tears on my cheeks I was unable to contain, I mumble, "Why aren't you mad?"

"Why would I be mad? A much-needed lesson was learned when I lost you. Now another lucky schmuck is reaping the benefit of my heartache."

When my bottom lip drops into a pout, Luke adds on, "Just like some lucky schmuck is reaping the reward of me discovering you have no gag reflex."

I slap my hand over his mouth as my eyes scope the area, wanting to ensure no one overheard his admission. Happy we are void of prying eyes, I slowly remove my hand from his mouth. "That isn't common knowledge," I whisper as if I am sharing guarded secrets. "Besides, it was a banana that ultimately discovered that skill."

Luke scoffs. "A banana might have started the investigation, but my cock ended it. Also, I guarantee you everyone in this house is aware of the fact you have no gag reflex. I was a teenage boy, Cleo; that was bragging rights," he mutters, his voice hindered with laughter.

He chuckles even more loudly when I smack him on his bare chest. "Go and put some clothes on. I'd hate for people to get the wrong idea."

"Too late," he murmurs under his breath as he stands from the couch.

I watch him in silence as he grabs a clean shirt out of a basket of laundry on the ground and slips it over his head. Luke has a fit, athletic body with perfect clumps of muscles to drive women crazy. His hair is a little longer than I remember, and his eyes are wiser, but he is still the same boy I thought of more as a best friend than a lover. I think that is where our relationship went wrong. We had the sexual attraction, but it arrived much later than our friendship did. We probably should have stayed friends instead of seeking an attraction that needed to be sparked. Sexual connection should come naturally and without effort. *Shouldn't it?*

"Call him. Text him. Email him," Luke suggests, nudging his head to a desk covered with paperwork. "If you don't want to be with him, tell him. But put him out of his misery, Cleo, as you know as well as anyone what it feels like being left in the dark."

I pick at a ball of lint on my dress as I nod my head, too ashamed to look Luke in the eyes. Those three hours between expecting my parents to arrive home, and the police arriving on my doorstep to inform me of their accident were the longest three hours of my life. I called my parents on repeat, leaving message after message. It was pure torture. Luke understands it as I called him in a state of panic numerous times in those three hours.

Luke's warm breath flutters my hair when he leans down and places a quick kiss on my temple. "I'll wait for you outside with a bottle of tequila and a tub of ice-cream. You just tell me which one you need the most."

I wait until I hear the door latch click into place before raising my downcast head. My legs shake when I stand from the couch and pace to the desk Luke nudged to. I first consider calling Marcus, but remembering how one-sided our conversations have always been, I decide to write to him instead. That way I can express everything I want to say in one fell swoop. It will be out there, exposed for the entire world to see.

When I sit behind the desk, the desires of my answer-seeking brain overrule my lust-driven heart. Instead of logging into my email account as predicted, my fingers type a web address I haven't used in weeks. Although I haven't used the Chains' chat forum in months, my login details remain active. I type a name into the search engine before removing my hands from the keyboard, needing a few moments to ensure I'm going to be strong enough to face the possible outcome my snooping may unearth.

Realizing no amount of time will lessen my devastation, I tap the enter key. I inwardly curse when my search returns a match. Master Chains' account is once again active. Even my too-forgiving heart releases a few choice curse words as I click on his account and open a messenger box.

Over the next ten minutes, I type every thought passing through my mind. My disappointment that he wasn't man enough to tell me I was no longer what he wanted. My anger at being betrayed. My annoyance at the constant lies I've been told. But most importantly, I express how angry I am that he wooed me so intensely, I couldn't help but fall in love with him.

I hate that you are so easy to love.
I hate that I fell in love with you even when my brain begged me not to.
I hate that you'll never love me back.
But more than anything, I hate that I can't hate you because I love you
too much.

After signing the bottom of my message, *from the one who wants the best of both worlds*, I hit send before I can talk myself out of it.

The room spins around me when three eclipses trickle across the screen not even a second later, advising that Master Chains is in the process of typing a reply. With how quickly his message is delivered, it is evident he didn't read my entire message.

Master Chains: *Stay where you are; I'm coming to get you.*

Chapter Seventeen

PANIC WELLS WHEN I SPOT A FLASHING RED LIGHT BLINKING IN THE middle of the laptop screen. I snap down the screen, mortified I'm being watched. My eyes swing around the space, seeking any identifiable markers Marcus could use to unearth my location. My breathing halts when reality dawns. He doesn't need to find recognizable pinpoints. He'd just have someone track Luke's IP address. *Shit. This isn't going to end well.*

I push back from the desk with so much force, the large leather office chair I'm sitting in sails backward, only stopping when it crashes in the bathroom door Luke exited nearly an hour ago. Bopping down, I gather my heels I kicked off during our heartfelt chat. I hop across the room on one foot as I slip my feet into the tight confines of my shoes. Either my feet are swelling, or my shoes shrunk, as it takes more effort than it should to slip them on.

A frigid breeze prickles my arms with goosebumps when I swing open the glass door of the pool house and step onto the paved footpath. My eyes frantically search the area, seeking Lexi and Jackson amongst the scantily clad pool crowd that has swelled in size the past hour. I spot them huddled together under a cabana on my right. They are clothed—barely.

"We need to go," I notify Lexi, hurling Jackson's jeans I gathered off the AstroTurf during my travels into their smooching faces. "Marcus is on his way here." My voice relays my absolute panic.

Luke's high school parties were famous for the number of attendees he could cram into one space; tonight is no different. The entire residence is jam-packed with partygoers; I'd easily say the figure is in the mid to high hundreds, so the chances of someone recognizing Marcus is immense. We had enough trouble evading the dozen paparazzi at his grandmother's residence weeks ago, so I don't like his chances of escaping the clutches of drunken fans by the dozen.

Even with her dramatic moves dampened by her inebriated state, Lexi jumps into action. She thrusts her legs into her skin-tight mini skirt before wiggling it up her goosebump-riddled thighs. Although I'm overcome with panic, a dash of gratitude pumps into me when Jackson shelters Lexi's half-dressed frame with the large beach towel they were snuggled under. His stern gaze is enough to retain most of Lexi's modesty, but an additional finger point is required to warn some lurkers to look away.

After pulling her shirt over her head, Jackson commences getting dressed. His jeans are barely covering his drenching wet boxer shorts when Lexi curls her arm around his elbow and drags him toward the house. Music blares into our ears when we enter. It doesn't take me long to realize my initial guess about Luke's guest count was way off. There would be a minimum of a thousand people taking up every inch of his family home.

Our efforts to leave are hindered by a large group of people lining the front porch, waiting to enter. You'd swear we were at the latest nightclub hotspot by the eagerness spread across their face.

I've just dodged a lady losing her biscuits in a hedge when I hear someone calling my name. Spinning around, I spot Luke standing at the foot of his front porch. Just as he promised, he has a tub of ice cream in one hand and a bottle of tequila in the other.

"I'm sorry, I have to go," I shout, aiming to project my voice over the deafening roar of partygoers.

Luke holds the bottle of tequila to his ear, soundlessly acknowledging he can't hear me.

"I'll call you," I mouth as I mimic making a call with my thumb and pinkie against my ear.

Luke holds his finger in the air, requesting a minute. I nod before turning my panicked gaze to Lexi. Although my intuition is screaming blue murder at me, the kindness Luke bestowed on me tonight deserves more than a minute of my time, so at the very least I should bid him a proper farewell.

"I'll meet you guys in Jackson's truck," I advise Lexi, whose eyes are bouncing between me and Luke's rapidly approaching frame.

"Tread carefully, Cleo," Lexi warns, her tone surprisingly smooth for how dilated her eyes are. "You're only supposed to aim for additional game time, not be sidelined for the rest of your career."

Stealing my chance to reply, she dashes to Jackson's truck, giggling the entire trip. I wait for Jackson to have her safely latched in the passenger seat before swinging my eyes back to Luke. Our long strides have us meeting in the middle of the sidewalk in two heart-thrashing seconds.

His eyes drift over my face as he stops to stand in front of me. "Hey, I thought we had plans?" he says, waving the scrumptious goodies in the air.

My nose scrunches up as guilt burrows into the black crevice in my heart. "I'm sorry, I need to take a raincheck. Maybe next week?"

Luke nods, graciously accepting my guarantee I'm not once again going to become a stranger, even though we've been out of touch for so long.

His heart-cranking eyes dance between mine for several moments before he asks, "It's him, isn't it? That's why you're fleeing?"

"Yeah," I faintly whisper, embarrassed I'm acting like a coward. "He knows I'm here."

Luke's brows scrunch for the quickest second before recognition dawns. "He tracked you?"

When I nod, he adds on, "You did say he was possessive. I didn't realize it extended this far, though." His last sentence is hampered by a dash of worry. "You're not running as you're afraid of him, are you, Cleo?" Now there is no doubting his concern. His words were drenched with worry.

I shake my head. "Not at all. Marcus would never hurt me. Not physically, anyway." I stiffen the instant I realize I said Marcus's real name.

Luke stares at me, unmoved by my disclosure. I shouldn't be surprised by his nonchalant reaction. I'm sure there are millions of men in the world named Marcus.

After promising I am in no way in fear for my safety, I say goodbye to Luke with a brief kiss on his cheek and a rub of his arm. "I'll call you. We'll do lunch next week," I assure him.

Luke smiles. "Great. Then I'll have the perfect opportunity to tell you about Rachel."

My heart swells to double its size when I see the twinkle of admiration in his eyes. If I still know Luke as well as I used to, it is the twinkle of love. "Rachel Dion? That has a nice ring to it." I run my hand down his forearm before walking back down the sidewalk. "Thanks for tonight. I can't wait to hear all about Rachel."

Luke rolls his eyes at the exaggerated waggle of my brows. When I reach the end of the sidewalk, I spin on my heels to face Jackson's truck. Luke waits for me to disappear behind a large bush before he returns to his house overrun by rowdy partygoers.

My quick strides to Jackson's truck slow when a sense of awareness washes over me. I curl my arms around my torso to ward off the icy chill running down my spine as my wide gaze floats around the space. Even though drunken guests have spilled out of the house and onto the front lawn, there is a weird, spooky feeling enveloping me. It reminds me of the times I've allowed silence to overwhelm me, but I'm surrounded by noise this time, and it is still spine-chillingly creepy.

The reason for my body's odd response comes to light when I return my eyes front and center. Even my poor vision can't encumber my recognition of the dark sports car parked two spots behind Jackson's truck. It isn't spotting Marcus's vehicle that has my heart slipping into my queasy stomach, it is detecting a flurry of blonde walking away from his passenger side door that makes me sick.

Keira is wearing a dress matching the one in the photos sent to me earlier tonight. The grin on her face is mocking and contrite, and her eyes are blazing with lust. Believing I'm stuck in a jealous trance, I tilt to the right, wanting to ensure I have correctly identified Marcus's car. I have. Not only does the license plate leave no doubt in my mind, the stern green eyes glaring at me from the driver's seat corroborate my findings.

Returning my body to its original position, I lock my eyes with Keira. Realizing I've spotted her advancing frame, her cheekbones incline before the most pig-headed smirk I've ever seen stretches across her face. She looks like a woman who not only baked the cake, but she also got to eat it too. Her arrogance is at an all-time high, sending my anger skyrocketing to a point I can no longer ignore.

Gritting my teeth, I spin on my heels and head it the opposite direction. I don't know where I'm going, but it is anywhere but here. The fact Marcus arrived to collect me with Keira in tow has my anger reaching fever pitch. I've never been so furious.

In the process of racing down the red cup-lined sidewalk, I spot Brodie approaching me from my left. His gaze is as stern as Marcus's. I change the direction of my course, hoping the throng of drunken guests bouncing on the lawn like they are at cheerleader tryouts will conceal me long enough to derive an appropriate action plan. I can barely breathe through the anger curled around my throat, much less think straight.

With my vision blurred with tears, I bump into more people than I skirt. I apologize on repeat as I continue for Luke's poolroom I can see on the horizon. My frantic steps stop when my forearms are suddenly clutched in a vice-like grip. My back molars grind together as I fight to be released from the person's firm grasp.

My wailing stops when a distinctly male voice says, "Hey, Cleo, I didn't realize you knew the Dions?"

Although the man's voice comes out with a slur of someone who has a few drinks under their belt, I still recognize who it is. *Dexter.*

"Damn, Cleo. Look at you. Always beautiful, no matter what the century." If I weren't so enraged, I could kiss him for his compliment. My ego is so battered I'd even accept a wolf-whistle from a bunch of dirty construction workers.

As Dexter bobs down to plant a greeting on my cheek, my eyes frantically dart between his hazy gaze and Brodie's rapidly approaching frame. I don't know why I do it. It could be a state of panic or a last-ditch effort to maim Marcus as painfully as his deceit gutted me, but before I can stop myself, I curl my shaking hands around Dexter's bristly jaw, tilt my head to the side to better align our lips, then seal my mouth over his.

The instant my lips brush Dexter's, I know I've made a stupid mistake, but there's no turning back when Dexter drops the bottle of beer in his hand so he can weave his fingers through my wild mane. He slides his tongue along my gaped lips before plunging it into my mouth. His hand holds me hostage as his tongue explores every inch of my mouth.

I don't return his kiss, but the patrons surrounding us can't tell. They call out and wolf-whistle, encouraging Dexter to deepen our kiss even more. His exploration of my mouth only comes to an end when an arm wraps around my waist, and I'm forcefully dragged back. Dexter's hold on my head is so firm, the roots of my hair pull from my scalp when Brodie yanks me away from him.

Before my body registers the pain rocketing through my scalp, my heart is hit with a much worse jab. Marcus arrives out of nowhere, his fist swinging as forcefully as his stern gaze pins me in place.

The strength of Marcus's unexpected hit is so strong, Dexter stumbles backward, landing on the ground with a sickening thud. Party-goers using the lawn as a dance space squeal while dashing out of the way of a red-faced Marcus. He fists the collar of Dexter's shirt before planting a second hard knock to his chin, sending his head flying to the side with a sickening amount of force.

"Marcus, stop!" I scream when his fist rears back to hit Dexter for the third time.

Thrusting out of Brodie's hold, I scramble closer to them on my hands and knees, only stopping when Dexter uses Marcus's distraction to lunge forward and head butt him in the nose. The fury lining Marcus's face matches the blood oozing out of his nose from Dexter's unexpected attack. The sound of cracking booms into my ears when the two well-built men slam onto the concrete sidewalk like a ton of bricks. They continue brawling like street fighters, going punch for punch, ignoring everyone's pleas for them to stop—mine included.

I stare at them, shunted into silence. Marcus's impressive fighting skills are expected since he is fueled by jealousy, but Dexter's have completely blindsided me. Most men would have been knocked out after Marcus's first swing, but Dexter holds his own, issuing several of his own blows to Marcus's unprotected body.

Hating that they could get injured because of my stupidity, I drift my eyes to Brodie and demand, "Stop them."

After taking a second to register my request, Brodie nudges his head to Jackson, who is standing on the sidelines of the large group watching the fight like they're at a private MMA match. Brodie drags Marcus off Dexter at the same time Jackson curls his arms around Dexter's wildly thrusting body. Once they have been pulled apart, Dexter and Marcus stare at each other with nothing but disgust radiating out of their narrowed gazes. It infuses the air with tension so thick I can taste it on the tip of my tongue.

With Marcus's composure more controlled than Dexter's, Brodie relinquishes him from his grip, but with Dexter continually fighting Jackson, Jackson remains holding on to him tightly, showcasing his impressive strength. Tears stream down my face as I stand muted, bouncing my eyes between the two furious men. Dexter's eye is already swelling so badly, it is nearly sealed shut, and Marcus has blood gushing out of his nose and mouth.

After running the back of his hand under his nose, Marcus drifts his eyes to me, exposing his recognizable face to the crowd standing behind me. It takes a matter of seconds for their chants for more to turn into murmured hums and excited whispers. The dozen or more camera phones capturing the fight double as the sizeable crowd swarms, hoping to get up close and personal with an idol.

Sensing he is moments away from being swamped by overzealous fans, Brodie locks his eyes with Marcus and says, "We've got to go." The sound of police sirens wailing in the distance amplifies his suggestion.

Marcus continues glaring at me, his eyes unforgiving, his fists clenched. Guided by the pleas of my aching heart, I pace to stand in front of him, my legs wobbling with every step I take. When my hands lift to cradle his blemished cheeks, he pulls away from my embrace, adding a brand-new nick to my already faltering heart.

Dropping my hands to my side, I advise, "You need to go." My voice cracks with emotion.

Marcus stares at me for mere seconds, but it feels like the moon circles the earth a thousand times. His eyes are dark and full of torment, matching the sludge sitting in my chest where my heart used to belong. A tear rolls down my cheek when he abruptly pivots on his heels and stalks back to his car. Although the crowd shows their excitement at seeing a famous rock star in the flesh, none approach him, his rueful glare compelling enough to dose their enthusiasm to ask for an autograph.

When Marcus disappears within the crowd, Jackson releases Dexter from his hold. Mumbling a string of gibberish under his breath, he fixes his crumpled clothing. Once his clothes are sitting right, he lifts and locks his eyes with me, spearing me in place. I've never seen him so angry.

"I'm sorry," I murmur, wishing I could offer him more than useless words.

Ignoring the snickered comments murmured by mainly female guests, I weave my way through the hundred or so party invitees camped on the front lawn. Unlike Marcus, the crowd doesn't part when they see me coming. I get elbowed and barged no matter which direction I take. When each jab into my ribs is made with a bitchy remark, I realize they're intentionally hitting me.

Noticing my struggle, Brodie's naturally engrained protective demeanor kicks into gear. He curls his arm around my shoulders before using his other hand to push people out of the way. The crowd grumbles when his rough approach knocks several cameras out of my face. Although I don't want him to damage equipment I can't afford to replace, I keep my mouth shut, grateful to get away from glares so heated they're burning me alive.

"Out of all the men in the world, you had to kiss that one," Brodie murmurs under his breath, nudging his head to Dexter, who is watching my escape from the sidelines. Brodie's question was quiet enough the people lurking around us didn't hear, but not soft enough for me to pretend I didn't. "Marcus is. . . I don't know, Cleo. Fuck."

"It was a stupid thing to do, but I wasn't exactly thinking straight when I noticed he arrived with *her*," I reply, my plummeting mood not enough to surrender the jealousy blackening my blood. "I might have kissed Dexter, but it was nothing compared to how Marcus deceived me."

Brodie stops walking when we reach the passenger door of Jackson's truck. I can feel the heat of Lexi's baffled gaze drilling into my temple, but I can't take my eyes off Brodie. He may not be speaking yet, but his forthright gaze is warning me to listen carefully to what he is about to tell me. It gives me this horrid feeling that my entire universe is about to be upended.

"Are you talking about Keira?" Brodie queries with scrunched brows. "The blonde watching your every move?"

When I crank my neck in the direction Brodie's eyes are peering, he pinches my chin and yanks my head back to him. "The first thing you need to learn about recon is don't let your target know you've spotted them." His eyes dance with mine before he glances back over my shoulder. "Is she wearing a satin dress just like the one in the photos you received earlier tonight?"

When I nod, Brodie's deep exhalation of air is unable to conceal the string of curse words that follow it. "Marcus didn't turn up with Keira. He spent the last three hours with me searching every street in Montclair for you. Keira was already here when we arrived. When she recognized his car, she came over to talk to him."

"What?" I ask, confident I've misheard him. "Marcus was at Chains —with Keira. That's why she was wearing his marks in the photos. They are together."

Brodie shakes his head. "Marcus was at Chains earlier tonight." My eyes rocket to his as horrid unease twists in my stomach. Spotting my flaming-with-anger face, he quickly adds on, "With investors. He is selling Chains."

"What? Why would he do that?" I barely whisper. "Keira was wearing his marks; you saw them, Brodie, you know what they are."

My argumentative tone loses steam when Brodie constantly shakes his head.

"That's what I was coming to tell you when I busted you sneaking out. The photos sent to you were photoshopped. Those marks on Keira's back weren't real. They were added recently. That photo was from a fundraising event over a year ago. A five-second Google search told me that."

I stare at Brodie, wishing he was lying while also incredibly grateful for his admission.

"For two people who work with words for a living, you are both shit at communicating," he chastises, his tone forthright.

"Then why did he pretend he was in Florida when he wasn't? That doesn't make any sense," I ask.

Brodie stares me straight in the eyes. "Once again, I'm not the man you should be asking. If you want answers, you have to go in there and get them." He jerks his chin to Marcus's car idling two spots up from where we are standing. "If you want to walk away and pretend today never happened, your chariot awaits." He opens the passenger seat of Jackson's truck.

I drift my eyes between Brodie, Lexi, and Marcus for numerous heart-clenching seconds. My first thoughts are to push off my feet, fall to my knees at Marcus's heel, and beg him for forgiveness. The only thing stopping my feet from moving was the way he rejected my touch earlier. Maybe I am too late? Perhaps the choice no longer belongs to me?

Seemingly reading my inner monologue, Brodie says, "He wouldn't still be sitting there if he weren't waiting for you, Cleo."

"How will you get home?" I query, mindful Marcus's car only has two seats.

"We'll take him," Lexi offers, the slur of her tone reminding me she is still intoxicated.

I peer at Brodie, gauging his reaction to Lexi's offer. He nods his head before requesting for Lexi to scoot.

I wait for Jackson to climb into the driver's seat before shifting on my feet to face Marcus. I fiddle with the hem of my dress before plucking at a ball of lint, doing anything to delay the inevitable. Once I've worked up the courage to survive his dismissal, I push off my feet and pad to his car.

His car remains stationary until I slide into the passenger seat, then all hell breaks loose.

Chapter Eighteen

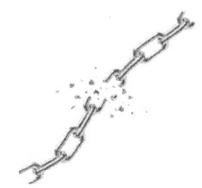

My fingernails bend harshly when I secure a tight grip on the leather seat of Marcus's sports car. His speed is so furious, when we hit a small dip in the driveway, his tires lose traction on the asphalt, and we go airborne. He whizzes out of Luke's parents' property so fast, Jackson's truck no longer tails us within a matter of seconds. An oncoming motorist honks his horn, unappreciative of Marcus's frantic swerve between cars when he illegally overtakes a sedan driving the designated limit.

"Please slow down," I request, fearful his anger will lead to a wreck. "You're scaring me." My voice displays my sheer horror. I'm not worried about me being injured as much as Marcus getting hurt.

Marcus's grip on the steering wheel turns deadly before his pressure on the gas pedal eases. Although his speed is still well above the limits marked on the side of the road we're careening down, it is a hell of a lot slower than it was initially.

Because he is gripping the steering wheel so tightly, the unnatural coloring of his hand is even more prominent. "Are you hurt?" I ask, scooting to the edge of my seat to inspect his hand more diligently.

When my fingertips brush the bruised skin angrily stretched over his swollen knuckles, he yanks his hand away as if he was burned by my touch. "Don't," he sneers, his voice brutal enough for me to recoil in my seat.

I stare at him, my stomach churning with both fear and regret. He keeps his gaze on the road, his jaw clenched, his eyes dark and lifeless. I want to express my sorrows nearly as much as I want to seek answers to my questions, but I do nothing. I just sit, gawking at him, willing him to speak, to say something. He says nothing. Not a thing. He just stares into the black abyss of a stormy night, unblinking and unspeaking.

I balk twenty minutes later when the sudden shrill of a cell phone rings through my ears. Marcus answers his call before the second ring.

"They increased the offer, but not to the amount you're requesting," says a thick, husky voice with a hint of maturity to it. "I'll continue squeezing them. They say they have reached their limit, but I know they have a few more millions up their sleeves."

When recognition dawns on what their negotiation is for, I close my eyes and count to ten, doing anything to ward off the tears threatening to spill at any moment. He is selling Chains just like Brodie said. *Oh my god, I'm a terrible person.*

My eyes pop back open when the gentleman on the phone says, "Mr. Everett, are you there?"

Air snags halfway down my throat when I comprehend the reason for Marcus's delay. He is watching me, his gaze intense and heated with an equal amount of anger and lust. The pain in his eyes triple when he drops them to my kiss-swollen lips. With his gaze white-hot, my tongue instinctively darts out to soothe the burn of his glare. A brutal pain stabs the middle of my chest when I taste the beer Dexter was drinking on my lips.

Ashamed, I twist my neck to the side and peer out the window, successfully hiding the handful of tears toppling from my eyes.

Even more tears glide down my cheeks when Marcus says, "Let them have it."

"That is not wise, Mr. Everett. They're still ten million away from your reserve. If you give me a few more hours, I can get them to the figure you are seeking—"

"I don't care about the money. Accept the terms," Marcus interrupts, his tone ensuring his caller is aware his decision is not negotiable.

I hear his caller gulp loudly before he mutters, "Okay, if you are sure?"

Ignoring his sneaky question, Marcus asks, "How long until handover can be finalized? I want this wrapped up as soon as possible."

His caller "ums" a few times as the noise of papers ruffling sounds down the line. "I've never sold a business of this manner before, so there isn't a specific time frame recommended. If the buyers are happy to move forward quickly, handover could be as early as Monday morning."

I peer at Marcus over my shoulder, my eyes expressing that I don't want him to do this. Chains is a part of who he is; if he sells it, he will lose a part of himself.

Not noticing the silent pleas of my eyes, Marcus's gaze remains locked on mine as he says, "Email me the contracts; I'll have them authorized and returned by 6 AM."

He disconnects his call, foiling his caller's ability to reply.

"Why would you sell Chains? It is a part of you, Marcus. It is also a part of Links," I blurt out before I can stop my words.

Marcus acts like he didn't hear a word I spoke, but I know he heard me, as the veins in his neck thrummed the instant I mentioned Links. Although I don't know the entire story behind Links, I know Marcus well enough to know how important it is to him. Chains' profits fund Links and many other worthy charity projects. Marcus's band is wealthy, but I doubt any rock group could amass the wealth Chains has the past three years. It is a sad but true notion—privacy is the most valuable commodity you own—only second to love.

"I'm sorry, Marcus. I'm sorry for hurting you. I'm sorry for everything I said—did—will do, but I don't want you to sell Chains. I'll do anything you want. I'll sign our contract. I'll publicly expose Global Tens' unwarranted investigation into Chains. I'll do anything you want if you'll reconsider your decision to sell Chains. I do *not* want you to sell Chains."

I angrily swipe at a tear rolling down my cheek when Marcus snarls,

"That is no longer your decision to make." His eyes drift from the roadside to me before he viciously sneers, "Any of them."

His confession ends our conversation in an instant.

Marcus's speed slows while he fields numerous calls from his lawyer, allowing Jackson, Lexi and Brodie to catch up to us twenty minutes later. They pull into Marcus's property not long after us. Detaching his cell from Bluetooth, Marcus clambers out of the driver's seat and climbs the stairs of his residence without so much as a glance in my direction. His conversation with his lawyer continues without pause as Aubrey assists him out of his coat.

I remain sitting in his car, sickened with grief. I may not have acted like it tonight, but I am an adult who can accept the consequences of her actions, but the people who rely on Links aren't as lucky as me. Most of Links' patrons are children stuck in a debilitating world of domestic violence. They don't deserve for my stupidity to ruin their chance of a normal upbringing.

I run my hands over my cheeks, collecting my tears when a brief tap sounds on my driver's side door. The outside temperature is so cold, white air puffs out of Jackson, Lexi and Brodie's mouth as they stand by the passenger side door of Marcus's car waiting for me to exit.

"Do you want me to stay?" Lexi asks when I peel out of the car to stand next to her.

The worry in her eyes grows immensely when I shake my head. "No. I created this mess, now I must fix it." I lock my eyes with Jackson. "Can I ask a favor before you leave?"

When Jackson nods, I add on, "Can you check Marcus's hand? I think the fight may have done some damage to the ligaments in his hand. It could be nothing, but he has a world tour scheduled next month, so I'd rather be safe than sorry."

"Yeah, no worries. I have my bag in my truck," Jackson replies, nudging his head to his vehicle.

Lexi, Brodie, and I wait in the living room of Marcus's residence for nearly an hour before Jackson merges from Marcus's office. My chest grows heavy from the gaunt expression on his face. If he wants to become the world-renowned surgeon he is striving to be, he needs to alter his facial expression. If he confronts his patients' families to update them on their condition after surgery like he is approaching me now, I have no doubt they would fall to their knees and howl. He has the same look on his face the surgeon did when he advised us Tate didn't survive surgery.

"He damaged his hand?" I ask, even though the truth is projected by his direct gaze.

Jackson nods. "I'm fairly sure he has broken the capitate and scaphoid bones in his hand. He has also done extensive ligament damage. I won't know the full picture until he has a set of x-rays done in the morning."

"Will he need surgery?" Lexi asks, her words as low as I'm feeling.

Jackson shrugs. "I won't know until I get the x-rays, but at a guess, I'd say no."

"Can he play guitar?"

Jackson's remorseful eyes peer into mine before he shakes his head.

"Jesus Christ," I mumble under my breath. "Like this night could get any worse. His band will cancel their tour."

Although I'm murmuring to myself, Lexi says, "Don't panic until you know the actual results, Cleo. His hand might not be broken. It could just be swollen."

When she peers up at Jackson, wanting him to back up her theory, he unconvincingly nods, making my guilt ten times worse.

After numerous assurances that I'll be fine, I bid farewell to Lexi, Jackson, Brodie, and Aubrey. My nerves don't fully kick in until the taillights of Brodie's car disappear over the horizon. It isn't just the eerie silence playing havoc with my emotions, it is the chaos equally numbing my heart and brain.

My steps down the hallway separating Marcus's office from the central living space are shaky and drawn out. I am exhausted, but my sluggish actions have nothing to do with tiredness. Marcus's head lifts from his desk when he detects my presence. I prop my shoulder on the doorjamb of his office, waiting for him to give me permission to enter.

My heart rate quickens to a brisk canter when he stands from his office chair and paces toward me. Although he has his cell phone pressed up against his ear with his taped hand, he doesn't speak a word. I close my eyes and inhale deeply when his unique scent overtakes the stench of desecration leeching out of my pores. My eyes snap open when a spark of electricity surges through my top lip. Marcus's touch is only brief but strong enough to fill me with hope.

The pain in his eyes turns lethal when he stares at my lips while roughly scrubbing them with his thumb as if he is trying to remove Dexter from my mouth. He scrubs and scrubs until my mouth reaches a point of blistering from his feverish touch.

When he steps back, I peer up at him, issuing silent apology after silent apology for my idiocy. When his hand moves toward me, I pray it is to pull me into his body and comfort me until the moisture leaking from my eyes stops running. I've always said I'm saving my tears for my darkest day—this is my darkest day.

My hopes are dashed when Marcus says, "You need to shower. You still smell like him." He then shuts his office door with me standing on the other side.

I stand frozen, staring at the white frosted door, confident the male scent on me doesn't belong to Dexter. Not wanting to stir any more trouble, I keep my mouth shut and wait for his shadow to disappear from behind the door. When it does, so do I. I don't go far, only to the bathroom in his master suite. I know running would ease the sting of his rejection, but I won't run. I'm going to face the consequences of my actions with a maturity I did not hold tonight. I just need to work out what that appropriate outcome is.

After taking a shower hot enough to hide the tears staining my cheeks and incinerate Luke's cologne scent from my skin, I pad into the massive walk-in closet. Although my clothes are stacked in a neat pile on my right, I veer to the left, allowing my heart to guide my steps. I dress in one of Marcus's bland white undershirts and a pair of his cotton boxers. Since the waistband of his boxers are too loose for my female frame, I roll them up until the cuff is sitting high on my thigh.

My toes grip the plush woolen carpet as I slowly pace out of the room. Instinctively, my hand darts out to run over Marcus's suit jackets hung in sequence of their color. I've done the same thing every day the past weeks, because even though his clothes have been laundered, they still smell like him.

My brows furrow, leaving a substantial groove in the middle of my head when I notice a folded-up piece of paper sitting on top of one of many black polished dress shoes. Bending down, I gather the note. I swallow away the bile burning my throat as I slowly unfold the unknown document. My heart stops beating when I read the hand-written message scripted inside.

A relationship can weather any storm
if the couple continues standing under the one umbrella.

I miss you.

Marcus xx

I search the note for any indication of whom the message was written for; it is void of any clues. The sluggish beat of my heart doubles when I stand mute, staring at the group of freshly pressed navy blue suits hanging in the closet.

Recalling the message Brodie shared last week, my jaw gapes. "Tell Cleo if she is cold, she can borrow my jackets. Navy blue is my favorite color."

In a hurry, I check the pocket of the first navy blue jacket I stumble upon. I find a matching folded-up piece of paper in the breast pocket. This note leaves no doubt whom the messages belong to. They belong to me.

The name Cleo is of Greek origin, it means "Glory."
Glory can mean many things: a victorious triumph, an award.
But for me, it recalls magnificence and great beauty.

That is what you are to me.
Wait for me, Cleo.
The storm will soon be over.
Marcus xx

I find another four notes hidden in Marcus's suit jackets, each one placed in one of his beloved navy blue suits. They all follow a similar tune—that we are stronger than the storm striving to overcome us. God—what I would have given to find these messages sooner, then maybe I wouldn't have acted so recklessly. I thought I was losing him; little did I know he was fighting to save us.

I sit on the edge of his bed for several minutes, my stomach churning, my mind at a loss on how to move us past this. Marcus is sacrificing everything, yet I've given up nothing. I've always maintained that I want our relationship on an even playing field; shouldn't that refer to both sides of the team?

I inhale a sharp, quick breath when an idea pops into my brain. There has only ever been one thing Marcus has requested during our negotiations—he wants me. If he still desires that, I can give him that —wholly and without reservation.

I stand from the bed and race across the master suite. My steps are weightless since all the heaviness on my shoulders lifted the instant I made my decision. That is how much I want this—not even my brain can cite an objection. I gather a fancy treasure chest-like key out of the wooden box sitting on top of a stack of drawers before exiting the main suite.

I pace across the hall, reaching the door of Marcus's playroom within two heart-thrashing seconds. The boom of the lock sliding out of place bellows down the hall when I shove the key into the door and twist. I move through the playroom in a flurry, wanting to have my ducks lined up in a row before the noisy clank of the lock mechanism announces my intentions to Marcus.

Remembering the rules associated with this room, I remove my clothing, fold them into a neat stack, then place them on a woven laundry basket on my left. The coolness of the air vents prickles my skin with goosebumps as I head for the trunk of goodies Marcus and I spent a week working through before our separation.

My hand rattles softly when I pry open the singular drawer above the chest, but I push aside my shaky response, knowing it is more based on exhilaration than fear. I place a new D/s contract on top of the drawer before hunting for a pen. Failing to find one, I dash back into the main room and gather one from in there.

I freeze halfway into the playroom when I hear Marcus climbing the stairs. With his shoulders still weighed down by my betrayal, his steps are clunky, sending every one of them booming down the hall. I race for the blank contract, flipping it over until I find the most significant section I need to fill in—my signature.

After scrawling my name across the bottom of the document, I set it square in the middle of the drawer before adopting a submissive stance. I lower to my knees, bow my head and rest my hands on my bare thighs, palm side up in an offering position. With my hair still wet from my shower, it clings to my naked back. I am exposed and utterly raw with nothing but remorse blanketing me.

I level my breathing before pricking my ears so I can listen to every step Marcus takes. I count his steps: *one, two, three, four, five*, until they stop just outside the playroom door. The hairs on my nape stand to attention, announcing his arrival, but I keep my head down low, waiting for my Master to issue any punishment he sees fit.

I wait.

And wait.

And wait.

Chapter Nineteen

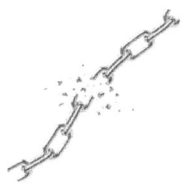

My muscles grow weary as I wait for Marcus to respond. Although the pain in my aching joints tells me I've been kneeling for some time, I know Marcus is still with me. Even strangled by remorse for my betrayal, my body's awareness of his closeness is still primitive. She knows her mate, and she knows him well enough to hear all the thoughts running through his mind right now. He is torn, stuck between wanting to punish me and wanting to walk away. His indecisiveness kills me more than believing Keira was his sub. I've laid myself bare to him, yet he is still considering walking away from me. That hurts—a lot.

I shut my eyes to ward off my tears at the exact moment Marcus steps into the room. With my head still bowed, I watch his feet slowly pace across the room behind a set of lowered lashes. He stops in front of the chest moments before the sound of paper sliding across wood trickles into my ears. I don't breathe—I can't, every muscle in my body is reserved for listening to any prompts Marcus may give when he realizes I've signed on to be his sub. A sigh. A murmur. I'd even take a grumbled curse word.

He does nothing. He remains perfectly silent.

I pull my chin in close to my chest when he spins on his heels to face me. Every stride he takes to lessen the bridge between us has my pulse quickening. His steps are slow, as if they are purposely torturing me. My hair falls from my face when he grips my chin and raises my head. He has my recently signed contract in his hand, his hold so firm it has a massive crinkle down the middle of it.

"This space may be known as a playroom, but you do not play games in here," Marcus mutters, his tone a stern warning that I'm no longer in the presence of Marcus. *Master Chains has arrived.*

"I understand, Master Chains," I respond, my quivering voice giving away the emotions pumping through me.

"Then why did you sign this?" He thrusts the contract to within an inch of my face.

I angle my body to the side so I can look him in the eyes. "Because I wanted to. I want to be yours. I want to be your sub. And I want you to punish me for the wrong I did."

"Disobedience does not get rewarded," he snarls, assuming I'm using my idiotic decision to kiss Dexter as a way of forcing him to dominate me.

That is not what I'm doing. I want him to punish me so we can move past this. If my research into the BDSM lifestyle is correct, once a punishment has been issued, the reason for the punishment is no longer valid. So once Marcus punishes me, he'll have no reason to be angry anymore. I'll also happily suffer through the pain my disobedience will bestow upon me, as I doubt it will be anything close to the ache gnawing at my chest.

"I was wrong; I deserved to be punished, and I'm willing to accept any punishment my Master sees fit." My words come out strong, hiding the turmoil brewing in my stomach from Marcus's rueful glare.

When he releases my chin from his firm grip, I return my head to its bowed position. My entire body quakes uncontrollably as I wait for him to make his decision. I honestly don't know what I'll do if he walks away from me. This is the furthest point I can reach to display my devotion to him; I can't do any more than this.

I sneakily run my hand under my nose to gather the contents spilling from it when Marcus pivots on his heels and paces away from me. To begin with, I'm panicked, assuming he has decided he is done with me and my Garcia antics.

I suck in a grateful breath when I realize my assumptions are wrong. "Because this is the first time, you, the sub, will be punished purely for pain instead of pleasure, I will allow you to choose your punishment and the severity of it." His voice is monotone and flat, unlike anything I've ever heard.

I nod, incapable of speaking through the heartache of him referring to me as "the sub" instead of my real name. He has always called me Cleo in the playroom. He has never addressed me as if I am not a real person.

When Marcus moves back to stand in front of me, I notice his feet are now bare, but his trousers remain in place, acknowledging that our session in the playroom is not about pleasure. If it were, he wouldn't be clothed.

"Look at me," Marcus demands, his voice throaty.

I swallow away my nerves before peering up at him. He has removed his suit jacket and tie, and his business shirt is undone at the front. Even with my mood suffocated by fearful guilt, my eyes can't help but drink in his smooth skin pulled tightly over the impressive ridges of his stomach and torso. His body is truly a masterpiece—one I'll do anything to make mine.

"First, you will choose what instrument you want to be punished with. Then you will choose the severity of your punishment. But be warned, if I do not believe the punishment equates to the level of your disobedience, our session will end, and your contract will be void. Do you understand?"

"Y-y-yes, Master Chains," I reply, idiotically stuttering like a fifth grader. It isn't panic about the pain I'm no doubt about to experience that has me stammering my words, it is the sheer darkness of Marcus's eyes. He honestly looks like he's lost his soul. I hate that I've caused him so much pain his usually vibrant eyes are dull and lifeless.

"Choose your punishment, C—" He stops himself before saying my name.

Following the direction of his gaze, I take in his wall of floggers, whips, and canes. When I first entered his playroom in Chains, I was honestly shocked by the apparatus I assumed would be as unpleasant as they looked. But the more weeks I spent with Marcus, the more I understood that in the right hands, even something as tortuous as a whip with pronged ends can be used to entice pleasure.

None of the toys Marcus has used on me ever solely caused pain. They walked the fine line between pleasure and pain, awarding me enough courage to try many of the floggers and whips in his collection. The only thing I haven't been brave enough to face is the canes. I don't know why, but they honestly scare me. So much so, they are the perfect instrument to prove to Marcus I am taking this seriously. I understand the severity of my disobedience, and I am willing to face the consequences of my actions.

"I choose the cane, Master Chains," I advise. My voice comes out with so much confidence, anyone would assume I'm choosing a dessert.

For the quickest second, Marcus's stern mask slips, exposing an emotion his face hasn't held tonight: panic. As quickly as his mask slipped, it returns. He paces to the wall, his steps fast and with purpose. After gathering the cane sitting in the middle of a stack of three, he moves back to stand in front of me.

"Now the severity," he asks, his voice demanding yet calm at the same time.

I peer down at my hands, trying to devise an appropriate number of strikes. I'm reasonably certain the cane will be painful, so the first number that pops into my head is deficient. But not wanting Marcus to null our contract, I continue racking my brain for a more appropriate number.

Once I have a number settled in my head, I lift my eyes back to Marcus. His face is stern, but his eyes show he is as bewildered as I am right now.

"I choose seven strikes, Master Chains," I advise, hoping the seven strikes will erase the seven seconds I kissed Dexter.

Seven may not seem like a high number, but when I realized seven seconds was all it took to unravel something magical, I'm hoping seven strikes with the cane will absolve my betrayal.

"Very well," Marcus replies, briefly nodding. "Stand from your position and move to the spanking bench."

I briefly nod my head, acknowledging I've heard him before doing as requested. The ache in my muscles grows with every step I take. It isn't just exhaustion causing their taut response, it is my body preparing for the next stage of our exchange.

Once I'm bent over the spanking bench where I received my first taste of anal play, Marcus moves to stand beside me. He leans the cane against the Saint Andrew's cross so he can adjust my position. His freezing cold hands are a stark contradiction to the heat roaring through my body. Our bodies seem on opposing sides of the spectrum—much like the massive sentiment bouncing between us. The uninhibited lust that always surges between us is still in effect, but it is stultified by anger and regret.

Happy I am positioned correctly, Marcus takes the cane in his hand. "What is your safe word, sub?" he asks, his voice barely a whisper when he reaches my horrid nickname.

I fight back tears before murmuring, "Pineapple."

"Repeat it."

"Pineapple," I choke out through a sob.

He waits for what feels like an eternity before reiterating, "If at any time you want me to stop, say your safe word. Do you understand?"

"Yes, Master Chains," I reply, nodding.

There is no chance of that happening. If I don't go through with the punishment I instigated, our contract will be void. I'm never going to let that happen. Nothing would be more painful than losing Marcus —not even seven strikes with a cane.

"I want you to count each strike. When we reach seven, this will be over, and tonight will never be mentioned again. Do you understand?"

"Yes, Master Chains," I repeat, thankful for his pledge that my punishment is in line with the severity of my deceit.

"This is going to hurt," Marcus warns under his breath as he raises the cane into the air, preparing to strike. "But it will be nothing compared to the pain I felt seeing you kiss another man."

I grit my teeth when the cane lands hard across my backside. Just as I had anticipated, the hit is intense, ten times worse than any I've been given in this playroom. Tears spring to my eyes in an instant as I cry out in pain. It is a sharp bite to my skin, one I'm certain I'll never relish.

I wait for the burn of his strike to release its grip on my throat before muttering, "One."

Marcus's second hit is just as brutal as the first—if not more severe. The tears looming in my eyes are so plentiful, they have no option but to slide down my cheeks and drip onto the floor near Marcus's bare feet.

I suck in mass gulps of air, fighting to breathe through the pain roaring inside my body. It does nothing to ease the agony spreading across my butt cheeks. This pain is the worst I've ever endured.

My body's big shakes echo in my tone when I stammer out, "Two."

I'd give anything for that number to be seven right now. I honestly don't know if I'll survive another five strikes of that caliber. It burns so much, it feels like my skin is on fire. I wouldn't be surprised if my ass is bleeding by the time we reach seven strikes.

When Marcus fails to strike me with the cane for the third time, I angle my head to the side and peer at him from under the veil of my hair which has fallen in my eyes. From the expression on his face, anyone would swear it was him being hit by the cane. His beautiful eyes are tormented and full of pain, his jaw open and quivering.

When he spots me peering at him, he murmurs, "Say it." His voice is so soft I barely hear his request over the thumping of my heart against my ribcage.

"Say it," he repeats louder, ensuring I can't mistake his request.

More tears fall from my eyes when I shake my head. "No."

"Goddamn it, Cleo! Say your safeword!" he shouts, his loud words vibrating in my heart.

"No," I reply, shaking my head more fiercely. "I kissed him. I deserve to be punished. I hurt you. Punish me. Make me pay for my mistake, then we can move on from this."

The last half of my sentence is muffled by a scream when Marcus strikes me for the third time. His hit isn't as firm as his first two, but with my backside still struggling with the agony of his first two strikes, it feels just as intense.

I try to ride the crest of pain, hoping to shift the fine line between pleasure and pain to a satisfying experience. It is a pointless effort. The endorphins pumping through my body from his strikes are curtailed with so much pain, I can't trick my brain into believing it's an enjoyable experience.

Swallowing down the bile scalding my throat, I murmur, "Three." I hiccup through a sob before whispering, "Four more to go."

Marcus stands next to me with his broken hand clenched so firmly, the tape Dexter wrapped around it is cracking and crumbling to the ground. His eyes frantically dart between my weeping face and my aching backside as he requests, "Say your safe word. You've reached your limit. Say it."

Hating the sheer agony in his tone, more tears roll down my cheeks. "No."

"Say it!" Marcus roars, scaring the living daylights out of me. "Stop being so goddamn fucking stubborn and say it!"

I balk at his rare use of a curse word before shaking my head. The pain shredding across my backside is brutal, but it is nothing compared to the pain his eyes held when he peered at me in the moments leading up to him hitting Dexter. I'm not going to say my safeword, no matter how much he begs. Four more strikes and tonight will be forgotten. I can live with that.

When I continue shaking my head, Marcus lifts the cane high into the air. I squeeze my eyes shut and grit my teeth, praying I'll be strong enough to endure another four strikes. I just want this over so we can move forward.

The bamboo sluicing the air breaks through my pulse raging in my ears. It is the sound of pure pain, equally evil and haunting. A loud crack booms around the room; it is the loudest one so far. I wait for pain to quickly follow it.

It never comes.

I crank my neck to the side, shocked and confused. I've only experienced subspace once before, and I'm certain this isn't it. I was barely lucid last time; this time I'm very much coherent.

I inhale a sharp breath when I spot the cane lying at Marcus's feet, snapped in two. It is as broken and mangled as Marcus's beautifully tormented eyes staring at me in shock. He briefly shakes his head before spinning on his heels and exiting the room without so much as a backward glance in my direction.

It is only when I hear him murmur the word "pineapple" as he gallops down the stairs of his palatial residence do I realize the man striking me with the cane wasn't Master Chains—it was Marcus.

Chapter Twenty

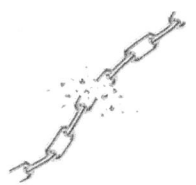

I WAKE UP SEVERAL HOURS LATER, CURLED IN A BALL IN THE MIDDLE of the four-poster bed in Marcus's playroom. This is where I crawled to and cried when the sound of Marcus's engine roaring to life echoed into the room within minutes of him fleeing. I had planned on taking a few moments to gather back the small skerrick of my dignity I had left, but I guess exhaustion eventually overwhelmed me.

I scoot down the bed, pretending I can't feel the sting of my naked backside when it glides along the smooth, satin sheets. A blanket I don't recall being there falls from my shoulders when I swing my legs over the bed and stand. My muscles squeal, unappreciative of taking the weight of my body. Unlike every other time I've walked out of this room, this time they aren't protesting from exhaustion, they are aching from dehydration. I swear every ounce of moisture in my body was shed last night—that is how much I cried. Losing something you love is never easy, whether it is by death or their choosing. Last night proved that.

Upon entering the main suite, I drift my eyes to Marcus's bed. I'm not surprised to notice it hasn't been slept in. The house has a dead-quiet feeling, like the entire world has vanished. I pace to the landline phone on my left and snag the cordless handset from its dock. While dialing a number I know by heart, I gather my suitcase from the foot of Marcus's bed and move into the walk-in closet.

"Hey, Cleo, you okay?" Lexi asks weakly, her weak voice exposing I've woken her up.

"Yeah, I'm fine," I lie, my tone low with guilt. "Umm . . . can you come pick me up?"

Lexi sucks in a sharp breath before she faintly whispers, "Of course I can." Her voice cracks as if she too is struggling to hold in her tears. "I'll be right there, okay?" I hear the shuffling of sheets before the sound of bare feet padding on tiles booms into my ears.

When I fail to answer Lexi's question, she asks, "Do you want me to stay on the line with you until I get there?"

Heat blooms across my chest, warming some of the black sludge sitting in the crevice where my heart used to belong. "No, it's okay. I'm going to take a shower, then pack."

"Alright," Lexi replies, her tone low. "If you change your mind, you know how to reach me. I'll be there as soon as I can, Cleo."

"Thanks." I'd like to express more, but the substantial sentiment in Lexi's tone isn't allowing it.

My hand rattles when I place the phone back onto the deck. Although I just told Lexi I am going to shower, I veer to the left instead of the right. Although Marcus didn't touch me very much last night, I can still smell his unique scent on my skin, and I'm not willing to wash it away just yet.

Nearly an hour later, I descend Marcus's curved staircase. The clatter of my suitcase wheels thumping down each step announces my arrival to Aubrey. I balk, shocked by her presence. The house was so padded-cell quiet, I assumed I was alone. After placing my bag at the edge of the entranceway, I shift on my feet to face Aubrey.

"Is Marcus here?" My heart may be shattered, but if he is home, I'm not going to be a coward who leaves without saying goodbye.

"No," Aubrey replies with a curt shake of her head. "He is

attending a press conference to announce the cancellation of Rise Up's world tour."

"His hand is broken?"

Aubrey smiles a reserved grin before nodding her head. "He had x-rays earlier this morning. He won't be able to play an instrument for eight to ten weeks."

I scan the room, seeking any type of clock. With Lexi's drowsy reply and the tired headache thumping my skull, I assumed it was still early. I startle, stunned by how high the sun is hanging in the sky. Without seeing a clock, I can quickly tell it is nearly noon.

"Come and have something to eat before you leave," Aubrey says, gesturing her head to the kitchen. "I have a fresh pot of hot chocolate waiting for you on the stove top."

My stomach churns. Its squishy response has nothing to do with the quality of Aubrey's hot chocolate and everything to do with her acknowledgment that I am leaving. She's acting like she is aware of my departure as if someone updated her hours before my decision. My stomach flips even more violently. Clearly, Aubrey and Marcus's relationship is more stable than I first perceived.

Aubrey's steps into the kitchen, stopping midstride when the sound of a doorbell ringing fills the silence bristling between us. When she heads for the door, I quickly mutter, "I'll get it." *It's for me anyway.*

Aubrey peers at me, reading the rest of my statement my mouth failed to produce from my eyes. With a shy grin, she dips her chin before continuing her trek to the kitchen. Her speed is so unchecked, anyone would swear her backside was as burning as mine. I wait for her to enter the sweetly aromatic room before heading for the door. Although I'm stunned by Lexi's quick arrival, I am also grateful. Every minute I spend in Marcus's house adds to my grief.

"I'll pay any speeding tickets you received in your travels," I mumble, swinging open the large glass door.

My breath traps in my throat when the vibrant chocolate eyes of my sister I was expecting to see have been replaced with the eyes of the devil. Satan has returned with a vengeance, her snarl as vicious as the sharp cut of her bob hairstyle.

"I'll be sure to take you up on your offer. . . *when hell freezes over,*"

Delilah retaliates before sauntering into Marcus's property without waiting for permission.

"Hell has already frozen over, Delilah; otherwise, why would you be here?"

Delilah accepts my snotty remark without protest as she removes her elaborate black fur coat. Considering how evil she is, I'd say that is the skin of a real animal—no fake fur for a woman as wicked as Delilah. She folds her coat over her rake-thin arm before moving to the edge of Marcus's entranceway. She inspects his property with the eagle eye of a person who is accustomed to wealth. From my research, I know she and money are close friends. That's probably because she leeched herself onto one of the wealthiest families in New York City: the Gottle's.

"You have five seconds to tell me what you are doing here, or I'll use the olive branch Mr. Gottle extended to me last week." My statement is a complete lie. Although Mr. Gottle assisted in my investigation of Keira last week, I've never personally spoken with him.

Delilah's utter stupidity rings true when she replies, "When you speak with Henry, be sure to tell him I said hello." She is clearly ludicrous. No one in a right frame of mind would taunt a mob boss.

She scrubs her hands together as if she is ridding them of dirt before locking her eyes with me. "Now that we have the idle chitchat out of the way, why don't we get down to business?"

My pulse quickens when she takes a step toward me. Because her strides are so long, she reaches me in one fluid march. "I knew it would only be a matter of time before you exposed Chains' identity. I was right. I just had to be patient."

She thrusts a folded-up newspaper into my chest. The paper has been so recently rolled through the printers, the ink is still sticky.

Air brutally sucks from my lungs when my eyes scan the headline on the front page.

Rise Up's Golden Boy Not So Golden

In a state of panic, my eyes frantically speedread the document. Every nightmare I've had the past three months comes true when detail after detail of Marcus's involvement in the BDSM community is presented before me. His ownership of Chains, its connection to Links —it even has reports from supposed ex-subs "brave enough to recount their horror of living with a sadist."

"None of this is true," I snarl, lifting my eyes to Delilah. "He is not a sadist or masochist. He doesn't instill pain for his own pleasure. He does it for his subs' pleasure. You are going to ruin a good man all because you are a vindictive two-faced bitch who steamrolls anyone who dares to have a different opinion."

Delilah shrugs off my admission, but the quickest blaze in her eyes exposes that some of my words cut deeper than she'd care to admit. "You should be privileged you were awarded the first copy. I thought it was the least I could do since you were the source of the story."

Horrid unease scorches my veins when her finger points to the byline under the scathing headline. Although I've dreamed of having my name printed on the front page of the New York Daily Express, I don't want to achieve it like this.

"You can't run this story, Delilah," I plead, my words the sincerest I've ever used with her. "I'm imploring for you to just once listen to the little voice inside of you telling you this is wrong. You know this is wrong. Please don't do this."

"It is too late," Delilah advises, spinning on her heels and heading for the door. "The special online edition is scheduled to be released at noon. The print edition will follow an hour later."

The mirrored frame hanging in the entranceway rattles furiously when she slams the front door of Marcus's property with force. I stand frozen, muted and confused. My paralyzed stance doesn't linger for long, only long enough for me to see it is three minutes past eleven. I might not be able to stop the story from going to print, but I can warn Marcus of its arrival, then maybe his media team will have a chance of mitigating the shit storm that is sure to follow.

I charge into the kitchen, startling Aubrey, who is standing near the stovetop. The brush of her hand across her wet cheeks is quick, but not fast enough for me to miss it. Although concerned about what has caused her to cry, my utmost priority must remain Marcus.

Snatching the phone from the cradle, I dial Marcus's cell phone number. It rings and rings and rings until his voicemail eventually picks up.

"I know I'm the last person you want to speak to right now, but please call me. It is urgent."

I hang up and redial his number.

When my calls reach his voicemail another three times, I place the telephone back on the cradle before my eyes stray to Aubrey. "Do you have a car?"

She barely nods before I trudge around the kitchen and curl my arm around her shuddering shoulders. "Do you know where Marcus's press conference is being held?"

Aubrey once again nods.

"Good, show me where it is."

While driving into the city, I borrow Aubrey's cell phone to update Lexi of my change in location. She warns me against approaching Marcus in public, but I shove aside her caution, mindful that things can't get any worse than they already are. I set up a google alert on Aubrey's phone for any articles mentioning Marcus's name with the inclusion of BDSM in the search field before calling his number on repeat.

Thankfully, no pings are received during my travels.

With me expressing the absolute urgency of my plea, Audrey's car circles the block of the hotel Marcus's press conference is being held at within a record-breaking forty-five minutes.

"Pull over anywhere, and I'll walk the rest of the way," I demand when traffic becomes so congested near the hotel, pedestrians are moving at a faster speed than vehicles.

"Thank you," I say to Aubrey when she maneuvers her car to the furthest lane.

I place a quick peck on her cheek before snagging her cell and my purse from the middle console.

"I'll get it from you later," Aubrey advises when my panicked eyes lock on her cell clutched in my hand. "Just go."

I nod my head before closing the door. The love I have for my sister city is tested when I push and barge my way through the mass of people mingling on the sidewalks. New York streets are always crammed with people, but with having one of the most prolific bands of all time gathered in one place, the swell of the crowd has doubled.

"Excuse me. Pardon me. Sorry," I continue to plead as I shove my way through the clog of paparazzi standing by the exit of the hotel.

The scene inside the hotel is nearly as frantic. Gushing guests, squealing fans, and over a dozen security officers line the foyer of the elegant hotel. My eyes scan the room, unsure of what direction to take. When I spot a man I've met before, I head for him.

"Hey, Hawke. I'm not sure if you remember me—"

"Cleo, right?" he greets as his face stretches into a welcome smile.

"Yeah. That's right." I reply, smiling. "I urgently need to speak with Marcus. I've been calling his cell nonstop, but he isn't answering."

"That's not surprising; Emily makes the guys hand in their phones before every press event or meet and greet. She wants them interacting with real-life people, not an electronic device."

He places his hand on the curve of my back before guiding me to conference room number three. Upon opening the door, a massive brute of a man with a shaved head and an angry snarl drops his gaze to me.

"This is Cleo. Marcus's girlfriend," Hawke quietly advises the snarling unnamed man.

In an instant, the sheer terror radiating out of him in invisible waves disappears. He smiles, softening the harsh lines on his face before gesturing for me to enter.

"Thank you," I whisper to Hawke before merging deeper into the room.

He nods his head before spinning on his heels and returning to his original position.

Since the press conference is well underway, I move to the far edge of the room, then skedaddle to the row of tables Marcus and his band-mates are sitting behind. Spotting my sneaky approach, Kylie and Jenni wave a greeting before gesturing to the empty seat next to them. I briefly shake my head before continuing my mission.

The confidence Marcus generally exudes by the bucket load isn't present today. His chin is tucked in close to his chest, and his unin-jured hand is cradling his bandage-covered one. He doesn't even lift his eyes when a reporter asks for details on how his hand was injured. He leaves Emily the task of responding, citing it was the result of an "error in judgment."

The only time his eyes lift from his hands is when I reach the edge of the table he is sitting at. His narrowed gaze doesn't swing around the room. They lock straight onto me, proving he can sense my pres-ence as easily as I detect his. I chew on the inside of my cheek when I see the pure devastation radiating out of his beautiful green irises. They are as cold and blank as they were in his playroom last night.

Before I get the opportunity to request to speak with him, the loud ding of a cellphone shrills from my pocket. I suck in a deep breath, conscious it could be my last chance to breathe before digging Aubrey's cell out of my pocket. The prompts of my body are proven accurate when the screen displays 138 alerts on my search of Marcus Everett and the BDSM lifestyle.

Just as quickly as my eyes rocket to Marcus's, the buzz of numerous cell phones sounds through the room. It is a tidal wave of horror, swelling in size and intensity with every beep. The quiet snickers are the first to arrive, closely followed by the hammering of paparazzi questions. Marcus leaps from his chair and lands in front of me as if magic.

He snatches Aubrey's cell phone from my hand before dropping his eyes to the screen. The more he scrolls through the dozens of stories on his hidden BDSM lifestyle, the firmer his jawline becomes.

His eyes missile to mine when he reads the name of the lead reporter of the investigation.

"I didn't do this. You know I didn't do this," I stammer out, my words choked by devastation.

"You're an investigative reporter?" Marcus questions, the roar of his words enough to silence everyone in the conference room.

"Yes." The brief nod of my head sends tears toppling down my cheeks. "But you know this. I told you I work for Global Ten Media." Unlike Marcus, I keep my voice low, striving to lose the attentive ear of the hundreds of reporters surrounding us.

"You told me you worked for Global Ten. You never mentioned you were an investigative reporter! You write obituaries for a living for fuck's sake! I've never seen your name in print," Marcus shouts, his voice so loud, I hear his screamed statement twice since it bounces off the stark walls before echoing back into my ears.

I stare at him, shocked and confused. I don't understand what he is saying. I never explicitly said I was an investigative journalist, but that was because I didn't need to. He knew about the Chains investigation. He knew I couldn't discuss the particulars of the case for fear of being prosecuted, so I don't understand why he is acting as if he doesn't know. He knows I'm an investigative journalist. *Doesn't he?*

"How many more coals do you want to drag me over, Cleo?" Marcus asks, his words as broken as his slit gaze. "First you cheat on me, and now this? Is nothing sacred to you?"

The crowd sighs in sync, just as stunned by Marcus's revelation as I am.

"I didn't cheat. Kissing isn't cheating," I deny, hating that I'm being forced to defend myself in front of hundreds of people watching my every move, much less doing it with the most pitiful excuse I've ever used.

Marcus takes one step toward me. He stands so close, the furious heat of his body dries the wetness on my cheeks. "Yes, it is," he snarls viciously.

The hotness of his breath bounces off my lips when he murmurs, "You should have packed an umbrella, as you never know when the next storm is about to brew."

As his eyes dance between mine, his hand slides into the pocket of his trousers. Two seconds later, he presents a folded-up piece of paper. My stomach violently flips when I realize what he is holding. It is the D/s contract I signed last night—the one thing still tethering us together.

I recoil when Marcus rips the contract in half, not stopping his onslaught until each section crumbles to the floor like rubbish. Once our agreement has been destroyed beyond recognition, Marcus sneers, "We're done. I never want to see you again. Do you understand?"

Incapable of speaking for fear of sobbing, I briefly nod my head.

"Good. Goodbye, Cleo," he bids me farewell, his tone flat and without hesitation.

With that, he spins on his heels and exits the conference room via a back entrance. His stunned bandmates soon follow him, leaving me defenseless against a bunch of ravenous journalists, desperate to unearth any tidbit of information on his recently exposed secret.

Chapter Twenty-One

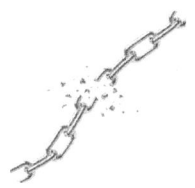

THE PAPARAZZI GO MANIC. I'M BOMBARDED WITHIN SECONDS. Cameras and microphones are shoved in my face as an endless stream of questions pummel into me. I raise my hand to shelter my eyes from the blinding camera lights as I endeavor to locate the door I entered mere minutes ago. The swarm of the paparazzi is so strong, for every step I take forward, I'm knocked back three paces. My full name, address, and date of birth are shouted between journalists eager to share their knowledge with the hope it will be returned full-circle when I pick which media company I'll award an exclusive to. That is never going to happen. Even stunned by what just occurred, I'll never share my story.

My endeavors to reach the exit are impaired when my hips are suddenly grabbed by a firm hold. The terror thickening my veins dulls to a slight boil when I recognize the smell of the man clutching me.

"Keep your head down," Brodie instructs, altering the direction of my course so we head toward the set of doors Marcus and his band-mates entered earlier.

I step on numerous black dress shoes and expensive high heels as Brodie guides me out of the hair-raising situation I find myself in.

Although the shouted questions continue when we enter a thin corridor of the hotel, the brutal elbows and shoves end.

As I gulp in deep breaths to quell the anxiety making me a clammy mess, Brodie pushes his finger to his ear and says, "Yeah, I've got her."

"Marcus?" I ask, my voice hopeful.

Brodie begrudgingly shakes his head. "It's Lexi. She's waiting for you outside."

I've barely recovered from my first brutal blow when I'm hit with another. Marcus is standing at the end of the corridor with his blazing-with-anger eyes firmly locked on me. When I take a step toward him, the curt shake of his head pins me in place, freezing me with both fear and remorse.

His eyes dance between Brodie and me for several heart-thrashing seconds before he angrily mutters, "Brodie, let's go."

Brodie's lips twitch, preparing to issue a reply, but his words stay entombed in his throat when Marcus adds on, "Now."

Brodie lowers his eyes to me, the remorse in them uncontainable. "Lexi is just outside those doors," he advises, his voice barely a whisper.

I swing my head in the direction he is facing. It looks like an emergency fire exit you'd expect celebrities to use when avoiding the paparazzi. When I return my moisture-filled gaze to Brodie, the tears ramp up a gear. Marcus is nowhere to be seen.

"I'm really sorry about all of this, Cleo," Brodie murmurs before he pushes off his feet and heads in the direction Marcus was standing.

Nursing my bruised ego the best I can, I make my way to the emergency exit door. I've barely merged onto the cracked sidewalk when the smell of rotten tomatoes streams through my nose. Lifting my eyes, I catch sight of a flurry of red charging toward me.

I dodge the soaring tomato, forcing it to land on my shoulder instead of my chest where it was aimed.

"Skank. Whore. Cheater." Numerous teenage girls scream from the other side of the alley as they continue pegging rotten food products at me. "You don't deserve a man like Marcus Everett. You are nothing but trash."

They throw hurtful words as if they are grenades as I race down the street to my baby poo Buick parked halfway down the alley. Hearing their taunts, Lexi emerges from our car, her face as red as the tomatoes being thrown at my head. When one lands on her stomach, she bends down and picks it up before pegging it back at the jeering teens.

"You better run," Lexi yells when her perfectly thrown tomato smacks one of my tormentors right across the face.

While she retaliates to their childish taunts with equal maturity, I slide into the passenger seat of my car and use my shirt to clear smears of egg yolk from my hair.

I've scarcely removed the eggshells from my hair when Lexi returns. She grumbles angrily under her breath as she snags her seat-belt and yanks it across her chest. Because she is tugging on the latch so hard, the seatbelt mechanism locks into place, foiling her endeavors.

"Goddamn motherfucker shit-box cock-sucking piece of crap!" Lexi yells, saying every curse word she was forced to hold back this week.

I don't know how I muster the strength, but a hearty giggle spills from my lips before I can stop it. It is another one of those cry or laugh moments. Considering I cried so much last night that I'm fresh out of tears, I must laugh.

Upon hearing my laughter, Lexi cranks her neck and peers at me. She stares at me like I am insane, which only makes me laugh even more. My laughter must be contagious, as Lexi soon follows suit. We laugh so much our car vibrates as if her rusted engine has been cranked. We laugh until our bellies ache, and our eyes fill with happy tears, then we laugh some more.

When my laughter loosens up my devastation, I slump into my seat. The deep sigh I release ruffles a strand of hair that has fallen in my face. "I royally fucked up," I murmur, more to myself than Lexi.

"No," Lexi replies, the shake of her head amplifying her short reply. "We fucked up."

I peer at her, confused by her statement. *What does she have to do with any of this?* She might have encouraged me to sneak out last night, but I'm an adult who could have said no at any stage. She also didn't kiss Dexter; the blame for that idiocy solely belongs to me. As much as this kills me to admit, Delilah was right. She knew my insecurities would get the best of me. By doing that, I not only exposed Marcus's involvement in the BDSM community, I also sacrificed our relationship.

Not reading the questions my eyes are relaying, Lexi picks a chunk of eggshell from my hair, dumps it into the cracked vinyl console between us, then fires up the ignition. When the radio begins broadcasting breaking news, she leans over and switches it off. Hating the silence as much as I do, Lexi commences whistling.

When she hears my disgruntled moan, she murmurs, "It's either face the music or listen to my whistling. Pick your team, Cleo?"

She whistles the entire hour journey home.

When Lexi pulls our rusted old Buick into the driveway of our family home, my eyes go crazy, frantically searching the hands of the dozen or so teens camped out on the sidewalk of our house. Thankfully, they are void of any molded fruit and vegetables.

"I know gossip on social media spreads like wildfire, but how did they discover my involvement so quickly?" I query, stunned.

Lexi unlatches her seatbelt before gathering my hands in hers. "The press conference was recorded live."

My pupils dilate. "They broadcasted my fight with Marcus." Although I appear to be asking a question, I'm not. I'm summarizing. "That's why they called me a whore. They heard what he said to me?"

Lexi's brows furrow before she nods her head. "They've also seen the video of Chains and Dexter fighting last night. They know the real reason his hand is broken," she discloses, her voice low with worry about how I am going to take her news.

"I'm going to be eaten alive. You know how crazy the Rise Up fans are," I mumble under my breath.

Lexi nods her head in agreement. "I also know how quickly things like this blow over. You've just got to keep your head down for a few days and weather out the storm."

"What's with all the storm metaphors lately?"

Lexi shrugs. "You've got to ride out a storm to see the rainbow at the end?"

Stealing my chance to reply, she cranks open her driver's side door and exits our Buick. Mercifully, the angrily snarls of Montclair locals aren't as vociferous as those in New York City. Things dampened down considerably celebrity-wise after Justin Bieber moved into town a few years ago. Hopefully, the fanatic teen fans continue camping out on his doorstep. It is the smart thing to do considering the chances of Marcus arriving at my property are slim to none.

As per Lexi's request, I spend the remainder of my week hiding away from the world. With her final exams ending Tuesday afternoon, we've spent a majority of our time watching Netflix and splurging on the occasional Passionflix movie. I haven't heard from Marcus at all the past six days. Honestly, I didn't think I would. He made it extremely clear during the press conference that he doesn't want to see me. And if that wasn't evident enough, the arrival of my packed suitcase via a courier company within the hour of me arriving home Saturday after-noon was a sure-fire indication.

Unsurprisingly, the news of Marcus's involvement in the BDSM community hasn't dampened the band's appeal in the slightest. If anything, it has made their fans more rampant. The press is going crazy, vying for exclusive interviews with anyone in the industry associ-ated with Marcus, and the band's popularity has soared to a level no one expected. My social media accounts were always filled with Tweets and Facebook posts about teens idolizing the members of Rise Up; now, it's not just teen girls posting those declarations. If I had a dollar for every time I read a post from a grown woman begging for Master Chains to spank her, I'd be a very wealthy lady.

The media and the public's reaction to Marcus's scandal proves I'll never understand this bizarre thing we call life. His secret may be exposed, but public awareness of the BDSM lifestyle has grown tenfold. Unlike Delilah, most reports have conveyed both sides of the coin. It truly is a win-win for Marcus. The band's albums from years ago are once again at the top of the charts, and the dialog about indi-viduals having the right to choose their own sexual prerogatives has been established. I'd give anything to go back and alter the decision I made last Friday, but since I can't, I'll take comfort in the fact the heartache I've endured the past six days has made it easier for women who are battling between their desires to be both feminist and submissive. Maybe now they'll realize they can have both.

I shut the screen of Lexi's laptop, hiding my umpteenth rejection letter for the week. Before Marcus's scandal broke, I was struggling to keep up with the number of stories my freelance journalism career had offered me. Now I am getting rejection letter after rejection letter. Although every rejection arrives with a letter of offer for me to do an exclusive interview about my relationship with Marcus, none have accepted the stories I penned in the hope of moving my name away from Marcus's.

"Another rejection?" Lexi asks, pacing into the living room.

I curl my feet under my bottom while nodding my head. Accepting the mug of hot chocolate she is holding out for me, I gently blow on the steamy goodness. "They increased their offer on an exclusive, though. If the rates keep climbing like they have the past six days, I'll reach seven figures soon."

Lexi timidly shakes her head. "If only you were interested in Chains solely for his money."

"Would you be tempted?" I ask Lexi, curious of her reply.

She considers my question while sipping on a glass of tea. "I don't know. Maybe?" She places her tea on the coffee table before swiveling her torso to face me. "If it were Chains, yes, I'd sell his story."

I peer at her, shocked by her admission. She's never been money-hungry before.

"But if it were Jackson, no, I wouldn't," she explains to my bewildered expression. "That's why you don't have to defend your decision not to make a profit out of this, Cleo. I may not have as many brains as you, but I get why you're remaining quiet. You loved him, so you'll protect him no matter what."

"I love him," I correct before I can stop my words.

Moisture looms in my eyes as my hand darts up to the pendant wrapped around my neck. Although I could use the chain's light weight as a reason for my constant checking, I know that isn't the case. Just like Cartier, I've resorted to seeking courage from a piece of jewelry instead of the man who gave it to me.

My stomach churns violently as I am plagued by another severe bout of nausea. The past six days have followed along a similar tune. I pretend the world doesn't exist until something shoves me back into reality. When the pain of my existence becomes too much for me to bear, the contents of my stomach reenter the world in the ghastliest way.

"Not again," Lexi mutters when I springboard from the sofa and race into the bathroom.

I've barely skidded to my knees in front of the toilet when the sweet brown goodness I enjoyed earlier resurfaces. Just like every time I've vomited the past week, its return isn't as pleasant as its consumption.

Once my stomach is void of any nutrients, I stand from my kneeled position, then move to the sink to wash my hands. While splashing fresh water on my face, I catch sight of Lexi's worried expression. The concern on her face stretches to mine when I notice she has my tattered old coat in her hand and a set of keys. "Are you going somewhere?"

"No. We are."

When I peer at her, blinking and confused, she paces into the bathroom to assist me into my coat. "A broken heart doesn't make you nauseated," Lexi informs me while pulling my hair out of the neckline of my coat. "But babies do."

"What? Don't be ridiculous. I'm not *pregnant*." I murmur my last word, fearful speaking it out loud will cause it to come true.

"Then you'll have no reason to deny my request for you to pee on a stick," Lexi fires back, her tone dead serious.

I'm not going to lie; a trickle of doubt entered my mind earlier this week when I recalled my period didn't arrive on my return from Ravenshoe. But with Richard's death and the stress of the investigation, I pushed it aside as an effect of the strenuous strain placed on my body. The week following our return was a rollercoaster ride of emotions that plagued both my mind and my body. I never figured my soaring moods had anything to do with being pregnant until the bouts of vomiting arrived.

When I fail to shadow Lexi out of the bathroom, she cranks her neck back to peer at me. Her eyes silently convey that her suggestion of purchasing a pregnancy test isn't up for negotiation.

"We shouldn't spend our money willy-nilly," I mumble, using any excuse I can not to face the truth. "After my disclosure on national television that I breached my contract with Global Ten, I can't be guaranteed Mr. Carson will pay the remainder of my salary as we negotiated. He might hold over that monetary amount until his legal team advises their next move."

"It's six bucks, Cleo. Stop being so cheap," Lexi replies, grumbling.

"It's not six dollars," I continue to argue, my Garcia stubbornness not allowing me to back down without a fight.

"It is when you know the pharmacist, and he gives you a *we used to fuck* discount."

My eyes bulge as the rest of my argument lodges in my throat. Using my frozen stature to her advantage, Lexi seizes my wrist and yanks me out of the bathroom.

After wading our way through a contingent of media still hounding me for an exclusive and a handful of teens still hoping to spot Marcus, we arrive at the drugstore Luke owns twenty minutes later. Just locating Luke's truck in the parking lot has my nerves hitting an all-time high.

"I can't do this, Lexi. I can't face Luke, and I also don't want to confront the truth. If I'm pregnant, nothing will change. I can't tell Marcus—"

"Why not?" Lexi interrupts, her tone high in shock.

"The media would tear me apart—even more than they already are. They will have a field day saying I trapped Marcus and am after his money. That gauntlet we just ran, it will double in size for every month of my pregnancy, then it would turn crazily stupid when the baby was born. I can't put a baby through that any more than I could do that to you or Marcus. This is my life, Lexi. It is not a circus."

Lexi flicks a rogue tear from my cheek before locking her eyes with mine. "What if I get it? I'll tell Luke it is for me."

"Then what?" I ask, loathing how heavily I'm relying on others to dig me out of the bottomless pit I'm in.

"Then we'll put one foot in front of the other until we work out which path you want to take." Her glistening eyes bounce between mine as she murmurs, "You don't need a test, do you? You already know."

I nod. "Life likes to display just how fucking cruel it can be, so why not throw another curveball into the mix?"

Chapter Twenty-Two

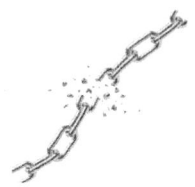

THE PREGNANCY TESTS GO PRECISELY HOW I PREDICTED. BUT instead of being baffled with color charts and a box of instructions, Luke gave Lexi top of the line pregnancy tests—three of them. All I had to do was pee and wait, then I discovered I'm six to eight weeks pregnant. *My fucking god.*

I place the third positive test back on the cracked vanity before resuming my frozen stance on the toilet. Lexi's nerves are so evident, Jackson joins our pity party in the bathroom, making the cramped space even more so. When his eyes lower to the positive tests, my first thought is the hide them before he reads the results, but I'm so lost right now, I'll happily accept advice from anyone.

"Are these tests yours?" Jackson asks, peering at me.

Although relief crosses his face when I nod my head, I swear a small dash of disappointment also filters through his eyes.

"The good news is you're only six to eight weeks, so you've got plenty of time to decide what you want to do," Jackson says, using his surgeon voice I've only heard a handful of times.

A whizz of air parts his mouth in a rough grunt when Lexi back-hands him in the stomach.

"What?" he asks when she glares at him.

"Cleo is not having an. . . *abortion*." She whispers her last word as if it is a curse word.

"I wasn't suggesting one. I meant for telling Marcus. With miscarriage statistics so high, doctors recommend you wait a minimum of twelve weeks before announcing a pregnancy. This will give you a few weeks to clear the fog from your head."

"I need a lot more than a few weeks," I grumble under my breath.

Jackson smirks softly, proving he heard my private mumble. "Do you have a preferred obstetrician you'd like to see?"

I roll my eyes before shaking my head. "I haven't been to the doctor's since the mandatory health check Global Ten employees get."

"And she wonders how she ends up pregnant," Lexi snickers.

She connects her eyes with mine, the angry cloud in them growing with every second that ticks by. "Did Marcus know you weren't on the pill?"

I shrug. "I don't know. He never asked, and I honestly forgot to mention it."

When the storm in Lexi's eyes triples, I add on, "I know, I know. Very stupid. But I'll be okay. From the way his D/s contracts were worded, it's clear his previous subs had a full medical exam before any contact, so I don't have to worry about diseases or anything."

"No, just one that requires food, shelter, and clothes for at least the first twenty-one years of its life," Lexi retorts.

"Alright, Lex, I think Cleo's got enough on her plate without us adding to it." Jackson's assurance lessens the severity of Lexi's glare, but it doesn't fully douse it. "There is a local obstetrician in Montclair, but I'd rather refer you to a specialist in Queens." He hands me a tattered card from his wallet. "I've worked with her a few times; she comes highly recommended."

The rueful glare Lexi is directing at me reverts to Jackson. Her gaze is white-hot, adding to the horrid mugginess of so many people in the small space.

"She is also fifty-eight," Jackson adds on, understanding the meaning of Lexi's suddenly cold demeanor. "If I didn't love your jealousy, Lex, I'd be pissed about your mistrust."

"I'm not the one who slept with half the interns during residency,"

Lexi fires back, shadowing Jackson out of the bathroom. "How am I to know if she is one on a long list of many?"

"Lexi, if we start this conversation, I'll mention my run-in with not one, but two of your ex-boyfriends at Luke's birthday party last week."

Their jealous bickering continues until they enter Lexi's bedroom. Their argument doesn't last long. I've barely hidden the pregnancy tests in the top drawer of my desk when the sound of shouted words is replaced with needy moans.

Not wanting another dash to the toilet, I snag my old cell phone off my desk and trudge to my bed. My phone is over four years old, but it is in perfect working order. Its extensive playlist has been a godsend the past six days. Although seeing Lexi deliriously happy with Jackson has made my heartache stronger, I'm also glad my foolish decision hasn't impacted them too significantly.

Another benefit of my outdated iPhone is its iCloud capabilities. All the sneaky photos of Marcus I took during our brief fling are stored on my phone. Although seeing what I've lost adds to the endless pit in my chest, I've perused our photos numerous times the past six days. I always start my trip down memory lane from the beginning of our relationship—at the snaps I took of Marcus with his bandmates the very first night we met. Tonight is no different.

The slideshow of photos goes from our first night together until the morning Marcus left for his supposed trip to Ravenshoe. They display that our time together was brief, but jam-packed with memories.

I still haven't worked out the reason for Marcus's deception on his location. The only person who can answer my questions is the same man who is avoiding me like I have the plague. Even Lexi has been unsuccessful in reaching him. If his face weren't splashed across every news program and article in the world, I'd assume he vanished.

When the montage of our brief relationship ends on a sneaky video I took of Marcus singing in his recording booth, I scroll back to the only photo I have of us together. It is a corny selfie I made him take in the minutes leading up to our dinner on the patio being disrupted by a sprinkling of rain, but it is a perfect representation of our relationship —fire-sparking and intense.

As I stare at our contrasting skin tones and eye coloring, I daydream about what features our baby could get from each of us. I wonder if he or she will have Marcus's alluring eyes—part of me hopes they will, whereas the other half wants the brown-eyed Garcia gene to reign supreme—then I can keep a part of my family history continuing even years after I'm gone.

When the creak of my bedroom door breaks through my pulse shrilling in my ears, I scrub away a rogue tear the curve of my lips is caressing. The pain crippling me dampens when Lexi slips into the bed and curls her body around mine, like she has done the past six days. I don't know if my quiet sobs aren't as silent as I aimed for, or if she just knows me well enough to know when I'm having a low, but she arrives at precisely the right time every single night.

"Shh. I've got you, Cleo," she guarantees when the shivers racking my body become too great to ignore.

The following morning, Lexi prances into the kitchen, her steps as upbeat as my mood. "Is that waffles I'm smelling?" she asks as she paces to the fridge to snag one of the many vitamin waters Jackson stacked in the fridge last night.

"Uh huh," I reply, accepting the bottle of vitamin water from her hand. "Jackson knows these are a waste of money, right?"

Lexi shrugs. "He thinks they will help with your nausea. He also wrote down a list of vitamins he wants us to pick up for you today."

"Are you going out?"

Lexi waits for me to check on the waffles before answering, "Yeah. I have a follow-up appointment with Dr. Spencer. He wants to see my results firsthand."

Ignoring my heartstrings painfully tugging, I smile. Dr. Spencer has been Lexi's CF specialist since the day my parents discovered she had CF. Dr. Spencer fought for years to get Lexi included in the Kalydeco program when the drug was first discovered, but his requests went unanswered. I'm certain if he didn't have four sons he was putting through medical school, he would have personally funded Lexi's inclusion in the program.

"Thank you." Lexi's eyes blaze with excitement when I carefully pluck two waffles out of the waffle maker and pop them onto the plate she is holding out. "I haven't had your waffles in years, Cleo. I'm dying to discover if they still taste as yummy as they used to."

She wasn't lying. She doesn't even add any condiments before taking a sizeable bite of the still steaming waffle. "Sooo good," she mumbles through a moan.

Happy the first part of "Operation Get Cleo Back" has been hatched, I pour another batch of mixture onto the waffle machine. I've had an entire week to mourn Marcus, and as much as I wish I could continue hiding away from the world, it is time for me to get my wheels back in motion. I'd like to say discovering I am pregnant is the catalyst for my new and improved attitude. Unfortunately, that would be a lie. It was waking up to find my bank account void of the salary I was expecting to be wired in there overnight.

If my accounting skills are correct, I have approximately fourteen days to find employment or I'll be homeless. With not just having Lexi's health to factor into my dilemma, any mourning must be pushed aside until I've dug myself out of the massive, ceaseless pit I'm sitting in.

My eyes swing to the side when Lexi asks, "Are you alright, Cleo?" Her words are mumbled by a syrup-slathered waffle.

"Yep" I reply, enunciating the P to add extra emphasis to my false statement.

Lexi's brows inch together as her eyes dart between mine. For the first time in a week, my weary gaze must portray the screamed prompts of my brain, as Lexi faintly smiles before returning her focus to tackling her breakfast.

I place the final plate in the kitchen cupboard when the distinct noise of knocking sounds from my front door. Snagging a tea towel off the drying rack, I apprehensively pace out of the kitchen. Although the brazen attempts of reporters have dulled down the past three days, I still receive the occasional cold calls from eager media companies vying for an exclusive interview.

"I'll get it," Jackson says, coming out of Lexi's room.

He throws a shirt over his shaggy hair as he bypasses me standing mute in the hallway. Jackson has been a godsend the past week. Even with his mother facing a terminal illness, he has been by my and Lexi's side during this entire ordeal. The tumor in the base of Janice's skull hasn't shrunk, but the optimism of her family has increased tenfold the past two months, as it hasn't grown either. Their family is proof that a positive attitude can sometimes be the only drug you need.

As much as I'm grateful for Jackson's assistance, I'm also worried he will burn out. His residency requirements at the hospital are already crazy, let alone handling creepy stalkers obsessing over how a plain-Jane member of society snagged a rock star and journalists who are inept at taking no for an answer.

I never thought I'd say this, but I'm really missing Brodie. He may pee with the bathroom door hanging wide open and tell crude jokes as if he is Kevin Hart performing on stage, but he is a great guy. I guess Brodie's disappearing act should have been my first clue that things were truly over between Marcus and me. For weeks, Brodie shadowed my every move. Then, suddenly, poof, he was gone. What Lexi said last week was true. Knowing Marcus had Brodie tailing me meant he still cared. Just like withdrawing his contact implies the opposite.

I snap my thoughts back to the present before they put a damp-ener on my recently formed go-get-'em attitude in just enough time to see Jackson open the door. My brows stitch when our expected caller's frame is covered by a large hamper of goodies. It is only when I hear the unique rumble of a recognizable male voice do I push off my feet and head into the foyer.

"Hey, Dexter," I greet, my tone apprehensive.

I haven't seen Dexter since our kiss last week. I did send him a quick text earlier in the week to apologize for my appalling behavior. When he replied saying I had nothing to apologize for, I ended our conversation. It wasn't that I was ungrateful for him loosening the knot of guilt wrapped around my throat, I just had too much going on to factor in another person's feelings. My priority was secretly nursing Marcus through his scandal—albeit unnecessary, but I didn't know that at the time.

When Jackson's wide eyes shift to me, silently asking if I am okay to be left alone with Dexter, I nod my head. Dexter is harmless. *Although my scalp still tingles from his rough hold.*

Dexter waits for Jackson to enter Lexi's room before drifting his dazzling eyes to me. "I wanted to get you flowers, but I've always thought they were pointless. They cost a fortune; they last a matter of days, then they end up as compost." He hands me the massive basket filled to the brim with food. "I thought this was more practical."

"It is great. Thank you, Dexter." My high tone relays the sentiment in my voice. After my calculations this morning, this food basket means way more than I can express.

I mosey into the kitchen. Dexter follows behind me, indiscreetly taking in my home on the way. "Your home is nice, Cleo. It has a real family vibe to it."

I set down the basket on the kitchen table before spinning around to face him. "Thank you. It has a lot of my mom and dad embedded in its bones."

"They bought this when they got married, didn't they?" Dexter asks, removing his coat and slinging it over the chair I am sitting next to.

I smile. "Yeah, they did. I can't believe I mentioned that to you." I'm usually more reserved with sharing information about my personal life.

I step into the hallway so I can see the heart of the home. "It was rundown, but while my mom sampled cakes and organized the seating chart, my dad spent his hours bringing her back to her glory days. My dad carried my mom over the threshold the night of their wedding."

My small smile increases when I recall how beautiful the molded-wood features look after a coat of paint. That is the first thing I'll do once I get settled. I'm going to return my home to a state my parents would be proud of. *One I'll be proud to raise my family in.*

"How come you're not at work?" I query, praying he won't see the stupid sentimental tears looming in my eyes.

He chews on the corner of his lip. "I'm on leave." He rocks back and forth on his heels, his nerves clearly evident. "Didn't feel like explaining my black eye and chipped tooth to my supervisor."

My pupils grow as guilt engulfs me. I don't know how I missed it earlier, but now that he pointed it out, his right eye is still wearing the effects of his fight with Marcus.

"You chipped your tooth?"

Dexter runs his tongue along his teeth before saying, "Yeah. Not that you can tell now. My dentist is a genius."

I cringe, loathing what his bill to have a chipped tooth repaired was.

"I don't have much, but if you are willing to accept installments, I'll pay your dentist bill."

My steps to gather my checkbook halt midstride when Dexter says, "I didn't come here to hand you my medical bills, Cleo." His voice is husky, strangled by either laughter or concern.

I spin around to face him. He has his arms crossed in front of his broad chest and an amused smirk etched on his face.

"You didn't?"

When Dexter shakes his head, I stammer, "Then why are you here?"

"To see if you are okay. I thought we were friends?" He shrugs his shoulders like it is no big deal. "I wanted to come last week, but decided to wait for the craziness to die down." His neck cranks to peer at the kitchen wall facing the front of my house. "But from what I saw out there, things are still pretty hectic."

Some of the heaviness on my chest lifts from him calling us friends. I was worried my stupidity last week damaged our recently formed friendship. "I'd like to say I'm surprised by the media's tactics, but we both know all too well the tactics reporters stoop to for a story."

"Hey," Dexter says, holding his hands out in front of his body. "Don't shove me into that cesspool. I might work for Global Ten Media, but I sure as hell ain't one of them." He nudges his head to the wall he was looking at earlier.

"Thanks for the sneaky stab at my career, Dexter," I grumble under my breath.

Dexter barges me with his hip. "You might be a reporter, but I don't see you pitching a tent on someone's front lawn so you can harass them day and night."

I remain quiet, unsure how to reply. What Dexter is saying is true, but if my career didn't nose-dive after the false story I approved on Noah in rehab, would I be one of them? Morally, I'd like to say I was raised better than that, but I can't one hundred percent certify that. My career was my life until it came tumbling down, so who's to say what I would have done for the story of the century?

The fact I attended an underground BDSM nightclub wearing nothing but a satin slip abundantly proves the lengths I will go to for a story. The only reason that ruse is more acceptable is because I continually told myself it was for my sister's well-being. Although part of me wonders now how true that was. Maybe I'm not as saintly as I like to portray. Perhaps I am just like Keira, displaying one façade to the world while poorly hiding another.

"Talking about jobs, have you decided what you are going to do yet?" Dexter questions, guiding me away from my negative thoughts.

"Honestly, no. I don't have a clue." Realizing there are products that require refrigeration in the basket, I pry open the saran wrap and gather them in my hands. "I'm going job hunting this morning," I advise, pacing to the fridge.

"Around Montclair?"

I place the orange juice and cream into the fridge before spinning on my heels to face him. "Anywhere, really. A job is a job. I'll take what I can get."

Dexter scrubs his hand over the stubble on his chin as he stares into space. Not wanting to interrupt his train of thought, I start packing away the items in the basket. Although most are products I've previously used, they are much fancier brands than the ones my grocer stocks.

I've just finished stacking the banana and walnut muffin mixture in the pantry when Dexter asks, "You studied personal relations, right?"

I screw up my nose. "Yeah, but just as a filler class as the creative writing course was full. I wasn't overly good at it."

"Did you pass?" Dexter asks with an arched brow.

I giggle softly before nodding my head. "Just."

Dexter checks his watch before questioning, "Do you have any plans next Friday?"

"Christmas eve?" I ask, certain he has his dates confused.

He doesn't.

"Yeah, my father's lifelong friend is attending Global Tens' Christmas Eve ball. I think he is someone you'd *really* like to meet."

My brows scrunch from the ambiguousness of his reply. It isn't what he said; it is the way he said it. It was showy and teeming with attitude, very unlike Dexter.

"Thanks for the offer, but I'm not interested in attending a function overrun with reporters." *That is the last thing I need.*

"Why not? The opportunity would be immense, Cleo. You could be walking away from something—"

"I'm not interested, Dexter," I interrupt, my tone stern and to the point. "I appreciate you looking out for me, but I don't want to work in that industry anymore. I can't handle the stress right now."

Even with my worry at an all-time high that I'm weeks away from being homeless, I'm not so desperate I'll fall to my knees and beg the people responsible for the demise of my career and relationship for any scraps they're willing to throw me. I'd rather scrub toilets for a living than lower myself to those standards. Furthermore, discovering I'm pregnant ensures I need to limit my stress. My baby doesn't deserve to be bombarded with out-of-control hormones and soaring emotions. If I don't lower my stress, the poor baby will have a mental breakdown before it is even born.

Dexter's lips twitch as he struggles to hold back further debate. I issue him a glare, warning him I've reached my quota on our conversation.

"Alright," he eventually breathes out. "But if you change your mind, I'm only a phone call away."

"Thanks, but there is no chance of that happening."

I lied.

Chapter Twenty-Three

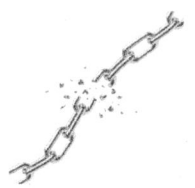

"No luck?"

I shake my head before closing our front door, blocking out the nagging questions from the paparazzi still following my every move. After placing my portfolio on the entranceway table, I sling off my coat and pad into the living room Lexi is gawking at me from. My steps are slow, weighed down by the intense amount of pressure I'm under.

I slump onto the sofa next to Lexi so I can pry my stilettos off my aching feet. Air whizzes from my thin, grim lips when I spot the mountain-sized blister on the back of my heel. I knew trekking the streets of Montclair in a pair of heels would be a tortuous feat for my ego, but I had no clue it would cause physical pain as well.

"Ouch. I'll get the iodine," Lexi offers, rising from the couch.

I've barely skimmed off my second shoe when she reenters the room, clutching a bottle of iodine and a box of Band-Aids.

"I think it is time to devise a new tactic," Lexi suggests, handing me the items she gathered.

Before I can announce a protest to her suggestion, she continues talking, foiling my attempt. "I'm not saying you have to accept Dexter's offer, but I think you should use his invitation as a way of confronting Mr. Carson. Your leave is not negotiable, Cleo. You earned those hours by working your ass off for his company the past five years. The least he could do is hear you out."

At Jackson's suggestion, I reached out to Mr. Carson after contacting my bank to ensure there wasn't an error processing my paycheck. There wasn't. I was informed by Mr. Carson's PA that he will be unavailable until next year, so I spent my week job hunting. I've yet to secure a position. It isn't because the companies believe I lack the skills for the job, nor am I overqualified, they just don't want the stigma attached to my name to negatively impact them. I can't say I blame them. Having a prospective employee arrive at an interview with half-dozen paparazzi in tow would have to be a major deterrent for any employer.

"When this dies down, come back and see me," is a quote I've heard on repeat the past five days. Little do they realize by the time the media's interest in me ends, I'll be homeless.

"Mr. Carson is on leave, so I doubt he'll be attending the gala," I reply, issuing any excuse to avoid being lured into agreeing to this plan.

Lexi leaps off the couch, startling me. "If the news printed by his own company is right, he will be at that gala."

She hands me a front-page article on Mr. Carson and a mystery blonde he was seen with at a racetrack event last month. Although the blonde's face in the photo is anything but pleasant, Mr. Carson's hold on her implies they are more than friends. He is holding her like a groom would when carrying his bride over the threshold.

"Rumors are they will be attending the event together."

I peer at Lexi, stunned by her snoopiness.

"What? My nosey-nancying is encouraging the media to shift their focus away from Marcus. . . which in turn will shift their focus away from you as well," she mumbles.

My heart rate turns calamitous when I flip over the paper to discover Marcus's handsome frame. With the recovery time of his hand being critical, he has been photographed entering and exiting a well-known physical therapist's office in lower Manhattan the past week. If the gossip articles are anything to go off, the band will resume their world tour as early as late January.

Lexi removes the article from my hand, practically prying it from my death-clutch hold. I'd like to say as the days roll on, my grief over losing Marcus is fading. It isn't. I miss Marcus just as much now as I ever have. I always thought the saying "absence makes the heart grow fonder" was a crock of shit. Now, I'm a believer. I miss Marcus for every second of every hour of every day. Years will pass, and I don't see that logic changing.

My eyes lift to Lexi when she hands me my cell phone. "Accept Dexter's offer."

My brisk headshake slows when Lexi adds on, "Or I'll sell my Kalydeco medication on the black market."

I stare at her, blinking and confused. "You can't do that. It's illegal."

"Yes, I can," she confirms, her tone firm. "With the price being so high, people are desperate. But you don't need me to tell you that, do you, Cleo? As you already know the steps people will take to protect the ones they love."

I huff. "I only considered it once. It was still out of my price range," I admit, unashamed. I'm not deceitful when I say I'll do anything to protect my sister, even going as far as risking prosecution for purchasing medication on the black market.

I lick my dry lips before accepting my cell from Lexi. My hands shake uncontrollably when I punch Dexter's number into the screen from the business card he handed Lexi last week. As the sound of ringing buzzes in my ear, I stand from the couch and pace to the front window to peer outside. The media's numbers have halved the past week and a half, but their presence is still highly notable.

"Cleo," Dexter greets, proving he has my number stored in his phone. "How are you? Good? I hope you're calling to accept my offer?"

I wait a beat to ensure his interrogation is over before replying, "Hi, I am good; thank you for asking, and in regards to your offer, if your plus one is still available, I'll happily tick the box." My words come out in a flurry, spurred on by the nervous butterflies taking flight in my stomach.

"But just as friends. I'm not ready for anything more than a friendship right now," I clarify, wanting to ensure he doesn't mistake my acceptance of his olive branch as a date.

Dexter chuckles softly. "That's understandable. It's not every day you're dumped during a live broadcast, so I don't blame you for being turned off at the idea of dating again." Although his tone comes out playful, it doesn't stop his words from brutally stabbing my heart.

"So. . .umm . . ." I cringe at my inability to produce words. Dexter's laidback approach to my public humiliation has me a little stumped for a reply. "What time do you want me to meet you there?" I force out through the unease gripping my throat, silently asphyxiating me.

"I'll come pick you up around 6 PM," Dexter replies.

"Oh, no that's not necessary. You live in New York. I'll come to you. It will be easier this way."

"Come on, Cleo, the gas prices are astronomical at the moment, let alone the parking fees. Are you sure that's an expense you want the day before Christmas?"

My ego absorbs his brutal maiming without a smidge of hesitation. "Fine. I'll see you at 6." Stealing his chance to reply, I disconnect our call. *Okay, maybe my annoyance was late to the party.*

Riddled with guilt that I'm being a cow to a man who deserves nothing but my admiration and respect, I quickly send Dexter a message.

Me: *Sorry, bad reception. I'll see you Friday at 6. Thanks for the invite.*

Dexter replies not even two seconds later.

Dexter: *I look forward to making you smile. That is one asset void of a monetary value, but also the most priceless.*

His reply has my worry sitting on edge, but I shut it down, too overrun with hormones to decipher cryptic riddles.

Me: *I look forward to once again smiling, thank you for taking up the challenge.*

My phone buzzes, indicating another message, but I ignore it, my mind too busy unscrambling why I feel so guilty. I have nothing to feel guilty about, but there is no doubt that was the emotion thickening my blood during my phone call with Dexter.

"Done?" Lexi queries, glancing up at me.

I give her an unenthusiastic nod. "Yes. Now I just have to find something to wear and work out a way to convince my heart it isn't wrong to go out with the man who aided in ending my relationship." A loud grumble spills from my lips as I flop onto the couch. "Oh, god, this isn't a good idea, Lexi. Maybe I shouldn't go? This will look bad."

"Bad to who?" Lexi argues, straightening her spine. "You've seen the articles, Cleo. Marcus has been on more dates the past two weeks than he has the past two years."

I grab one of the cushions from the couch and mash it into her face, muffling her heartbreaking words. Although everything she says is true, I still don't want to hear it. I'd rather keep my head stuck in the sand than believe the rumors circulating about Marcus's new playboy status. The idea of him with previous subs was an uphill battle, but it is nothing compared to seeing him night after night on *E News* with a new beautiful woman on his arm.

"I swear on our parents' graves, if he attempts to have our little boo-boo call one of those bimbos Mommy, I'll cut his balls off," Lexi warms, nudging her head to the TV broadcast of an exclusive interview with a woman whom Marcus went on a date with last week.

My heart swells and painfully squeezes at the same time. I love that Lexi calls my baby "our little boo-boo." She has done it numerous times the past five days—even Jackson caught on to the trend. But the gouging sensation inflicting my heart is from her admission that another woman could be a part of my child's life. That wouldn't really happen, would it? Stepmothers and fathers only enter the equation if the child is an orphan, right?

Right. So why is a horribly bitter taste scorching the back of my throat?

"Oh no," I mumble, fighting to hold back the sludge in my stomach racing to my lips.

Realizing I have no chance of ignoring the ghastliness of Lexi's admission, I slap my hand over my mouth before I go running into the bathroom for the third time today.

"Do you have wet wipes and mints?" Lexi queries.

I stop rummaging through my tiny purse and peer up at her. "Why would I need either of those things?"

Lexi rolls her eyes before gathering breath mints from the vanity cabinet in the bathroom and wet wipes from under the sink. "You vomit a minimum three times a day, Cleo. Today you are only at two. Breath mints are essential."

I arch a brow. "And the wet wipes?"

"Who wants to dance with a girl with vomit on her chin?" A big shake hampers Lexi's tiny frame. At first I think it is caused by laughter, but I soon realize it is vileness. Lexi can't stand the word vomit, much less actual vomit.

"I need a bigger clutch," I mumble, glancing down at the tiny black sequin purse I'm holding.

Lexi nods her head in agreement while pacing to the clutches stacked in my closet. "What is he doing in here?" Lexi asks, twisting her body so I can see Mr. Bunny clutched in her hand.

"I don't know. I swear he has a mind of his own lately." I remove him from her grasp and place him back on his rightful spot on the shelf above my desk. The dust circle where his fluffy backside sits reveals he hardly moves from my shelf, but I've noticed him in weird locations the past two weeks.

Shrugging off my confusion as Jackson playing tricks on me, I help Lexi hunt for a clutch to match the dress I'm wearing to the Global Ten Media Christmas function. My pulse accelerates when she pulls out a plain black clutch from the very back of my closet. I shoved it in there, hiding it from the world as I wish I could my face. It is the purse I used at the fundraising gala I attended with Marcus.

"It's just an accessory, Cleo; it has no sentimental value whatsoever," Lexi assures my mortified expression.

"Here. Look." She clicks it open and yanks out all the crap hiding inside. Most is the standard accessories every girl has: lip gloss, compact powder, a few loose notes, tampons, and an emergency condom stash that is so outdated it expired two years ago.

"Guess you won't be needing these anymore." Lexi jeers, turning the clutch upside down to dump the dreaded products without having to touch them.

In the flurry of dumping my possessions, a burst of white captures our attention when it flutters haphazardly in the air. Our eyes follow a folded-up piece of paper as it slowly floats in the air, its pace so whimsical it has trance-like qualities.

When it lands on the ground, Lexi's eyes rocket to mine. "What's that?" she asks, her interest unmissable.

"I completely forgot about it," I admit, bending down to gather the item. "It's from Andy."

Lexi's brows stitch. "Andy? As in Andy who broke into my room when I was sleeping Andy?" she queries, her voice fretful. "The same Andy who broke into Marcus's house? What ever happened to him?"

I shrug. "I don't know. I never got an update. I'm assuming we'll be informed of his hearing date when his case goes to court, but other than that. . ." I stop talking, having no real explanation to give.

"What does the note say?" Lexi asks, her interest notable.

My lips quirk. "I never read it."

Lexi snatches the paper out of my hand before hotfooting it to the other side of the room. I don't bother chasing her. I can barely walk in my heels, let alone chase down my barefoot and more energetic sister.

My eyes swing to the side when Lexi sighs heavily.

"His phone number?" I ask. I've hardly dated the past four years, but I never have any trouble gaining a collection of phone numbers when I do go out.

"No," Lexi replies, shocking me. "It's some sort of riddle."

Peering down, I read the note.

The master commands. The submissive obeys.
Look closer, Cleo.
The people surrounding you aren't who you think they are.

There is an address for a property in East Village scribbled under the handwritten quote.

"That's not a riddle. I've heard that before." I stop talking, giving my brain time to summarize. The air brutally sucks from my lungs when reality dawns. "Richard said that to me in the hours leading to his death."

"Something like this?" Lexi only speaks three words, but her eyes aren't as reserved. They hammer me with questions so hard and fast I'm nearly knocked onto my ass.

I shake my head. "No. He said exactly that."

"What does it mean? Shian said Richard and Andy were as thick as thieves; do you think he is playing games? Or. . ." Lexi leaves her question open, hoping I can fill it in. I can't. I have no clue what this message means. I'm assuming the address at the bottom doesn't belong to either Richard or Andy, as they lived in the same apartment building in East Harlem, so I'm truly at a loss about what this means.

"Maybe you should cancel tonight. Something about this doesn't feel right," Lexi discloses.

Before I can reply, the sound of knocking booms into my room. I drop my eyes to my watch; it is three minutes to six.

"It's too late to cancel now," I mumble, grabbing the clutch from Lexi's grasp and harshly shoving my belongings inside.

Although my intuition is screaming as loudly as Lexi's, my curiosity is also piqued. With Global Ten's function being held in the financial district, with a little persuading, I may be able to convince Dexter to detour past the address on the note Andy handed me.

My fast strides out of my room are halted by Lexi seizing my wrist. No words spill from her mouth, but her eyes issue her doubts.

"I'll be fine," I assure her before wrapping her up in a big hug.

Chapter Twenty-Four

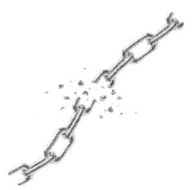

WITH TRAFFIC AT ITS ABSOLUTE WORST, MY REQUEST TO ALTER THE direction of our course is never relinquished by my tongue. We've been sitting in standstill traffic for nearly an hour. It is probably best Dexter hired a limousine company to transport us to the function, or I'm confident his patience would be wearing thin. Driving in New York is already a challenge, much less on Christmas Eve.

"No, thank you," I reply when Dexter offers me a drink from the small crystal bar tucked under the windowsill of the stretch limousine. My mouth is parched, and I'd love a drink, but considering any liquid in the bar is alcohol-based, my quenching my thirst must wait until we arrive at the Christmas party.

After Dexter fills his glass with a generous serving of whiskey, he sinks back into his chair, cautious not to spill any liquor on his expensive tailor-fitted suit. When I swung open my front door to greet Dexter, my eyes bugged out of my head. Compared to my simple satin long-sleeve dress and plain black pumps, Dexter was dressed to the nines in a tailored suit and bowtie. Mortified I'd mistaken the dress code, I rushed back into my room, hoping to glam up the bland design of my dress with a few intricate pieces of jewelry and a new take on my hairstyle.

Although time was against me, I wrangled my wavy locks into a twisted French braid that slides down the right side of my neck. Although Dexter's appearance still screams wealth, my hasty mini makeover compliments his sophistication.

"Do you know if Mr. Carson is attending tonight?" I aim to keep the hopefulness out of my voice. My attempts are borderline.

Dexter's brows bow high into his hairline. "Yes. Since he hasn't attended the past five years, a conscious effort was made to assure he was at tonight's event."

"A conscious effort? By whom?"

Dexter shrugs. "That's just the gossip around the water coolers."

"Any other gossip I've missed out on?" I twist to face him. Even though the main purpose of our date is to make contact with Mr. Carson, I don't want to be rude. Dexter has made an effort to impress me tonight, and it would be ill-mannered of me to pretend I haven't noticed.

"Hmm," Dexter murmurs, his voice giving the hint he guzzled his whiskey too quickly. It is raspy and thick, and if I am being totally honest, pulse-quickening. "Keira and Delilah no longer work at Global Ten.

"Oh." I'd like to say more, but my words are trapped in my throat.

"No one knows why or how; Keira just failed to turn up the Monday morning following. . ." He locks his eyes with me. ". . . you know."

Still unable to talk, I nod. He is referring to the night we kissed.

"And Delilah hasn't been seen since she was seconded to a secret assignment the start of last week. She didn't even pack her office. It is like she has vanished off the face of the planet."

My brows furrow. "She's probably torturing a whole new set of defenseless interns at another Global Ten office?" I don't know why my reply comes out sounding like a question. Delilah is the bane of my existence, but I'm still shocked by Dexter's nonchalant disclosure of her supposed disappearance.

"Did you know Keira was at the party the night we kissed?" Dexter queries, placing his empty glass on the bar.

I wait for him to refill his drink before answering, "Not at the start, but I spotted her as I was leaving."

"Figured as much," he murmurs under his breath before taking a sizeable gulp of the brown liquid inside. He screws up his face, unappreciative of the burn of liquor rolling down his throat. "I don't know what burns more: the whiskey or knowing you only kissed me to get back at him."

"Dexter. . .I . . . ah." I can't formulate words as every one I try to force out of my mouth is a lie. I did kiss him to get back at Marcus, but I never figured I'd be confronted by his honesty.

"Don't feel bad," Dexter demands, plonking his half-consumed whiskey on the bar. "I can think of much worse ways to be used. Hell, you're welcome to use me anytime you like."

I elbow him in the ribs when he waggles his brows excessively.

"I just hope you aren't seeing me in the same shady light you're seeing him. Our kiss might have added ammunition to the failure of your relationship, but that couldn't have been the only downfall." His voice softens at the end, a unique mix of confusion and regret.

"Our kiss didn't help, but there were a lot of misunderstandings before that," I admit before I can stop my words.

Dexter runs his fingers through his thick hair as he returns his eyes to mine. The unease in his gaze sets me on edge, but I hold my ground, acting like I am still the strong-willed Garcia my parents raised to me be.

"Can I speak freely?" Dexter asks, his tone forthright.

Appreciating him seeking permission, I reply, "Yes. Please."

"Marcus embarrassed you in front of millions of viewers, sat by and watched the media call you every vulgar name known to mankind, then paraded around town as if you were nothing more than a blip on his radar, yet, you still wear his trademark. Why? Did he knock your confidence so low you can't see how much you're worth, Cleo? Despite what you're thinking, you're better than this. You deserve better than *that*." He nudges his head to the chain link pendant curled around my neck.

My hand instinctively darts up to cover my pendant, protecting it from the harshness of his slurred words. Although everything he says is true, it doesn't make it any easier to hear.

"It's complicated," I murmur, using the same excuse my heart has argued with my brain over and over again the past two weeks.

The remainder of our trip is made in silence, our conversation as barren as the bottle of whiskey Dexter emptied during our two-hour trip. When we arrive at the gala, I force a smile onto my face before following Dexter out of the limousine. Thankfully, with Dexter attached to my side, it takes the paparazzi glancing in my direction three times before they realize who I am. By then, it's too late. Dexter and I have already entered the lobby where the Christmas function is being held, and they are trapped outside by the big burly bodyguards manning the doors.

A flurry of black in the corner of my eye gains my attention when Dexter moves through the crowd of people gawking at us. Although the stranger's glance is one of hundreds directed at me right now, my body is responding differently. His gaze seems familiar—*hauntingly familiar.*

While Dexter chitchats with a man and an elegantly dressed lady, my eyes scan the crowd, seeking the person who set my heart rate rocketing with a single glance. It takes me several moments to lock in on a razor-cut jawline concealed by a turned-up trenchcoat collar. I hold my breath when his head shifts in my direction. For the quickest second, time comes to a standstill. I'm certain I've seen that face before, only now it belongs to a ghost.

"I need to use the washroom," I advise Dexter as my eyes follow the black blur careening through the crowd as if he is panicked by my wide-eyed glare.

Dexter loosens his grip enough I can slip my hand out of his grasp, but not quite enough to not project his disappointment I'm fleeing his company so early. When his eyes lower to mine, a stabbing pain hits my chest. His eyes are teeming with remorse and silent pleas. They nick my heart, but don't diminish my naturally engrained inquisitiveness. My desire to hunt down the man mere moments from evading me is so strong, nothing could stop me—not even Marcus.

"I'll be right back," I assure Dexter, loathing how many people I've made feel terrible the past three months.

I wait for Dexter to reluctantly nod before dashing in the direction the suit-covered man went. My pace quickens when the man I'm chasing peers back at me, pinning me in place with his murky blue eyes. My frozen stance comes to an end when he darts down a concealed corridor at the edge of the hotel foyer. I take off after him, my fear overrun by curiosity. Even with a cap hanging low on his head, I'm certain I recognize those eyes.

When I reach the entrance of the eerily black corridor, I glance over my shoulder, back to the large gathering of people lingering in the foyer. My intuition is screaming at me to spin on my heels and return to Dexter, but no matter how loudly it pleads, my inquisitiveness reigns supreme.

Exhaling a deep breath, I step into the dingy and cramped space. My heart rate doubles when my poor vision locks in on a blob of black halfway down the hall.

"Richard?" I query, my voice equally scared and hopeful. "Is that you?"

Ignoring my interrogation, he shuffles further down the dingy corridor. The hiss of overworked boilers adds to the squealing in my ears as I cautiously step down the brick-lined corridor. Murmured voices sound over the creaking of old water pipes when I stop at a T intersection halfway down the corridor. I glance in three directions, unsure which way to go.

My head snaps to the side as my heart smashes against my ribs. Something just darted past the hallway on my right, scaring the living daylights out of me.

"Hello?" I call out, praying I'm not going to be front page news again tomorrow—its headline more horrendous than the ones I've endured the past two weeks. "Is anyone down here?"

My shouted questions stop the murmured voices in an instant while adding to the sweat slicking my skin. I pivot on my heels, preparing to leave, too paralyzed by the fear scorching my veins to continue my mission. Just before I exit, I spot a man halfway down the corridor wearing a black trenchcoat. I push off my feet and race down the hall before my brain can cite an objection.

"Richard," I mumble in disbelief as I grip the man's shoulder and spin him around to face me.

I take a step back, frightened. The man I've approached isn't Richard. It is Mr. Carson.

"Cleo?" I don't know why, but his greeting sounds like a question. "What are you doing down here?"

"Oh. Um. I was looking for a friend. Have you see anyone else down here?" When the nape on my neck prickles, I straighten my spine and take a step back, moving out of Mr. Carson's hold. When I leaped in fright, his hands must have shot out to stop me from falling, otherwise what other reason would he have for holding me?

"No, there isn't anyone else down here. You shouldn't be down here either, Cleo. It isn't safe." Not giving me a chance to reply, he places his hand on the curve of my lower back and directs me toward the foyer. The way he moves us through the dimly lit corridors with ease exposes he is familiar with the floorplan of this establishment.

"Is this one of your properties?" I inwardly gag, hating my obsessive need to know everything.

"Yes," Mr. Carson answers, his tone direct and to the point.

"That must be nice."

He drops massively dilated eyes to mine, seeking silent clarification on my riddled statement.

"Having enough money to buy half of New York," I answer.

He smirks. "Not quite half, but I'm getting there."

"By forcing people out of their homes they have lived in their entire lives? Who said chivalry was dead?" My voice is laced with unusual bitchiness.

Mr. Carson's long strides come to an immediate halt. The glare he directs at me would make grown men shiver in their boots, but I hold my ground. All my nerves were so rattled out of me while chasing ghosts down dingy corridors that I'm fearless.

"What are you talking about?" Mr. Carson queries.

"Where shall I start?" I murmur, tapping my finger on my pursed lips. "The fact you didn't keep your pledge to pay for my sister's health and schooling for the remainder of her life? Or the part about how you increase your bank balance by swindling your ex-employees out of their rightful entitlements?"

"A check for your sister's full tuition was mailed over a month ago. I addressed the envelope myself," he replies, his tone giving no indication of deceit. "And in regards to your entitlements, your salary was paid this morning, along with the other twenty-eight thousand employees I pay every week."

"Unless some money-hungry dust bunnies came in and cleared out my account, both this week and last week's salaries were not deposited into my bank account." If I wasn't being swarmed by embarrassment, I'd not hesitate to whip out my phone to show him how dire my bank account is. It is the lowest it's ever been.

When Mr. Carson glares at me with confusion etched over his face, I push aside my embarrassment and hunt for my phone in my clutch.

"I don't need proof," Mr. Carson assures me, stopping my manic rummaging by placing his hand over mine. "Your eyes are the only proof I need."

I snap my clutch back together, hoist it under my arm, then lift my eyes to Mr. Carson, using my soul-baring eyes to my advantage. Tears prick in my eyes when he nods before guiding me into an office at the end of the hall so he can secure a checkbook from the top drawer. I watch him in silence, too stunned to do or say anything. He writes a check for ten thousand dollars before handing it to me.

"That's way too much. My weekly salary is only—"

"We'll work out the details properly Monday morning. Until then, take that as collateral and my word as your guarantee. I've never backed down from a pledge. I am a man of my word, so you can be assured I'll find out who caused this error, and I'll personally fix it," he promises, staring straight into my eyes.

Incapable of speaking for the fear of crying, I store the check in my clutch, dip my chin in thanks, then spin on my heels. I may have shamefully bombarded him outside of working hours, but my pride is too great to allow him to see my tears.

"And Cleo?"

I force a neutral expression on my face before cranking my neck back to peer at him.

"I didn't get to the position I am in by sitting on a perch and shitting on those below me. I used to be one of those unknowns on the bottom rung, so I understand the struggle it takes to reach the top." I smile when some of his Jersey boy heritage rings true in his voice. "My offer from weeks ago is still valid. I need people like you to bring Global Ten back to its glory days."

I gently shake my head, knowing no amount of agony will ever have me working for a company that so hideously invades people's right to privacy.

Spotting my disagreeing gesture, Mr. Carson says, "I don't need an immediate answer, Cleo. Think about it over the weekend, a week, a month. Take as much time as you need. My offer will remain as long as it takes for you to realize mistakes were made, but I'm doing everything in my power to fix them."

"Okay," I agree, accepting his guarantee with the confidence his eyes are relaying. "I'll consider your offer if you'll consider one of my own."

Mr. Carson stores his check book in the drawer before pacing around the desk to stand in front of me. "Hit me with it," he says, crossing his arms over his broad chest.

"Talk to your niece."

He balks as his pupils dilate to the size of dimes.

"I don't know why you are keeping your lineage a secret, but I have a feeling even you don't know the entire story. Any good journalist will tell you there is only one way to get answers—"

"By asking questions," we say in unison.

"Exactly," I confirm, nodding. "I know the importance of protecting your family, but there comes a point where you need to make sure the people you're protecting are being shielded for the right reason. I saw the photos of Keira. I understand how hard they would have been for you to see. But the voice of the majority is no proof of justice."

With that, I exit his office, my steps more spirited than the ones I took earlier.

Chapter Twenty-Five

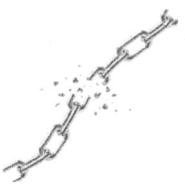

NEEDING A FEW MOMENTS TO SETTLE MY ERRATIC HEART, I slip
into the women's restroom at the side of the foyer. With most of the
guests in the main ballroom, a peaceful silence has fallen over the
elegant space. I do my business in one of the vacant stalls before
heading to the sink to wash my hands. Thankfully, this time I'm not
bombarded by any unwelcomed guests.

As I wash my hands in the sink, I take in the way the little secret
nestled safely in my womb has added to the rosiness of my cheeks. My
eyes are wide and bright, spurred on by both excitement and fear; and
my hair is extra glossy thanks to the overload of vitamins Jackson has
been feeding me the past week. Although my insides feel like they are
in a million pieces, my outside appearance successfully conceals their
shattered remains.

After tucking a few strands of rogue hairs back into my braid, I
trail my fingers down my cheek, stopping once they reach the diamond
pendant sitting in the little groove of my neck. While I stare at the
necklace, I recall what Dexter said in the limousine. Although his
sneered statement hurt to hear, every word he grinded out was true.
I've been slaughtered in the media, called names I'll never speak. I lost

my job, my freedom, and my right to privacy the instant Marcus ridiculed me in front of not only millions of viewers, but his fans and bandmates as well, yet I'm still wearing a gift that symbolizes I am his. This needs to stop—the pain, the anger, the remorse—it all needs to stop.

I feel the shudder of my hands all the way up my arms when I slide them around my neck to release the white gold latch on my nape. I exhale deeply when my necklace descends down my chest, puddling around the neckline of my dress. Gathering the thin chain in my grasp, I fist it tightly before placing it in the hidden nook of my clutch.

I peer back at the mirror, feeling oddly naked. The necklace was thin, but its significance was immense. "You've got this," I declare to the stranger staring back at me.

I hold my head high as I weave through the throng of people mingling in the opulent space. My ruse of using the washroom took longer than I anticipated, and the mood of the crowd has greatly improved since I left. Not only is alcohol enticing a carefree sentiment amongst the cheerful group, so is the beloved Christmas bonus disbursed in every Christmas card Mr. Carson awards. From the gleaming smiles of numerous partygoers, this year's bonus must have vastly improved over last year's.

I find Dexter sitting at a bar at the side of the dance floor. His expensive suit jacket has been removed, and his bowtie is draped around his slumped shoulders. I quicken my pace, eager to discover what has caused his low composure.

"Hey. Sorry it took me so long. I got lost." I don't know why I lie. It just came out of my mouth before I could stop it.

"Cleo?" Dexter peers at me like I am a ghost. I understand the look he is giving me as I just wasted twenty minutes I'll never get back chasing a ghost. Perhaps that is why I lied to Dexter? As it wasn't an utter lie? I did get lost—chasing pipedreams. "I thought you'd left. That I pushed you too hard, and you decided to leave."

"No," I reply, shaking my head. I place my clutch on the bar before facing him. "What you said hurt, but it was true. See?" I brush my hand down my naked neck.

The dark gleam in Dexter's eyes clears away as he drinks in my bare neck. "It's gone," he murmurs, running the backs of his fingers down my neck.

"Yes," I answer, barely choking back a sob.

Dexter's glassy gaze bounces between mine. "You're free of him!"

It is the fight of my life not to lower my hand to the non-existent bump in my stomach. What Dexter said is a lie. My baby guarantees I'll never be fully free of Marcus. But with time, and assistance from my family and friends, I'll eventually be okay with that. *I hope.*

"I'm so proud of you, Cleo."

When Dexter leans in to place a kiss on my lips, I crank my neck to the side, forcing his lips to land on my cheek. Dexter doesn't protest my snub of his contact. I don't know if it is because he's encircled by women fluttering their excessively long lashes and pursing their lips as they strive for his attention, or because he is too drunk to notice it. Either way, I'm glad to have dodged another bullet directed at me tonight.

"Come on, we better work off some of this whiskey lacing your veins before you end up in bed with Meeka from Classifieds," I mumble, helping Dexter from his chair.

"What's wrong with Meeka?" Dexter answers, winking suggestively at Meeka, who is giving him kissy gaga faces.

I curl my arm around Dexter's waist and guide him to the dance floor. My initial thoughts about his intoxication ring true when he sways and stumbles with every step we take. "One, she's married. Two, she's married. And, three—"

"She's married?" Dexter chimes in.

"Bingo."

Dexter laughs, forcing the flock of women circling him to hover closer.

"If you laugh again, you're on your own, Mister."

Dexter hiccups. "Mister, hey? I like the sound of that."

It takes nearly an hour of dancing before the excessive alcohol Dexter consumed burns off. You'd think dancing someone back to sobriety would be a torturous endeavor, but it has actually been a lot of fun. For once, I just let go. I shimmy and shake my caboose without a concern in the world, realizing that no matter what I do, or how well I behave, it won't change people's opinions of me.

Even before I precariously tiptoed into the world of BDSM, I was ridiculed and mocked by people I thought were better than me. Only now do I know that nothing will alter people's desires to ridicule one another. We live in a world full of judgmental people who speak before they consider how their mockery will be absorbed by the person they are taunting. It is unfortunate, but true.

"I need a drink," I shout, ensuring Dexter can hear me over the music booming out of the speakers hanging above our heads.

Dexter's eyes bounce between mine. "Do you want me to come with you?"

"No, I'll be fine. Do you want some water?" I query.

When he cups his ear, signaling he can't hear me, I move in closer. "Do you want some water?"

"I'd rather have whiskey, but if water is all you're offering, I guess I'll take it." His husky voice sends a flurry of goosebumps racing to the surface of my skin. Although his lips brushed the shell of my ear with every word he spoke, I'm still shocked by my body's response. My body has only ever reacted like this with one man—that man isn't Dexter.

Since I'm numb and in a trance of confusion, I don't notice the rapid advancement of Dexter's lips until it is too late. His kiss is brief —only swift enough for his tongue to slide halfway across my mouth— but long enough to consume me with horrid grief.

Yanking back, I muster a fake smile on my now whiskey-scented lips. "Water. I'll be straight back."

I pivot on my heels. Not trusting my stomach, which is flipping with unwarranted guilt, I race for the washroom instead of the bar. When my black pumps step off the makeshift floor, the reasoning behind my body's peculiar response to Dexter's closeness comes to fruition. Marcus is standing at the edge of the dance floor with his heavy-hooded gaze firmly rapt on me. He is wearing an impeccably tailored suit that showcases every perfect ridge of his mouthwatering body. The dark circles around his alluring eyes display his sleep the past two weeks has been as lacking as mine, but he is still the most handsome man I've ever seen.

My brain signals for me to look away before I get stuck in a trance by his tempting eyes, but it's too late. I'm frozen, dazed by the thick sentiment firing the air with heat. The tension bristling between us is so hot, it hisses and crackles over the loud roar of guests mingling between us. It switches my flipping-with-unease stomach to somer-saulting-with-excitement.

I can't believe even after weeks of absence, the attraction between us is still so intense. It feels like we stepped back in time, back to the night we officially met. God—what I'd give to go back to that day. To forget the furious storm raging between us—to fix the mistakes I made.

The pleas to forget the world around us fall on deaf ears when a perfectly polished blonde intimately drapes her arm over Marcus's broad shoulders—a blonde who looks remarkably identical to Keira in every way. When Keira snootily glances into my eyes while whispering in Marcus's ear, I grit my teeth, then spin to face the opposite direc-tion. She looks so cozy with him, like they are perfect for one another.

After breathing out my despair, I head back to Dexter. The anger boiling my blood has made quick work of the nausea twisting my stom-ach, meaning I no longer need to use the washroom.

"We need to leave," I tell Dexter, stopping at his side.

Dexter stops dancing with a curvy brunette. The angry glare she is directing at me extinguishes when I say, "I need to leave. Thank you for tonight. I'll call you tomorrow."

Before I get two steps away, Dexter grips my elbow and pulls me backward. The more his worried gaze roams my face, the closer his brows stitch together. Seemingly reading the blatant fury pumping out of me for what it is, he lifts his eyes in the direction I came from. His jaw gains a quiver when he spots the cause of my sudden fury.

Dexter returns his eyes to me. "If you leave now, you're letting them win."

"No," I deny, shaking my head. "If I leave now, I'm letting them live," I snarl through clenched teeth.

The unnamed brunette waiting impatiently for the return of

Dexter's attention snickers over my bitchy remark. I'm glad she can see the humor in my situation. I am anything but amused.

A girly squeal topples from my lips when Dexter bands his arms around my back and unexpectedly dips me. Dizziness clusters in my brain just as quickly as confusion clouds me.

He flips me back up while saying, "You want him to feel what you are feeling? Give him a taste of his own medicine."

Dexter plasters his body to mine, allowing me to feel every inch of him—*every inch*. He draws me in so vigorously, we share the same breath. He grinds his pelvis against mine, his moves as surprisingly fluid as his fighting skills. Feeling the heat of Marcus's gaze scorching my skin, I close my eyes and meet Dexter's dance moves step for step. We move together glibly, like two people who know each other intimately well.

I don't know how much time passes before I lose the heat of Marcus's gaze. It is long enough for my thirst to become dire, but not long enough for my anger to be fully subdued. When my eyes slowly flutter open, I inconspicuously scan them around my surroundings. Marcus is nowhere in sight.

My eyes stray back to Dexter. "If I didn't know any better, I'd swear you've played these games before."

Dexter doesn't agree or dismiss my claims; he merely smirks before guiding me off the dance floor so I can satiate my parched throat. While unscrewing a bottle of water, Dexter peers past my shoulder. The color of his overheated cheeks drains to the soles of his shoes as his throat works hard to swallow. I glance over my shoulder, seeking the person who has caused his gaunt appearance. My first thought is it must be Marcus, but I soon realize that Dexter's peacock feathers fan out whenever Marcus is in his presence—they don't cower away.

Unable to spot the cause of Dexter's worry, I drift my heavy-lidded gaze back to him. I forgot how tiring dancing can be. I'm truly exhausted. Dexter's eyes frolic between mine for several moments before he asks, "Will you be okay if I leave you here for a minute? I've just seen someone from a past life I'd like to buy a drink for."

"Sure," I reply, placing my half-guzzled bottle of water on the counter.

Relieved by my agreeing gesture, Dexter presses a quick kiss to my cheek before ambling in the direction he was looking. When I return my baffled gaze to the bar, I notice Dexter has left his wallet on the counter.

"Dexter, you forgot your wallet." I twist my torso to face him. I can't pinpoint him in the sea of black. "It's a little hard to buy someone a drink without any money," I mumble to myself.

After using my crumpled-up twenty-dollar note to pay for my and Dexter's water, I push off my feet and head in the direction he went. There are only two bars in the room, so he couldn't have gone far.

My unsteady pace grows more wobbly when my elbow is suddenly clasped and I'm dragged into a room concealed by a thick curtain. My screams are cut off when a hand clamps over my gaped mouth, stealing my pleas for help. As quickly as my panic rises, so does my anger. Not only do I recognize the scent of the man accosting me, my body is also activating with primitive awareness of its mate. *Marcus.*

I attempt to spin around to face him. His clutch on my hips firms, foiling my endeavor. My spine straightens when he burrows his nose into my hair and inhales deeply.

"God, I've missed your smell," he mutters ever so quietly.

The scent of hard liquor filters through my nose, displaying he is heavily intoxicated.

"Let me go," I sneer, my words choppy, clogged by the inane lust curled around my throat.

I'm appalled by my body's reaction to his meekest touch. He is only conversing with me as he is drunk, yet I'm clammy and hot, and don't even get me started on the improper thoughts running through my mind.

Marcus complies with my request by loosening his grip on my right hip, but instead of dropping his hand to his side, he slides it up the planes of my quivering stomach before cupping it around my breast. My disloyal nipples bud, adoring his touch after weeks of absence.

"Don't." My one word is barely audible since it was forced out of my mouth against my body's wishes.

"You know what to say if you truly want me to stop," Marcus

murmurs into my ear before he places a peppering of kisses down my neck.

"I don't need a safe word, remember? I'm not your sub."

My knees shake when Marcus rolls my nipple between his thumb and index finger. His pinch isn't overly painful, but my body responds as if it is. When he twists them for a second time, this time more firmly than the first, my clutch and Dexter's wallet falls to the floor with a clatter.

"Always so responsive," Marcus mutters, revealing he is aware of my body's silent pleasure in his meekest touch.

As his fingers uncoil the tight weaves of my braid, his lips glide down my exposed neck. My core spasms when he sinks his teeth ever so slowly into my shoulder. My nostrils flare as I fight with all my might not to give any indication to the fire raging out of control in my womb. I can't believe how treasonous my body is. I am boiling with unbridled anger and lust at the same time. *How is that even possible?*

I yank away from Marcus, sickened that I've become so lust-crazed I've lost all my morals. Marcus splays his hand across my stomach and yanks me back. I shamefully moan when our rough collision allows me to feel how aroused he is. His cock is thick and long, straining against the zipper of his trousers, dying to break free.

"You seem to have a dilemma. Do you want me to fetch Keira for you?" I viciously snarl, my words doused with so much jealousy they are drowning in it.

"Why would I want Keira when everything I need is right in front of me?" My breathing turns manic when his hand splayed on my left hip drops to my aching sex. "You're saturated, and no matter what you say, I know every drop of this goodness is for me. Your pussy doesn't ache with need when he grinds up against it; your neck doesn't flush when his lips brush past it, and your heart doesn't race at triple the speed when he walks into the room. Those prompts of your body belong to me. They've always belonged to me. *They'll always belong to me.*" He growls out his last sentence in a thick and raspy groan.

I remain quiet, incapable of denying his egotistical remark since every word he spoke was true. Even when Dexter kissed me, my body didn't react with a tenth of the intensity it did when Marcus clutched my elbow. Marcus owns my body—and he knows it.

"Stop," I plead through a quiver when he slips my panties to the side so he can run his finger through the folds of my soaked sex.

"No," Marcus mutters into my ear, his one word sharp and precise. "That's not the right word."

A wave of excitement rolls over my stomach when he slips his finger inside me. I softly mew, overwhelmed and heightened beyond belief. My pussy ripples around his stationary digit, encouraging the continued defiance of my adulterous body.

"Tell me what you want, Cleo," Marcus commands. His hot breath hitting my neck causes a smattering of goosebumps to form in its wake.

I remain quiet, too conflicted to form a response. After the two weeks I've endured, I should be demanding for him to release me from his clutch this instant. I should be marching out of this room and announcing I'm perfectly fine living my life without him in it. I should be doing anything but whispering, "I want you."

Marcus growls, pleased by my response. His husky groan sends my libido into overdrive. I'm panting and hot, crazed by an emotion like no other: the desire to be loved.

A cluster of dizziness rushes to my head, making me giddy, when Marcus suddenly spins me around. Any concerns of me crashing to the ground are a forgotten memory when he cups his hands around my thighs to band my legs around his waist. My back braces against one of the many shelves lining the small room we are cavorting in. Leaning me back, he lowers the zipper of his trousers.

While Marcus frees his hard cock from his trousers, I pry open the buttons of his dress shirt to expose the rippled abs and firm pecs I've missed ogling the past two weeks. Our movements are frantic—almost possessive. I honestly feel like I'm drunk, even though I haven't had a drop of alcohol in weeks.

With his eyes locked on mine, Marcus snaps my panties off my body and pockets them in his trousers, which are hanging dangerously off his hips. I throw my head back and moan in delight when he impales me with one ardent thrust. The pain of taking a man his size without preparation is excruciating, but I welcome the pain—I relish it.

I claw at his back with my nails as he pumps in and out of me at a furious speed. My pussy adores every crazed thrust, meeting him grind for grind. I use the sturdy shelving as a tether to keep me upright so I can slam down on his barely exposed cock over and over again. We are fucking so manically, industrial products topple off the shelves I'm braced against, landing around Marcus's feet.

Marcus rolls his hips with every precise thrust of his magnificent cock, ensuring his pelvic bone stimulates my throbbing-with-desire clit. The sensation is overwhelming—unlike anything I've experienced. I moan on repeat, incapable of caring if anyone can hear me. I've wanted this for weeks, so I'm not going to let anything stop me from cherishing every perfect sound.

A brutal tidal wave crests at my stomach before plunging into my tightened coil. I can feel my orgasm growing, and growing, and growing until it reaches a point I can no longer hold it back.

"Give it to me, Cleo," Marcus demands, showing he is as intuitive with my body as ever.

My eyes snap shut as I quiver and shake. I grunt a string of indecipherable words, loving that we've reached this stage of our exchange without any additional stimulation needed. When the exhausting shudders wreaking havoc with my body fade, I tighten the walls of my vagina around Marcus's densely veined cock, begging for the heat of his spawn, wanting him as unraveled as me.

Marcus thrusts into me another four times before answering the silent pleas of my body. He stills as the hotness of his cum roars out of him in raring spurts. With his eyes tightly shut, he growls my name in a feral grunt, pushing me into my second climax—this one more powerful than the first. I clench the walls of my pussy around him, graciously milking every drop of his cum as I shout his name on repeat.

After coating the walls of my throbbing sex with his cum, Marcus opens and locks his eyes with me. He rests his sweat-drenched forehead on mine as his beautifully tormented gaze bounces between my lust-crammed eyes. After silently reviving my heart with nothing more than an amorous glance, he carefully places me back on my feet. I brace against the shelves since my legs are wobbling like Jell-O on a plate. We remain quiet for several moments, struggling to regain our breath.

After curling a piece of my wild hair around his finger, Marcus bends down to gather his trousers, which are furled around his shoe-covered feet. My bottom lip slumps into a pout when he tucks his cock, still firm and glistening with my arousal, back into his boxer shorts. Air snags in my throat when he returns his eyes to me; they appear more haunted than mere minutes ago. I pant, panicked he is already regretting his decision.

My knees curve inwards as his index finger gathers the moisture my full-to-the-brim pussy couldn't contain. With his wide gaze dancing between the hum of activity outside and me, he drags his cum-covered finger across my neck. I remain still, motionless and in shock when he follows the same routine another two times.

Once his cum is smeared in the exact position my diamond collar used to sit, Marcus locks his dark gaze with mine. My heart breaks from the desolate look in his eyes. He appears truly broken. I hate that our exchange has filled him with remorse when all I'm feeling is euphoria.

His sweet breath fans my lips when he mutters, "This is one collar he'll never be able to remove. Even if he can't see it, he will smell it."

After one last prolonged glance of my flushed and disheveled appearance, Marcus spins on his heels and stalks to the door.

"Marcus?" I ask, dazed.

He acts like he doesn't hear me as he continues his trek without pause. His long strides have him crossing the room in two heart-thrashing seconds. I stand frozen, unmoving and unspeaking. My muted stance doesn't last long. Only as long as it takes for my anger to steamroll back in. Who does he think he is that he can treat me in such a way? I'm not a worthless whore he can dispose of like trash. I'm going to be the mother of his child, for crying out loud.

Fuming with out-of-control rage, I grab one of the many toilet paper rolls knocked down during our exchange and peg it at Marcus's rapidly retreating frame. "I hate you!" I scream, my voice hoarse from my previous erotic cries.

I continue throwing insult after insult at him, telling him I don't need him in my life, and I never want to see him again. Every word I scream is a lie, but I'm praying one will nick his gigantic ego enough to force him to retaliate.

None of them work. He just exits the room without so much as a sideways glance in my direction. Then I slump to the ground and cry.

Chapter Twenty-Six

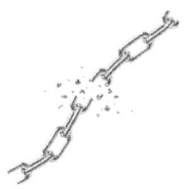

My HAND FURIOUSLY SCRAPES ACROSS MY CHEEK TO GATHER MY tears when the clunk of a lock sliding out of place booms into my ears. I still as my body seeks signs of the trespasser's identity interrupting my private sulk. Failing to hear any signs, I lift my eyes from the ground to see Dexter is entering the room. His brows furrow, and his lips quirk when he spots me sitting on the ground.

"Are you okay, Cleo?" he queries, his voice rife with suspicion.

I rise from the ground, my legs still shaky from the mind-hazing climax I endured minutes ago. The squares of toilet paper I used to wipe some of Marcus's cum off my neck drop to the floor like feathers floating in a warm summer breeze. "Um. Yeah. I just needed a minute."

Dexter remains quiet. He doesn't need to speak for me to know what he is thinking, though. The room reeks of sweaty, lust-fueled sex. It is so pungent, even if Marcus hadn't smeared his cum on my neck, I'm confident Dexter would still know what occupied our hour apart.

Embarrassed by him catching me getting down and dirty in a storage room, I tuck my chin in close to my chest, not just hiding my flaming red cheeks from Dexter, but my grossly collared neck I was only halfway through cleaning up when he arrived. My slumped posture has me catching sight of my purse and Dexter's wallet dumped in the middle of the room.

"Let me," Dexter says when I bob down to gather the articles off the floor.

He swoops down and collects the items before a syllable can escape my lips. "Thanks," I murmur when he hands me my clutch.

My brows stitch when his hand rummages through his wallet, as if he wants to assure nothing is out of place.

"I didn't touch anything," I assure him, equally shocked and appalled he'd think I'd steal from him. I may have been close to homeless before bumping into Mr. Carson, but I'd never resort to such levels of stealing just to put food on the table. There is desperate, then there is *desperate*. I'm still on the first step of desperate.

"It's not you I'm worried about," Dexter mutters under his breath, his words so soft I'm not sure he wanted me to hear them.

Happy his wallet is in its original condition, he slides it into the pocket of his trousers. His change in position conveys even more wariness.

"I take it the person you wanted to buy a drink for was a woman?" I ask, my voice smeared with relief that I'm not the only one who struggled to be respectful in public. Dexter has a large red smear on the collar of his dress shirt. If my hunch is right, it appears to be vibrant red lipstick. For how high on his collar it is, it could have only been put there one way.

Dexter's wide, confused eyes bounce between mine for several heart-clutching seconds before he shrugs, indicating he is unaware what my question refers to. I'm not buying his innocent act. His pupils expanded to the size of saucers the instant I insensitively probed, plus the quiver in his jaw tripled.

"The lipstick on your collar? Unless Meeka cornered you unaware, I can't think of another way that mark could have gotten there." I waggle my brows, happy to use his gasping expression to detract from the awkwardness of him finding me sitting on the ground bawling in a storage room in the middle of Christmas Eve celebrations.

Dexter's cheeks turn a hue of pink as his hand darts up to his neck-line. When his fingers immediately graze the area I am referring to, my assumption is proven dead on point. "It was an interesting opportunity I'd be a fool not to take advantage of," he murmurs, his tone laced with innuendo.

Stealing my chance to chastise him further, he bands his arm around my sweat-drenched back and guides me out of the storage room. I flinch, expecting him to react to the sticky mess on my body. My worry is unwarranted. He doesn't even notice my change in hairstyle, much less that every inch of my skin smells like Marcus. That probably has to do with the fact his own skin is a sweaty, sticky mess.

My long strides out of the storage room come to a dead halt when my eyes lock in on a pair of alluring green eyes across the room. Just like earlier tonight, Marcus doesn't hide his skin-roasting glance. He just stares at me, unashamed and without remorse. While Keira blubbers nonstop in his ear, he sips on a glass of whiskey. My throat feels scratchy when his other hand slides into his trouser pocket—the same pocket he stuffed my shredded panties in. I can tell the exact moment his fingertips graze the damp material, as his nostrils flare, and the lust-incited gleam in his eyes doubles.

Sickened that he is thinking of me while he has Keira plastered at his side, I break out of Dexter's hold and head for the door. I can't handle this anymore. My hormones are too out of whack to continue with this rollercoaster ride. I *want* to get off. I *need* to get off. I thought I was strong enough to handle this, but I'm not. Marcus doesn't just rule my body, he rules my heart as well, and every day I spend without him shrivels it more and more. If I don't stop this crazy ride soon, there isn't going to be any of me left to love. Our baby deserves better than a heartless mother. *My* baby deserves the world, so if I must cut ties with its father to give him or her that, so be it. Just like Lexi, I'll do everything in my power to protect my baby. Even denying my heart its greatest wish.

"Cleo, wait!" Dexter shouts, following me onto the sidewalk. "He is playing games with you, and you are letting him win."

I angrily wipe at the tears streaming down my face, loathing that they are making me look weak. Once all my tears are cleared away, I spin around to face Dexter. "I'm not letting him win. I'm forfeiting the game. It's different."

"No, it's not. You're giving him all the power, letting him play you like a pawn."

I viciously shake my head. "No, I *gave* him all the power. Now I'm taking it back."

"Until he corners you in another storage closet for a cheap fuck," Dexter roars, the viciousness of his words shocking me.

My nostrils flare as my eyes rocket to Dexter. "Until you've walked a day in my shoes, you have no right to judge me. That was *not* fucking—"

"Then what was it?" Dexter interrupts as his wild eyes dance between mine. "Because you sure as hell look like you've just been fucked. Real classy, Cleo. Arrive at an event with one guy to wander off and fuck another."

"Oh, how convenient for your morals to arrive now. Where were they when you were guzzling down whiskey like it was water? Or when you got lipstick on your shirt?!"

The hushed whispers of those around us advise that our little spectacle is gaining us unwanted attention, but unable to back down without having the last word, I take a step closer to Dexter and sneer, "It is not classed as fucking when it is with someone you love."

Dexter snarls, bearing teeth. "He treats you like a whore. That's not love, Cleo. That's treating you how you're acting."

"Whatever," I immaturely retaliate, flicking off his cruel comment as if it is a piece of lint. Nothing he could say will pain my heart any more than its already hurting. "Maybe one day you will understand the difference between fucking and love. Until then, stick to what you know, Dexter. As a man who won't date women with a certain hair color shouldn't be giving relationship advice. "

When I spin on my heels, Dexter grabs my wrists and drags me back. Air whizzes through my gaped lips when he yanks me into his raging-with-anger body. If it weren't for our hands stuck between us, we would be plastered together even closer than we were when dancing.

"I already know the difference between fucking and love. But since I'm foolishly chasing a woman who can't see her worth, I have to sit by and watch her make mistake after stupid mistake."

My eyes bounce between Dexter's as shock makes itself known. Although he didn't directly name names, his blazing eyes tell the entire story. He wants me.

"Dexter. . . I. . ." Of all the times for words to fail me, I wish now wasn't the time. "I'm sorry. I like you, but we will never be a couple—"

"Why?" Dexter interrupts, his anger growing. "Because I'm not a billionaire rock star with a fucked-up obsession with kink? Or because I don't treat you like a whore? What the fuck has he given you that I can't?"

My lips twitch, but I remain quiet. I can barely breathe, let alone speak. I've never been confronted with such a furious glance as the one Dexter is giving me. Not even when I was assaulted in the alleyway months ago.

"Give me a reason, Cleo! One fucking thing he's given you that I can't, and I'll drop my entire campaign. I'll walk away, knowing the better man won," Dexter yells, sending his loud voice roaring into the eerie quiet.

"A baby," I murmur before I can stop my words. "He gave me a baby."

Dexter balks but remains as quiet as a monk on a vow of silence. I would have assumed he missed my snapped comment if he wasn't clenching his fists opened and closed.

"You're pregnant?" Dexter queries, his tone high. "With *his* baby?" His voice sounds disgusted when he sneers "his."

Before a syllable is fired off my tongue, I'm slammed with a barrage of personal questions. I'm not just talking about a handful of Global Ten Media employees assuming we are a prime example of an office romp gone wrong; I'm talking about the dozen or so paparazzi absorbing and categorizing my every move.

"Did she say 'baby?' He gave her a baby?"

"Is the baby Marcus Everett's?"

"Can you repeat your pregnancy confirmation louder?"

"Cleo, would you like to confirm reports you are the reason for Rise Up's latest world tour cancellation?"

Ignoring the screamed questions being thrown at me left, right and center, I lock my eyes with Dexter's brimming-with-disappointment eyes. "I'm sorry," is all I murmur before pushing through the throng of paparazzi cramming the sidewalk to signal for a taxi. Thankfully, one pulls to the curb almost immediately, saving me from the onslaught of painful elbow jabs and even more probing questions.

"Are you famous?" the driver asks when I slide into the backseat and beg for him to go.

"No, just a case of mistaken identity," I assure him before connecting my pleading eyes with his in the rearview mirror. "Please go."

The gentleman's eyes glisten, then he pulls away from the curb. "I'll still get your signature just in case," he murmurs before throwing a used napkin and pen over the partition.

My scribbled signature didn't save me the exorbitant fee for the cab ride from New York to my home in Montclair. If I didn't catch sight of Mr. Carson's handwritten check in my purse while rummaging for a non-maxed out credit card, I might have cried when the driver announced the fee.

"Thank you," I say to the driver, paying his tip with the last of the crumpled-up bills in my purse.

He smiles softly before unlatching the locks. Although annoyed at his belief I was going to stiff him on his fare, I can also understand his hesitation. I spent the entire trip with my head resting on the chilly window while peering out at the starless sky. With my mind in a state of panic on how I'm going to dodge the latest scandal engulfing me, the expression on my face no doubt displayed my desire to flee.

I can't believe I blubbered out my news like that. If it isn't bad enough I've shared my pregnancy with everyone before Marcus, I did it in front of a group of reporters. I'm not only going to be slain by the media, but the diehard Rise Up fans as well. They already hate me after watching the video of Marcus and Dexter fighting. There are even shirts being sold in local stores emblazoned with "I wouldn't kiss Cleo for a million dollars" or "Who said pirating was the demise of music? It was a woman named Cleo." Now they will hunt for blood. It is my fault, though. If I had just kept my mouth shut, none of this would be happening.

I take a deep breath, mentally preparing for my second run through the shards of hell before cranking open the taxi door. Although the media has been camped out on my lawn the past two weeks, their presence has tripled from when I left earlier this evening. Clearly, gossip circulates even more quickly than a taxi ride from Manhattan to Montclair.

The questions thrown at me are oddly similar to the ones in New York, but instead of asking me to repeat my confirmation, they are requesting for me to confirm the rumors that Marcus is denying the paternity of our baby.

I keep my head down and my lips clamped shut as I struggle to push my way through the media. How can this be legal? They are trespassing on private property, yet when I called the police to complain, I was treated as if I were the criminal.

Their crushing onslaught continues until I enter the foyer of my home. Taking a minute to clear my nerves, I lean my back on the entranceway door and suck in lung-filling gulps of air. I pretend the wetness glistening my cheeks is sweat from the blinding paparazzi lights scorching my skin as I made the trek from the sidewalk to my front porch.

My heart rate doubles when the crazed frenzy outside the door replicates ones heard inside. Pushing off my feet, I hesitantly pace into the living room, gathering an umbrella out of the nightstand on the way. The reasoning behind the ruckus comes to light when I see the program Lexi is watching on TV. It is a live broadcast of my arrival home, slightly delayed as per national standards.

Lexi cranks her neck to peer at me. "I knew something was wrong the instant the media swarm grew in size. I wanted you to tell Marcus you're pregnant, Cleo, but not like this." She nudges her head to the TV.

Before I can request for her to switch it off, she rewinds the footage until it stops outside the building I fled from an hour ago. I dump the umbrella I gathered to defend myself before taking the empty seat next to Lexi. Just like I was, Marcus is swamped by the paparazzi as he leaves Global Ten's Christmas function. Although my heart is still in tatters, I take comfort in the fact he is minus the blonde he had plastered to his side most of the night.

Lexi takes my hand in hers when Marcus and his lawyer stop in front of the media. His lawyer—a man matching the picture Marcus showed me after my attack in the alleyway—advises he will be releasing a brief statement. I scoot to the edge of my chair, wanting to ensure I can hear what he has to say.

Standing to the side with his head held high but his eyes elsewhere, Marcus allows his lawyer to speak on his behalf. "As per speculations, Mr. Everett has recently become aware that an old acquaintance of his, Ms. Cleo Garcia, has announced she is pregnant."

The media go crazy, nearly drowning out the rest of his statement. "Although Mr. Everett wishes Ms. Garcia well, until such time as her pregnancy is confirmed and DNA tests are arranged, Mr. Everett will act under the assumption Ms. Garcia's child is not his. Any further questions in regards to the alleged pregnancy and paternity should be directed to my office." He hands a bunch of business cards to the media contingent in the front row before gesturing for Marcus to leave before him.

The paparazzi follow Marcus down the stairs, asking question after question until he slides into the back seat of a blacked-out SUV. Lexi switches off the TV as her wide, shocked eyes stray to mine. Her lips twitch, but not a peep escapes her mouth. I'm just as dumbfounded. Although I hate that Marcus was informed of my pregnancy via the media, his denial is shocking.

"How can he deny little boo-boo is his?" Lexi asks, reading my private thoughts.

I shrug, a better reply above my comprehension.

"That's bullshit, Cleo. That—"

"Hurts," I stammer out, my one word muffled by a sob. "I saw him tonight," I admit, not caring that my tears are falling freely. "We. . ." The horrified expression on my face speaks on my behalf.

"Tonight?" Lexi asks, certain she heard me wrong.

I nod. "The building he was standing in front of was the location of Global Ten's Christmas party. He was there as Keira's date." My voice displays my disgust in myself. Even though I had him first, tonight I technically became the other woman. That is one label I've never wanted.

"I tried to stop our exchange, but I'm defenseless when it comes to him," I blubber while running the back of my hand under my nose. "I still love him, even when he is tearing my heart in two."

"Oh, Cleo. . ." Lexi murmurs softly while pulling me into her arms, where I stay for the next several hours, crying about a man I love, but never wholly owned.

Chapter Twenty-Seven

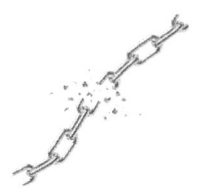

THE CLATTER OF A CHAIR SCRAPING ACROSS THE FLOOR AWAKENS ME from my restless sleep. Rubbing my tiredness from my eyes with the back of my hand, I crank my neck to peer at the clock on my bedside table. It is 4:17 AM. I've been lying in bed the past six hours, but have barely slept two. I slump back onto my pillow, hoping to block out the world long enough to ease the thumping of my temples.

My endeavor to get more sleep fails when the softest tickle of fur brushes my forearm. I jackknife to a half-seated position, sending a flurry of dizziness to my head. My hands shoot up to my temples, circulating them to soothe the nausea roaring to my throat.

Once the desire to vomit has eased, I drift my eyes to the cause for my startled response. Mr. Bunny is lying at my side, tucked into the blankets. He wasn't there when I went to sleep. I'm certain of it. I stop staring at Mr. Bunny when a second scuff-like noise booms into my ears.

Slipping out of bed, I pad to the door. My footing is unsteady, shocked by Lexi's early awakening. She hasn't seen the sun come up since the day Jackson dragged her to *Fosterfields Living Historical Farm*. I lighten the tap of my feet when a male moan breaks through the sound of my pulse shrilling in my ears.

I clutch at my chest, equally revolted and relieved. My darn sister and her propensity to get naughty in any spot other than her bedroom nearly gave me a heart attack.

Not wanting to bust Jackson and Lexi in a compromising position, I tiptoe backward. "Shit," I grumble softly when I unexpectedly crash into something halfway down the hall.

"Cleo, what the hell are you doing sneaking around so early?" Lexi asks, her voice groggy as if she has just woken up.

Lexi's drooping eyelids pop open when a painful sounding grunt echoes down the corridor.

"Where's Jackson?" I don't know why I whisper my question, but my intuition is screaming at me to remain quiet.

"He was called into surgery a few hours ago," Lexi answers, her voice as shallow as mine. "Something about a mass casualty. . ." She ends her sentence with a shrug.

Our eyes rocket to the kitchen entrance when a second groan resonates into the corridor, this one sounding like a man in pain.

"Go into Mom and Dad's room and lock the door," I instruct, shoving Lexi down the hall.

"No, Cleo. I'm—" The rest of her sentence is drowned out when I cup my hand over her mouth.

My desire to keep her safe fuels me with so much strength, I drag her down the hall without breaking into a sweat. Throwing open our parents' bedroom door, I roughly push her inside. With adrenaline thickening my veins, my shove is more powerful than I anticipated. Lexi lands on her backside with a sickening thud. I grimace, hating that I've hurt her, but determined to keep her safe, I tuck away that flare of emotion. Lifting my finger to my lips, requesting she remain quiet, I quickly scamper out of my parents' room, shutting their thick wood door behind me.

My hand rattles out of control when I twist the key, locking Lexi inside. She bangs on the door, her hits loud enough for me to hear, but not sufficient enough to stop the man in our kitchen from groaning once more.

"Cleo, let me out," Lexi begs, her voice breaking into a sob.

I place my hand over the area her banging is coming from before whispering. "Call the police. Tell them we have an intruder and stay on the phone with them until they arrive. Do not come out of this room for anything. Do you understand me?" My last sentence is laced with worry.

"Cleo, please," Lexi begs ever so quietly.

"I love you, Lexi the Leech." *So much so, I'll never let anything bad happen to you.*

With my stomach lodged in my throat, I spin on my heels and head toward the man groaning. My heart thrashes against my chest with every step I take down the eerily black corridor. I keep the lights off, knowing the floorplan well enough to use it to my advantage. The hairs on my arms stand to attention when I stop at my bedroom door to collect the stainless steel baseball bat I keep hidden behind my door.

You know that feeling you get when someone is watching you? It's overwhelming me right now. I freeze, paralyzed with fear when I lean on my bedroom door too hard, hurtling its loud creak down the hall.

Straightening my spine, I pull the bat behind my back when a large shadow fills the entrance to my kitchen. From the build alone, I can tell it is a male, much less the overpowering testosterone sucking oxygen from the air.

"Cleo," gargles a voice I've heard many times before—of one who plunged to his death weeks ago.

I take a step backward, crashing into my door when Richard steps out of the alcove, allowing the street lights beaming in the living room to illuminate half of his face.

"It was you? At the gala tonight?" I ask, hating that my quivering voice exposes the nerves making my skin a sticky, clammy mess.

"Yes," Richard replies, nodding weakly. "And the pizzeria. And Toloache. And the fundraising gala--"

"And the notes in my room," I interrupt, my words as bewildered as my facial expression.

Richard locks his eyes with mine before shaking his head. "No, those notes were not from me. I only left you one note. The one Andy gave you."

I gingerly shake my head when he steps closer to me, bringing the knife he is clutching to within striking distance. My fear could be unwarranted since he is fisting the knife at his side, but the fact he is approaching me in my house, armed, and weeks after his supposed death has my panic surging to an alarming level.

He lowers his eyes to my stomach. "Are you pregnant like the reports said?" he questions as his Adam's apple bobs up and down.

A tear falls from my eye when I timidly nod my head. *Is that what caused his sudden reappearance? News of my pregnancy?*

Richard returns his eyes to mine, the worry in them uncontainable. "Why didn't you read my note, Cleo?" he asks as his massively dilated gaze bounces between mine.

"I did," I reply, pulling the bat out from behind my back to display I'm armed.

Although his eyes are tainted with dread, there is a gleam in them warning me of impending danger. He looks more fearful now than when I was dangling precariously off a cliff months ago, but instead of looking like a man who is seconds away from rescuing me, his composure is exuding a man who is about to wreak havoc on another.

A ghost of a smile cracks onto Richard's mouth when he spots the bat clutched in my hand. "Good girl," he murmurs, sounding pleased. "I've got you. We'll get out of this together. You've just got to trust me. Do you trust me, Cleo?" Half of his confident declaration is lost to a wheezy bout of coughing.

He stumbles down the hall, bracing himself against the wall as if he can't walk without support. My panic surges to an all-time high when my vision clears enough to see large droplets of blood on his chin and the neckline of his shirt.

"Do you trust me, Cleo?" Fear clutches my throat when I notice his teeth are smeared with blood. "We won't get out of this alive if you don't trust me."

My head instinctively nods, causing tears to roll down my cheeks. I don't know if it is panic forcing me to cowardly nod, or the plea in Richard's massively dilated gaze. Just like the minutes leading up to his death, his eyes are open and raw, exposing he is a man I should trust, not fear.

"Good. Then run!" Richard roars, startling Lexi so much she furiously bangs on our parents' bedroom door over and over again. "Run, Cleo, and don't look back!"

Richard pivots on his heels and charges down the hall with the large knife held out in front of his blood-stained body. His steps are more furious than the ones he used mere seconds ago. Paralyzed with fear, I watch him tackle a second man I didn't see hiding in the shadows. The concealed man grunts when he crashes into the entranceway table; Richard's hit was so firm, he knocked him nearly twelve feet.

"Run, Cleo, Run!" Lexi screams at the top of her lungs.

Her frantic scream pushes me into survival mode. Spinning, I race down the hall as fast as my shuddering legs can take me. I fumble over my feet when a loud boom echoes down the hall two seconds later. "That one was in his stomach; the next one will be in his head," warns a deep, masculine voice hindered with pain.

The audible click of a gun's hammer freezes my heart. "What do you want? I don't have much, but I'll give you everything I have."

A chill of dread runs down my spine when a familiar voice replies, "I want you. I've always wanted you."

Through a wobbly pair of knees, I turn around to face a man who just became a stranger to me. Even cloaked in darkness, I am confident my rattled brain has correctly identified the man standing before me. I'm so sure, I'll boldly confirm he is the man I was dancing with mere hours ago without even seeing his face.

"Dexter, what are you doing?" I lower my panicked eyes to Richard, who is slumped on the floor. Although he is motionless, I seek comfort in the fact his chest is rising and falling.

"No," I plead softly when Dexter emerges from the shadow to yank the knife out of Richard's grasp, not caring that he slices his hand in the process. "He isn't a part of this, Dexter. He has nothing to do with anything happening between us."

My chin quivers when Dexter lifts his eyes to me. They are almost lifeless, black and hollow. "No? Then why did he give you this?" A piece of crumpled paper floats across the floor before landing at my bare feet. It is the slip of paper Andy handed me at the gala three weeks ago. He must have stolen it out of my purse when he gathered our belongings off the floor in the storage room.

"It's just a riddle; it doesn't mean anything," I assure, my voice shaky yet confident.

Dexter laughs. It is the laugh of an evil man. "A riddle with my love's address and phone number on it means nothing?! Don't treat me like an idiot!" he roars before backhanding me.

The bat falls to the floor with a clatter when I raise my hands to protect my face from another blow. My first instinct is to fight back, but the lights beaming through the glass paneling on the side of my entranceway door ensures I can't mistake what Dexter is aiming at me. He has the barrel of his gun pointed at my stomach.

"I *know* Richard went to Florida to show you want he found. I *know* he's been sending you sneaky messages." My roots pull from my scalp when Dexter fists my hair and yanks me to within an inch of his face. "And I *know* he wants to make you his," he sneers in my face, covering my throbbing cheek with spit.

I painfully hit the wall when he throws me backward as if I am as light as a feather. "The only thing he hasn't worked out is, you don't belong to anyone but me. I suffered the loss. I endured the pain. I get the reward for years of heartache. Not Richard. Not Marcus. Not the fucking man who stole the love of my life. Me! I get it! He took the woman I love, so, in return, I get to take his."

I flinch when he crouches down in front of me to curl his hand around my throat. "An eye for an eye. A death for a death. A love for a love. That's how life works, isn't it?" He drags the barrel of the gun down my cheek, his pressure so firm, a trail of blood follows its wake. "Now there is just one problem I must take care of first. If he had just followed the rules as I had instructed, all of this could have been avoided."

His eyes stray to Richard, who is gagging on his own blood. "But since he is too pathetic to do as asked, I must take care of business myself. You think Stephen's death would have warned him I do not appreciate being double-crossed. Richard was supposed to fix the error made while I watched from the wings like I did the night you were attacked in the alley."

My chin quivers when he returns his evil eyes to me. They are dark and lifeless, but also display what he is saying is true. "Stephen was supposed to rattle you until I arrived as your savior. I didn't give him permission to touch you the way he did. But be assured, my sweet Cleo, your face was the last thing Stephen saw before I sent him to hell for touching what is mine. Nobody touches what is mine! Nobody!" he roars through gritted teeth.

His nostrils flare as anger lines his face. "He should have walked away as instructed, then I wouldn't be forced to fix his mistakes." I assume he is still talking about Richard until he replaces his gun with the knife he took from Richard as mumbling, "If my research on the female anatomy is correct, right about here will fix the errors Marcus made while keeping your vital organs intact."

My eyes widen when the coolness of a blade digs into my lower stomach. My pleas for clemency trap in my throat when he tightens his grip, stealing my ability to breathe, much less talk.

As his eyes frolic between mine, the evil in them grows. "Sit still. I don't want too much damage done, as you never know, one day we may want children of our own."

I spit in his face, my last fighting defense since his hold on my neck has me drifting in and out of consciousness. My vision blurs and white spots dance in front of my eyes. I slump against the wall, floating into darkness when he tightens his hold around my neck even more.

My eyes bulge when the searing pain of a knife slicing my skin forces me back into consciousness. The pain is intense, ten times worse than anything I've experienced. I don't just feel the pain in my stomach, but in my heart as well.

Dexter stares into my eyes, enjoying watching the life inside me vanish with every inch of the blade he painstakingly slants into my stomach. My hands wrap around his, willfully fighting to stop him harming my unborn baby, but I'm too weak to compete against a man his size. I'm barely conscious, much less lucid enough to comprehend that the more I fight, the further his knife inches in.

I wheeze uncontrollably as sticky, warm liquid covers my hands. I drift between blackness and light as Dexter whispers in my ear, updating me on all the places we're going to visit during our relationship, and how happy I'll be now that I've stopped fighting him. He apologizes for hurting me before expressing his undying love for me, and how in time, I'll understand why he went to such lengths for our relationship.

"When you love someone, no one stands in your way. In time, Cleo, you'll thank me for what I did. I've saved your bastard child from a lifetime of misery, like my parents should have done for me."

My head slumps forward when he releases my neck from his grip. My lungs fight to fill with oxygen but the blood oozing out of my stomach hinders their efforts. Feeling the blackness rolling in, I lift my head and stare into Dexter's eyes. My first lot of words are garbled by the bile sitting in the back of my throat. They are incoherent and breathless.

Realizing I'm trying to talk, Dexter tilts his head to the side. My blood-stained lips tickle his earlobe when I faintly whisper, "I'll never be yours."

Dexter rears back suddenly, stunned by the callousness of my sneered words.

Wanting him to feel the pain searing my heart in half, I add on, "I hate you."

Happy my Garcia stubbornness has reigned supreme, I allow the blackness to take over.

Chapter Twenty-Eight

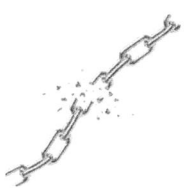

"REQUESTING ASSISTANCE TO 160 VALLEY ROAD, MONTCLAIR. WE need a trauma unit and multiple first responders. Officer down. I repeat, officer down."

A ragged groan expels from my lips when someone pushes hard on my stomach. My eyes pop open as a furious pain scorches my veins. I thought having my wisdom tooth extracted without anesthesia was painful. This is ten times worse. It's not just the pain of the knife still stabbing my stomach causing tears, it is wondering if my baby and sister are safe.

Seeking an update, my lips move. Nothing but painful grunts escape my blood-stained mouth. Fear clutches my heart, stricken with grief my unborn baby has been seriously injured by the knife still stabbed in my stomach. Suddenly panicked I'm still in Dexter's presence, I attempt to sit up, my desire to protect my sister and unborn baby more dire than dealing with the pain swallowing me whole.

"Stay down, baby, an ambulance is on its way," requests a deep, thick voice from above.

I slump back onto the floor where I'm sprawled, certain I'm dreaming, as that voice sounded remarkably like Marcus.

I'm not dreaming. The ashen face of Marcus enters my peripheral vision not even two seconds later. "Stay awake, baby. Keep your eyes open and on me," he pleads, staring at me with hollow, black eyes. "You're going to be okay. Both of you. Just stay with me. Alright?"

Weakly nodding, I do as requested, gasping through the pain striving to overwhelm me. My breathing is garbled, weakened by the panic curled around my throat, and my vision is hazy from an incalculable number of tears swamping my eyes. The pain in my heart is as horrendous as the stab wound to my stomach. I can't believe this is happening. Nothing makes any sense. Other than foolishly kissing Dexter two weeks ago, I haven't done anything to warrant this type of retaliation, much less my innocent unborn baby.

Seemingly reading my inner monologue, Marcus mumbles, "The battleline between good and evil runs through the heart of every man; some just aren't capable of ignoring the temptation." The pain in his words cut me raw. They are tinged with regret, sorrow, and remorse. His voice is the most devastated I've ever heard.

Before I can issue him silent comfort with my eyes, Shian drops at his side. "How is she?" she asks as her gaze dances between Marcus and me. Her dark eyes are as wide as Marcus's, and they are also brimming with as many tears.

"Losing too much blood; where are the paramedics?" Marcus answers, his voice laced with uncontrollable worry.

"They're on their way." The sound of sirens wailing in the distance strengthens Shian's assurance.

"Brodie?" Marcus asks, his voice as weak as I feel.

I feel like an angel floating on a cloud, both woozy and free. Attacks of dizziness are as regular as breathing for me the past three weeks, but this feels different; it almost seems unreal.

Shian swallows harshly before replying, "He got shot three times. One in the arm, one in the spleen, and one in the chest. Fellow agents are working on him. He is still with us—*barely*."

I swallow the horrid taste in the back of my throat before forcing out, "Lexi?" My one word is so garbled I can hardly understand what I said.

Thankfully, Marcus can read the silent plea in my eyes. "Lexi is okay; she is safe and uninjured," he assures me.

Shian jerks her chin up at someone across the room. Two seconds after her nod, Lexi appears at my side. Her face is marked with hot, ugly tears, and her entire body is quaking. I realize how frighteningly cold I am when she gathers my blood-stained hands from my stomach to rest them in her lap.

"You silly, silly, girl. You should have locked yourself in the room with me," Lexi chastises, her voice more a plea than an angry snarl. "Don't ever do that to me again!"

Before I can reply, two first responders arrive at my side. One replaces Marcus's hands with his own while the other searches for a vein in my arm. The mumbled request for an immediate blood transfusion sounds through my ears as the white spots dancing in front of my eyes double in size.

"Please be careful, she's pregnant with my baby," Marcus advises them, his eyes drifting between the first responders and me. "She's due August 29th."

I peer up at Marcus, blinking and confused. How could he know my due date? I haven't even been to the doctor's yet, so I have no idea the date our baby is due. But he just blubbered it out like he is so in tune with my body, he knows precisely the moment we conceived.

I inwardly snort. *He probably does.*

My confused eyes drift to one of the first responders when he chuckles under his breath, "I guess we know what you were thankful for Thanksgiving weekend." He spiritly winks before jotting down the information Marcus handed him in my file.

Marcus glares at him, stunned by his cheerful demeanor. I also stare, but I'm not startled by his response. I know he's attempting to ease the tension thickening the air by using his charismatic personality. I'm just glancing at him in bewilderment, wondering how he knew what Marcus and I were doing Thanksgiving weekend.

Noticing he has me baffled, he places down my file, then explains, "The 29th of August is exactly 40 weeks following Thanksgiving weekend. Obviously, someone gifted you something you'll always be thankful for."

My pulse skyrockets as my eyes snap back to Marcus. Not expecting my rushed movement, my woozy head cites an objection to my unannounced crusade. My eyes roll into the back of my head as I'm overcome by a severe bout of nausea. I feel like I'm floating, even though the rigidness of the tiled floor is digging into my aching back.

"Cleo, keep your eyes open, baby," Marcus demands, his tone indicating the arrival of another savior at my side, this one more demanding than any before him. *Master Chains has arrived.*

I try to do as my Master requests. I try to instill the obedience our time in his playroom taught me. But no matter how hard I fight—no matter how much I beg for my body to listen to its Master—the blackness comes steamrolling in so hard and fast, I don't have a chance of stopping it.

As I'm swept away by a bright white cloud, my thoughts stray to my first sexual encounter with Marcus.

"You make me so reckless," he said that morning. "You make me irresponsible and careless. I don't know whether I should punish you for making me reckless or punish myself."

When I told him I could handle any punishment he wanted to give, he said, "Be careful what you wish for, Cleo."

No. . . he wouldn't have purposely forgone protection, otherwise why did he deny our baby earlier tonight? He doesn't want me so much he is willing to tie himself to me for eternity. *Does he?*

"Cleo, stay with me, baby," Marcus demands, gently shaking my shoulders, dragging me back to the present. "Keep fighting. Fight for our baby, Cleo. Fight for us."

I struggle against my heavy eyelids, wanting to peer into Marcus's eyes so I can read the truth from his forthright gaze. But no matter how hard I fight, I can't keep my eyes open.

"Our baby. You want our baby?" I faintly murmur, my words barely audible as my veins are deprived of adequate oxygen.

"Yes. Always," is the last thing I hear as I fall into unconsciousness, closely followed by,

"Move, she's flatlining!"

Chapter Twenty-Nine

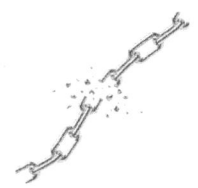

Marcus

What started out as a dream, turned into a nightmare.

I LIFT MY BURROWED HEAD FROM MY HANDS WHEN THE CREAK OF A
door sounds through my ears. I'm not Cleo's family, but I refused to
leave the waiting room for next of kin attached to the operating room
she was wheeled into three hours ago. I keep my eyes locked on
Jackson as he cautiously approaches Lexi and me, refusing to look at
the amount of red blood covering his white scrubs. His face is as gaunt
as mine and his eyes as glistening.

When he briefly shakes his head to my silent question, a part of me
dies. The hope, the optimism the world couldn't be so cruel to one
person—it vanishes in an instant. I drop my head back into my hands,
denying the vultures of the media to get one more picture of me with
tears streaming down my face. Although Lexi's sobs drown out the
incessant clicking of their long-range cameras, I know they are still
there.

People often believe that members of the BDSM lifestyle are sick,
worthless people. This past few weeks, I've witnessed more unspeak-
able behavior than I've ever seen in my club. Not only did I see the

woman I love lying lifeless on the floor, cradling the blood-soaked area our baby was nestled safely in mere hours earlier, I also saw vultures more concerned about getting an image worthy of the front-page news than letting the first responders do their job. The scum of the paparazzi would rather a woman and unborn baby die than miss out on the opportunity to harass me one more time. They'd rather watch a man fall to his knees and howl than offer him comfort. They are pathetic human beings, not me or anyone in my lifestyle.

Overwhelmed with anger I've been harboring for months, I stand from my chair before sending it hurdling across the room. Incapable of holding in the rage tearing my heart out of my chest, I do the same with the chair standing next to me. I did what he asked: I let her go so she'd be safe, yet he still hurt her.

If I knew weeks ago what I know now, I wouldn't have been so goddamn stupid.

Upon arriving at Stephen's house to question him for the assault on Cleo, police stumbled onto a crime scene. Although a body wasn't discovered in the vicinity, it was apparent it would only be a matter of time before one was found. When police linked a connection between Stephen's murder and a series of death threats I had received for Cleo two days earlier, I panicked. After filling Lexi in on the investigation, she packed Cleo's belongings, and I shipped her off to Florida.

The initial plan was for me to stay with Cleo in my sub house in Ravenshoe, but I couldn't do it. No matter how many times I fought my hands to turn left when we exited the airport hangar, I turned right. Cleo wasn't my sub, and I wasn't going to treat her as if she were. Don't get me wrong, I did fill in a contract months ago; I wanted her to be my sub, but that was because I feared losing her more than anything. I know BDSM; I don't know relationships, so having a piece of paper guaranteeing Cleo was mine for a stipulated amount of time was almost everything I could have wished for—there was only one thing I wanted more—*her*.

When the local law enforcement office in Ravenshoe caught wind of Richard knowing Cleo's location, they hatched a plan to catch him red-handed. It took the guarantee of Abel and his daughter, Regina, that they would keep Cleo safe for me to leave that morning. I thought seeing Cleo leave with Richard would be my worst day—it is nothing compared to how I am feeling now.

When Richard plunged to his death, the FBI assumed the death threats I'd been receiving for Cleo would cease. They did for the first week, but the morning of Anna's arrival to fit Cleo for a dress to wear at the Serena Scott Fundraising Gala brought the arrival of new threats —these more gruesome than the first.

Her stalker was clever—generally one step ahead of the FBI with every move he made. Although stumped by his caliber of computer knowledge, the agents working the case believed the evidence was clear-cut. Richard's body was never found, so their focus remained on him and anyone associated with him—i.e. Andy.

I'll admit, I overreacted the day Cleo walked to Links after dining with Dexter, but with my security team receiving images of her entering and exiting Toloache within seconds of Serenity advising me of her arrival, panicked anger was my first emotion. The pictures didn't contain a threat like the other correspondence I had received, but they still displayed Cleo was being watched.

The night of the gala was the first time I received a digital threat firsthand. Usually, they'd go through the servers at Chains, but that one came directly to my cell phone. That threat not only warned of ill-harm to Cleo, it also had a picture of her sitting at the bar where she lingered the first hour of her arrival. The threat gave statistics on how it would only take a few drops of poison to kill a woman of Cleo's size, and that all I had to do to save her was walk away and never look back. Since that was something that seemed impossible for me to do, my security team launched into action.

As my men worked behind the scenes, Cartier moved Cleo to a safer location. Although the booths were in the far corner of the ballroom, Cleo was flanked by undercover FBI agents and members of my security team. She was safer that night than anyone else in the country.

When Keira called me to advise she had information on a man at her work harassing Cleo, I should have requested for her to give me the details over the phone. Unfortunately, I've always had a weak spot for Keira. Not because I want her to be my sub, but because of injuries she sustained in my club during my watch.

I created Chains so members of my community would have a safe, sane, and consensual place to play. My guarantee was voided the day Keira's Dom failed to acknowledge her repeated use of her safe word. I still recall the look in her eyes when she stumbled into my office, draped in a blanket and crying. The horrified cloud in her eyes that night nearly haunted me as much as seeing Cleo's face the night of her assault. They are two images added to many I'd give anything to forget.

Keira didn't extend any more information on the man threatening Cleo than I already knew. She advised of the exchange between Cleo and Richard months earlier and mentioned them meeting up in Florida. With her knowledge lacking, it soon became apparent Keira had staged a ruse to secure my utmost attention. Conscientious of her mental well-being, I endorsed caution while handling the matter.

Although shocked at discovering Keira was wearing a chain link pendant, upon further questioning, I believed her reasoning behind it. Still rattled by her exchange at Chains only weeks earlier, she believed wearing my trademark would ensure no other Dom would approach her. It is a logical action, but one I'd rather not explain to Cleo. I hated keeping Cleo in the dark, but the confidential indemnity I guarantee my clients ensured I was unable to update her on all the details regarding my exchange with Keira. *Now I wish I wasn't so damn stubborn.*

Just as they had done throughout the night, my security team kept me updated via a transmitter device lodged in my ear. During my argument with Cleo in the computer facility room of the hotel, my security team received another credible threat. Although watching Cleo walk away from me with her face etched in devastation, it was my safest bet to ensure she'd leave the gala uninjured, as just like all the other threats the prior two weeks, this one was adamant Cleo would be safe as long as she wasn't with me.

The night I returned home and thought Cleo had left me. . .that was one of my hardest days. I don't know what you call the weird fluttering thing my heart does every time I'm with her—the one I've never experienced with anyone before her—but it was thumping to an entirely different beat that night. *It's pumping a similar rhythm now.*

I'm going to be upfront: when Cleo asked me to make love to her, I felt threatened. Not because I didn't want her to know what she meant to me, but because I'd never done it before. My confidence exudes in a playroom environment. I know my strong points, and I confidently exploit them during scenes, but making love was a whole new ball game for me. Don't get me wrong, I'm not saying I didn't enjoy it, but it was unlike anything I've ever experienced before.

While Cleo was recovering from our night of lovemaking, Shian introduced me to an FBI profiler who specialized in the type of stalking Cleo had endured the past year. He discovered a distinct pattern with her stalker's tendencies, proving this was something he had done before. On his advice, I left Cleo in New York while I pretended to return to Ravenshoe, hoping her stalker would believe we had separated.

Little did we know at the time, Cleo had arranged to meet her real stalker the day of my departure, and during their conversation, she exposed that our relationship was still going strong. So, as much as I believed my absence would diminish the threats to Cleo's life, her stalker's rage grew, angered by my attempts to defraud him.

Although I firmly believe in Chains and what it represents for members of the BDSM community, my reasoning behind selling it far outweighed my desire to keep it. With the FBI's investigation into Richard being the most in-depth Shian has conducted, several missing pieces of a puzzle started falling into place. *Well, so it seemed at the time.*

The Dom who assaulted Keira is believed to have been Richard. Although he used an alias to initially gain access to Chains, when his annual membership application wasn't endorsed by the party member who invited him, Chains' staff took extra precautions to ensure the safety of its party members.

Richard was the only Dom suitably matched to Keira the night she was allegedly assaulted. Their compatibility test scores were shockingly similar, making them ideal D/s candidates. Wanting to discover if my assumptions were accurate, I met with Keira for brunch the week of my separation from Cleo. Although Keira denied knowing the identity of her Dom due to being blindfolded, her eyelashes excessively fluttered when I showed her an image of Richard I'd found on the Chains servers.

But with Keira's continued request for anonymity, and the lack of cameras in the playrooms, my assumptions were merely hearsay. Believing it was my decision to cut Richard from the Chains community months ago as the reason for Cleo's death threats, selling Chains felt like the right thing to do at the time. I wasn't lying when I said I'd kneel before I'd give up Cleo. I'll give up everything I have before I'll lose her.

Have you ever had an out of body experience? That is what it felt when I was standing in the playroom with Cleo while punishing her for kissing Dexter. I was there, but I wasn't. I've struggled many times the past few months with aspiring to exert my power over Cleo, while also wanting to cherish her at the same time. I suffered the same torture that night.

I watched Cleo kiss another man, knowing it was the perfect ploy to lessen the severity of her stalker's threats. But instead of embracing the opportunity, I let it eat me alive. I should have manned up. I should have absorbed my anger with the steel rod my father lodged in my back since the day I was born. I should have been a man. Instead, I acted like an idiot.

I never knew what blinded by love meant, but if I had known the identity of Cleo's stalker the night she kissed Dexter, and I had a weapon capable of issuing him the torment I went through, I would have killed him. I would have made him suffer as horrendously as I did. That's how much it cut me raw seeing Cleo kiss another man. I've traded subs. I've walked away from women kneeling at my feet, begging to be loved the instant the flare in their eyes told me they were getting too close. But never in all my life have I experienced the pain I felt seeing Cleo kiss another man.

I thought the kiss would be the ultimate proof to her stalker that Cleo and I were no longer together, but do you know what happened? The threats worsened—instantly. They were so horrific, even Jackson had a hard time stomaching them when he caught the quickest glimpse of one on my computer monitor when he was checking my hand. I struck Dexter hard—*now I wish it were even harder*—but my hand isn't broken. It merely presented the perfect opportunity for me to walk away from Cleo once and for all.

Going against the advice of my lawyer, I anonymously released my story to the public before organizing a press conference I knew would allow me to shame Cleo in front of millions. Cleo is a stubbornly beautiful opinionated woman I knew wouldn't stand by and watch a person she cared about be slaughtered without first trying to intercept her attacker's play. But instead of embracing Cleo's determination, I used it against her.

I tore her heart out for the world to see, then I let her be ridiculed and called horrid names no one with a soul as beautiful as hers should ever be associated with. I gave her up to save her, yet it was my inability to fully let her go that has brought us here today.

I never went to Global Ten Media's Christmas function with the intentions of doing what I did. When Cleo removed her collar, Shian needed another wireless tracker placed on her. Knowing where Cleo was at all times was our only chance of keeping her safe. I knew I could get close to Cleo. And I did. But my desire for her was even stronger than I could have anticipated. For just an hour, I wanted to believe I could save her from anything. I wanted to raise two fingers in the air and tell the world to get fucked. I wanted Cleo to be mine and only mine. Now, I ruined everything because I thought right would always triumph over wrong. I should have known better—my childhood shows that isn't the case.

Deep down inside, I know I'm not entirely to blame for today's outcome. Dexter caught everyone by surprise. He disarmed Shian's usually guarded persona by giving her unlimited access to Global Ten's servers when she was investigating Stephen's assault of Cleo and Richard's stalking case. He befriended Brodie by hacking into the security servers at the hotel where the gala was held when Brodie believed he saw Richard in attendance. He even called in a possible sighting of Richard at Global Ten's function last night. He embedded himself in every aspect of Cleo's life by befriending those closest to her.

The only person he failed to woo was me.

I knew something wasn't right with Dexter the moment I saw him enter the fundraising gala. He had his arm wrapped around Delilah a majority of the night, but his eyes never left Cleo. He watched her all night, often moving positions to ensure he could surveil her from afar.

But he was clever, purchasing his drinks with cash, and familiarizing himself with the location of the security cameras around the ballroom.

That was his first downfall. I know from experience, only men who have something to hide shield themselves. My security team's prime focus that night was Dexter. Their attention was only diverted because a facial recognition scan of the area received a positive match to a man the FBI had been searching for the prior two weeks: Richard.

Richard was trying to help Cleo, but more often than not, his assistance had the opposite effect, because instead of looking at the main players, the FBI was constantly chasing a ghost. Their focus was sidetracked from the man they should have been watching.

Dexter is obsessed with Cleo, there is no doubt about that. The only thing we can't work out is why. The FBI profiler said there is usually some deep-seated connection that triggers stalking cases of this caliber. Although it is still early, no credible link has been found as to why Dexter is so obsessed with Cleo.

I get his fascination—any red-blooded male would. Cleo is a beautiful woman with a heart of gold, but what makes a man hurt someone he claims to love? What drives him to such a brink of insanity that he believes it is acceptable to stab a knife into a pregnant woman's stomach without fear of prosecution? What society do we live in that a story is worth more than a life?

Exhausted from throwing chairs across the room as if they are tennis balls, I crouch down on the floor and suck in ragged breaths. My body is slicked with sweat, successfully concealing the two tears my brimming eyes couldn't contain. The little flutter my heart makes every time Cleo is in my presence has been doused, leaving a hollow, empty space in its place.

My eyes raise from the ground when a familiar scent lingers in the air. Same brown eyes, same straight nose, and same angelically beautiful face meet my curious glance. Cleo and Lexi are so similar; the only thing that separates them is their scent. Cleo's smell is refreshing and clean, where Lexi's is wild and carefree—much like their personalities.

"Jackson said we can go and see Cleo if we want. I think you should go first," Lexi murmurs, her usually smooth voice choked by tears. "Do you want to see her?"

Not trusting my voice not to break, I nod my head, then stand. I tug Lexi to my side before placing a quick peck on her hairline. When I first arrived on scene at Cleo's attack, Lexi was standing at the end of the hall with a loaded gun uncontrollably shaking in her hands. Her need to protect her sister and unborn nephew was revealed when I saw how poorly the door she was standing in front of was splintered. Lexi is tiny, a little smaller than Cleo, but the adrenaline surging through her body saw her kicking open a thick wooden door before firing at the man assaulting her sister.

Her first shot missed, but her second hit of Dexter's shoulder was a through and through. If Shian and I hadn't arrived when we did, I have no doubt Lexi would have killed Dexter. She had a fire in her eyes that mimicked mine to a T. She wanted him dead as much as I did. The only thing that stopped both of us was when Cleo suddenly gasped in a wheezy breath, exposing she was still alive. That led us to where we are right now—to the hospital where Jackson works.

No matter how much my heart is breaking, I know Jackson did everything in his power to help Cleo. He loves Cleo as much as he loves Lexi, so I was sure he would take care of her when Lexi suggested him as the surgeon to operate on Cleo. He did everything in his power. I know this, and I will continue telling myself this as I face my darkest day.

"I'll be back soon," I assure Lexi, knowing how difficult it is for her to let me see Cleo first.

I follow Jackson into the hallway of operating rooms, my heart rate lowering with every stride I take. They have Cleo in a private suite in the west wing. She is lying in a large hospital bed that makes her appear much younger than her twenty-six years. Her hair has been brushed straight, stopping just below the swell of her breasts. She looks peaceful and rested, even with only sleeping a few hours every night the past three weeks. Although Cleo isn't aware, I was with her every night the past month. Maybe not in the capacity she needed, but in spirit I was with her every night.

"I'll be in the hall if you need anything," Jackson advises before exiting Cleo's room, leaving me alone with her.

I stand at the side of her bed with my hands, which are itching to touch her, balled at my side. She has been through enough today I don't want to risk hurting her anymore.

"I'm so sorry, baby," I whisper, my voice barely audible over the beeping of machines. "I was trying to protect you when I should have been protecting us. All of us." I peer down at her flat stomach, sending a flood of moisture back to my eyes.

Unable to withstand the desire to touch her, I gently run my index finger down her exposed forearm—the one without tubes and wires. When the hairs on her arms bristle from my touch, my heart stops beating. I lift my eyes to her face, then take a step back, stunned. Cleo's eyes are open and peering straight at me.

"Hey. How are you?" It is a stupid question to ask, but I'm too shocked to articulate more.

As Cleo's hand slowly creeps down to her stomach, her eyes silently question the results of her surgery. Cleo was assaulted by Dexter fifteen days ago; since that day, our baby has been hanging on by a thread. The knife wound Cleo sustained during her attack did significant damage to her uterus. Although our baby was unharmed, the wound still threatened its life. Doctors were adamant Cleo would eventually miscarry. Today was our last ditch effort to save our baby. We knew the odds were against us, but both Cleo and I agreed to try was better than sitting by and doing nothing. Unfortunately, our hopes were dashed, leaving us both devastated.

Although the tears streaming down Cleo's face tells me she read the answer from my eyes, I softly murmur, "I'm sorry, baby; Jackson did everything he could, but the damage was too much. Our baby didn't make it."

Cleo's entire body quakes as fresh tears roll down her cheeks unchecked. Although Jackson was upfront about the chances of our baby surviving, we were both optimistic that life couldn't be so cruel to one person. *How wrong were we?*

Careful not to agitate her still-healing body, I slide into the bed next to Cleo and gather her in my arms. She nuzzles her head into the groove of my chest, using my shirt to catch her tears. For every tear she sheds, I issue her a silent promise that it will be one of her last.

I've seen her cry more the past two months than I ever wanted to witness. If I see her cry again in this lifetime, it will be too soon.

After the shudders wracking her tiny frame have eased, I gently pull her back by her shoulders. Balls of moisture are beaded on the top of her extremely thick lashes, and her cheeks are white. I kiss away her tears before scooting down the bed to meet her eye to eye.

"Heaven may have held our baby before us, but it is just keeping him safe until we meet him again."

Her brief nod sends more tears trickling down her face. I let these stay, knowing they are a part of her grieving process. We all grieve in our own way. Cleo shows her grief on the outside, in the tears she sheds and the pain etched on her beautiful face, where my pain is felt on the inside. No matter which way you show it, it doesn't make it any less significant. Grief is grief.

I pull Cleo in close to my chest, careful not to cause her any more harm. "Every tragedy has a lesson equal in significance to its heart-break. We will work through this, and hopefully find the reason behind it in the near future."

Cleo draws her head off my chest so her eyes can bounce between mine. She looks both confused and horrified. I slant my head to the side, silently reading her soul-baring eyes. I come up stumped as to why she looks so panicked.

"What is it?" I ask, deciding a more direct approach is needed.

Her lips quiver as she begins to speak, "That saying you just said, have you heard that before?"

"Yes," I reply, smiling softly. My heart thwacks my chest as I prepare to share a snippet of my life I don't often tell. "My grand-mother regularly said it after events in my childhood. Why? Have you heard it before?"

"Yes," she replies, gently nodding her head. "Dexter said it to me after I told him about my parents' accident. He said the exact same quote."

Her admission mystifies me. Although I've heard similar quotes before, I've never heard it quoted in the exact manner my grand-mother used to say it.

As I sit in silence with Cleo safely wrapped in my arms, my mind drifts back to the first day we met. The beautiful brunette who stole my attention with one glance of her angelic face wasn't the only person I comforted that day. When I was leaving the hospital, I spotted a man in the parking lot, mumbling and cursing to himself. Although he was angry, his grief was also clearly visible. I shared that quote with him that afternoon, hoping the words I failed to say to Cleo could help another.

That couldn't have been Dexter—*surely*.

Cleo has often quoted how intermingled our lives have been the past four years, but it wouldn't extend this far.

Would it?

Chapter Thirty

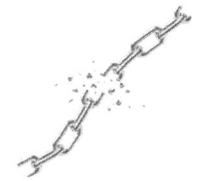

Two years later....

Cleo

RESOLUTE SILENCE FALLS OVER THE LARGE GATHERING OF PEOPLE surrounding me when I step out of the alcove I'm standing in. Although I'd like to say their gaped-mouth expressions are due to the one-of-a-kind J Holt creation I'm wearing, that isn't the case. It is the soulful voice of Marcus breaking through the hum of chatter. Our guests sit in silence, marveled by a voice that can make me swoon and scream in ecstasy at the same time. My smile beams as I glance at the two men standing on each side of me, both silenced in awe by Marcus's acoustic serenade. When he proposed, Marcus said he was going to sing at our wedding. I just had no clue he would do it in front of a hundred of our closest family and friends.

Abel's eyes twinkle with moisture as he walks me down the white rose petal aisle with another man I've always seen as family. Miguel dips his chin at his wife's appreciative ogle of his suit-covered body. Although two years ago the world proved how cruel it can be to one person, I'm glad that logic hasn't come true for Miguel and Janice. Her tumor hasn't just stopped growing; it is shrinking in size as well. Doctors still caution Miguel not to get his hopes up, but optimism has always been his strong point.

As we continue slowly pacing down the aisle, my ears drink in every perfect syllable of Marcus's beautiful voice as my eyes absorb our guests. Shian, forever the rebel, is sitting in the very back row. Although her tailored pantsuit gives her a tough exterior, the glistening moisture in her eyes softens her not-to-be-messed-with persona.

I arch a brow at Richard, who is sitting a few spots up from Shian. His cocky attitude is beaming out of him as brightly as ever. Even two bullet wounds within a month couldn't squash his peacock demeanor. Although it took the FBI several months to solve the riddle of a man as psychotic as Dexter, when they did, they also discovered that Richard, although arrogant, isn't a murderer nor a stalker. I don't even believe he is a Dom who doesn't understand he needs to stop when being given a sub's safeword.

When Marcus confronted Richard about any prior exchanges with Keira, Richard never denied his interaction with Keira the night of Keira's alleged assault. He agreed they did act out a scene that night at Chains, but he adamantly refuted not stopping when she safeworded. He's adamant she never spoke a word, much less something as important as a safeword.

Although new to Chains, Richard had been in the BDSM lifestyle three years before his exchange with Keira. He openly expressed an eagerness to gag his subs, but assured Marcus he never muzzled a sub until he had extensive knowledge of her limitations. Trust is a significant factor in the BDSM lifestyle, so casual playmates rarely perform scenes that require an immense amount of trust.

When Richard's account of events is stacked with Keira's desire to be Marcus's sub, doubt of Keira's accusations surfaced several months ago. Although Keira could have been assaulted by another Dom that same night, I highly doubt it. I don't believe Keira was the victim of wrongdoing at all. I believe her entire ruse was solely devised to get her close to Marcus. She knew how important a safe, sane and consensual environment was for him, so guilt hit him hard when she was allegedly assaulted in his club. It is just lucky Marcus is a shrewd man who saw past the ruse—albeit a little later than I would have liked.

Considering Richard is an invited guest of both Marcus and me, I'd say I'm not the only one who doubts Keira's claims. Marcus must believe Richard is innocent, or he wouldn't be here. Admitting he was wrong is a massive step for a man as dominant as Marcus, but just like the FBI, he is discovering not everything is always as it seems.

After going to such lengths to protect me, the FBI looked further into Richard's alleged stalking and murder charges. They soon realized all the evidence they had on Richard was planted by Dexter. Even the image of Richard and Stephen together in the elevator was discovered to be fraudulent.

Although Richard went about it in the wrong way, he was trying to help me the morning he arrived at Florida. His impressive hacking skills that he remarkably kept under wraps had him unearthing Dexter's ruse faster than Shian's skilled team. Unfortunately for all involved, Dexter was always a few steps ahead of everyone.

The quote Marcus said to me the day we lost our baby was the final piece of the puzzle to understanding Dexter's obsession with me.

Overwhelmed with grief, I never considered the consequences for anyone else involved in my parents' car accident. From the police report, I knew when my dad hit a section of black ice, he veered into oncoming traffic. What I didn't know was that his car struck another, killing a twenty-three-year-old San Francisco native who had recently moved to New York. After further investigation, it was discovered that Shelly Christian had moved to New York to escape the clutches of her manic stalker. She did everything the police had requested—doctoring any contact they had, filing for a restraining order, changing her phone number and address. When nothing worked, Shelly became so desperate, she drove to the other side of the country. Her stalker was just as determined as she was. He never gave up. His name was Dexter Elias.

Dexter—believing he'd lost the love of his life—took vengeance on the person he felt responsible: my dad. The desire to get back what he lost made him move to New York and seek employment at the same company of the person he sought vengeance on: me. His plans to make my life miserable stayed on track the first few months. . . until we met in person. The FBI believes that is when Dexter's revenge shifted to obsession. Shelly and I have a lot of similarities. We were both of Latin heritage, both orphans, and we were both looking for a break in life. Shelly never got hers—I found mine in Marcus.

Some believe if I'd just denied Mr. Carson's request to go undercover at Chains all our heartache would have been avoided. I don't believe that is true. If I hadn't gone to Chains, I would have never met Marcus again. He would have never paid for my sister's inclusion in the Kalydeco program, and I would have never felt as loved as I do right now having him serenade me in front of our guests.

Marcus's grandmother's quote is true: every tragedy has a lesson equal in significance to its heartbreak. I'd give anything to lessen the pain I endured losing my family and our unborn baby, but I'd also give anything to keep Marcus in my life. He is my reward for years of unhappiness, as I am his.

When I reach the end of the aisle, the crowd breaks into rapturous applause, as appreciative of Marcus's singing talent as I was the first time I heard him sing. Miguel and Abel place a kiss on my cheek before handing me to the groom, who is waiting impatiently next to his long line of groomsmen. Unsurprisingly, Marcus's bandmates all have a prime spot at the end of the aisle, just as their wives—my very dear friends—have a place on my side of the church.

There are also two extra inclusions on Marcus's side that wholeheartedly deserve to be there. The man who saved me when I nearly bled out on the floor of my living room, and soon-to-be husband of my baby sister, surgeon extraordinaire, Jackson Collard. And Brodie, the man who took three bullets for me when Dexter lured him out of the safety of his patrol car by telling him Richard had broken into my home. I knew Brodie's love of his job was more deep-seated than a standard bodyguard. I just had no clue he was an undercover FBI agent. I shouldn't be surprised—his acting skills are the best I've seen.

"Hi," I greet Marcus when I stop to stand in front of him.

His eyes dance between mine as the back of his fingers run down my cheek before faintly hovering over the scar in my top lip only he can see. After the loss of our baby two years ago, Marcus pledged me a lifetime of happiness. He has strived to achieve that every day since.

The rollercoaster ride we endured the first two months of our relationship has been just as thrilling the past two years, but instead of having
soaring highs and devastating lows, we are on a ride that never stops
gliding.

The past two years have been magical, unlike anything I could have
imagined. The death of our unborn child was a horrible experience I'd
give anything to change, but our loss also brought us closer together,
bonding us in the same way I'm sure our son would have if he had
survived our attack. Although our baby never had the chance to take
his first breath, he will always be a part of our lives. Marcus and I even
have his date of conception and due date tattooed on our wrists.

Sensing where my thoughts have drifted to, Marcus runs his index
finger over the Roman numerals etched on my wrist, drawing my eyes
to his.

"Hi," he greets me.

He only says one word, but he doesn't need to say more. His eyes
express everything his mouth fails to articulate. As Marcus quoted the
day we lost our baby, heaven may have held our baby before we did, but
they are keeping him safe until we meet again.

Marcus's lips curve when a loud squeal breaks the silence encom-
passing us. I giggle softly before following his amused gaze to our six-
month-old daughter Tatum, wooing the crowd with her adorable black
ringlet curls and unique hazel eyes. Although Tatum's pregnancy was
an unexpected surprise, even more so considering the significant
damage Dexter did to my womb, news of her impending arrival was
handled more pleasantly than our unborn baby.

I still get the occasional gripe on social media about trapping
Marcus by getting pregnant, then using his grief to sink my nails into
him more deeply. But for the most part, the media and fans have
welcomed me into the Rise Up family with open arms—*mostly*.

Marcus's obvious grief the two weeks following my attack was
broadcast around the world. The loss of our unborn baby hit him
harder than he'd ever admit, but his relief that I was spared any life-
threatening injuries was also visible. Just like our first meeting, it was a
beautifully tormented moment in time.

The media played out the entire charade like some sort of morbid re-telling of Cinderella. I was cast the part of Cinderella and Marcus was Prince Charming. The fans gobbled it up, adoring that a modern-day harlot could have a prince whisk in and rescue her from her miserable, decrepit life. Although my feminist side hates the idea of being cast as a damsel in distress, I'll never express my disdain out loud, preferring headlines full of half-truths than ones entirely based on fiction.

Realizing she has captured the attention of her daddy, Tatum blows a loud raspberry—her way of awarding him kisses from a distance. After scrunching up her nose and snarling a toothless grin, she attacks the silver spoon Aubrey gifted her with unbridled fury. Her teeth have been giving her hell the past week. No. Correction. Her teeth have been giving *us* hell the past week. Unlike her mother, Tatum doesn't appear to be a fan of pain, which is very well, because that is one conversation I'd prefer to avoid in the future.

Although I am an orphan, and Marcus has no contact with his parents, Tatum doesn't notice the absence of her grandparents. Miguel and Janice, as well as Abel and Aubrey, have stepped into the roles so well, Tatum will never miss cherished family memories.

I met Marcus's parents the month following my near-death experience. It wasn't a pleasant meeting, one I'd prefer not to share on the happiest day of my life, so it must wait for a future story. Serenity keeps them updated on events in Marcus's life, but I'd expect to see pigs fly before a reunion occurs between Marcus and his parents.

"Are you ready, Cleo?" Marcus asks before pivoting on his heels to face the wedding celebrant.

"Uh huh," I answer, smiling a grin that displays my utter joy.

Although our wedding is occurring nearly a year after Marcus wanted, I'm glad I held my ground and adjusted the dates. I wanted to ensure I had time to lose my baby weight before squeezing into the gorgeous satin and lace gown Jenni handcrafted for me.

While handing my bouquet of white roses to Lexi, I playfully wink at Serenity, soundlessly revealing I didn't miss her bug-eyed expression regarding the hottie seated three rows back when we arrived at the church. Serenity rolls her eyes before sticking out her tongue. Her nonchalant approach is blown out of the water when her wide gaze immediately returns to the man she hasn't taken her eyes off the past ten minutes.

"Try not to scare this one off," I playfully chide to Marcus, moving to stand next to him.

"If he grasps how to treat a lady like a lady, I won't have to scare him away," Marcus replies, his tone a unique mix of commanding and nurturing.

I smile, adoring his protectiveness of his sister, while also feeling sorry for Tatum when she reaches dating age. When Marcus slips his hand over mine, my smile enlarges. His palm is clammy and wet—he is just as nervous as I am.

When I shift my eyes to peer at him, his massively dilated gaze meets mine halfway.

"Are you ready to have the best of both worlds, Master Chains?" I whisper ever so quietly.

Marcus's eyes flare as the corners of his lips curve high. He looks happy, intrigued, and if I'm being totally honest, smug as hell. The reason behind his pompous attitude comes to light when he slides his spare hand into his pocket to activate the tiny device he has hidden inside. My knees curve inwards as a ferocious wildfire ignites in my womb. I stand perfectly still, praying our guests are clueless to the vibrating jolt turning my sex into a sticky, heated mess.

Happy I'm on the brink of orgasm, Marcus switches off the device before drifting his eyes to me. "As ready as I'll ever be," he croons, his voice causing even more dampness to puddle between my legs.

There he is: the man I fantasize about every night.

Master Chains has arrived.

Epilogue

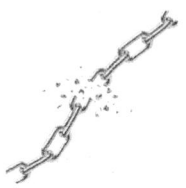

Marcus

"Slow down; anyone would swear you've been away from home for a week."

I sling my arm into the air, too eager to return home to bother bantering with Cameron about my obvious excitement. I've been away from Cleo and Tatum for a week; I am well past eager. As I gallop down the stairs of my private jet, the flashing of bulbs in the distance flicker in the droplets of rain falling from the pitch-black sky. Unlike the Florida temperatures I've become accustomed to the past seven days, the night is cool and summer is now a distant memory.

"Thanks," I say to Tripp, one of the many men who work at the private airstrip I own on the outskirts of Montclair, when he throws a set of keys across my expensive pride and joy.

My muscles sigh when I slide into the driver's seat, appreciating the way the vibrating leather pads Cleo had installed relieve the tension of a long week. The past week has been the longest week of my life. In the past three years, I've never been away from Cleo more than a night, so to spend seven nights without her by my side, I'm not only restless, I'm extremely fatigued.

With modern technology, I kept in contact with Cleo and Tatum as if they were right in front of me—but there is one thing missing no technology can replicate: their smell. Just like every other sensory outlet in my body, my sense of smell has improved since I met Cleo. Smell has a direct link to the limbic system. The limbic system is responsible for the processing of emotions and memory. That is why when I smell the scent of pollen on a dew-crisp morning, I can recall Cleo in crystal clear form: her beautifully plump lips, the generous swell of her breasts, her alluring curves that capture the attention of every man when she walks into the room. One smell and I'm trapped, caught between a man wanting to parade his most valuable asset in public for the world to see, and the Master who wants to possess every inch of her so thoroughly, she'll feel me with every breath she takes.

Tonight, I'm not stuck. I know exactly what I want.

My tires lose traction on the wet asphalt when I increase the pressure on the gas pedal. I go whizzing toward the exit manned by a four security guard-strong team. Paparazzi rush toward the exit when they spot my sports car gliding down the pavement. I flash a grateful smile to the two security officers braving the wet weather to clear a path through the media circling me. With my family's time equally shared between Montclair and Bronte's Peak, the paparazzi isn't as dense as normal.

I'm thrusted into my seat when I spot a clearing between the flashing lights. My engine roars to life, showcasing its power with a grunt every man loves. There is only one purr more intoxicating than the rumbling of my high-powered engine: my wife's.

My excessive speed has me eluding the paparazzi by the time I'm halfway home. I lower my speed to a more appropriate level, but it remains above the designated limit marked on the road, my eagerness too powerful to contain.

As I roll down the curved driveway of our family home, my eyes scan our palatial mansion for any signs of life. With a live-in nanny, a housekeeper, and two bodyguards, I'm surprised to find my residence plunged into blackness. I can't often escape the constant bustle that has become my life the past three years. Silence is a hard limit for Cleo —meaning I am forever surrounded by noise. I'm not going to complain. After living the first sixteen years of my life restrained with silence, I relish every beautiful sound. The whispered I love yous, the screams of ecstasy torn from my wife's mouth, and the coos of my daughter when she covers my chin with slobber. I cherish every perfect noise. To me, they are more beautiful than any song I've produced.

I park my car at the edge of our entranceway, my patience too thin to park my vehicle in the garage. Dots of rain fall on my suit-covered shoulders as I climb the stairs of the home I bought in the months following Cleo's recovery. It is a large estate nestled in a gated community of Montclair. This town is my wife's home; it was her refuge after having all the sounds she loved cruelly torn from her, so it was the right place for her to recover after the loss of our unborn baby.

As I toss my keys on the wooden table in the entranceway, my eyes catch sight of the Roman numerals on my wrist. "One day, little man, one day," I murmur to myself, reminding our son we will meet again one day.

The tapping of my feet as I take the stairs two at a time booms into the eerie silence filling my house. Years ago, I would have panicked about a lack of fanfare for my arrival home, but now, I appreciate that Cleo has her hands full chasing a toddler and manning all the charity organizations she boards as part of Chains' charity efforts.

As per Cleo's request, I remain the sole owner of Chains. Except now, instead of having one BDSM club cloaked by secrecy, I have fifteen well-represented clubs dotting the coastline from New York to Florida. The exclusivity and guarantee of privacy are still two of the utmost priorities of my clubs, but having a safe, sane, and consensual place for people of my community to play will always be my number one focus.

My brisk speed down the dark corridor of the main residence of my property slows when I stride past a fluorescent pink-painted door. Although I'm dying to smell my wife's indescribable scent, I carefully pry open the ghastly-colored door and step into the room. Tatum is sleeping in the top corner of her crib, sucking on her thumb. She stirs softly when

I run my hand over the sprout of black curls on top of her head. Other than her angelic face, Tatum is the perfect mix of both Cleo and me. She has her mom's curls and my black hair. Her skin tone is a mix of us both, and her eyes are the perfect combination of Cleo's and mine. She truly is the best of both Cleo and me mixed into one adorable little package.

I snag the fluffy rabbit Cleo arrived home from the hospital with when she was a baby and tuck it under Tatum's arm before exiting the room. Eager to slip into bed with Cleo, I remove my suit jacket and tie as I finalize my strides down the end of the hall. My steps halt midstride when a surge of adrenaline roars through my veins. I stop just outside our bedroom door when a flicker of light in the corner of my eye garners my attention.

The heat thickening my veins migrates to the lower half of my body when I turn my head in the direction the light is coming from. There are four small candles dancing around a room that makes my chest puff with smugness every time I enter it. Although the candles are dim, they are bright enough to erotically showcase the visual of my naked wife kneeling at the entrance of our playroom. Her chin is tucked into her chest, and her hands are resting on her bare thighs, palms side up in offering. Although she is perfectly still, I know she has sensed my presence as the hairs on her nape are prickling with attention.

When I pace into the room, my eyes swing sideways. Just as I had suspected, Tatum's baby monitor is sitting on the drawers above the chest of toys and gadgets we've made good use of the past three years. My cock thickens painfully as I turn around to close our playroom door, not only blocking out noises from outside, but also locking Cleo's erotic screams inside the soundproof walls.

As I remove my clothing, my eyes drink in every delectable curve of my wife. The smug grin on my face turns into a genuine smile when I spot a splatter of paint on the ball of Cleo's foot. Although I offered to have an interior designer return Cleo's family home to its prior glory, Cleo was adamant she wanted to do it herself. Because it is a feat of love more than a chore, she has spent the last year sanding and painting every wall herself. Her love of her family shines through in that property, as it does with our daughter's name. Tatum is named after Cleo's little brother, Tate.

If security wasn't an issue, I would move us in into Cleo's family home the instant Cleo finishes her renovations, but with her and Tatum's safety my utmost priority, my dream must remain precisely that—a dream.

Once my clothes are removed, folded and sitting on top of Cleo's nightgown, I move to stand in front of her. She is kneeling next to a cart Aubrey generally serves breakfast on every Sunday, but instead of it being covered with scrumptious savories, it is filled with even more delicious products. Nipple clamps, vibrating butt plugs, a riding crop, and a pinwheel are a small handful of the instruments she has laid out.

Placing my hand under her downcast chin, I lift her head. The thrill of the hunt scorches my veins when her beautiful chocolate eyes lock with mine. Cleo's eyes are the reason I've grown an obsession with blindfolding her. They are my eternal weakness, potent enough to unravel me with a single glance. I've learned to limit my need for control outside of this environment, but in this room, there is no compromise. Although Cleo continually breaks the boundaries outside of this domain, she is well aware of the rules associated with this room.

Cleo hates the title of submissive, but she has many submissive qualities. She loves being dominated and pleasing her Master. She is cautious of the rules and is eager to explore the BDSM lifestyle, and she challenges me to be the best Master I can be. She is the perfect submissive—the best I've ever had, even without the official title.

"What is this?" I ask, my voice throaty as I struggle to ignore the heat of her lust-filled gaze hardening my cock even more.

Cleo licks her lips as she follows my gaze to the instruments laid out on the cart. "We only got halfway through our list last night, so I thought we could finish it tonight, Master Chains." I feel the soft purr of her voice all the way to my balls.

"We are well overdue to adjust your hard and soft limits, but that is not usually done while utilizing the instruments associated with them."

"Why not?" Cleo questions, returning her eyes to me. "It will be more fun this way."

"Eyes," I demand when her amorous smirk instigates a wild recklessness to run through me.

Only Cleo can make me throw caution to the wind. I've never been as heedless with another woman as I am with her. I have had subs who went above and beyond to please, ones who never wanted to leave my side, and ones who would bend to any will to keep me as their Master. But there has only ever been one woman I altered the rules for. She was the one who walked into my world and amazed me with her strength and determination. She was the one who truly proved I can have the best of both worlds. She is my wife.

A husky growl rolls up my chest when Cleo drops her eyes to her hands the instant my command leaves my mouth. *See—perfect submissive.*

"Because I am feeling generous, I will approve your request." I don't need to see her face to know she is smiling. I can feel it deep in my bones. "But be warned, I am restless, so my patience is thin. Today is not the day to test me. Do you understand?"

"Yes, Master Chains," Cleo replies without delay.

Her agreement makes me want to pull her into my lap and ravish the mouth I've been dying to taste all week, but I won't. The day I became her husband, I not only promised to love and cherish her every day of my life, I also promised that every time we stepped into this room, her every desire, wish, and craving would be fulfilled. Cleo loves being dominated; so much so, I'll push aside my need to fuck her hard and fast on the floor she is kneeling on to ensure she is dominated in the way she needs.

"Very well. Move onto the Saint Andrew's Cross," I instruct, my voice stern.

"Yes, Master Chains."

Keeping her head tucked into her chin, Cleo stands from her kneeling position and moves to the Saint Andrew's Cross in the middle of the room. Her pert tits lift high on her erratically panting chest when she stretches out her arms to rest them on the polished wood. Her legs soon follow suit. After gathering a blindfold from the chest on my right, I pace toward her, my strides purposely slow so she has plenty of time to see how hard she has made me.

Just as she has done every time I stand before her naked, Cleo's eyes run over my body, categorizing and memorizing every inch of me as if it is the first time she has seen me naked. Her attentive gaze makes me even harder. For every step I take, the shimmer between her legs becomes more apparent. She is so wet, her arousal glistens on her thighs.

My hands twitch to touch her when I stop to stand in front of her, but I keep them balled at my side—barely. Cleo's eyes remain arrested on mine as I shackle her wrists and ankles with the leather cuffs on the cross. I restrain her tightly enough her skin gets the pinch she loves, but not firmly enough to hinder the little squirms she makes. Happy she is safely locked in, I crank the handle on the cross until she is inclined to a forty-five-degree angle.

I take a step back to appreciate the beauty of my wife bound and erotically staged in front of me. The Saint Andrew's Cross is the perfect instrument to expose every inch of her gorgeous body. The rosy pinkness of her nipples, the beautiful little ripples in the bottom of her stomach from growing our daughter, and the angry scar that reminds me every day of how lucky I am to still have her in my life. She is undoubtedly beautiful—perfect in every way.

Incapable of waiting a minute longer to touch her, I move to stand in front of her. Cleo's minty breath fans my hungry lips when I slide a blindfold over her ravishing eyes, dampening the firm grip she has on my balls and throat.

A trail of goosebumps follow in my wake when I track my finger down her blemished cheek, then over the chain link nestled in her neck, before dropping it to the swell of her breast. Her thighs squeeze together when my fingers' trek over her body has me reaching the bare mound of her glistening pussy.

"Spread your legs wider," I demand as my finger glides through the wet folds of her soaked sex.

The pants of her breath grow as she does as instructed. "Good girl," I praise as I slowly inch my index finger inside her. The walls of her vagina ripple around me, silently begging me to lose control. I push into her so deep, I hit the little nerve inside her that drives her wild.

Cleo braces against the restraints holding her tightly as a throaty purr simpers through her lips.

I pump my finger in and out of her as I gather one of the instruments she left out in offering off the silver cart. With her mind stuck in a lusty haze, the air leaves Cleo's body in a hankering grunt when the unexpected intrusion of latex replaces my finger. She stills for the quickest moment before her husky growl advises me she is aware of the instrument I am priming. For a woman who had never experienced anal play before me, my wife has become obsessed.

After coating the anal plug with Cleo's arousal, I move it to the crevice only I have claimed. I circle the plug around her puckered hole before slowly inching it inside.

"Stop squirming," I demand, using my voice that only belongs in this room.

I swivel the anal plug, stretching her more, as I sink it deep inside her. Cleo moans when I flick on the switch at the end, sending a pleasing vibration over every inch of her body. When I slide my fingers back into her pussy, she squeezes around me. She is even tighter now—clenched with arousal. Her soaked sex is hot and begging to be consumed. Unable to deny myself for a moment longer, I lower my mouth to her clit.

"Oh. . .yes. . ." Cleo hisses when my tongue circles her throbbing bud before I suckle it into my mouth.

She quivers against me as her delicious arousal engulfs my taste buds. I roll my tongue down her pulsating sex before plunging it inside. Cleo's pussy clenches around my tongue as she fights to stave off her orgasm. She has trained well the past three years, learning that orgasms released after an immense battle are often the most rewarding.

"Do not come until I say," I warn, ensuring she is aware of the rules. My domain. My say. "If you come, I will punish you."

Her frustrated grunt thickens my cock even more.

After driving her to the brink of climax three times, I pull my mouth away from her aching-with-need pussy. She whines softly. She isn't the only one disappointed. I could eat her greedy cunt all night long.

Cleo's disappointed moan switches to an animalistic grunt when the leather tassels on my favorite flogger run over the taut skin on her stomach. I flick the handle of the flogger slowly, preparing her skin for the sting of its touch before increasing the pressure of my taps. Cleo's nipples harden to the point of cutting diamonds when the leather cracks against her puckered buds. Her nipples have always been responsive and nursing our daughter hasn't altered that fact.

I work the cat o' nine tales over the skin on her stomach, breasts, and inner thighs until they are covered with gorgeous pink welts and Cleo's cries of ecstasy have reached a stage of begging. "Please, Master Chains. I can't hold it back much longer."

"Not yet," I reply, placing the flogger down to secure another instrument.

I continue working through each of the items until the desires of my body can no longer be ignored. Watching Cleo orgasm three times ensures I have played my role of Master well, so there is no need for me to continue depriving myself. The paddle I'm grasping drops to the floor with a clatter as I line my engorged knob with the entrance of my wife's saturated pussy.

"Wait, please," Cleo demands softly, her voice exhausted.

Our chests compete against one another when I'm stilled by her request. Usually, Cleo follows the rules of the room to a T, trusting my ability to read her needs; she's never had to voice her desires before. I tug her blindfold off her forthright eyes, fearful I've misread the signals of her body. I did have her gagged until mere minutes ago, so maybe she wanted to safeword but couldn't.

Cleo blinks several times in a row as her eyes adjust to the brightness of the room. "Hey," she greets me with a grin, her lips curving upwards.

"Hi," I reply, shocked by her carefree response.

Although her eyes reveal her exhaustion, they are brimming with so much love, I'm tempted to re-cover them.

I secure my first full breath in over a minute when she says, "Sorry for stopping you. I know it's against the rules. I just. . ." She lowers her eyes, fearful she's going to be punished for disobedience.

Her glossy black hair falls from her face when I lift her chin to its original position. "What is it?" I ask, reminding both myself and her that she isn't my sub—she is my wife.

Her throat works hard to swallow before she faintly whispers, "I just really want to touch you. I haven't touched you in a week, so I'm dying to feel your skin against my hands." She swivels her restrained wrists to enhance her request. "Please," she frailly begs, equally turned on and panicked by the idea of being punished.

Her deep exhalation of air fans my sweat-drenched face when I say, "Okay." It is quickly redrawn when I add on, "But first we are going to negotiate."

Cleo stares into my eyes, her gaze unreserved and without fear as she replies, "I do not need to negotiate. I'm willing to accept any terms my Master sees fit."

See—the perfect submissive.

One I'll happily command for the rest of my life.

The End. . .

Afterword

I hope you enjoyed Restrained as much as I enjoyed writing it. I am planning on writing a book from Marcus's POV. He has so much to tell.

Cheers Shandi xx

Join my Facebook page:
www.facebook.com/authorshandi

Join my READER's group:
https://www.facebook.com/groups/1740600836169853/

Join my newsletter to remain informed:
http://eepurl.com/cyEzNv

My Amazon Page:
https://www.amazon.com/Shandi-Boyes/e/B01D8C13WU

If you enjoyed this book - please leave a review:
http://a.co/eHWUFq4

Acknowledgments

Thank you to all the wonderful people who have supported me in my new endeavor. I'm incredibly grateful to have been blessed with such wonderful family and friends.

The time and effort it takes in writing a book are immense. You sacrifice your family, your hobbies, and yourself to produce a book that you hope your readers will enjoy. If you have enjoyed this book, please leave a review. A review is the only way you can truly thank an author for all the effort they put in.

Not many people are aware, but I'm a mother of five. I have four boys and one little daughter. I'd never be able to produce these books without the support of my husband. He comes home from working ten hour plus days to shower the children and get them ready for bed, never once saying a negative word. He is my rock, my inspiration, and my everything.

Also thanks to my mum Carolyn, for reading and assisting me when I call you crazily saying a scene isn't working. I appreciate everything you do. And last, but not at all least, my editor, Krista. Thank you for making my manuscripts extra sparkly. I appreciate everything you do!

Once again, thank you for your support and messages. I read every single one received. Please leave a review, and I'll see you on the flip side.

Cheers Shandi xx

Also by Shandi Boyes

Perception Series - New Adult Romance

Perception of Life - (Noah & Emily)

Reality of Life - (Conclusion of Noah & Emily)

Fight of Life - (Jacob - standalone)

Player of Life - (Nick - standalone)

Beats of Life - (Slater - standalone)

Enigma Series - Steamy Contemporary Romance

Enigma of Life - (Isaac)

Unraveling an Enigma - (Isaac)

Enigma: The Mystery Unmasked - (Isaac)

Enigma: The Final Chapter - (Isaac)

Beneath the Secrets - (Hugo - Part 1)

Beneath the Sheets - (Hugo Conclusion)

Spy Thy Neighbor (Hunter - standalone)

The Opposite Effect - (Brax)

I Married a Mob Boss - (Enrique)

Second Shot (Hawke's Story)

Bound Series - Steamy Romance & slight BDSM

Chains (Marcus and Cleo)

Links (Marcus and Cleo)

Bound (Marcus and Cleo)

Restrain (Marcus and Cleo)

Russian Mob Chronicles

Nikolai: A Mafia Prince Romance

Nikolai: Taking Back What's Mine

Nikolai: What's Left of Me

COMING SOON:

The Way We Are (Ryan's Story)

The Way We Were

Printed in Great Britain
by Amazon

81993313R00180